INNER SANCTUARY

D Jordan Redhawk

Bella
BOOKS
2012

Bella Books, Inc.
P.O. Box 10543
Tallahassee, FL 32302

Printed in the United States of America on acid-free paper
First published 2012

Editor: Katherine V. Forrest
Cover Designer: Linda Callaghan

ISBN 13: 978-1-59493-310-3

Other Bella Books by D Jordan Redhawk

The Sanguire trilogy:
The Strange Path
Beloved Lady Mistress

Dedication

To Anna Trinity Redhawk—it might be broken, but it's ours. I love you.

Acknowledgment

As I've said before, no book is created in a vacuum! Here is the list of people who helped me along with the Sanguire series:

Janet Redhawk (no relation), Agatha Tutko, Carol Dickerson, Teresa Crittenden, Jean Rosestar, Jac Hill—you guys stuck through years and years of manuscripts, rereading and rereading as you went. Thank you for your comments and criticisms!

Anna Redhawk (every sort of relation!), Anita Pawlowski, Shawn Cady—first readers, one and all. You're my first line of defense! I couldn't do this without your love, friendship and support. Thank you!

Bella Books—Karin Kallmaker, Katherine V. Forrest, Linda Callaghan, & Jessica—I appreciate your taking a chance on me! It's been the best couple of years working with you folks, and I hope to have many more!

About the author

D Jordan Redhawk lives in Portland, Oregon where she works in the hospitality industry. (But don't make the mistake of thinking she's hospitable.) Her household consists of her wife of twenty-four years, two aging black cats that provide no luck whatsoever, and a white buffalo Beanie Buddy named Roam.

For more information on D Jordan Redhawk, visit her website: *http://www.djordanredhawk.com*

CHAPTER ONE

"It has been five months! Certainly by now the situation has become stable enough for us to demand Davis's return." Bertrada Nijmege thumped the heavy oak table to emphasize her point, rattling the water glasses set out for this meeting. Her hawk-like visage was even more pronounced as she glared down her sharp nose at her fellow counselors. "Or do we wait until our traitor decides it's safe for another attack?"

"Bertrada is right." Dark of hair and eye, the young man seated beside her had a solemn expression more reminiscent of an earnest high school student than a member of the *Agrun Nam*, the powerful ruling council of the European Sanguire. When Samuel McCall spoke, his demeanor wasn't as aggressive as his compatriot, though no less stern. The black leather of his chair creaked as he leaned forward. "Whoever hired the assassin, whether it's someone in our employ or one of us, hasn't made another attempt. We've all taken great pains to stop information leaking from our offices, and I think this lack of action indicates our 'traitor' isn't one of us at all."

Lionel Bentoncourt smothered a sigh, repressing the desire to look up at the vaulted ceiling in private supplication. He and the other members of the *Agrun Nam* had heard the same tired outburst from her nigh onto every blasted moment of those five months of which she complained. It was becoming tedious. Rather than respond, he scanned the familiar walls of the council chamber as he considered his words. Framed images of all of the counselors hung on the ivory colored walls, each portrait stern and unyielding. Nijmege's didn't look much different than she did now though the photographer had taken the picture six decades ago. Bentoncourt focused on the largest frame directly across from him, an old painting of the former leader of the *Agrun Nam*, Nahib. He had been Nijmege's lover and Bentoncourt's friend, and his execution had ultimately created the hateful woman glaring at Bentoncourt from across the table. Those snapping eyes brought him back from his dithering. His dark eyebrows bristled beneath the shock of white atop his head, the contrast making it difficult to pinpoint his true age. "Perhaps so, Samuel. Regardless of who hired the Human to kill Davis, the fact remains that we cannot compel her to attend us. She's not our servant; maybe not even European at all."

Nijmege snorted, her aquiline features narrowing into a grimace. "So sayeth the great *Ki'an Gasan* Margaurethe O'Toole." She snapped her fingers to indicate her opinion on that particular point.

Across from her, a man with pleasant demeanor leaned forward, his wavy brown hair brushing his shoulders. He wore a black three-piece suit, golden cufflinks and tie clip flashing in the overhead light. "You do not believe the *Ki'an Gasan*?"

The lone woman on the council glared down her nose. "Why should I, Aiden? I wouldn't put it past Margaurethe to bend the truth to suit her agenda. We all know how unbalanced she became after Elisibet's death."

Aiden Cassadie frowned, his handsome features turning even that expression into an agreeable appearance. "What would be the purpose in deluding us?"

"Who can fathom?" Nijmege dismissed the question with a wave. "Perhaps to forestall our direct intervention. Perhaps she truly believes this tripe. Perhaps it's a ruse to keep us at each others' throats, unsettled, uncertain. I never understood what she ever saw in the Sweet Butcher to begin with."

Bentoncourt, lips thinning, said, "I cannot believe *Ki'an Gasan* Margaurethe would be so crass as to play a charade such as this. She believes as she says—Ms. Davis is the *Ninsumgal* Elisibet Vasilla reborn."

Beside Nijmege, McCall expressed disbelief with the narrowing of his eyes. The woman harrumphed, opening her mouth to rebut Bentoncourt.

Cassadie cocked his head. "Certainly you cannot also discount the reports obtained from *Sublugal Sañar* Valmont and indirectly from Father Castillo? We have three separate accounts from three separate people, two of whom are not willing to work together in any civil manner. If Davis was not who *Ki'an Gasan* Margaurethe insists she is, then Valmont would have happily denied the claim."

"Not to mention Father Castillo's independent corroboration. His was the initial report." Despite his words, Bentoncourt wished he had never heard word of the hapless young expatriate who had first discovered Elisibet's reincarnation in Seattle. He found it abhorrent to think so, but it would have been easier for Davis to have been found by someone with a grudge against Elisibet—someone who could have killed her before she could defend herself, saving everyone the trouble.

"Reported to you." Nijmege arched an eyebrow.

Bentoncourt fell to temptation and rolled his eyes. "Which brings us back to the conspiracy theory. It's a never ending circle of deceit, corruption and power mongering brought on by too much control and the desire to keep it." His voice sounded tired, even to him. "I'll not explain how I came across his report again."

Nijmege sniffed and tossed her thick black hair from her shoulders.

Cassadie chuckled. "Well, we can now discount Bertrada as the likely traitor." At her dangerous glance, he winked. "If you don't believe Davis is who she is, you wouldn't need to hire an assassin to kill her."

The final member of the *Agrun Nam*, Ernst Rosenberg, had remained silent until now. His blond hair closely cropped, his angelic features contrasted sharply with a thick and muscled body. Heavy lids sheltered the intelligent gray eyes that scanned his companions. "It cannot be both ways. Either Jenna Davis is who she claims to be, or she is not. We cannot yet order this youngling to attend us, yet we also cannot put the life of an innocent in jeopardy."

McCall leaned back in his chair, elbows on the armrests, fingers steepled together. "We've spent the last five months preparing for her arrival. I shan't say 'return' as we don't know the validity of her claim. We have a full contingent of guards waiting, a palace prepared, and servants thoroughly scrutinized in the hopes of keeping her safe. Regardless of 'is she, isn't she,' Davis would be imminently safer here."

"So, everything hinges on whether or not she is Elisibet reborn."

"She's not." Nijmege's jaw jutted low in physical denial of Bentoncourt's words.

Bentoncourt grimaced. "Then we'll put it to a vote. If this esteemed council concludes that Jenna Davis is Elisibet Vasilla, we accept the invitation to her *Baruñal* Ceremony, and send a representative. If, as some of us have announced, she is only a young Sanguire trapped within a web of deceit, we order her to report to us where we can keep her safe until we can decide what to do with her." He scanned the others, noting their indications of approval.

"Those who believe Jenna Davis is Elisibet reborn?" He raised his hand. Cassadie followed his lead, an expression of surprise blossoming on his attractive face when no one else voted. Not pleased, Bentoncourt nevertheless forged onward. "Those who believe she is not?"

Nijmege and McCall provided a united front, both simultaneously raising their hands.

Everyone turned toward the fifth of their number. Rosenberg's beatific gaze regarded his peers. "I abstain."

Nijmege cursed roundly.

Bentoncourt relaxed. For now, Davis would remain in the colonies. "As we are no closer to a decision, might I suggest a recess?"

Nijmege snatched up her paperwork and stormed from the room, her footfalls echoing into the distance. Close on her heels, McCall gifted the others with an apologetic tilt of his head and followed, leaving open the conference room door.

Cassadie appeared amused at the woman's outburst as he slowly gained his feet. "That was most entertaining." He met Rosenberg at the door. "Are you busy for lunch? I'd like to pick your brains about your abstention."

Grim but polite, Rosenberg bowed his head, gesturing for his companion to lead the way.

Alone, Bentoncourt stood and closed the door before returning to sink back into his chair. Small wonder they had difficulty arriving at anything conclusive with five different personalities and personal agendas in play. Such was the nature of a monarchal parliament without a monarch. The *Agrun Nam's* decision to retain control over their people after Elisibet's assassination had been a stopgap measure that had evolved into an institution.

Bentoncourt stared at the empty chairs of his comrades, settling on Nijmege's. He had no illusions about her true aspirations. The youngling Davis in America was in danger of more than just a stray assassin hired for political causes. For all intents and purposes, Davis seemed to be the reincarnated tyrant responsible for Nahib's death. Since that horrible execution so many centuries ago, Nijmege had become a shattered and bitter woman. Bentoncourt had rarely spoken with her prior to her appointment as a *Sañar*, making her grief and rage his only point of reference. As one who knew only the broken woman, he marveled at the ferocious vitality that she had exhibited since her discovery of Davis's existence. If her passion had been this substantial when Nahib had known her, it was no wonder they had become lovers. Nahib had always surrounded himself with strong, lively people.

His gaze shifted to the seat beside Nijmege's. Odd. He had never considered McCall one of her prospective allies. He had always assumed Rosenberg would support Nijmege's desire for vengeance, having at least had the benefit of experience with the Sweet Butcher. Yet the longer this debate went on, the stronger the bond grew between McCall and Nijmege. McCall had missed Elisibet's reign by several hundred years. Historical documents and past *Agrun Nam* meeting minutes shored up his lack of firsthand knowledge, and perhaps a healthy dose of prejudice. His family had come to power after the Purge, one of several clans that had gained political clout as Elisibet's hardliners were destroyed. He had always seemed levelheaded, though, austere and analytical, rarely jumping to decisions without a thorough understanding of the situation and repercussions. Bentoncourt wouldn't have thought him set on vengeance even if there was some historical background for it.

Certainly Bertrada isn't compelling him? Bentoncourt fiddled with a pen on the table, a frown creasing his face as he decided this was not the case. Compelling another required constant attention, and the two *sanari* could most often be found in separate offices involved in different activities. Had she been responsible for directing McCall's decisions, he would know it the minute her control wavered.

Rosenberg's abstention was the astonishment of the day. Bentoncourt could count on one hand the times the man had declined to vote on an issue. Stacked up against several hundred years of experience, Rosenberg's refusal to choose was inexplicable. Rosenberg knew the truth of Davis's existence—Nijmege argued the finer point only to get Davis within reach of her talons, not because she denied the woman's claim. Hopefully, at lunch Cassadie would get to the bottom of Rosenberg's refusal. Bentoncourt needed to bypass Nijmege's murderous intent, and soon.

As Nijmege had said, it had been five months. Five months since Valmont had thwarted the Human assassin, Rufus Barrett—the man who had said Bentoncourt had hired him. No one who knew Bentoncourt believed it, but Davis didn't know him, did she? His disgust at the slander nearly rivaled his dismay at hearing

Valmont had been named her advisor, and had sworn fealty not long after the foiled attempt. Bentoncourt had expected Davis to be a political innocent, but his opinion of Margaurethe had taken a slide; certainly she was aware that Valmont and Nijmege remained in contact with one another. Margaurethe had always struck Bentoncourt as a shrewd young woman, not given to stupidity. How could she have allowed the murderer of her lover back into the fold, knowing he often spoke with the one European Sanguire who most hated Elisibet?

The questions followed a well-worn path in his mind, pacing through the topics and connections with no urging as he continued manipulating the pen in his hands. The assassination attempt still clouded the *Agrun Nam* with distrust as they all wondered who had set it in motion. At the time of the endeavor, no one but the *Agrun Nam* and a handful of aides had known of Davis's presence. Only Rosenberg seemed to have little need for her death. Nijmege and McCall, bound tight as lovers, wanted Davis to pay for the Sweet Butcher's sins. Cassadie, next in line as *Nam Lugal*, would benefit the most by Bentoncourt's implication in the assassination attempt, giving him the edge to take over the council.

Bentoncourt himself had no fear of losing the authority given him upon Nahib's death. Since Elisibet's assassination the *Agrun Nam* had ruled in her stead. He had found the job a migraine producer. He remembered the way of things immediately after Nahib's execution. Everyone had dreaded Elisibet's next foul mood or bloody desire. Her inability to feel compassion had crippled her as a decent and just ruler, and it had been Bentoncourt's fault. He had given the primary argument to start her on the *Ñíri Kurám* before the age of majority after her father had died in a hunting accident. The rite of passage had warped her preadolescent psyche for all time, creating the monster she had become. Should Davis have a modicum of Elisibet's feelings of betrayal along with those memories she was touted to having, Bentoncourt would gladly suffer the same fate as his predecessor for his mistake.

He tossed the pen down and sat back with a frustrated sigh. Would Davis see how these last months had been spent in keeping her safe from harm? Or would she decide the *Agrun Nam* refused to assist her because of guilt and fear, hiding behind the banner of genealogy to thwart her claim to a crown she had no proof of owning? How much of Elisibet did Davis possess? Only memories, or something more?

Having no answers, he rose and gathered his belongings. "I'm getting too old for this sort of thing."

CHAPTER TWO

"I think I'm going to be sick."

Margaurethe clicked her tongue, giving Whiskey a slightly exasperated look. She adjusted the mid-length cuff of her silk jacket, unknowingly revealing her own case of nerves though she hid it with casual grace. The jacket, like the floor-length dress it accompanied, was a deep forest green that set off her eyes and contrasted the auburn highlights in her hair. "No, you're not. Your introduction will last all of five minutes; you won't have time to be ill."

Whiskey debated arguing the point. If she was the *Ninsumgal* of the European Sanguire, future leader of all Sanguire, she could order everyone to make time, right? Her stomach would thank her, though the janitorial department might have some reservations. Rather than argue the point, she tossed her long blond hair over her shoulder with a shake of her head. Elevator doors opened, spilling the two women and four of Whiskey's *Ninsumgal* Guard, the *Aga'gída*, out into the ballroom level service area of The Davis Group building. Two of their brethren already stood in place, bristling with weaponry. One blocked access from the foyer and another stood near a long hallway to their right.

"This way, *Ninsumgal*." *Ugula Aga'us* Anthony, Whiskey's captain, indicated the hall. "We've cleared a path to the foyer."

Surrounding Whiskey and Margaurethe, the personal security officers briskly walked toward the banquet kitchen with their cargo. Whiskey couldn't decide whether the delicious aromas wafting toward her made her feel better or worse. She hadn't had anything but toast for breakfast this morning, her nerves playing havoc with her stomach despite all of Sithathor's attempts to entice her. *Did* she *ever feel this nervous before?* Somehow, Whiskey doubted Elisibet Vasilla had ever experienced such anxiety. If she had, she would have executed whoever had caused the sensation. For a moment, Whiskey almost felt closer to the Sweet Butcher.

The hallway opened up to an area with three walk-in coolers. They rounded a corner, almost physically forcing themselves through the wall of noises and smells of a fully operational commercial kitchen. Cooks and assistants called orders to each other as a team dished up plates, covered them with metal lids, and stacked everything in rolling hot boxes. Meanwhile, others remained at the stoves and ovens, adding more chicken and steak and potatoes and steamed vegetables to the works. Off in one corner, the banquet maître d' and Margaurethe's master chef conferred over a crisis of some sort, hardly noting their passage. Whiskey had been through here before, though never during such an industrious display. The kitchen crew hardly batted an eye when she and her entourage whisked by, focused entirely upon the chaos around them. Past a giant rack of decorative desserts, a set of double doors led out to the back hall. Two more *aga'usi* waited there, saluting before opening the door to let them through.

In the public area, the rumble of eight hundred guests and a hundred staff became clearly audible, though this corridor was as far from the action one could get without going into the service aisles. The main foyer near the public elevators held the main reception. From the sound level of the voices, many of the guests had remained to enjoy the hosted bar rather than take their seats inside the ballroom. Another four guards were stationed in this corridor—two at the doors Whiskey would use to enter the ballroom, one blocking access from the service aisle behind, and the fourth directing stray guests back toward the reception in the foyer. *If all my personal security is here, who's taking care of the rest of the place?* She knew that almost half the building staff was devoted to security, but did there need to be this many *aga'us* to babysit her for this function?

A Human server burst through from the service aisle, a tray with teapot in one hand, nearly running into the guard stationed there. She gasped in surprise at the sudden animosity directed at her. "I'm sorry! I forgot!"

Four of Whiskey's guard interposed themselves between her and the Human. One grabbed the woman, tumbling tray and pot to the ground with a crash. Anthony began to drag a struggling Whiskey back into the kitchen. Whiskey attempted to push his hands away, but he was physically stronger. Instead, she flicked at him with her mind, not enough to do more than cause a sting. "Stop it!"

Anthony released her. "But *Ninsumgal*—"

Whiskey straightened her rumpled shirt. "Let her go."

Released from the grip of two Sanguire men, the woman shivered, blinking at the crowd of suspicious stares. At her feet, tea water soaked into the carpet.

"Step back. Clean this mess up." As someone was dispatched to take care of it, Whiskey approached the server, hands out in a calming gesture. "It's okay. You made a mistake. I understand."

Her compassion triggered the Human's relief. "I'm so sorry, *Ninsumgal*!" she babbled. "They said not to use this hallway after five, but I didn't realize what time it was. I was in a hurry. I mixed up an order at my table, and this was the quickest way. I'm so sorry! I didn't mean to—"

Whiskey smiled. "It's okay. It's all right." Her hands rested on the thin shoulders. She felt the woman tremble beneath her touch, smelled the fear coming off her. "You'll remember next time, I bet."

The server nodded adamantly, a skittish chuckle escaping her as she edged toward the doors leading back to the service area. Whiskey waved her security away, letting the Human flee through it to safety.

"Well, that was entertaining. Can we get on with it?"

Whiskey turned and grinned at Margaurethe, watching her feign annoyance as she brushed lint from her dress. "The sooner the better."

Margaurethe smiled, linking her arm through Whiskey's. She gave Anthony a nod, and he spoke into the small microphone at his sleeve. Inside the ballroom, the music changed from a gentle background to something more commanding, and the voices of the people faded in anticipation. Around Whiskey the *Aga'gída* shifted, the original four flanking her and Margaurethe while the others returned to their posts.

Patting Margaurethe's hand, Whiskey smirked. "You know that sounds like the *Star Wars* theme, right?"

Margaurethe sniffed. "Hardly. Though it'll have to do until we can hire a composer." The haughty exterior faded, and she gave Whiskey a real smile. "At least that little accident made you forget to be sick, yes?"

Whiskey felt Margaurethe's essence slip over her, wood smoke and mulled wine soothing the sudden jump of nerves at the reminder. She was about to agree, but the rousing music had faded. Father Castillo's voice announced her over the loudspeaker. As her *Aga'gída* pulled the doors open, and the lights from the stage wash blinded her, Whiskey wondered what sort of reaction there would be should she upchuck onto her boots in full view of a number of Mayan, Indian, African and Japanese Sanguire diplomats.

The wood smoke grew stronger, strengthening her. She gave Margaurethe a wan smile, and stepped forward onto the stage.

CHAPTER THREE

Margaurethe patted her mouth with her napkin, setting it on her plate to indicate she was finished. Beside her, Whiskey poked and prodded her food without interest. Feeding the guests came first, followed by Whiskey's *Baruñal* Ceremony. Margaurethe doubted Whiskey would relax until she had an opportunity to flee. *I certainly hope Sithathor has a late dinner planned. She'll be starved when she can finally relax.*

Reaching beneath the table, she lightly stroked Whiskey's thigh, receiving a smile in return. The aroma of roses with a hint of blood filled her. Whiskey rewarded her by taking a healthy bite of food. The server came and removed Margaurethe's plate, offering her favorite after-dinner tea and dessert. While she awaited his return, she looked out over the ballroom.

Close to eight hundred guests filled the room. The majority of them were Sanguire local to the west coast of the United States and Canada, or hangers-on of various political factions that had deigned to attend. Others came from Human families that had served the Sanguire for generations, vassals and *kizarusi* alike. A constant low rumble of conversation merged with the sound of silver on china and ice rattling in glasses. To dramatize the dais lighting, the rest of the room was kept at a lower illumination. Regardless, Margaurethe easily spotted the *Ninsumgal's* guests.

In the past six months, Margaurethe had succeeded in making contact with a number of world governments—it had helped that her companies, though largely based in the United Kingdom, had enjoyed success worldwide. Over the centuries, she had lent a hand to the Mayans of South and Central America and the Indians on the subcontinent. These two governments stood on the verge of following the example of the American Indians in signing treaties with Whiskey. The Mayans had some territorial issues with their northern neighbors, but Margaurethe hoped they could settle their differences soon. Once they did, The Davis Group would have a growing coalition of mutual support.

The political delegates had reserved tables closest to Whiskey's. The Japanese ambassador had insisted on seating twenty people at the front of the room. Aware of their prickly honor, Margaurethe had obliged. They took up two tables, creating a blot of black business suits and implacable faces. Next to them, the Africans wore colorful ethnic clothing, their flamboyant movements and speech contrasting with the controlled Japanese. Bold yellows and reds splashed across the warp and weave of the feasting fabric lying on all the tables across the room.

One table held the American Indian contingent. Four of the *Wi Wacipi Wakan* and their spouses dined here. They held a place of honor, directly beneath the *Ninsumgal's* seat, central to the front row of tables. They had signed a treaty with The Davis Group months ago, the only government yet to do so. Sitting with them were Whiskey's only known living relatives—her aunt

Zica and grandmother, Wahca. The Mayans sat three tables away, a move by Margaurethe to discourage any arguments between the two factions. Border skirmishes had been the norm for so long, it had taken concerted effort of diplomacy to keep them from "counting coup" on one another. Separating the two were the Indians from the subcontinent. They had arrived three days ago, and hadn't had the opportunity to meet with Whiskey.

The *Agrun Nam* of the European Sanguire had declined to answer their invitation. Margaurethe had expected the snub, though Whiskey had exhibited wistful hope that they would at least send a representative. Rather than gloss over the rebuff in front of their guests, a number of whom were European expatriates, a single empty table sat at the periphery of the front row. Margaurethe had made certain others knew for whom it had been reserved, knowing gossip was the lifeblood of most Sanguire. If she were a betting woman, she would lay odds that the *Agrun Nam* already knew about their seating arrangements.

Giving up on her dinner, Whiskey sat back and tossed her napkin onto the uneaten food. She refused dessert, though did ask for peppermint tea. Margaurethe leaned closer. "It's almost over."

"Not soon enough." Whiskey grimaced, glancing down the head table at her advisors. "How much longer?"

Margaurethe let her gaze stray over the others. The only one not present was Reynhard Dorst, Whiskey's *Baruñal*, in charge of the ceremony proclaiming her an adult in the eyes of the European Sanguire. A podium divided the head table, standing to Whiskey's immediate left.

On the far side of it, Father Castillo and Chano remained in animated discussion, having become fast friends since the American Indian's induction to the Board of Directors. The priest's dark head bent toward the elder Indian, contrasting the sparse whiteness of the elder's hair, and he wore the black cassock of his order. Chano's nod to this ceremonial event was a red shirt with wide green bands embroidered at collar and cuff. A fringe of green cloth tassels cascaded from his shoulders and across the front of his chest. Beyond them, Valmont slumped in his chair. Despite his insolent slouch, he was a good-looking man with mahogany skin and neatly trimmed beard. His dreadlocks spilled haphazardly across his scalp, hanging to his shoulders. Rather than a standard Western-style suit, he wore a black midlength collarless jacket, perhaps to impress the Indian delegation. He currently levitated his dessert fork to combat his boredom, the utensil flashing in the stage wash as it whirled in a slow circle an inch above the tablecloth.

Ignoring the desire to mentally goose Valmont, Margaurethe reached for Castillo's mind, sensing dark chocolate. He looked her way, nodded, and waved one of the regular security officers over to begin the next step. "How about now?"

Whiskey swallowed, her color fading.

The lights in the ballroom dropped to their lowest setting, and the hubbub of discussion quieted. Servers disappeared into the service aisle, silently closing the doors behind them. Since Whiskey had followed the European manner of Turning, it had been decided that her ceremony would reflect that despite her American Indian heritage. The Sanguire from other nations had exhibited keen interest in being able to observe as each tribe-faction had its own ways. Spotlights centered on the doors at the back of the room, drawing the attention of eight hundred pairs of eyes.

An altered Dorst stood bathed in the brightness. His facial features remained the same—gaunt and pale, the capacity for withering sarcasm resting in the curve of his generous lips—but everything else had changed. He was *Gúnnumu Bargún*, a shape shifter, one of the most talented and experienced of the European Sanguire. Gone were the three black mohawks that normally adorned his pate, replaced with shoulder-length brown hair. His clothing remained black, though it was no longer leather and spikes. Instead he wore clothing more appropriate to the 1300s, trousers and boots, tunic and cape. He strode toward the stage, the silver embroidery in his clothing catching the light. A baldric across his shoulder held the large silver and burgundy patch of Whiskey's sigil—not the raven of Elisibet's rule, but a stylized scorpion.

Scorpions were solitary hunters, vicious and poisonous, apt to sting first and investigate later. Whiskey had researched the topic for weeks before deciding upon the scorpion. Margaurethe had argued for something less...sinister, but Whiskey had been insistent. Despite her aversion to all things Elisibet, she wanted to make certain everyone knew how dangerous she could be if necessary. Margaurethe wondered how the *Agrun Nam* would react to the representation.

All eyes upon him, Dorst stalked to the front of the room, radiating strength. Not many knew his identity, but all Sanguire present noted his age, his power. Beside Margaurethe, Whiskey shivered. Margaurethe reached over to pat her shoulder. She wondered if anyone would bolt from the room when he introduced himself. With easy grace, he stepped onto the stage, standing in front of the podium dividing the high table. He bowed once toward Whiskey, and spun around to face the gathered assemblage. "I am *Sañur Gasum* Reynhard Dorst, advisor and *Baruñal* to *Ninsumgal* Jenna Davis." An exclamation of surprise washed across the audience, and a playful grin crossed his face as knowledge of his notoriety filled the room. "I am here to proclaim that *Ninsumgal* Jenna has completed the *Ñíri Kurám* of the European Sanguire." He turned with a wave toward Margaurethe's side of the table, one of the spotlights sweeping across to illuminate Whiskey. "Come to me, child."

To her credit, Whiskey didn't look as terrified as she had professed herself. Margaurethe watched her rise without stumbling, and circle around the high table to approach Dorst. She was proud Whiskey didn't display the awkwardness she'd shown earlier in her apartment when preparing for this dinner. She wore a fitted silk suit of dark lavender with an off-white blouse, the satin texture shining beneath the lights. The garb was far outside of Whiskey's comfort range, she being at home in baggy cargo pants and revealing camisoles, but she moved with elegance. Again Dorst bowed low to her in deference to her rank, not as part of the ceremony. Rising, he smirked at Whiskey's grimace, and turned back to the audience. "I have guided *Ninsumgal* Jenna on the Strange Path, instructed her on her role among her people, and now proclaim her an adult. Do any Sanguire challenge this?"

Margaurethe tensed. One of the proofs of Sanguire adulthood was the ability to mentally defend one's self against attack. The European ceremony required a ritual challenge period where a peer called out the youngling in a mental duel before witnesses. Official challenges could be made and had to be accepted at this point. It was rare that someone utilized this opportunity for grievances, but it had happened in the past. Margaurethe glanced down the table at Valmont. He seemed as restive as she, his fork no longer spinning in the air, eyes scanning the crowd for potential danger just as Castillo did. Chano seemed oblivious to the danger, having never seen a traditional European ritual before.

After a moment's grace, Castillo stood in preparation of fulfilling his assigned role for the evening.

"I call challenge!"

Again Margaurethe tensed, staring out over the audience. Her gaze didn't go far, finding one of the Japanese contingent standing at his table. She silently cursed, but didn't otherwise react. Whiskey took the sudden change in stride, turning to face the man's table. The question in Margaurethe's mind was whether or not the challenger was doing this for his empress or some other reason. Had the *Agrun Nam* wanted to attempt something underhanded, this was when they could legally do so.

The stranger came round his table and approached the stage, stopping when the *Aga'gída* blocked his way. Dorst smiled benignly down upon the Asian.

"Let him pass," Whiskey commanded.

The guards followed Whiskey's order, stepping back. As the challenger came onto the stage, the lights illuminated him. He was tall among his people, with blue-black hair pulled back into a long tail at the base of his neck. His dark business suit was impeccable, silver cufflinks flashing under the brightness.

"Your name, sir?"

"I am Motoori Sadao, servant of Tairo-no-Mitsuko, long may she reign." He bowed low, eyes remaining on Whiskey who stood across from him.

Dorst bowed and turned back to the audience. "Motoori Sadao, you challenge the right of *Ninsumgal* Jenna Davis?"

"I do."

Dorst nodded and stepped back, leaving the two combatants at center stage. "Prepare yourselves."

Motoori bowed to Whiskey, who returned the respectful gesture. She straightened, chin lowered. Motoori assumed a martial arts stance, causing Margaurethe to tense. Did the Japanese realize this was not a physical challenge? Or was this just the way they squared off in their culture? Her mind feverishly tried to remember, but it had been centuries since their damnable empress had graced Elisibet's court with her presence.

"Lay on," Dorst called.

Every Sanguire in the room felt the first volley between them. Whiskey had practiced with Dorst over the weeks, and her strength had grown dramatically with the familiarity of useful strategy and tactics. She didn't use her full power on Mootori, knowing this was just a test even if he didn't. The intense mixture of their essences floated around them, plain for any Sanguire to feel. Whiskey had been instructed to draw the fight out for a few minutes, to ensure everyone in the room witnessed her potency. That alone would keep future conniving to a minimum, especially from the European expatriates who would report this to their friends and family back home.

Margaurethe relaxed her diligence as Motoori didn't physically attack. She remained on alert, and a quick glance down the head table told her that Whiskey's other advisors were doing the same. The Japanese empress had probably instructed her man to do this in order to gain information on Whiskey. The tactic both galled and impressed Margaurethe; she'd been prepared for an attempt by the *Agrun Nam*, but not this.

Motoori attempted a breach, and Whiskey blocked him. She didn't attack, letting him pound against her defenses for several seconds. He found what appeared to be a weakness, zeroing in on one area. She drew him in, luring him with the potential for success before abruptly wrapping around him. Motoori broke into a sweat, completely concentrated on breaking free of her control. When it was clear he would be unsuccessful, he straightened and took one step back, indicating he yielded. Whiskey immediately released him. He bowed low, then wavered. She reached out to stabilize him, and they smiled at one another. "I rescind my challenge, *Sañur Gasum* Dorst. *Ninsumgal* Jenna Davis is as you say she is, an adult in her own right."

Dorst smiled and stepped forward. "Thank you, Motoori Sadao."

Motoori bowed and shakily returned to his table. His immediate companion leaned over to whisper to him, offering a glass of water. Valmont smiled derisively at their table before noting Margaurethe's attention. With a grin, he lifted his wineglass in toast. She scowled and focused once more on the ceremony.

"Again, I proclaim *Ninsumgal* Jenna Davis as an adult. Do any Humans challenge this?"

Margaurethe heard a growl from a number of the dinner guests. Those who had gone through this ceremony were the most inclined to be offended, while the other nations would simply think the idea of a Human challenging a Sanguire an oddity of the Europeans. Whiskey had demanded this change from tradition. Normally a Human was brought forward, and the new adult fed from him or her while the adult Sanguire sat witness. In the dark past, the Human was "wild," one captured for the purpose of illustrating the youngling's ability to suppress his or her prey. These days, a *kizarus* normally stood in, making it more of a custom than a qualification of hunting ability.

"I call challenge." One of the spotlights swept to a side table, where a *kizarus* stood. The slender young man was one of the young Humans attached to Whiskey's pack. Despite the formal dress of most the attendants, he wore jeans and a leather jacket, his dark curls unruly. He threaded his way through the tables, making his way to the stage, smelling as nervous as he looked. Margaurethe had to respect his courage for volunteering to wade through a crowd of outraged Sanguire to reach his destination.

Dorst sneered at him. "You, a Human, challenge the right of *Ninsumgal* Jenna Davis?"

The young man's Adam's apple bobbed. "I do."

Dorst backed away. "Then do so at your peril."

Whiskey, more relaxed after her spar with Motoori, glared at the contender. Though this part had been rehearsed earlier that afternoon, he swallowed audibly under her gaze. His heart raced within his chest, and the aroma of anxiety tipped the scales into fear. Whiskey closed the distance between them, reaching up to grab him by the back of the neck. He tried to duck away, but she was faster and stronger, holding him tight. They stared into one another's eyes, and he capitulated, turning his head to reveal his throat. She accepted his invitation, and bit him, the smell of blood permeating the air. She didn't take much, only enough to prove her claim. Still gripping the back of his neck, she stared at him again.

"I rescind my challenge."

Dorst returned to their sides. "As well you should, Human."

Whiskey released her hold, and the young man bowed before leaving the stage. He went to the side of the stage, and circled behind the high table where Whiskey's *Aga'gída* waited to escort him to safety. No doubt a number of European Sanguire would want to get their hands on him to remind him of his place in the scheme of things.

"*Ninsumgal* Jenna Davis has been victorious over both a Sanguire and a Human challenge. You are all witnesses to what I proclaimed in the beginning—*Ninsumgal* Jenna Davis is an adult Sanguire, legally responsible for her decisions and actions, and bound by law." He stepped to one side, relinquishing the center stage to Whiskey, and bowed. "I introduce you to *Ninsumgal* Jenna Davis."

Margaurethe felt a swell of pride and love fill her heart as the applause began. Standing, she added hers to the thunderous sound, clapping in celebration.

CHAPTER FOUR

Tucked into a dark corner, the man watched the lazy dance of patrons wandering through the private club. The establishment radiated the ambiance of a small public house from the 19th century; no dance area marred its floor plan, wooden kegs and casks shared space with dusty bottles of liquor behind the bar, and musicians in the corner played a song popular in the late 1800s. A prevailing odor of absinthe and opium resisted attempts to be smothered by cigarette smoke and beer. His eyes remained on the door. Had his potential employer gotten cold feet? It was past time for their appointment. He frowned and nursed his scotch.

The bouncer, a whip thin man whose bare arms bulged with ludicrous muscle, responded to a tap at the door. He eased off his stool and peered through the peephole. Satisfied with whatever credentials were presented, he slid the bolt and opened the thick oak door to allow a newcomer inside.

In the corner, the man scanned the new arrival with a practiced eye as the doorman closed and bolted the entry. He nodded to himself, watching the cloaked and hooded person pause to inspect the crowd. When the unseen gaze met his table, he raised a chin in supplication.

His invitation accepted, the stranger approached the table, stopping in a swirl of dark cloth. "Trust no Future, howe'er pleasant."

Glad to hear the phrase and end this interminable waiting, the businessman nodded. "Let the dead Past bury its dead." His guest satisfied, he waved at the chair across from him. "Won't you sit down?" He watched the man sit—if man it was—amused to see every inch of skin hidden beneath black cloth. Dark gauze masked the stranger's face, distorting the lamplight reflecting from Sanguire eyes. Even the stranger's essence was tightly wrapped; his own mother sampling the pub's patrons would be hard put to identify him.

"Would you like something to drink?"

The stranger shook his head. "I'd much rather get these proceedings over with."

Feeling safe in the knowledge that the one across from him couldn't retaliate for fear of revealing himself, he chuckled and raised his glass in salute. "It's not easy rolling in the gutter with the rest of us, is it?" He swallowed his scotch, setting the empty glass on the table between them. "Who do you want dead?"

Shifting, the head turning to ensure their privacy, the stranger appeared nervous.

"No worries, guv. No one here gives a tinker's fart about our business."

Affronted, the stranger stiffly brought his attention back to the table. From the folds of his cloak, he produced two manila envelopes and set them on the scarred surface. "Half your payment, and information on the target and her location."

He collected the envelopes, and peeked into each one. One held a single sheet of paper, a bank statement showing the transfer of a large amount of money to his offshore accounts. The other contained several sheets of paper—a name and address, a thorough biography and background check, and two small photographs. He recognized both women, and glanced sharply at his visitor. "The target is one of these?"

"Yes, the blonde. The other will be most likely to interfere."

"She's much younger than portraits I've seen." The bio seemed extensive enough.

The stranger refused to be drawn into small talk. "All the information is there."

Studying the photo, he considered his position. The difficulty would not lie in infiltration. Unquestionably, the problem would be his unveiling by someone who knew either the person he imitated or he himself. Still, he enjoyed a challenge, and the amount of money being offered signified this would be quite the lark. "So, is she who she appears to be?"

"A pretender. Do you agree to the terms?"

He smiled at the stranger's impatience. He was someone influential then, someone whose control was threatened, for power was far more important to the Sanguire than anything. Power lasted throughout the ages, an intriguing game for people who lived hundreds of years. Money only greased the wheels and made the long life comfortable. *And knowledge, knowledge is the ultimate in strength, isn't it?* Discovering the secrets of this woman outweighed the contract for her death.

"I agree."

***

Only when he was well away from the squalid club did he remove his coverings. He pulled the stolen car into a parking lot crowded with vehicles, quickly doffing the cloak and mask. Wrapping them into a bundle, he scanned the lot for unwanted company before exiting the vehicle, and striding away. He walked briskly down a narrow sidewalk with the clothing tucked under one arm. A few hundred meters farther, he deposited the now-useless disguise into a trash bin. Half a kilometer beyond that, he arrived at his waiting limousine. The driver jumped to open the door.

As his chauffeur pulled into traffic, he pondered the day's events. Last month's vote with the *Agrun Nam* had gone poorly, and didn't look to change any time soon. The abstention had stalemated the entire proceeding. Despite intelligence reports that Davis had approached several Sanguire governments to begin diplomatic proceedings, Bentoncourt remained on the fence. The *Agrun Nam* had been split in half with one balancing between both sides of the argument. Nijmege had been livid at being thwarted yet again from bringing Davis to Europe. None of the *Sañar* believed she wanted Davis returned to the defunct throne. Davis had to die before she could officially be "returned" to her people.

Planting evidence against Bentoncourt would be dead simple. The *Nam Lugal's* adamant opinion that Davis remain in the Americas seemed good enough cause. Bentoncourt's politicking indicated he believed Davis was Elisibet reborn. The naive bastard protected her by taking his current stance, but he also had the most to lose upon Davis's ascension. Why wouldn't he want to keep her far away until someone could remove her from the picture? Once the goal was met, all fingers would point to their intrepid leader. O'Toole and her people would stop at nothing to slake their bloodthirsty fury, and this *Nam Lugal* would meet the same fate as the last.

Chewing his lower lip, he stared out the tinted window at passing countryside. The Human idiot he had hired had gloriously failed. Now on her guard, Davis was constantly flanked by O'Toole and Valmont, surrounded by her revitalized personal guard, the *Aga'gída*. Hopefully this time of peace would pave the way for his new attack dog. That and growing rumor of Elisibet's return would simplify matters. The European Sanguire whispered among themselves these days, their jaded attentions having turned to an incongruous piece of gossip from friends in the colonies, news of the Sweet Butcher's return. Their talk had not grown so loud that the *Agrun Nam* needed to make an official statement, but that time was fast approaching. Through the tangled network of families and houses, certain individuals had been put on notice, searched for, and asked to take a trip to the New Country. Rumors came from other countries, filtering through the Europeans, of invitations to discuss a new corporate foundation, one begun independently of any nation.

Time was running short. If his plans were to succeed, the Sanguire assassin must finish the job Rufus Barrett had begun.

***

Whiskey drifted toward the balcony of her apartment. She spent the majority of her free time there. It was the only place she could go outside to enjoy the day without a hundred *Aga'usi*, building security, and three hours of logistics planning. Of everything about her new lifestyle, the lack of freedom and spontaneity were the hardest to endure. It was high summer here after a too-long spring. Past the summer solstice, the nights were longer. At nine o'clock in the evening, twilight lay a blanket of gray across the river below.

So many things had changed. Early last year she had lived wild on the streets, never knowing where her next meal would come from, always in danger of police intervention or attacks from homeless predators. Now, here she stood—clean, well fed, and rich beyond her comprehension. She had gained her high school equivalency diploma, and had started college business courses last month. After years of living anonymously on the streets, so many people now knew her true name. It was a rags-to-riches tale like one seen in a Disney movie.

She chuckled. She doubted Disney would approach her for movie rights even if they knew about the Sanguire. Translating blood-sucking parasites to a Human-loving G-rated flick would be extremely difficult. Though they'd done it with a lot of Grimm's tales, hadn't they?

Whiskey saw something dark flicker across her peripheral vision and looked up. Her superior sight found one of the *Aga'gída* on the roof, placed there for the duration of her *Baruñal* Ceremony and feast. Waving, she saw him return the greeting. Building security was made up of an equal mix of both races, though all of Whiskey's personal guard were Sanguire. The other staff kept their distance, whether from ignorance of her political position or knowledge of it, she didn't know.

Among the Humans working in the building, she had become a local celebrity. Father Castillo insisted on treating her as royalty whenever they met, invariably in front of some employee or other. Dorst had gleefully informed Whiskey that current rumor among the unwashed masses was that she was the by-blow of royalty, though no one had been able to pin down who had fathered her. As time went on, more and more people referred to her by her royal title, *Ninsumgal*, rather than as president of the company. Gareth Davis's family had yet to be located, so even the Sanguire on the payroll had cause to wonder about Whiskey's parentage. At least she no longer had to explain her nickname; it had taken several weeks of constant explanation of the connection between her initials—J.D.—and the Jack Daniels brand of whiskey.

The only European Sanguire who didn't treat her as if she wore an unwieldy crown were Margaurethe and Valmont. Margaurethe, of course, had very good reasons—friend, confidante, and potential lover. Whiskey couldn't stand the thought of her bowing and scraping in deference. Margaurethe only did so when it was required for form's sake. Valmont's reasons were unknown. He kept his secrets well and Whiskey didn't pry. They both knew she could overpower his will in an instant; they flirted back and forth with words and gestures, he never quite giving cause for her to do so, and she searching for where she stood with him. At first Whiskey had felt relief at his lack of royal acknowledgement, though not at all comfortable with the emotion. Now, she held a grudging respect. The Valmont Elisibet remembered—teasing and profane—remained beneath a thick shell of sarcasm and self-deprecation. Despite having assassinated Elisibet, and regardless of Whiskey's native mistrust and anger at that betrayal, Valmont's presence among her advisors...completed things. Nothing felt right without both he and Margaurethe at her side.

She still didn't trust him.

Behind her, she heard the soft snick of the door. Without turning, she smiled, knowing who approached.

"Father Castillo says you've done him justice."

Whiskey turned toward Margaurethe, reaching for her hand. "I have a good teacher."

They balanced and complemented each other well. Where one was dark, the other was light. Margaurethe stood a little taller than Whiskey, her dark hair reflecting red highlights from the interior lamps as she stepped closer. Olive skin and high cheekbones suggested a Mediterranean descent though she insisted her blood sang for Eire and nowhere else. Emerald eyes, alight with pleasure, twinkled.

Raising the hand she held to her lips, Whiskey kissed the palm, lingering a bit longer than politeness dictated. "Is everyone still partying?"

"A good number of them." Margaurethe moved closer, sliding an arm around Whiskey's waist. She peered down the building at the busy front drive below. "The bulk of the major players have taken their leave."

Whiskey followed her gaze, watching as the valet staff hustled back and forth to deliver cars to the delegates. Only the *Wi Wacipi Wakan* had taken up the offer of rooms. "I hadn't expected to see *Saggina* Bescoe," she said, referring to the leader of the local European Sanguire embassy.

"He called at the last minute, asking if he could attend. I think his desire to not offend you outweighed his duty to the *Agrun Nam*."

Grimacing, Whiskey returned her attention to the woman in her arms. "In other words, he wasn't here in an official capacity."

"Politics isn't all wine and roses."

Whiskey smiled at the musical lilt of Margaurethe's accent. "Remind me to order all the wine and roses in the city for you."

"I shall."

She laughed at the matter-of-fact tone.

With a sigh, Margaurethe leaned against her. They stood, heads together, as they stared out at the river. "Rather a nasty day for you today, hasn't it been?"

Whiskey almost nodded but stopped, not wanting to upset their stance. Moments of quiet between them were few and far between, and she wanted to enjoy this for as long as possible. "It wasn't too bad, even that change of challenge," she allowed. "I don't know that I'll ever get used to all the—" She stopped, unable to come up with the right word.

"Pageantry."

"Yeah, that." She closed her eyes, recalling the momentary terror that had engulfed her when the doors had opened, and again when Dorst had brought her forward. "I'm just glad I didn't make a mess of things."

Margaurethe tightened their embrace. "You were marvelous, love. I don't think anyone knew how nervous you truly were."

A bark of laughter escaped Whiskey. "Sithathor did. She had a huge dinner waiting for me."

"Ah, I'd hoped so."

A fond smile for her chambermaid remained on Whiskey's lips. As time passed, Sithathor's maternal instincts had wormed their way into her heart, forging a connection between them that Margaurethe seemed to find distressing upon occasion. Small wonder considering the constant threat of danger. It was anyone's guess where the next attack would come from, and paranoia had become Margaurethe's watchword.

"Where would you be right now if everything had remained the same?"

Used to the sudden change of subject when Sithathor was discussed, Whiskey considered her response. "It's Tuesday, right?" After an answering nod, she continued. "Well, I would have spent all night at Tallulah's, and grabbed breakfast at Mickey D's. I'd probably hang out at the library to keep busy. If I didn't have much money, I'd spange downtown."

"Spange?"

Whiskey smiled. "Spare change. Beg for cash."

"A sad life."

Pulling away, Whiskey looked at Margaurethe. "Not unless you make it one. There are lots of kids out there who become family for one another. Street moms and street dads help the younger ones learn the ropes of survival."

"Did you have a street mom?"

A grin tugged at her lips. "For the first year, yeah. Her name was Shadow. She was a couple of years older than Gin and I, found us about a week after we met each other. We were both scared to death and nearly starving. Never would have survived without Shad."

"I'm glad someone was there for you. Where is she now?"

"Don't know. We left Portland for Seattle about five years ago. Haven't heard from her since." Whiskey felt her smile fading as she lost herself to the memories. "I guess it is a sad life, isn't it?"

"Not unless you make it one."

Chuckling, Whiskey pulled Margaurethe close once again. "Have I told you that you looked ravishing tonight?"

Margaurethe feigned preening, using one hand to brush at her hair. "Not today."

"You. Look. Ravishing. Tonight." Whiskey cupped her cheek, caressing with a thumb.

"As do you."

Whiskey's thumb slid along Margaurethe's cheekbone, her fingers brushing the golden earring dangling from an earlobe. She leaned closer, glad that though Margaurethe was taller the difference between them wasn't awkward. Her lips brushed Margaurethe's, her mind caressing the mulled wine and wood smoke of Margaurethe's Sanguire essence. Whiskey felt a deep, abiding love, a wordless welcome, and a sense of joy she'd never known she'd missed until this woman had arrived at her side. As they languished within each other's souls, Whiskey could only liken this feeling to a homecoming.

Eventually the kiss ended, though the mental connection between them remained strong. Margaurethe cocked an eyebrow at her, a smile on her lips. "I'll have to wear this dress more often."

Chuckling, Whiskey brushed her knuckles across Margaurethe's temple. "No complaints here."

Margaurethe caught Whiskey's hand, stepping back to put some space between them. She retreated within their bond, as well. Her expression remained one of love, though Whiskey saw and felt a sense of closure between them. Margaurethe kissed the back of Whiskey's hand and released her. "It's been a long night."

Whiskey accepted the reticence for the uncertainty it was, pulling mentally away from Margaurethe as she nodded. They both had hurdles to cross. Margaurethe needed to reconcile the woman she loved centuries ago with the woman who stood before her now. Whiskey's baggage came in the form of memories and assumptions gleaned from Elisibet Vasilla's memories, and the fear that Margaurethe saw more of Elisibet than Whiskey when they were together. She and Margaurethe had been dancing back and forth for months, ever on the edge of consummating a relationship only for one or the other to retreat at the last moment.

They strolled back into her suite, not touching. "I'll see you tomorrow?"

Margaurethe turned and smiled. "Of course, *m'cara*. Another busy day in the international world of business." She reached out and recaptured Whiskey's hand, tugging her close for a final kiss. "Good night."

"Good night, Margaurethe." Whiskey watched until the door closed quietly. Spinning around, she brought both her hands to her head, running fingers through the golden strands. "Argh!"

CHAPTER FIVE

Whiskey frowned at the textbook, working her way through the finer points of American Literature, her laptop open beside her. She and her pack had permanently taken over one of the open sitting areas on the third floor of The Davis Group. The move had been her idea, making her visible to the people who worked for the company, and thus more approachable to Human and Sanguire alike. She was constantly underfoot, always available to chat, and more than willing to help maintenance take out the trash or lend a hand in the copy room on one of the floors. The ploy had worked well with the more conservative members of her workforce, staid older Humans who frowned on the tattoos, piercings and wild hair of the younglings among them. They were less inclined toward scandalous gossip this way.

Cora and her new boyfriend, an off-duty security officer, whispered and giggled with each other on the couch, not quite slipping into impropriety. Zebediah cast withering glances in Cora's direction, his spiked red mohawk moving like a weather vane in heavy wind as her behavior interrupted his video game. Three of Whiskey's *Aga'usi* idled about the room, keeping tabs on their charge. Alphonse had gone to an electronics store with Dorst to look for parts for one of their mutual projects. Daniel, his dark blond mohawk laying across his scalp, sat at the table with Whiskey, playing blackjack with Nupa and Chaniya. Nupa, an American Indian, had the only full head of hair of the men, the dark brown locks brushing his shoulders.

The newcomer, Chaniya, was another reason for the move to a more public venue. As various governments sent representatives, invariably someone's son or daughter ended up hanging with Whiskey's pack for a while. No longer using Whiskey's apartment as a hangout eased the stress on her personal guard. She didn't have to have security with her in her own quarters this way. Margaurethe hoped to create a diverse atmosphere within The Davis Group as treaties were signed. Chaniya's mother was the ambassador of their people, here to hammer out an agreement with the Board of Directors. Once a treaty was signed, an African Sanguire would join the board—no doubt Chaniya herself would remain here, a member of Whiskey's pack of younglings. She got along well enough with the others, and Whiskey held out hopes that the adults would follow their children's examples.

"Whiskey."

Looking up from her book, she smiled as she spotted Margaurethe. Whiskey closed the book and stood, walking forward and taking Margaurethe into her arms. She could never be in the same room with her without touching her in some manner. "Hi." She kissed warm lips. Margaurethe squeezed her, but broke off the kiss before it became inappropriate. Only then did Whiskey realize Margaurethe hadn't come alone.

Father Castillo and two strangers stood just inside the room. Castillo appeared no more than twenty-five years of age. His curly dark hair hung to his shoulders. He wore the cassock of his order, though he wasn't a practicing priest these days, having taken a leave of absence to become Whiskey's advisor.

The first stranger smiled at Whiskey. He stood tall, with broad shoulders, casually confident in his body, indicating he knew how to defend himself. His bronze skin tone and jet black hair marked him as Mayan, as did the colorful shirt he wore. Beside him, an older man stared at the ground, vigorously wringing a tweed cap in his hands. His hair was iron gray, and a bit ragged. His downturned face made it difficult for Whiskey to identify him, but a vague tickle of memory feathered along the back of her mind. He wore a brown suit, frayed about the hem of his jacket, and a barely visible bow tie.

"I'd like you to meet some people." Margaurethe drew Whiskey toward the new arrivals. "This is Pacal, your new man-at-arms."

"It is a pleasure to make your acquaintance, *Ninsumgal* Davis." Pacal bowed in the proper European manner, tilting his head to one side. "I hope to serve you well in the years to come."

Man-at-arms? What's that? "Thank you, Pacal." Whiskey's puzzled gaze flickered to Margaurethe. She didn't ask, not wanting to display her ignorance.

Castillo answered the unspoken question. "Pacal is one of the foremost warriors of the Mayan people. It's time your education included hand-to-hand combat as well as strategy and tactics." He patted Pacal on the shoulder. "He will be your beginning instructor, and eventually we'll expand your repertoire of weapons to include melee weapons and conventional armament."

Whiskey's eyebrows rose. She felt the collective interest of her pack behind her, knowing that Nupa and Zebediah paid special attention. "Of course." Returning her attention to the man-at-arms, she reached out and shook his hand. "I hope you don't mind a few extra students." She nodded over one shoulder to their avid audience.

Pacal smiled graciously, looking beyond Whiskey to the others. "Of course. It's much easier to practice with a number of students rather than one."

Margaurethe cleared her throat, indicating the nervous man

waiting to be introduced. "This is Andri Sigmarsson. Do you remember him?"

This man reeked of nervousness as he stumbled to his knees. "My *Ninsumgal*."

He spoke almost inaudibly, but a prickle of memory teased Whiskey's thoughts. She tilted her head to stare at him. "Look at me, Mr. Sigmarsson."

Neck stiff, Adam's apple bobbing as he swallowed, he forced his head up to reveal his features—a too-large nose, black eyes, and bushy sideburns going as gray as the hair on his head—and she recognized him.

Flash.

"I want him." Her voice held a higher pitch, the tone petulant and childish. She stared greedily at a litter of puppies suckling at a bitch. The squirming mass of canine life held a single all-black pup on which she was focused.

"Of course, Aga Gasan," *a man said. "But he is newly born. He will die if you take him now. You must wait a few weeks before he will survive without his mother."*

"I do not care!" She stamped her foot. "I want him now." Glaring at the man in servant's livery, she lowered her chin as she had seen her father do upon occasion. "Do not vex me, Andri. I will have him now or you will answer to the Usumgal."

Andri cast a resigned glance at the dog's owner, and nodded stiffly to the young princess. "Yes, Aga Gasan. *The black one you said?"*

Flash.

A young Margaurethe floated across the dance floor, splendid in her emerald green gown.

"I want her."

"Yes, Ninsumgal," *Andri said. "I'll see to it."*

Flash.

"Andri?" Whiskey stared. "You're Andri, her valet."

The man's eyes tried to shift away at her recognition. He was clearly discomfited. "Ja, *Ninsumgal*."

Whiskey knew what this man had gone through during his tenure as Elisibet's valet. He had been with the Sweet Butcher from her childhood and through the most vicious stages of her rule. It was no wonder he appeared nervous, not knowing what he was getting into or whether or not Whiskey would be as cruel and cold as her previous incarnation. She had intimate knowledge of what entertainment Elisibet enjoyed. Taking his trembling hands into hers, the cap he held and all, she lowered her voice to a soothing register. "I'm very pleased to make your acquaintance, Mr. Sigmarsson."

His brow furrowed, and his shivering hitched in surprise. "Uh, *danke*, *Ninsumgal*. I'm pleased to make yours."

"Andri has come to offer his services, Whiskey." Margaurethe glanced at Castillo.

Whiskey kept her eyes on the man before her. "Are you certain, Mr. Sigmarsson?" She frowned. "I know how unpleasant your job was before. I don't want you to be here if you wish to be somewhere else."

Again a flicker of puzzlement crossed his face. He opened his mouth to speak, and had to clear his throat before finding his voice. "I'm certain, my *Gasan*. My family has served yours for generations. I'll not shirk my duties now."

A smile graced Whiskey's features, and she held his hands tight before releasing them. "Thank you, Mr. Sigmarsson."

Margaurethe hooked her arm through Whiskey's. "Father, if you'd be so kind to show them to their rooms? And, Pacal, check with Helen regarding Whiskey's schedule. Let's get her started as soon as possible."

Castillo and Pacal both nodded agreement before turning to leave, but Sigmarsson remained in place, the nervous wringing of his cap his only movement. It took a moment for Whiskey to make the connection. He waited for her to dismiss him. "Oh! Yes, please do as Margaurethe says, Mr. Sigmarsson. We'll...um... meet later to discuss your duties."

Proper etiquette shown, he bowed. "My *Gasan*." He backed toward the hall, and followed Castillo and Pacal.

Whiskey turned to Margaurethe. "You could have given me some warning."

"I could have. It was much more fun to do it this way, though."

"Wench."

"Yes, I am." Margaurethe drew herself up, haughty in her pride, before falling to the laughter that infected her.

Whiskey loved to hear Margaurethe's laugh. She took the woman in her arms, risking decency with her roaming hands, regardless of their audience. "Just for that, I'm going to kiss you senseless."

"Oh, such a threat." Margaurethe rolled her eyes, failing in her attempt to appear disgusted. Behind them, her pack returned to their diversions. Even Cora no longer acted resentful of losing her place at Whiskey's side. Instead, she instigated a tickle attack on her current beau that more than irritated Zebediah beside them.

"A promise." Whiskey gave Margaurethe a light kiss, not allowing herself to fall sway to temptation. Later when they were alone she could indulge herself, but not now. Even the most liberal Humans in her employ would frown at finding the company's president and CEO heavy petting in the corridor outside the childcare facility. "When did Andri get here?"

"A few days ago." Margaurethe led them farther away from the pack.

They strolled down the corridor. "I thought he had died in the Purge. Where has he been?"

"Hiding in Switzerland."

Whiskey shook her head. "For four hundred years?"

"A number of Elisibet's former staff have been successful at hiding. Very few of us could afford to be seen in the public eye. Whole families went underground." Margaurethe shrugged, hugging Whiskey's arm. "Now that word is spreading of your existence, several are coming out of the woodwork."

The idea that Elisibet's supporters were revealing themselves didn't ease Whiskey's anxiety. Anyone who supported the atrocities his or her leader had perpetrated wasn't someone Whiskey wanted beside her. Elisibet had been as good as Hitler in developing a sense of terror in her people, and had cultivated the most cruel of them. Had Elisibet had as good a propagandist as the Nazi leader, she would have brought about a warped sense of nationalism. The idea of a fascist Sanguire state made Whiskey shiver. *This world would be a very different place.* She pushed away the thoughts. "What are we going to do with Andri? I don't need a valet, and I'm not going to toss Sithathor out on her ear."

"Actually, you do need a valet. Sithathor can continue her duties as chambermaid, and Andri will take care of your clothing and appearance. His past history and security clearance will allow it. He can assist Sithathor, and help with Anthony's apartment if there's not enough work to go around for him."

Whiskey nodded. "And Pacal? Are we closer to a treaty than I thought?"

"No." They reached the corner, and Margaurethe veered to the left toward the doors leading to the patio. She nodded to the guard at the security desk, waiting for Whiskey to open the door before stepping outside. "But he was between employers at the moment, and offered his services. I thought it would behoove us to start integrating their people with ours as soon as possible."

"Ah, an example." The sun was bright, and Whiskey grimaced at the sharp stabs of pain in her eyes. Fortunately, the maintenance staff had an excellent gardener on hand, and she escorted Margaurethe toward a shaded haven beneath a number of small saplings. They sat on a wooden bench.

"Not just an example, *m'cara*. He really is the best of his people." Margaurethe tangled their fingers together. "Now that you're officially an adult, you can be challenged. You need to be able to defend yourself should that occur."

"Are you saying I couldn't be challenged before last week?" Whiskey scoffed. "Did you forget Fiona?"

"You challenged her, Whiskey. There's the difference. You no longer have the luxury of being considered a child."

Margaurethe's serious tone dampened Whiskey's humor. She studied their entwined hands. "Do you think Valmont will challenge me?" The silence between them grew long enough that she looked up at her companion.

"I don't know."

Despite his history, Valmont had shown no indication of repeating his actions any time soon. If anything, he appeared to be in for the long haul. He gave his opinion on the board with acerbic wit and voted his conscience, though Margaurethe would argue he had none.

Whiskey said, "I don't think he will." Margaurethe gave an uncommitted murmur, this issue being the major point of contention between them, and Whiskey squeezed her hand. "If he does, it won't be for years, yet. I don't know why he's here, but he could have killed me when we first met, and didn't."

Margaurethe didn't offer her usual argument, probably aware it would make no difference. Instead, she smiled and changed the subject. "I hear Sithathor's making baklava tonight?"

Whiskey allowed herself to be distracted by discussions of her favorite dessert. She set aside her worries, trusting her people to keep her safe as she invited Margaurethe to join her for dinner. There was a time and place for politics and business, and a time and place to let such topics go for the sake of sanity. Elisibet had made paranoia an artform, and Whiskey refused to allow that to happen to her.

Even if it killed her.

CHAPTER SIX

Whiskey stood in the foyer on the second floor, elbows planted on a wooden rail as she gazed out upon the front drive. The marble in the lobby below made every voice and footstep echo, creating the illusion of a multitude though few employees were present on a Sunday afternoon. A foreign car pulled onto the drive from the street. The tinted window on the driver's side dropped down to reveal Valmont, grinning at the first of three guards converging upon him. He said something, and winked, evincing pleasure at verbally yanking the chain of the supervisor on duty. As he climbed out of the vehicle, two of Whiskey's *Aga'gída* arrived in the lobby to meet him. He made small talk, mirthful as he handed over the car keys.

Since his "return to the fold," Whiskey had kept him close, meeting with him three or four times a week. Her argument to Margaurethe had been one of education; she wanted Valmont to assist her with relearning the Sanguire. He held a different view of the political and social situation; Whiskey needed as many contrasting opinions as possible to put together a whole picture of a people she hadn't known existed two years ago. Margaurethe absented herself from these meetings in protest. Unwilling to leave Whiskey to Valmont's tender mercies, she had left standing orders to both building security and the *Aga'gída* to ensure Whiskey and Valmont were never alone together. Whiskey understood Margaurethe's reticence—a wild card, untrustworthy, Valmont had murdered before though Elisibet had borne the brunt of that death, not Whiskey. Still, it had been several months with no threat in evidence. The extra guards had become less a deterrent and more an insult, not so much to Valmont who gave an air of expecting such abuse, but to Whiskey. Other than his flippant, acerbic tongue, he had minded his manners at the board meetings, slowly becoming a contributing member to The Davis Group. The extra security insisted upon gave the impression that Whiskey was weak, and unable to defend herself in her own home.

Once inside the building, Valmont looked up and saw her. He gave her a sardonic wave and grin before disappearing beneath her feet as he was escorted toward the elevators. His words bounced readily off the marble flooring. "No strip search today?"

One of his escorts responded. "No, *Sublugal Sañar* Valmont. Not today."

"Ah, I'm wounded. I so enjoy those meaningful moments with you."

One of the guards chuckled. "I'm sure you do. The *Ninsumgal* is up—" The words cut off as the elevator doors closed on their conversation.

Whiskey laughed as well, pushing away from the railing. She turned and crossed her arms, leaning back against the wood. Up here, the carpeted floor muffled their footsteps, though she heard the elevator's soft chime and the doors open.

Valmont rounded the corner, her personal guards trailing.

He gave her a light bow. "Good morning, Whiskey. How are you today?"

"Not bad. Are you hungry?" She gestured toward the Executive Dining Room to her right.

He glanced in that direction, a grin playing across his face. "I could do with a bite." Showing off his teeth, he clicked them together without unsheathing his fangs.

Whiskey smirked. "Come on then. I have some sandwiches heading our way. Do you like ham and cheese?"

Falling in beside her, they entered the dining room. "It'll do for the moment."

Behind them, the two *Aga'usi* followed. One remained just inside the door, and the other placed himself at the fire exit. Whiskey ignored them, but decided it was high time to have a word with Margaurethe. "Have a seat."

From the kitchen, Andri appeared with a tray of sandwiches and sodas. Behind him, Whiskey saw another guard loitering there, and scowled. *Maybe a reminder to Anthony about who's really in charge.*

Valmont eyed the server. "New hire?"

Whiskey frowned a moment before catching the hint. "Something like that. This is Andri Sigmarsson. He used to be Elisibet's valet. Margaurethe found him, and brought him here yesterday."

"Ah, yes. I remember now." Valmont watched him set down the tray. "How are you, Andri? It's been quite some time since I've had the pleasure."

The homely man swallowed, eyes flickering about the room as he bowed again. "I'm quite well, *Sublugal Sañar* Valmont. Thank you for inquiring."

"Thank you for lunch, Andri." Whiskey smiled softly. "You can go now." Andri bobbed, and backed away before disappearing in the direction he had come. "We've hired him back as my valet, but he's insisted on fixing my food when I'm away from my apartment. He's been skittish like that since he got here. I hope he'll loosen up eventually."

"Considering your predecessor's disposition, you may have a long wait."

"Did Elisibet... Did she do anything to Andri?" Whiskey leaned forward. "I don't recall much, but a lot of my memories are spotty."

Reacting to her earnest tone, his flippant expression sobered. He chose his words carefully. "I don't think Elisibet did anything but be Elisibet in his presence."

"That would be enough, wouldn't it?" Not expecting an answer, she pushed the tray to the center of the table. "Have one. I had him make up enough for both of us."

Valmont helped himself to a sandwich and a soda. Whiskey offered food to her personal guard, and Valmont smiled when they sternly declined. Whiskey found their stiff reaction humorous, knowing that it was Valmont they attempted to impress. She had no idea why, nor did she think they had succeeded with instilling a sense of danger. All three would have to link together to take Valmont down. None were old enough to do so on their own.

They ate mostly in silence, occasionally speaking of weather and business. Each time she met with him, she had something new she wanted to ask, something she felt uncomfortable bringing up to anyone else, even her aunt and grandmother. It was easier with Valmont—he was a predator like Elisibet and Dorst. Margaurethe and Castillo would feel alarm at some of Whiskey's musings, and Dorst was too much a servant. He would never lie to her, but his responses would be filtered by what he thought she wanted to know, not the truth she desired. She had to ask these things of someone who would tell her the truth without sugarcoating or becoming agitated. It felt odd to realize Valmont was the one person to fill the bill, but over the months she had become used to their strange relationship. "Why do you hunt when there are *kizarusi* to be had everywhere?"

His eyebrows rose. "Because we are born to hunt, not feed off Humans like cattle."

Whiskey lifted a shoulder, and looked away as if bored. "What difference does it make? Blood is blood. A *kizarus* is always available."

Valmont smiled. "So says one who has never hunted."

"Then what's the attraction?"

Instead of answering, he posed a question. "Do you enjoy feeding from a *kizarus*?"

She pursed her lips, looking inside for the answer. Since her initial feeding from Aleya during the *Ñíri Kurám*, she had fed from a number of Humans. As a youngling, she required more blood than an older Sanguire, and feeding from the same *kizarus* over an extended time was unhealthy for the Human. "I feel better when I've finished. I enjoy it to the extent that I enjoyed eating this sandwich. It fills the need."

He edged forward on his seat, and placed his elbows on the table, hands crossed before him. "But it tastes different when you go to the kitchen and make it yourself, doesn't it? You can pick and choose the ingredients depending on what appeals to you at the moment. Some days you use a bit more mustard than others, other days Swiss cheese instead of cheddar. You have control to please your palate."

Whiskey considered his point. "I understand the analogy."

Valmont smiled. "I much prefer rummaging through the refrigerator to having my meals served upon demand."

She felt the rightness of his words. "I've noticed differences in flavor." His gaze sharpened, and she allowed a little of her uncertainty to show through. "At first I thought it was, you know, different blood types. But now I'm not so sure."

"Why?"

She searched for the words, feeling them out in her mind before pronouncing them. "Because I've fed from two different people with the same blood type. They tasted very different from one another."

"Have you figured out why?"

"I think so."

"Tell me."

"One is a *kizarus* whose family has served the Sanguire for generations. It's an honor and a privilege for him to do this. He feels pride. The other is a woman who gets off on it; to her it's a form of sex."

"That's it exactly." Valmont's grin was one of pride. "Humans feel emotion. Their bodies pump out chemicals in response to these emotions. Fear, arousal, anger—all color the blood in different ways."

"Some days a bit more mustard than others."

He winked at her. "There you have it."

She studied him, though he remained nonchalant under the examination. Nodding her head once, she turned to her security force. "You're dismissed."

Valmont's eyebrows lifted to his hairline, his expression echoed by the others.

"My *Ninsumgal*, our orders are to remain in the room when *Sublugal Sañar* Valmont is present."

Whiskey dropped her chin, glaring at the one who had spoken. She reached out to him and his immediate companion, gathering their essences to her with little effort despite the age differences between her and them. The one who spoke paled, and the other stumbled. Valmont shrank into his chair to avoid notice. "You forget who is the one in charge here." Whiskey's low voice carried a whip crack of authority. "You swore your allegiance to me, not *Ki'an Gasan* Margaurethe. You will obey me."

The *Aga'us* swallowed once, and bowed. "Yes, my *Ninsumgal*." He hastily backed toward the door Andri had used, waving at his companion to leave the other way.

"And tell your friend in the kitchen to leave as well."

"Yes, my *Ninsumgal*."

Whiskey frowned. "I don't think we have long. He's probably gone to report to Margaurethe."

"Have long for what?" Valmont asked, tentative. "Having pissed Margaurethe off many times in the past, I'm not too keen on the idea of repeating the adventure."

Whiskey smiled. "Well, an adventure is exactly what I'm thinking." She laughed at his suspicious expression. "I want you to take me hunting."

"I beg your pardon?"

"I want you to teach me to hunt," she repeated slowly. "There's something missing and I need to find it, or I can't rule effectively."

"And I'm to teach you?"

"You're the only one I can trust in this matter."

Valmont barked out a laugh, and pushed his chair back from the table. "You must to be kidding! I'm the last person to trust, Whiskey. You've remembered enough of Elisibet's past to know that."

"Maybe." She paused, wondering how to word this. "But you've had ample opportunity to do the deed again, and you haven't. I think the *Agrun Nam* played you. They twisted your natural anger and mourning for your mentor to convince you to assassinate Elisibet." She tilted her head. "And I think you've figured out I'm not her."

She must have read him well enough, because he scowled back at her. "So that makes you think I'm trustworthy enough to escort you on a hunting trip?"

"Yes."

"What about the security? Enough dogs mucking about ruin the tracks."

His argument sounded hollow. She had sprung the idea on him so thoroughly that he still struggled to catch up. "It'll just be you and me."

Valmont snorted, half amused and half incredulous. "You're serious."

Whiskey nodded. "Very much so."

He considered her request, and she left him to his thoughts. If Margaurethe got wind of this before they pulled it off, they both knew she would kill him. The longer Whiskey spent time with Valmont, however, the more she missed the Valmont of her memories. He had stood tall and proud at Elisibet's side once, and that was the man Whiskey admired. In the end, he had stood up for what was right, regardless of the centuries their friendship had enjoyed. He had attempted to sway Elisibet from the path she had chosen, and faced her down when nothing else worked. He had been counted a hero to his people, and been denigrated ever since among those whom he had once considered friends. "We both know I can force obedience, Valmont. But I won't compel you if you really don't want to do this."

Her words interrupted his thoughts. He looked sharply at her, then flicked a glance toward the main entry. She heard approaching footsteps, and Margaurethe's angry voice as she asked questions of the dismissed *Aga'usi* outside. "Yes," he said.

She smiled and relaxed in her chair. "Thank you."

The door flew open, stopping more discussion on the matter. He quickly assumed his devil-may-care pose for the new arrival.

"Margaurethe." Whiskey stood and held out her hand.

Valmont rose and bowed in greeting. He liked tweaking his nose at her with courtly behavior, and employed it generously whenever she was near. "Dearest Margaurethe, what a surprise." His tone left no question that he lied.

Suspicion coloring her movements, Margaurethe approached the table and took Whiskey's hand. She ignored Valmont. "Alan told me you dismissed him."

Here it comes. "Yeah, I did."

"Certainly you can understand that being alone with this... man can be dangerous?"

Valmont's grin widened.

Whiskey's disappeared. "His name is Valmont, Margaurethe. And I believe I know how dangerous he can be." She sent a tendril of her essence to Margaurethe, caressing the wood smoke and mulled wine with her mind.

Margaurethe's lips thinned, eyes snapping. Whirling about, she glared at Valmont. "I don't trust him. He assassinated Elisibet, and will do the same to you. You must never be alone with him."

Valmont sobered at the attack, but he didn't defend himself.

Appalled, Whiskey stepped between them. "Margaurethe!" Startled by the keen authority in her tone, both older Sanguire turned to stare at her. "Thank you, Margaurethe. Your opinion is noted. Please, leave us."

Margaurethe gaped. Her skin blanched as she realized she had crossed a subtle line between them. She opened her mouth to speak.

"Please." Whiskey's expression softened. "I'll be fine."

After a minor hesitation, Margaurethe lifted her chin. She swept past Valmont, who remained silent until she was gone.

"She loves you, and only wishes to see you safe. I can't say she doesn't have cause to be concerned."

Whiskey smiled. "You haven't killed me yet. Besides, if I'm to be this *Ninsumgal* you all want me to be, I can't be kept safe, can I?"

Valmont shook his head. "No. Unfortunately not." After a moment of silence, he winked. "Now if you will excuse me, I've some things to attend to."

"Of course. I'll see you in a couple of days."

"I'll show myself out."

Whiskey nodded. As soon as he was gone, she rubbed her temples. She fully understood the origin of Margaurethe's worries. The fear of losing Elisibet had made Margaurethe overly protective. The differences between the Margaurethe of Whiskey's borrowed memories and the one of today seemed shallow on the surface. Beneath the calm and loving exterior was a depth of helplessness Margaurethe refused to be a party to ever again. It colored everything.

And Whiskey couldn't let it stop her.

CHAPTER SEVEN

Whiskey paced. Hunger gnawed at her belly, an unfortunate consequence of being Sanguire. The biological impetus was both strength and weakness. Blood activated her endocrine system in ways unknown to Human scientists. Her studies had gone past general biological sciences and into the systems specific to Homo Sanguirus. There was an enzyme in Humans that Sanguire lacked. That complex protein boosted a Sanguire's physical abilities and speed, and assisted other internal functions down to the molecular level. The failing came from starvation—Whiskey could eat and drink day and night, but without feeding from a Human she would die as surely as if she had refused any sustenance at all.

She circled the room and considered what Valmont had discussed with her. Prior to their conversation, she thought the idea of hunting a Human seemed archaic. Certainly, with *kizarusi* always available, she had no need to find her own sustenance. Besides, she had lived on the streets, knew its denizens and the dangers inherent there. Who did the Sanguire hunt if not the helpless and hopeless of society? She couldn't hunt a street person down; she would feel too much compassion for her victim. Whomever she targeted would live, certainly; the Sanguire needed only a small amount of Human blood every few days. Stories of vampires draining their victims of their last drop illustrated myth, not reality.

On the flip side, she felt disassociated from the Sanguire despite being surrounded by them. During any number of political discussions with old-timers on the streets, she had heard the argument that the politicians ruling the country had no sense of their constituents. They sat in their gilded mansions, receiving hundreds of thousands of dollars in annual salaries as they passed incomprehensible laws, and couldn't understand the poor man's point of view. Whiskey had begun to think that her exalted position as president of The Davis Group and burgeoning high *Ninsumgal* of the Sanguire had created the same political schism. She knew nothing of the day-to-day existence of her people, not having lived with them for most her life. Her current level of protection against potential danger had made it all but impossible to learn anything about them.

She recalled Valmont's analogy of food from a refrigerator.

Up until now, she had been fastidious in her meals; she took what she needed to survive without fuss or dramatics. The *kizarusi* brought to her were all handpicked by Margaurethe or Father Castillo. Either the Humans had served Sanguire families for generations, or they received a certain level of enjoyment from the exchange. She had never manipulated the *kizarusi* coming to her, and she wondered if actively enhancing the experience would create a difference in taste as Valmont had suggested. Today was the day of enlightenment.

Whiskey stopped roaming the room when she heard the soft chime of the elevator in the hallway. She smiled as she picked up a familiar scent. Aleya had been her first *kizarus* during her Turning. It seemed appropriate that she should also be Whiskey's first attempt at enhancing their meeting. Her taste was well known to Whiskey, and any experimentation would be noticeable. She responded to the light knock on the door with a call to enter.

"My *Ninsumgal*. May I present Aleya."

"Thank you, Sasha. You can leave us." She kept her back to the room until she heard the door firmly close. Turning, she smiled at the plump Goth woman. "How are you, Aleya?"

The young woman's heart-shaped face flushed, her eyes widening at Whiskey's sultry purr. "I'm...fine." Her bag remained on her shoulder, and she clutched the strap with one hand. "Are you okay? You seem different."

"I'm quite well." Whiskey's eyes focused on the woman's throat, and she padded closer. Though she portrayed a sexual energy to her prey, her thoughts focused more on a giddy enjoyment of the game and the ending of her hunger. Aleya's scent changed, and subtle differences indicated her arousal. Their previous exchanges had always played out with Aleya as the aggressor. Her usual forward demeanor fled in light of Whiskey's active seduction. Whiskey circled behind, not quite touching as she inhaled deeply. Aleya shivered in response. "You look nice." Whiskey came back around, allowing her gaze to roam the curvaceous body. "Is that a new blouse?"

Aleya swallowed, and nodded. "Yes, it is." Flushing, she smiled, reminiscent of a teenager given a compliment by her high school crush. "I was hoping you'd like it."

Whiskey traced the low neckline of the clothing in question, drawing her finger along the shoulder, down the exposed flesh across the collarbone, caressing the top of Aleya's abundant breasts, and dipping into the hollow between them. She found it interesting that Aleya found her seduction so intense though Whiskey felt nothing but curiosity and hunger. A stray thought passed through her mind; did Sanguire and Humans ever become involved in lengthy relationships? Were there half-breed Sanguire?

Her stomach twinged, and she returned to the game.

Eyes closed, Aleya stood still, white-knuckled hand still

gripping her purse strap. She jumped when Whiskey lifted the bag from her shoulder. Before she could react, Whiskey kissed her for the first time. Aleya groaned at the wet invasion into her mouth. Her heart pumped fast, and her scent changed dramatically, causing Whiskey's mouth to water. Aleya had always enjoyed their time together, finding the entire process sexually arousing, but Whiskey's active participation magnified Aleya's responses. The *kizarus's* breasts heaved as she panted, and her hands slid up Whiskey's back, demanding in their pressure.

Whiskey continued to play with her food, teasing incessantly, her lips and hands alternating between gentle caresses and rough gropes. At no time did she touch Aleya in an overtly sexual manner except with kisses. That hardly seemed to matter to the woman as her arousal escalated. Whiskey reached the point where her hunger would not be denied. Walking Aleya backward, they bumped into the wall by the door. With a growl, Whiskey planted her thigh between Aleya's, knowing the woman needed the contact. Her teeth already extended, she buried them in Aleya's neck. Hot blood splashed across her tongue. Aleya's hand buried itself in her hair, holding her close as she surged against Whiskey's thigh. Whiskey drank her fill, marveling at the difference. It seemed richer, fuller; it was hard to describe. Feeding always soothed her, filled her, sharpened her edges and boosted sensations. This time it did the same only more extensively.

When she finished, Whiskey pressed against the now slumped form in her arms, her forehead resting on the wall, nose nestled at the crook of Aleya's neck. "Are you all right?" she whispered.

There came a groggy chuckle, and Aleya nodded weakly. "Yeah."

Whiskey eased away, giving Aleya time to reacclimatize herself to standing alone. She helped her into one of the chairs scattered around the room, and retrieved her bag. With gentle motions, she found the first-aid supplies Aleya always carried for her visits, and carefully bandaged the slowly seeping wounds. By the time she finished, Aleya had regained more of her senses, and watched her with curiosity.

"What the hell was that?" The smile on her face indicated she wasn't upset.

"An experiment." Whiskey sat beside her, holding her hand. "Did you enjoy it?"

Aleya reddened and rolled her eyes, fanning herself with her free hand. "Whew! Very much so!"

Whiskey grinned. "Good."

"What about you?"

She licked her lips, still tasting the aftereffects of her test. "Oh, yeah."

Aleya smiled impishly. "I suppose I should go now."

"No. Stay awhile. I'll have Sithathor bring you something to eat." Whiskey brought Aleya's hand to her mouth and kissed it. "You can leave when you're ready."

"Are you sure?" Her brow furrowed.

"Yeah. You fed me. It's only right I return the favor."

Aleya laughed, and Whiskey joined her.

CHAPTER EIGHT

Whiskey had finished a hot shower and now wore a thick, warm robe. Ignoring her reflection, she stared unseeingly out her apartment's office window. Lights illuminated the east side of the Willamette River, darkness speckled with silver flashes of falling rain. The low clouds reflected a glowing yellow street-lit backdrop upon which headlights and taillights from the overpasses and bridges danced across her vision. Through the glass, she smelled the wet earthiness from the planters that Andri had insisted upon setting on the balcony; she saw them through the patio door into her sitting room. She always thought of home as the scent and sound of rain on greenery and pavement.

A light tap at the door drew her away from the window. "Come in."

Sithathor entered, smiling. "My *Gasan*." She entered with a tray that smelled suspiciously like hot chocolate and baklava. "Is there anything else I can do for you?"

Whiskey smiled. "No, thank you, Sithathor. Why don't you get some sleep?"

"Of course, *Ninsumgal*. Thank you." She bobbed once and left the room.

Margaurethe had remained away since Valmont's visit. She hadn't joined Whiskey for dinner which had become their usual habit. Whisky wondered if Margaurethe absented herself out of anger; she had appeared to take Whiskey's order regarding security during Valmont's visits well enough, but there was no telling. Margaurethe had utilized the cold shoulder with Elisibet in the past. They needed to discuss the situation, preferably before this rift between them grew wider.

Returning her gaze to the view outside, Whiskey opened her mind, searching. She felt the tickle of others nearby—*Aga'gída* and servants, residents on the floor immediately below hers—and ignored them. The essence for which she sought was near. Margaurethe occupied her apartment, only a few feet of space and a vast gulf of emotion separating them. Whiskey brushed a gentle query across the surface of Margaurethe's mind. In answer, wood smoke and mulled wine reached out to strengthen the connection.

Margaurethe didn't knock. She let herself into Whiskey's apartment, a shadowed wraith crossing the sitting room as Whiskey observed from her post at the window, disappearing out of sight. Moments later, the office door eased open, and Margaurethe slipped inside. She, too, wore a robe—burgundy with silver lining—her dark hair flowing along her shoulders in damp waves. Her natural spicy scent mingled with the soap and shampoo she had used in her shower.

"I missed you at dinner."

Margaurethe regarded her with a hint of uncertainty. "I wasn't sure I was invited." She moved closer.

Whiskey tilted her head and looked away, pained. "I wouldn't turn you away, Margaurethe. We've had misunderstandings before and will in the future. I don't want to let them separate us before we've had a chance to explore things."

"I'm not sorry for this afternoon." Margaurethe thought a moment. "I've spent the day thinking, and I know my feelings remain the same."

Her tone held a note of steel Whiskey recognized. When she had first heard it, she realized that Elisibet never had. Margaurethe had changed dramatically from the sweet young consort of the *Ninsumgal* all those centuries ago. Upon closer inspection, Whiskey had decided she much preferred this version of the woman to the one of her unsought memories. "I understand. Your goal is to keep me safe."

"Yes, it is."

She turned and studied Margaurethe. "You know that's impossible."

Margaurethe bristled. "No, it isn't."

Whiskey barely resisted rolling her eyes. "The very nature of my position prevents you keeping me from harm. You can't protect me all the time. I've got to start acting like the *Ninsumgal* if I'm going to be one." She watched Margaurethe struggle with the argument, wanting to further deny the truth. "What kind of ruler would I be if I allowed you to continue as you have?"

"Alive."

She chuckled despite Margaurethe's acid tone. "No, not alive. Less than alive. And just as susceptible to assassination as Elisibet." She offered to link with the woman, but was rebuffed. "God, you're stubborn."

"As would you be had you been in my place!" Margaurethe immediately flushed, and turned away. Marching to the other side of the room, she stared at the desk.

"I won't allow a guard present when he visits anymore."

Margaurethe's lips drew into a tight line. "I trust you to take care of yourself. But I don't know that you have the ability to defend yourself against physical attack."

Whiskey moved closer, breathing her words into Margaurethe's ear. "What do you mean?"

Margaurethe gave a start at the proximity. "How many times have you had to physically fight? You have no training in the martial arts. Swords, knives, none of it." She sighed as Whiskey's arms wrapped around her stomach. "That's why I hired Pacal, to teach you these things. You may be able to mentally take on most people you meet, but physically you're unable to stop a knife from piercing your heart."

"In this day and age, I can't defy death. A sniper rifle from a rooftop can do the job just as well, regardless of how much training I have in swords and knives."

With a grimace, Margaurethe conceded the point, but not the argument. "Perhaps. But the same could have been said for arrows and siege engines. Elisibet knew about and protected against these things, and still Valmont succeeded in killing her."

It always came down to her. Whiskey sighed. *When will people see me for who I am rather than who she was?* "Elisibet was a fool. Her status blinded her to reality."

Margaurethe stiffened at hearing criticism of her dead lover. It was a knee-jerk reaction that Whiskey had grown used to over the months, made worse because it was Elisibet's voice that spoke the words. She tightened her grip into a hug. "I'm sorry. I know you don't like to hear things like that."

Turning in Whiskey's arms, Margaurethe smiled reassurance. "Something I need to get over." She leaned her forehead against Whiskey's.

"You never liked it when Elisibet talked smack about herself, either."

Margaurethe grinned at the modern statement. "You're right."

Whiskey pulled back, and peered into her eyes. "Did you ever disagree with her or her methods?"

"Yes, I did." Margaurethe's smile faded. She stepped out of their embrace, and returned to the window alone, wrapping her arms around herself. "I always knew she had the ability to do such wonderfully good things. Valmont and I were prime examples of her generosity and kindness. I had such hopes she would mature into the loving ruler for which I knew she had the potential."

"I don't know that she had all that much potential." Whiskey couldn't help her sour tone. Regardless of which European Sanguire she spoke to, they all measured her using Elisibet's tyrannical yardstick. Some found Whiskey lacking.

Margaurethe looked over her shoulder. "Your memories are sketchy. Perhaps as time goes on, you'll find that Elisibet did indeed have a heart. I know. I loved it well enough."

Though not actively linked, Whiskey saw tears threatening Margaurethe. Chagrined, she approached, lightly caressing Margaurethe's upper arms. "I'm sorry. I know how helpless you felt then. I know it can't be easy to feel that way now."

"You don't know what it was like after she died." Margaurethe's voice was low enough that Whiskey had to strain to hear. "Everyone fell upon each other in anger and distrust. Our people attacked one another for any reason. The Purge was a horrible bloody time in our history."

"And much of it was Elisibet's fault for cultivating fear and violence in her reign. I can't say I understand thoroughly. I wasn't there. I don't have any basis for comparison. But, Margaurethe..." Whiskey turned the woman around to face her. "I can't change that if I can't be trusted to lead."

She sniffled. "I trust you to lead."

"Then let me do so."

Margaurethe seemed about to argue.

"If you must disagree with me," Whiskey interrupted, "then do it privately, okay? I don't want a repeat of what happened today."

Margaurethe blushed, and dropped her head. "I understand."

Whiskey sighed, and wondered if Margaurethe would concede her next request. "Will you apologize to Valmont?"

Emerald ice shot up to glare at her. Margaurethe's jaw worked a moment before she finally spoke. "Yes, of course. I was rude."

"Thank you. I would like my advisors to at least be civil to one another."

"But I'll not apologize for distrusting him. He assassinated Elisibet, and has not received proper punishment for his deed. I still believe he's a coward and a traitor." She held her chin low in defiance, as if expecting an argument.

"Of course. I'm not asking you to change who you are. Just remember proper etiquette." Whiskey ventured a smile. "You are always harping at me about proper etiquette."

Margaurethe's Irish temper hadn't been completely soothed.

She sniffed once in response, her tears like stained memories on her cheeks.

"Again, I'm sorry. Maybe someday I will have other memories to balance out my feelings." Whiskey shrugged a shoulder, feeling like the ill-prepared young woman she was instead of the monarch everyone proclaimed her to be. "I do know she had love for you. I remember that."

Something in her words eased the last of Margaurethe's hurt. She felt arms wrap around her waist. "When we started this, you said we should take it slow. You didn't want me to see Elisibet when I looked at you."

"I meant it. I know how much you cared for her. I'm selfish. I want you to love me."

Margaurethe smiled. "But I do see you, Whiskey. I think the real issue is that you fear you see me with Elisibet's sight and not your own." She hugged Whiskey. "How much of Elisibet do you carry within your heart?"

Whiskey flushed, unable to meet her gaze. "I don't know. Sometimes I can't think for wanting you. I keep seeing you dancing at court or the first time I—she bedded you." She sighed, and attempted to pull away. "I was drawn to you before I met you. But those are her memories, not mine."

With a sigh, Margaurethe tightened her grip, forcing Whiskey to remain in her arms. Whiskey felt the touch of mulled wine and wood smoke, falling into the comforting essence. Speaking without words, Margaurethe soothed the erratic jumbling of Whiskey's soul. This connection had become so familiar over the months. Her words were a whisper, barely audible. "I think you were intrigued by me because of Elisibet. But I don't feel her here. I only feel you."

Reassured, Whiskey relaxed into the embrace, opening her mind for a stronger connection. Though the bond between them only shared that part of their Sanguire nature that any could see, Whiskey believed she felt a deep well of love in Margaurethe as she cradled Whiskey's mind. Hardly conscious of moving, Whiskey caressed Margaurethe's cheek, using her thumb to brush the tear stains away. "*I want her.*" Elisibet's voice echoed in her mind. "I love you."

Along the joining, Margaurethe seemed to soften. "I love you, as well."

"I have plans for you tonight."

"Do you now?" Margaurethe's face pinked. "And what if I've already made plans?"

Whiskey smiled. "Maybe I can persuade you to change them." She leaned closer, still caressing Margaurethe's cheek. "I don't want to go slow anymore. I want to taste you."

Margaurethe raised startled eyes. Whiskey heard her heart begin thumping rapidly. She swallowed, and licked her lips. "Really? What changed your mind?"

Closing her eyes, Whiskey drew in a slow breath. "All the best memories I have of you are Elisibet's. I think it's time I made my own." She didn't mention her belief that perhaps by consummating their relationship, her fears of becoming Elisibet might lessen.

"Making new memories sounds like a wonderful idea."

Their lips met and mingled, the physical connection bursting along their mental joining with sparks of fire.

CHAPTER NINE

Valmont sipped his brandy.

He sat in the dark of his apartment. Streetlights cast shadows across the walls, and the occasional rumble of the local transit system interrupted his thoughts. The rain had stopped some time ago, leaving streaks on the plate glass window overlooking the city. He hated the amount of rain here, and the chill breezes that cut through his clothes during winter. He wished he were back at his winery in Brazil. At the very least, it would be warmer. He had his suspicions, however, that it would be quite some time before he could return home.

A cell phone lay smashed in one corner of the room, the result of his last conversation with Bertrada Nijmege. Valmont had been able to hold off his anger and frustration until after he had disconnected the line. If she knew the direction of his thoughts lately, she would probably make the trip over here herself to see the job done properly. He thought he had handled their conversation quite well. He had calmly spoken of what happened since the last time he had reported, minus Whiskey's request to take her hunting. If Nijmege knew of the planned excursion, she would be straining at the end of her chain to get Whiskey brought to her, a rabid junkyard dog intent on shredding a trespasser. Valmont had argued with her about timing and transportation, insisted kidnapping Whiskey now was dangerous, that things remained in a state of flux at The Davis Group. A bunch of lies, really, but what choice did he have? The other option was to agree to Nijmege's demands, and see that Whiskey made her rendezvous with a destiny she didn't deserve.

So he brooded, half drunk from brandy, the darkness in his soul mirrored by the shadows surrounding him.

Valmont remembered the bright days of his youth. Not that he spent a lot of time dwelling in the past, but Whiskey's presence tended to facilitate such things. Nahib had fostered Valmont after his Turning; both he and Nijmege had taught him the ways of Elisibet's court—the formal manners, which of the *sanari* and *gasani* to avoid for their iniquity or ineptitude, which were honorable and decent. He had forgotten all his lessons when he was presented to Elisibet; all he could see were those icy blue eyes.

The more Valmont thought about it, the more he knew he fell in love with her at that moment. He wondered what would have happened had he been delayed in his presentation. What if it had been a few more decades before they had met? Would he have felt the same, knowing how Elisibet murdered her own people as viciously as she did Humans? Certainly by then he would have known Nahib's political complaints regarding Elisibet's rule, and perhaps would have been swayed by his mentor's politics. Of course, Valmont knew Elisibet preferred feminine company when he met her. Her predilections were hardly secret with *Ki'an Gasan* Margaurethe constantly at her side, on the dais or in her bed. He knew his love for this stern *Ninsumgal* would never result in a dalliance. Valmont satisfied himself with being in her presence, enjoying her companionship, and becoming her friend. He satisfied his lusts elsewhere, never settling on one woman, for only one woman ever held his attention.

Valmont realized his glass was empty. His fingers found the bottle on the floor beside his chair and he picked it up, pouring another drink.

He had long ago claimed his fair share of guilt. He had no doubt that much of what had happened with Elisibet had been magnified by his presence. The pair of them seemed to urge each other on to greater depravities as time had passed, daring each other to invent more gruesome punishments and executions. Valmont wondered if Elisibet would have reached those heights —or depths—without him there to escalate matters. Poor Margaurethe had little recourse but to leave the room when the pair of them got started; she had learned earlier on that arguing ethics and morals only annoyed her lover.

Valmont frowned. Had Margaurethe been as jealous of him as he had been of her? There was a thought. Why had it never occurred to him before? It would certainly clarify her behavior. After these last months, she couldn't still be worried he would murder Whiskey. Perhaps she saw the dangerous potential more clearly than he, saw how easy it would be to slip onto the same path they had all been cursed to follow before.

The execution of Nahib had changed everything. Valmont had never felt such rage. The woman he had considered a close friend, a sister, a potential lover, murdering the man who was like a father to him had been too much for Valmont to bear. He hardly believed it when Elisibet turned on him, threatening to call her guards, refusing to listen to his argument. And then Nijmege whispered her vile poisons to the *Agrun Nam*, insisted something be done before they were all murdered by the Sweet Butcher. It was she who had brought Valmont in on the planning of Elisibet's assassination, vouching for him to Bentoncourt. It was she who had twisted his fury to match hers.

But it had been Valmont who made the final decision to betray his oath, his friend, his family.

Another Max train rumbled past on the street below. His

brown eyes flickered to the digital readout of a clock. It was late; that was the last one. But he couldn't drag himself away from his thoughts. Some days his thoughts were a slow-motion car wreck holding him in its fascinating and horrible sway. When Nijmege had contacted him several months ago, her plan seemed a good idea. Certainly, the return of the Sweet Butcher was something no one wanted. Valmont had already killed her once. His honor had long been shredded by the winds of politics. What was one more murder? Besides, Nijmege had always resented that the *Agrun Nam* would not let her personally avenge Nahib's death. She had only included Valmont in the plan to live vicariously through his actions. Here was her chance. But Jenna Davis was not *Ninsumgal* Elisibet the Sweet Butcher.

Or is she?

He shook his head, the only movement in the dim room. Some days he saw an achingly familiar Elisibet so clearly, half expecting her to demand he cheer up with a quick hunting trip to some province or other where the Humans would stampede like cattle, and the blood would drip with their fear. At other times a very different young woman stood before him—uncertain, confused, ignorant of her people and their ways. The problem he saw was that the anger and fury and guilt he had carried for hundreds of years had not burned out his true feelings for Elisibet. Valmont found himself still loving her. Even killing her hadn't taken away the emotion or diluted its intensity.

And now he was falling in love with Whiskey.

The guilt had haunted him for centuries. He felt responsible for Nahib's death and Nijmege's twisted soul. He had killed his best friend, someone as dear to him as his very flesh and bone. He had destroyed his honor, his integrity and his heart, leaving him a dried out husk that should have blown away before now.

How could he betray her again?

***

Whiskey watched her pack with an unfamiliar sense of pride. They had come so far since she had first met them, been through so much disruption, defied their leader, and—in some cases—suffered outright torture for her. Yet they still played with abandon as they frolicked in one of the pools. A series of four current pools had been installed here, each large enough to accommodate two or three swimmers and space outside the flow for people to lounge in the water. Chaniya and Alphonse had challenged each other to a "race." They furiously swam against the current, Alphonse's impressive blue mohawk falling limp in the water, while the others egged them on. Daniel, the recognized neutral and most mature of the lot, sat by the controls with his feet dipped in the water, presiding over the match. Zebediah and two off-duty security guards floated on the side, yelling encouragement to their favorites.

Nupa was the only one not fully involved in the competition. He stood beside Zeb, arms crossed over his broad chest as he watched impassively. Every so often his somber gaze would scan the area, brushing over the room's other occupants. Whiskey looked over her shoulder at the hot tubs. A trio of Mayans lounged in the hot water, speaking in low voices that couldn't be heard above the sounds of the water jets. One of them was Pacal, the man-at-arms Margaurethe had hired. He and his companions sneered and jeered with each other, not quite stepping over the line. His eyes seemed cold though he remained pleasant and professional when he spoke to Whiskey. She hoped that the age-old feud between the nations could be put to rest; until then, she doubted there would be a Mayan youngling hanging with her pack. *Has anyone told Pacal that I'm half American Indian?*

She turned back to watch the race. The integration of the African Chaniya had been interesting. Though all present were Sanguire, there were such contrasts between the various national cultures that Whiskey hadn't known what to expect. Nupa had arrived before Margaurethe had come to build The Davis Group, but his laid-back nature blended well with Whiskey's pack. Younglings as a whole were much more vicious than their elders, their oversized competitive streaks displayed for all to see. Chaniya might be a woman, but she was as savage as the men that made up Whiskey's entourage. Whiskey had presided over any number of contests and brawls as the group dynamics settled into place, and Chaniya sat about middle of the pack. Daniel and

Alphonse had become her lieutenants. Despite his younger age, Alphonse had a level head and was physically stronger than most the others. In a battle of wills, he was woefully shortchanged because of his youth, but in physical battle he came out the winner most often, gaining him a level of respect from his peers that Whiskey had learned to make use of.

She glanced around the poolroom, not seeing Cora. Reaching out with her mind, Whiskey ignored the Mayans, tasting the strong smell of ashes. Cora was near. Climbing out of the pool, Whiskey grabbed a towel and dried off before wrapping it about her waist. Nupa, ever aware of her presence, looked up from the contest, and she waved him back to the entertainment. Up a few steps, she traversed through the cardiovascular room and into the hallway. Two *Aga'usi* fell into step with her. Other than greeting them and the building security guard stationed at the patio door she ignored them, having almost become inured to their presence. She never would have thought it possible six months ago.

There was a lot she hadn't thought possible back then.

Cora's essence strengthened as Whiskey walked through the rooftop garden. It had been ingeniously designed, and only the sound of traffic on the street three floors below indicated it wasn't located in the country. Stars winked above her head, and she scanned the side of the building. Most the lower floors housed offices and labs, and were dark except for the occasional light for the janitorial staff. The upper half of the building contained residences, and sparkled like a Christmas tree as it indicated how many were still up and about.

She paused and waved her escort back. They glanced at one another before acceding to her request, not quite on the verge of denying her order. She was going to have to remind them again who was in charge. In the beginning Margaurethe had left standing orders, an excellent strategy since Whiskey had no idea how to properly utilize a personal guard. Not any more. She stepped forward and around a bend, finding Cora bathing in moonlight on a wooden bench. "Hey."

Cora turned and smiled. "*Aga ninna.*" She patted the bench beside her in invitation.

"Thanks." Whiskey settled down, and looked at the orb glowing above them. "Pretty night."

"Yes, it is."

"I missed you inside." She watched Cora's profile, a series of conflicting emotions stirring her heart. Cora had been a key part of the beginning of all this, the willing carrot to draw Whiskey into Fiona's pack, the promise of intimacy and affection for a homeless teenager who had been living in deprivation for a dozen years. Half the time, Whiskey felt protective of Cora, knowing how Fiona had manipulated all the people in her pack. Cora had shown great devotion long before Whiskey knew who she was destined to become. She wanted to reward that dedication with lavish gifts, keep Cora safe, and never allow anyone to run roughshod over her again. Then Cora would do or say something so...*Sanguire* that Whiskey, with her Human-reared sensitivities, was hard put not to reveal disgust.

"I'm right here." Cora glanced at her, then back up. "I'm just not in the mood for all the excitement."

Whiskey took her hand with a laugh. "Don't I know it. I had no idea Chaniya could be as ruthless as the boys."

"Isn't she, though? She reminds me of Bronwyn in a way."

The image of a dark-haired girl came to Whiskey's mind, one of the two that had remained at Fiona's side, never wavering in their loyalty. The last time Whiskey had seen Bronwyn, Whiskey had slammed her headfirst into a concrete wall to escape a trap. "Really?"

Cora grinned at her and clarified. "She has a similar brutal streak."

"Oh." They sat in comfortable silence for a bit. "So, how's Mateo?"

"Mateo? He's old news." Cora sniffed.

Whiskey frowned, trying to remember the list of people Cora had been enjoying liaisons with since she had broken off their own romance. "Old news? Wasn't he sitting at our table last week at dinner?"

Cora wrinkled her nose in response, her naturally feline features becoming more so in the process. "We were already finished by then. These days, I've been seeing Anthony."

"My *Ugula Aga'us*?" Whiskey smirked at the thought. "No wonder you're sitting alone. His image would completely be blown if he started hanging out with the wild kids."

Cora returned the smile. "He's a sweet man. I like him a lot better than the others."

Curious, Whiskey tilted her head. "You think he'll last longer than they did?"

"I think so. He's...different than the others." Cora turned toward Whiskey, pulling their joined hands into her lap. With her free hand, she flicked her fingers vaguely away from them. "The others were just passing time. Not like you."

A faint sense of guilt whispered through Whiskey's gut. Before Margaurethe's arrival, she had been content to let things ride with Cora, though she knew Cora held deeper feelings for her. As soon as Whiskey caught sight of Margaurethe, however, everything about Cora paled. It didn't matter whether it was her own interest or the infernal memories of Elisibet's; Cora hadn't stood a chance. The death throes of their relationship had been horrendous, causing serious strife amidst the pack during a very stressful time. Her grip on Cora's hand tightened. "Then I wish you luck, *lúkal*. You deserve someone who will make you happy."

Cora's smile was bittersweet. "Thank you, *aga ninna*. I hope he will."

Unable to think of anything else to say, Whiskey opted to keep silent. They sat in the semidarkness, watching the stars overhead.

***

Valmont drummed his fingers against the steering wheel of the sedan. He glanced around the parking lot, wondering what was taking so long. He had received a phone call from Whiskey an hour ago, telling him to come to this lot and wait. Obviously, she wanted her hunting lesson tonight. Valmont had never been allowed to take her off the property before, and it was a sure bet Margaurethe knew nothing of their plans. He wondered if Whiskey was experiencing difficulty breaking away with discretion.

As he peered out the window in the direction of The Davis Group three blocks away, his heart thumped a little harder as he spotted her, a dark wraith flickering along the shadows. She wore only black, a slim figure against the white of the building, her blond hair shining like a beacon in the streetlights. The first time he'd met her, the ends had been dyed black. Since then, she'd trimmed off the coloring, leaving her hair its natural hue. He scanned beyond her for pursuers and found none. If Margaurethe discovered her absence, all hell would break loose. His smile widened at the thought, and he blinked his headlights.

She glided toward him and opened the door, easing into the seat with a grin. "Hi."

"Hi." He nodded back the way she had come. "Any trouble?"

"Nope. Just a gentle reminder of who runs the show."

Valmont chuckled, and put the car into gear. "Be sure to remind Margaurethe of that when we return."

"I will."

Her voice held a hint of vehemence, and he glanced at her in surprise as he pulled out onto the street.

As soon as they were away, Whiskey leaned back and sighed. "I haven't been out of that building for months."

"My sympathies. I've never liked being caged up for long." He drove through downtown Portland. It was still early enough that there were plenty of pedestrians and traffic. "Anyplace in particular you want to stop?"

Whiskey gave him a speculative look. "I don't think I have enough time to goof off. Perhaps if this expedition turns out well, I'll be able to con Margaurethe into allowing an occasional reprieve."

Valmont clicked his tongue in disbelief. "Highly doubtful. She's got quite a lot invested in your well being."

"I know. But I can't be kept safe if I'm to lead."

"No. You can't. You'd be ineffectual at best." He wondered why he continued this charade. He knew Whiskey would never be allowed to be in power, not with Nijmege slavering for her blood. Even if he came clean with Whiskey right now, Nijmege would simply find another way to attain her goals. His brow furrowed as he drove, not liking this turn of thought.

"So where are we going?"

He placed his melancholy aside. "That depends on what you want. There are several avenues we can explore, fear and lust being the most basic and easiest to obtain."

"There are more?"

Valmont laughed. "Oh, yes. The seven deadly sins are truly a Sanguire's menu. Avarice, anger, gluttony—all have their particular taste treats." He pulled into the heavier traffic of a main thoroughfare. "You have to be careful with gluttony, however. The blood will taste strongly of the thing in which the Human overindulges."

She pursed her lips as she studied him. He saw her eyes glowing in the dark, regarding him. "Why are fear and lust the easiest to get?"

"They take the least amount of effort. If you're good at seduction in either case, you can hype a Human up to the perfect level with little effort. With the others, you need to lay a bit more groundwork." Valmont winked at her. "Depending on your bias, it's well worth the wait."

"What's your bias?"

He gave her a mocking grin. "I prefer fear. Something I picked up from your predecessor."

When she didn't respond, Valmont glanced at her to find her eyes distant as they stared out the windshield. Another memory? He entertained himself with conjecture about which one. Her expression was chill as she remembered, and Valmont felt another tremor in his heart at his *Ninsumgal's* reappearance. She felt so much like Elisibet at this moment. He half expected her to turn, and give him a sarcastic smile and comment.

Whiskey turned to him, her face solemn. "I don't think I'm able to induce fear like her."

The illusion shattered, Valmont swallowed and turned his attention to his driving. Somehow the admission made her seem far more real. "I think you can. You just need the proper motivation."

They continued in silence, both wrapped in thoughts and memories.

CHAPTER TEN

Whiskey got out of the car and stared at the club. "Are you sure about this?" They had parked down the street from a small mob idling outside. Two burly people manned the door, a man and a woman, each wearing a radio headset as they kept the unlucky and, by extension, unpopular people waiting.

He grinned. "Of course. I remember you telling the priest you wanted to come here. No time like the present."

Her heart flipped in her chest. Tribulations was to Portland what Malice was to Seattle; a Goth-style club that a number of Sanguire used for a hunting ground. She questioned her wisdom in following him inside, reaching for a legitimate argument that didn't weaken her in his eyes. "I'm not legal age, yet. I don't even have a fake ID."

If anything, his smile widened. "The *Ninsumgal* of the European Sanguire doesn't need identification."

Still uncertain, she allowed him to take her arm and lead her to the establishment's door, the name of the club splashed across the black glass in bold white letters. A handful of Gothic posers loitered to one side, all too young to get in; they smoked illegal clove cigarettes and watched the older set waiting patiently to enter the packed business. She remembered many a Friday night doing the same outside Malice. The memory warred with reality as her steps took her past the teenagers, her feet wanting to step aside from her path to take her rightful place beside them.

Valmont swept past those waiting in line, ignoring the bitter comments and snide remarks as he pushed up to the doorwoman, Whiskey at his side. The woman's eyes glittered in the dark as she studied them. No words were spoken, but Whiskey sensed her mental touch. It felt amazingly like she was being frisked without the physical gesture, a quick pat down of her psyche to ensure...what? That she was Sanguire? Before she had opportunity to become offended, it was over. Apparently she had passed some test. The woman removed the velvet rope from the stanchion that blocked access, and allowed them through. The waiting crowd complained at the preferential treatment of the newcomers, but she promptly returned the rope to its place and glared them down.

"How many of these places are there?"

"As many as needed to support the population." Valmont gave her a wild smile. "Even 'vampires' need a place to relax."

Whiskey laughed, still apprehensive as they went inside. She wasn't sure what she anticipated, something along the industrial lines of the Seattle club, perhaps. For all its Gothic hype, however, Tribulations failed to meet her expectations.

The only dark thing about the place was the floor, black as night, stained and polished concrete that reflected the overhead lighting. As Valmont paid the cover to a Human male just inside the door, she scanned the oversize room. Past a large seating area was a dance floor. The music was comparable to what normally played in the youth club she used to frequent, though the beat was more sedate. A number of people writhed together, oblivious of watching eyes. Curtains lined the wall behind the dancers, and she wondered if a stage lurked there. She stepped further into the room, locating two bars, one on the wall beside her and the other opposite, both built of pine. Brass footrests gleamed against the black floor. Several occupied tables were scattered around the room. What little she saw of the walls was white. Tapestries and drapes of varying colors and designs blanketed most of them. Whiskey glanced to her left and frowned.

"What do you think?"

She glanced at Valmont beside her. "Is there another business here? I thought this building was bigger." She jabbed her thumb at the decorated wall to her left.

He chuckled into her ear. "Not exactly." Guiding her forward by the elbow, he reached one of the tapestries, and brushed it aside. A dimly lit corridor hid behind it, several doors sprouting from the hallway. A thin man sat on a chair, watching them. "Not everyone here is Sanguire. And most of the Humans who do come here aren't aware of us."

"So this affords a bit of privacy for those intimate moments." Whiskey was impressed. Malice hadn't boasted a back room.

"Yes." Valmont acknowledged the doorman, and twitched the tapestry back into place.

She turned back to the crowded room, a grin on her face. Simply being away from The Davis Group lightened her heart despite her unease; it had been too long since her last outing. She could almost forget who and what she was. Scanning the room, she caught hints of reflective irises like hers, and realized the fragility of the illusion. With a conscious effort, she refused to allow the awareness to interrupt her excitement. As the music thumped, she began to sway with the beat.

"Would you like to dance?"

Whiskey chuckled and turned to Valmont. "I dance alone."

He laughed, conceding the point. "Then perhaps we can get something to drink, and see what's on the menu."

She readily followed him to one of the bars, aware of many eyes watching her. Gentle brushes against her mind indicated the number of Sanguire present, and that they were curious about her. She lightly rebuffed their advances. If she announced herself now, what would happen? How many of the Sanguire here would decide to tear her apart? No one must have realized who she was, not yet. She felt a trickle of fear down her spine. Cocking her head, she stared at Valmont's back as he ordered drinks. It would be easy for him to put out the word of who accompanied him. The likelihood of her being torn limb from limb before she could get three steps was high. He turned toward her, a glass in each hand, hazel eyes dancing in pleasure.

"What's on the menu?"

Her tone washed away the amusement. Valmont's brow wrinkled once and cleared. "What do you mean?"

"I'm just clarifying what's on the menu. We both know the danger here. Do I give you my trust, or do I leave now?" She doubted she could even get to the door if she chose the second option.

"Whiskey." Valmont's jaw twitched as he ground his teeth. Setting the drinks back on the bar, he stepped closer to her. His voice low, so as not to be overheard by others of their kind, he said, "If that was my aim, we wouldn't be here now."

"Remember what I told you at our first meeting." Her words whispered between them. *"Don't let your guard down. The second I think you're holding back or are a danger to me and mine, I'll gut you quicker than anything."*

"I remember." With a subtle gesture, he bared his throat. "I brought you here because it's the easiest hunting ground. If you wish to try something different, we leave."

She studied him, weighed his words against her memories. After months of verbal sparring and joking, she had nearly forgotten how dangerous he was, and that Margaurethe had every reason to distrust him. Whiskey didn't know which made her angrier—that she had wanted his smooth words to lull her, or that she was slapped in the face by this need to be suspicious of his motives. Her memories of Valmont and Elisibet fueled a camaraderie that didn't exist with her current self. She was here because she felt a yearning for something she had never had.

But he told the truth. She saw it. He was a powerful Sanguire man, no doubt older than three quarters of those in this room. Yet he lifted his chin to her before them all with no concern for his reputation. Whiskey had no idea if anyone here knew his name or history. Would they be surprised that the great *Sublugal Sañar* Valmont capitulated to a youngling? She glanced around the immediate area, catching the interested gaze of several people. Father Castillo had once said that gossip was a mainstay of the Sanguire. Those with long lives clung to even the smallest thing to remain entertained. Perhaps they would think Valmont had an apprentice, for why else would he be showing her how to hunt? Or did some make the connection of her strength and her appearance? Not every Sanguire here was European, but those that were had to have seen Elisibet's official portraits. *Too late now. The damage is done.* "We'll stay."

He stared at her a moment before nodding. She thought she saw a flicker of sadness before he turned back to the bar and retrieved their drinks. Handing a glass to her, Valmont displayed the usual devilish quirk to his lips. He seemed to have already forgotten the incident, and a stab of pain pierced Whiskey as she wondered about the damage she had exacted upon him with her sudden suspicions.

Valmont guided her to a table. The three Sanguire seated there looked up at the interruption as he smiled, revealing his fangs. Deciding he wasn't one to pursue for an apology over his atrocious manners, they vacated their chairs and moved off.

Whiskey forced a light tone. "Rank has its privileges?"

"And they are many and varied." Valmont slid a chair out for her.

She grinned and sat. He had chosen well. Their acquisition put them right on the edge of the dance floor. From here, she watched the people gyrating to music, smelled the rich aroma of Human sweat and desire. The odors ignited her hunger. She caught herself licking her lips, anticipating the coming meal. As she watched, she began to note the disparities between Human and Sanguire. Before she had Turned, she had been oblivious to the existence of her people. She had been drawn to Castillo when they had met with no idea why, and knew no others. Since her *Níri Kurám*, she had been mostly sequestered away for her safety, the aborted assassination attempt by Rufus Barrett giving credence to the threat against her life. Surrounded by Sanguire security ever since, her only Human contact had been people who worked for her and the *kizarusi* brought to feed her.

The differences were subtle, hardly noticeable to someone not looking for them. The Humans, of which there were many, acted as they always did in this sort of atmosphere. They focused on drinking, dancing and having a good time. Their short lives necessitated a certain level of franticness to their actions, as if they subconsciously knew they could die any day and wanted the most possible experience before that happened. Their mode of dress ranged from Euro trash to historical garb as they pretentiously attempted to express vampiric personas, completely unaware of the Sanguire among them.

Whiskey's people, on the other hand, had hundreds of years on their hands, and it showed. They moved fluidly and at a more decorous pace. Their voices were low, and their gestures smooth as they conversed, flirted and seduced their Human prey. When they danced, it was for themselves; when they made eye contact, it was to pass hidden messages to their friends; when they focused on a Human, it was only partly an elegant hunt for food.

The idea of a Human/Sanguire pairing came to Whiskey's mind again. She saw that at least here such a relationship would be impossible. Her people saw Humans as prey, nothing more. This was a hunting ground. Was it biological predisposition for a Sanguire to feel superior to Humans, the natural predator's viewpoint? Or did this supremacy come about from years of indoctrination into Sanguire society?

"What do you think so far?"

Her reverie interrupted, Whiskey glanced at Valmont. "Interesting." She didn't elaborate, dubious of his reaction to her musings. She made a promise to herself to speak to Father Castillo. His radical opinion of Humans as more than a food source made him the most likely with whom to discuss such things. "What now?"

"Now we find a likely target. Any suggestions?"

Whiskey scanned the dance floor, noting there were more Humans than Sanguire. "Not really. You know what you like and how to attain it. I leave the decision to you."

Valmont glanced over the offerings, humming in thought. "What about...her?"

She followed his gaze to a young woman standing alone near the stage. White blond hair piled haphazardly on her head, the effect made her look adorable rather than sloppy. Her round face was pale, her full lips painted dark red. She wore a dress that seemed more tatters than cloth. Despite her apparent youth she seemed hardened, jaded. "Looks good."

He grinned and stood, leaving the table. Whiskey sat back to watch. Approaching the woman he introduced himself, made small talk, and flirted outrageously with her. It was nothing that Whiskey hadn't done on many occasions throughout her adolescence. As time passed, he cajoled the woman out onto the dance floor. At first distant, he pressed her until they were wrapped about each other. He spoke into her ear, causing her to laugh. Finishing her drink, Whiskey ordered another from a wandering barmaid. She frowned in vague disappointment. She had thought Valmont would act differently. He had said his bias was fear, not lust; she was curious how he instilled fear in his prey. As she looked around the room, however, she noted seductions everywhere. Apparently lust was the easiest to attain.

"Jack."

She looked up at a smiling Valmont, the Human woman held closely to his side. It took a moment for her to realize he was talking to her, and another to understand that Jack referred to the brand of whiskey she preferred. Answering his smile with one of her own, she cocked her head.

"This is Misty."

"Hi." The woman licked her lips as her eyes wandered over Whiskey. "Val says you like to watch."

Whiskey saw a burble of humor in Valmont's eyes. She took up her cue. "I do. Are you offering?"

"Could be." Misty ran her hand up Valmont's shirt, and caressed his neck. "It'd be cool to have someone like you watching. Maybe you could join the fun."

Her eyes flickered to Valmont, finding a raised eyebrow and questioning look. "I'm game."

"Good. I know just the place." He winked at Whiskey. "Come on."

As expected, he led them to one of the tapestries, brushing

it aside to reveal a dimly lit corridor. Misty acted surprised by its existence, and commented that she would have to come here more often. The hall guard nodded them toward an open door, and turned away as Valmont pulled Misty into the room. Whiskey followed, quietly closing the door behind her.

"Lock it."

Whiskey was taken aback by his sudden rough tone. She fumbled the two locks into place, hearing the click of metal and a gasp of surprise from Misty before she turned around. She hadn't gotten a clear look at the room upon entering. She saw it was a small dungeon, the concrete walls decorated with various restraint devices. She inhaled deeply, receiving a rush from the aroma of indistinct blood that permeated the air. Valmont already had his prey bound, her hands manacled together behind her.

"Wait a minute." All of Misty's coyness was gone, a hardened expression on her pretty face. "I'm not into this shit, okay? If you guys get off on this, you need to find another girl."

Valmont smirked. "I don't think so. You're just the sort of girl I'm looking for."

Misty struggled ineffectually with her bonds. "I'll scream," she warned as Valmont paced before her.

If anything, his grin widened. "Have you noticed the walls? Do you think you'd be heard? Surely if a room like this exists here, the establishment would have it soundproofed." He stepped closer and pinched her breast. "Besides, why do you think there's a guard in the hall?"

The woman swallowed, her annoyance fading to fear, her eyes blinking rapidly as she looked around the room.

"Don't worry. I'll pay what you asked, and throw in a bonus."

Whiskey abruptly realized that their victim was a prostitute.

Misty's eyes were green; not quite the shade of Margaurethe's, but close. Her smell altered as Valmont poked and prodded her. The scent was almost familiar, and against her will Whiskey felt her teeth extend in anticipation. Though her wrists were pinned behind her, Misty moved freely about the room. Valmont used his gifts well, following as she backed away, using inhuman speed to poke and prod her as he spoke of all the gory things he wanted to do. He described flaying her skin from her body until the blood ran sweet and her voice carried her screams to the heavens. He told her of others he had taken over the years, detailing the methodical breaking of bones or techniques of evisceration. Producing a blade from somewhere, he drew a line of blood along the woman's exposed breast.

Misty began to cry, her sobs punctuated by pleading. She had all but forgotten Whiskey's presence until inadvertently bumping into her as she tried to avoid Valmont. Terrified, the woman gasped and jerked away, then decided to appeal to another female. "Please! Don't do this. Don't let him do this."

Whiskey staggered from a wave of hunger. The fear from Valmont's prey was strong, rolling away from her like ripples in a disturbed pool of water. She had never felt anything like this. The desire to sink her teeth into their prey's flesh hit her with such strength that she bared her fangs.

The woman recoiled, eyes wide. She attempted to put as much space between them as possible. Backing into Valmont, she shrieked as he wrapped his arm around her. Using his free hand, he pulled their struggling prey's head to one side. "Would you like first taste?"

Whiskey felt the aching desire to appease her hunger battle with absolute revulsion. Unable to speak from the ongoing war within, she shook her head.

"Suit yourself." Valmont promptly bit the woman holding her tight in his arms as she fought against him, ignoring the screams piercing the room as he suckled the blood from her neck.

Misty passed out, the abrupt silence deafening. Whiskey's ears still rang with the sound, and she swallowed thickly against her need. Stumbling forward, her body had its own will. The smell of fear and blood swept over her. Valmont finished, a grin on his lips as he licked them. He held the woman's slack body in his arms and readjusted her, revealing the other side of her throat. "Go ahead. It's still good."

Unable to hold back, Whiskey sank her teeth into the offering. The blood was hot, and it tasted of smoke and seared flesh and tears. It soothed an ache deep within her she hadn't known existed, one that had always dwelled in the darkness of her soul. Or was it in Elisibet's soul? When she had drunk her fill, she disengaged. Valmont had pulled away at some point, removing the manacles, and Whiskey held the unconscious Misty in her arms. The woman seemed on the verge of wakefulness, murmuring weakly, brow flickering with confusion. Whiskey glanced around the room and carried her to a table, gently laying her down.

"Well, that was nice." Valmont went to the door and unlocked it. "Come on."

"What about her?" Whiskey frowned. "We can't just leave her here. Besides, she can identify us if she wants to press charges."

Valmont grimaced. "Don't worry about it. She won't want to press charges." He laughed, pulling money from his wallet, and tucking it into Misty's bra. "Who'd believe her anyway?"

Still worried, Whiskey allowed Valmont to lead her from the room.

CHAPTER ELEVEN

The drive back to The Davis Group was quiet. Whiskey's mind reeled as she faced a part of herself of which she hadn't known. *Or is this a part of Elisibet?* She had hoped this expedition would put to rest her fears regarding her previous incarnation. Idealistically, she had wanted to see that her fears were irrational, that Elisibet didn't live within her soul, that the Sweet Butcher was dead and gone, merely a memory bank to be plundered upon occasion as Whiskey learned to rule. She now knew the siren call of inducing terror, the taste of it still on her tongue, the scent of it still in her nostrils. The thrill of it still thumped hard in her chest as she reconciled this modern vision of herself with a monster that enjoyed torturing innocents, a monster wearing

Elisibet's face, her face. Stinging self-recriminations battled with the fact that her body remained flushed with exhilaration after her meal.

"Are you all right?"

She glanced at Valmont. "Fine."

He gave her a skeptical look. "I take it you weren't impressed with a taste of fear?"

She sighed, knowing he wouldn't let the subject drop. "Actually, I was too impressed."

"What do you mean?"

Irritated, Whiskey grimaced as she stared out the window. "I liked it. Too much. I'm also disgusted by liking it."

"Why be disgusted? It's the way we were made, the way we evolved. It's the natural progression for our species."

"It's horrible, putting a person through that sort of scare. It's...revolting. That woman did nothing but go to a club tonight, expecting a fun time. We ruined that for her." Whiskey considered for a moment. "Not only that, we scarred her for life. She's been completely destroyed, her world turned upside down. We might as well have raped her. Hell, we *did* rape her!"

"That Human was a prostitute who was paid for her time and effort. She's no more traumatized than from any other rough trade she's picked up in her life. Probably less so." Valmont sighed, clicking his tongue. "You've spent far too much time among Humans, my friend."

"Maybe."

"No. Really. You identify with them far too much. You cannot deny they are the key to our survival. Without Humans, we die. There aren't enough *kizarusi* to feed us all."

"There aren't?" She looked at him.

Valmont shook his head. "No. You, of course, wouldn't see the truth. Margaurethe keeps you hidden away and ensures your needs are met as quickly and painlessly as possible." His eyes flickered to hers and held her a moment. "But you'll note, the same *kizarusi* are rotated past you at every feeding. When's the last time you had someone new?"

Whiskey tried to recall the last new face she had seen. "It's been a few months."

"Months. That's because all the *kizarusi* in the area are already in use by others who don't hunt, as you don't. They can only give so much of themselves, they need to rest in between feedings to replenish their blood."

She mulled over his words, connecting them to the wisps of observations and stray thoughts she had entertained before. If such was the case, then the idea of Sanguire and Human working together toward a common goal would be almost insurmountable. Supply and demand alone made it unlikely. Her people didn't hunt to appease some ancient genetic code that required such activity; they hunted because it was the only means available for survival. "So what happens to Misty?"

"Who?" Valmont took a moment before recognizing the name. "Oh! Misty." He shrugged. "She'll wake up and go home, I'd imagine. Or see about another trick if the money she received wasn't enough for her pimp."

"Don't you care what happens to her?"

He frowned in confusion. "Why should I? She's still alive, a little smarter about the real world and its horrors. She'll probably never put herself into the same situation, will she?"

Valmont's callous attitude infuriated her, but she could find no argument to sway him. His world and hers were too different. He had as much difficulty seeing her point of view as she did his.

He must have read her mind, because he said, "Come now, Whiskey. Do you really care that much about the cows in the field that are slaughtered for the hamburger you eat at McDonald's? What about the chickens placed in cages for their entire lives, fattened up to the proper weights before being killed and plucked, sitting in the meat department at the grocery?"

"Humans are not cattle or chickens."

"Maybe not to Humans. But even Humans survive off the death of others, be it plant or animal. Some have distanced themselves from the process, but there are always those who get their tags every autumn and try to land that big buck. It's in their nature to hunt, just as it is in ours."

It was a compelling line of reasoning. She snorted at a sudden vision of Sanguire lining up at a counter to purchase hunting licenses for Humans. Recrimination quickly followed as her Human-based conscience went into play. Their conversation ended as Valmont pulled into the driveway.

The main door guard's eyes widened. "*Ki'an Gasan* Margaurethe is waiting for you in your sitting room, *Ninsumgal*."

Whiskey blinked, her current moral conflict fading in light of the coming confrontation.

"If you don't mind, I believe I'll sit this one out."

She chuckled at Valmont. "Coward."

"Discretion is the better part of valor, or so I'm told. I've had a few more years of Margaurethe's anger to deal with than you." He watched the guard open the passenger door. "She loves you. She's just worried about you being in my evil presence."

"I know." Whiskey sighed. She put one foot on the ground before turning back to Valmont. "Thank you for taking me. I've got a lot to think about now."

"Any time. Let me know if it's not safe to return for tomorrow's advisor meeting."

"I will."

Whiskey climbed out of the automobile and watched as Valmont drove away. Swallowing her trepidation, she strode into the brightly lit lobby.

***

Whiskey braced herself before opening the door. She entered her apartment, her manner calm and matter-of-fact. Margaurethe sat in an armchair in the corner, barely visible in the darkness. Her dark dressing gown consumed what little light there was, her eyes glittering in the dark.

"Where have you been?"

The strength of her accent measured the depth of her anger. Whiskey knew by the tone and the level of Irish lilt that Margaurethe's fury wasn't something set aside quickly, nor would she be cajoled out of with any ease. Regardless of the danger, Whiskey felt an abrupt wave of love for this outraged woman staring at her. "I missed you, too." She removed her jacket and hung it on a stand by the door. Normally, she'd toss it on a chair. No need to piss Sithathor off, too. "I didn't realize how late it had gotten."

Not willing to be enticed with inane chatter, Margaurethe rose and continued to glare at her. "You haven't answered my question."

Whiskey sighed. "I went hunting with Valmont."

Margaurethe seemed unsurprised. "That's what Anthony said when I asked where you were. He also said you had forbidden him and the others to report this fact to me."

"Yes, I did."

"Because you knew it was wrong!"

Whiskey stepped closer, and took Margaurethe's stiff hands into hers. "No. It wasn't wrong. I have to know everything about my people if I'm to rule them fairly. I just didn't want to worry you."

Margaurethe scoffed and pulled away.

Whiskey stared at her back, seeing the reddish hue in her hair. Her heart ached at Margaurethe's pain, knowing she was the cause yet again. It occurred to her that she had been right to not love another person since her parents had died. It was too painful, a raw open wound shooting agony through her soul with even the gentlest of touches. Too late now. "Margaurethe." Whiskey received no response, and she stepped closer. She caressed the stone of her lover's upper arms, lowering her voice to a whisper. "Margaurethe. I can't be kept safe from all dangers. You must know that."

Stern, brittle, Margaurethe said, "I most certainly do not know that. You are the culmination of a prophecy. Of multiple prophecies! You must be kept safe at all times, or they will never come to fruition."

"Mahar's prophecy was spoken four hundred years ago, and here I am. Did she say the returning *Ninsumgal* would be a tyrant like Elisibet?"

"No. Of course not."

Whiskey continued rubbing the woman's arms. "Did she say that the returning *Ninsumgal* would fail and die?"

"You've read the prophecy. You know as much as I."

"If her prophecy was correct, then how can I die now? I have to fulfill my destiny before that can happen." The argument was one she had heard often from her aunt to describe why so many cultures had similar prophecies and myths. It was arrogant to think they all culminated with her, but she would take any talking point she could get in winning this debate. She squeezed Margaurethe's arms. "I'm a long way from that point."

"You've spent entirely too much time with your family."

Whiskey didn't deny it as she dropped her forehead to Margaurethe's shoulder. "I told Anthony not to tell you because I didn't want you upset. I know how you feel about Valmont—"

"With good reason!"

"—and it was something I had to do."

Margaurethe spun around, causing Whiskey to sway at the loss of support. "And where did he take you?" she demanded. "I smell cigarettes, cloves, perfume. He took you to a bar, didn't he?"

Whiskey straightened, but she did not lift her chin. "Yes. He took me to Tribulations."

Margaurethe's eyes widened, a fleeting disbelief, of true fear, followed by the returning heat of fury. "It's a gods-be-damned *warren*!" Unable to stand still, Margaurethe paced the room. "What the hell was he thinking? No. He wasn't thinking, obviously. He never does. It's always the same thing, do what needs doing to ease the itch without care for the consequences." She stopped and glared at Whiskey. "And you! Do you have any idea how close you came to being torn apart? Tribulations is crawling with Sanguire, none of them loyal to you."

"I know, Margaurethe. I saw." Whiskey recalled that single moment of distrust, wondering if Valmont had set her up for just that purpose. "Valmont said it was the easiest hunting ground, that was all. At no time did he put me in danger."

"No. You did that all on your own, didn't you, love?"

The accusation burned with sarcasm. Whiskey grimaced at its sting, her temper slipping. "I'll do what I have to do to rule."

"Elisibet said the same thing. Usually right after some hideous atrocity she and Valmont had committed in her dungeons."

The spoken words splashed coldly across them both, dousing their fury. Through the soggy ash of it, their eyes met; Margaurethe's wet with unshed tears, Whiskey's wide and surprised. Coming so soon on the heels of her self-discovery at Tribulations, the statement made Whiskey feel hollow. Margaurethe's words hurt worse because Whiskey thought they might be true. They stood in silence for several moments. "You still see the potential for Elisibet within me, don't you? You don't see me at all."

"No. Whiskey, no." Margaurethe came forward, her body relaxed and responsive, unlike the marble of before. She pulled Whiskey into her arms. "I see you, Whiskey. I do."

"Not completely. You see a youngling Sanguire who has no experience, and must be protected like a child. You see how easy it would be for her to slip into the terrible behaviors of her predecessor." Whiskey's heart felt thick, cold, as if it had stopped beating at Margaurethe's hurtful words.

"I see how easy it would be for Valmont to lure you to your death," Margaurethe corrected. "He cannot be trusted, *m'cara*. He has no honor. He lulls you into a false sense of security in his presence. I'm afraid he'll succeed in whatever he plans to do."

"But a part of me trusts him." Whiskey sighed, feeling very tired.

Margaurethe hugged her. "I know."

Whiskey held on tightly. If Margaurethe echoed her innermost fears about Elisibet, there had to be a shred of truth in them. Who was she? Would she have to battle the Sweet Butcher every day of her life? Or should she succumb to the desires, the lusts of Elisibet? So many memories crowded her head, memories that weren't hers. Yet they were as strong and as authentic as those she held of her current life as an orphan and wanderer. What was real? What was truth? Every vision from Elisibet brought a sense of power, followed by a wave of disgust and revulsion for enjoying the strength pulsing through them. Tonight's episode had further alienated her from herself. Watching Valmont play with his prey made her nauseous with conflicting emotions. She wanted to do so much more to that poor woman, enjoyed hearing her sobs and shrieks, lusted after the scent of her fear.

What kind of monster am I?

Margaurethe whispered calming words, and led her into her bedroom. There she helped Whiskey undress. The tenderness, the comforting voice, the soothing caresses made Whiskey more ashamed of her horrible desires. She climbed into bed, tears stinging her eyes. Margaurethe doffed her robe and slipped beside her, holding Whiskey as she began to cry.

CHAPTER TWELVE

The hour was late yet Margaurethe remained awake. Whiskey had finally succumbed to a weary sleep only an hour before, her lips turned down in her slumber. Margaurethe held her close, pillowing Whiskey's head on her breast, petting the blond hair, and committing to memory the feeling of their entwined legs.

It had been so long since they had been together. Centuries had passed with Margaurethe ever diligent as she awaited the return of her lover, the return of her soul. She had to admit that she had idealized Elisibet through the decades, romanticized the reality of the *Ninsumgal*, and lost herself in the love filling her. With Whiskey's arrival Margaurethe found those heartfelt fancies to be wisps of fairytales, her recollections challenged on a daily basis. Now she remembered the sheer bullheadedness of Elisibet, the desire to do things her way. She had always been cruel, a spoiled child tossed into a pack of rabid wolves slavering for her power. Somehow, the little girl had picked up this diseased yearning for dominance, and had realized that to keep control she had to be more ruthless than the best of them.

Or perhaps that was another idealization on Margaurethe's part.

Elisibet had been content to merely have a heavy hand with her people. After Margaurethe had arrived at court, the *Ninsumgal* had actually begun to mellow. The next two centuries of her rule had become less a constant scrabbling for control and more a true kingdom of laws, strict though they may have been. Margaurethe had always been proud that perhaps she had been the one to begin teaching Elisibet the nature of compassion.

It all changed when Valmont had been presented at court. He was a man who reminded Elisibet of the youth she hadn't been allowed to have, the freedom to make mistakes and experiment without concern for repercussions. Margaurethe hadn't recognized the danger until long after the pair had committed several atrocities on both Human and Sanguire alike. Valmont magnified Elisibet's cruelty, and she in turn encouraged his bloodthirstiness. The worst of it was that Margaurethe had truly liked Valmont. They had become tight friends, the three of them, regardless of the constant escalation of tortures for which he and Elisibet were responsible. Margaurethe had always hoped she could talk sense into her lover, calm her irrational furies, and guide her along a less gory path. That chance had been violently taken away from her when Valmont murdered Elisibet. *Agrun Nam* orders or not, Valmont had succumbed to the ultimate brutality. He not only killed the ruler of his people but his best friend. His tragic whining about his loss of honor and his broken heart were useless to Margaurethe. Hers had been the worst pain. She had been left alone, bereft, the dark light of her heart no longer shining.

And here he was, to do it again.

Whiskey sensed Margaurethe's tenseness and shifted, mumbling. Instantly, Margaurethe accommodated her, forced herself to relax. Her lover sighed, hugging Margaurethe until she drifted further asleep, breath causing goose bumps on Margaurethe's flesh. *Gods, how could I have forgotten this?* Whiskey's skin against hers, the warmth radiating between them, the tingle of arousal always on the edge of her body, things she had vowed to never forget as she had mourned Elisibet's death.

Margaurethe had had other lovers over the decades, none for any length of time. After a century of mourning, she finally succumbed to her body's physical desires. None of those lovers ever held her heart, for that part of her had already been claimed though it wilted on the vine of her grief. They had been invited into her bed solely to relieve a bodily yearning she couldn't ease alone. It had been so long since Elisibet, that Margaurethe couldn't be certain of the differences between her and Whiskey. Their lovemaking was sweet and generous, not quite up to the rough standards Elisibet occasionally employed. They hadn't exchanged blood and Margaurethe wasn't certain whether it was Whiskey's innocence or the newness of their relationship keeping such from occurring. Was Whiskey truly Elisibet in a new body? Would she fall to the depravity Elisibet had welcomed with a full embrace? Would Valmont succeed in warping her yet again with his twisted soul?

Margaurethe had to do everything in her power to keep that from happening again. What else would stop Valmont from reenacting the past, urge Whiskey on to plumb her moral depths, and become outraged at the result? That was what had happened before. He had been the cause for Elisibet's downfall as well as her death.

Perhaps she needlessly worried. Whiskey seemed quite nonplussed after her escapade. Elisibet had never been upset after spending time hunting with Valmont; she had always been exhilarated, her passions ignited with the bloodlust that she quenched with Margaurethe. Maybe Whiskey's innate sense of compassion was strong enough to deny the temptation Valmont placed before her. It could happen. Margaurethe knew that Whiskey was right when she said she needed to know all aspects of her people to rule them. She had been detached from them for her entire childhood, inexperienced, unsophisticated; in danger simply due to her willingness to assume her people's culture aped Humanity.

The time had come to open the doors. Security had had plenty of time to finalize their training; the building was as safe as it was going to get, and operating procedures were in place for travel and exterior security. Other than the *Baruñal* Ceremony, the function levels had been empty of diplomats long enough. It was time to begin the process of lifting the stranglehold and allowing Whiskey and her pack a little freedom to act their age. At least Margaurethe would have more control over Whiskey's safety with her total involvement in the process.

Margaurethe felt a tremor in her heart. Would Whiskey appreciate the sacrifice? As much as Margaurethe didn't want to do this, Whiskey was right. She needed to be seen by her people, needed to interact with them all, not just the diplomats and ambassadors. Whiskey needed to experience everything the Sanguire had to offer. And perhaps the activity would thwart Whiskey's desire to go hunting with Valmont again.

She glanced at Whiskey sleeping beside her, noting the unrestful expression on her face. *I know one way to stop that from happening.*

***

"Are you all right?"

Whiskey blinked, looking up from her barely touched breakfast, feeling a tendril of cool rain brushing against her mind.

Chano, the leader of the *Wi Wacipi Wakan* and newest board member of The Davis Group, studied her. "You are far from here."

Since learning of the existence of her mother's family several months ago, Whiskey had made it a point to have breakfast with the old man at least three times a week. Normally, she enjoyed their time together, listening to stories about her people's history and mythology, but not today. Shying away from the familiar touch of his essence, she opened her mouth to proclaim she was fine, stopping as she looked at him. One thing she had learned was that her ability to spot a lie came from her native blood. Whiskey had vowed to never lie to any of them as a result. "I'm just unsettled."

Chano grunted acceptance. "The security guards were upset last night, and you could not be found. Did something happen?"

Whiskey rolled her eyes. How could she explain her fears of becoming an abomination? The American Indians never knew the Sweet Butcher, had no frame of reference for the heinous behavior for which Whiskey held potential. She returned his expectant gaze, knowing she might as well confess her actions; he would hear of it soon enough. "I ditched the place last night, and went hunting with Valmont."

Chano cocked his head, brow furrowed. "And this distresses you?"

"Yeah." Whiskey pushed her plate away, not really hungry. "We went to a bar, picked up a woman, and tormented her."

Silence reigned for a moment. Chano responded with hesitation. "Would you feel better had it been a man?"

Whiskey's head came up to stare at him. "Don't you understand? We hurt her, scared her half to death, then left her unconscious when we were done."

He paused a moment, studying her. "Was she permanently damaged? Did you cripple her in some manner, leave her to die?"

Horrified, Whiskey felt the blood leave her face. "No! Of course not!"

Now he looked puzzled. He reached out and took her hand. "The first hunt is always distressing. It is difficult to remember that our Human brothers and sisters are necessary for our nourishment. They can be friends, allies, and enemies, but they are also our sole source of survival."

Whiskey didn't pull away. "That's not it exactly."

"Then what is 'it'?"

She stared at Chano's hand upon hers, the darker skin contrasting against her lighter hue. *It should be the other way around. My soul is darker than his.* "I'm afraid."

He squeezed her hand. "There is nothing to fear in hunting for sustenance. I think you fear the pleasure of the hunt, not the hunt itself."

"Yes, that's it. It was..." Whiskey paused, a sensation of pleasure washing over her at the memory. "It was exhilarating." Dismayed, she pushed the joy away, not wanting to experience such things.

"Many find it so. And some lose themselves on that path, falling sway to the powerful feeling it gives."

"Yeah." Whiskey nodded. "That's what happened with Elisibet."

"Ah." Chano used his free hand to pat and cover hers. "Now you come to the heart of the matter. It isn't that you enjoyed the hunt, but that you remembered the past hunts of the woman you were."

Those memories came alive in Whiskey's mind, and she shivered at the strength of them. Her response was a mere whisper, though it seemed to echo loudly in the dining room. "Yes. It scares me."

"There is nothing to fear. You are not her."

"How do you know?" Whiskey clutched Chano's hand. "How do you know I won't become just like her?"

He smiled. "Do you remember Elisibet ever questioning herself in this way?"

Whiskey scowled, wanting to pull away from him, a perverse part of her wishing to continue her personal chastisement without interruption. Though he was ancient in appearance, his grip was iron. There was nowhere to go. "No. Sometimes she wondered if she was doing the right thing, but she enjoyed herself too much to stop."

"There is your answer." Chano again patted her hand. "You do question. You analyze what happened, and feel remorse for your feelings. Did Elisibet ever feel remorse?"

The question distracted Whiskey from her self-castigation. Though many of her memories of Elisibet were sketchy, a few were quite strong. "I think..." She trailed off, puzzling through the mix of recollections. "Yeah, once."

"And what did she regret?"

An image of young Margaurethe, tears sparkling in her eyes as she hovered within sight filled Whiskey's mind. "She regretted leaving Margaurethe when she died." Odd. She hadn't expected that answer. Sometimes things just blurted out of her mouth like this, leaving her both wiser in the ways Elisibet's mind worked and confused as to where the words came from. She puzzled over it as Chano squeezed her hand.

"Maybe her last feeling is what prompted you to have such compassion for the people around you," he ventured. "I think that you have nothing to worry about—you can never become like Elisibet."

Still stricken, Whiskey stared at her friend and advisor. She tried to say something, but a lump clogged her throat. When she spoke, her words came out in a croak. "Why not?"

Chano smiled. "Because you feel so much compassion for a stranger now. So long as you hold on to that awareness of others, both Human and Sanguire, you will never need to worry about becoming Elisibet."

"Can it be that easy?"

He nodded. "Yes, it can. Besides, there is something you have that Elisibet did not." His smile widened. "Elisibet did not have family who would gladly take her to task. I will stand by your side, support you on your path, and swat your behind when you make mistakes like any good grandfather should."

The image caused Whiskey to release a watery chuckle. She could well imagine Margaurethe's outrage should it ever happen. A sense of rightness filled her heart, pushing the anxiety aside as she belatedly realized that she wasn't alone. Overwhelmed by Elisibet's memories and desires, she had forgotten. Elisibet had fended for herself for two centuries before Margaurethe had joined her, and had continued out of habit to block any attempt at easing her burdens of leadership. Buried beneath learning other cultures as well as how to guide them, Whiskey had begun relying too much upon Elisibet's tactics. Last night's escapade had been a lesson, nothing more. Whiskey couldn't allow herself to wallow in guilt over Elisibet's choices; that emotion had magnified her feelings, nearly choking her.

"Your family may not always be at your side, but I am your family, too. We are all One People created by powerful spirits in the world." He gave her a rare wink. "We must stick together to confound the European invaders."

Whiskey chuckled, shaking her head. Only an old American Indian Sanguire would still consider the European expatriates invaders. Sniffling, she strengthened her hold on Chano's hand before releasing it. "Thank you."

"It is what a family does."

CHAPTER THIRTEEN

Castillo rose as the door opened, and smiled welcome. "*Ki'an Gasan* Margaurethe, good morning." He noticed the pinched look on her otherwise beautiful face, and her stance indicating a preparation to go into battle. Subduing his naturally cheerful demeanor, he pulled her usual chair from the conference table, offering it to her.

"Father." Margaurethe waited for him to return to his seat. "Thank you for being here."

"Of course."

"I appreciate you taking the time."

He tilted his head. Her jaw flexed as if the need for routine politeness grated upon her. Something had clearly annoyed her.

Right now, the one person capable of that was *Sublugal Sañar* Valmont. *Lord, have patience. What has he done to incur her wrath this time?* His musings were interrupted by the next arrival.

Chano hobbled into the room with a carved walking stick for support. Castillo automatically stood and went to the coffee station where he filled a cup for the elder Sanguire. "Good morning. How are you today?"

"Still kicking." The craggy Indian reached his chair and sank gratefully into it. "Old age ain't for sissies."

Castillo chuckled, bringing the cup and the sugar container to him. Chano enjoyed it strong and sweet, similar to the Basques in the Old Country. Considering Chano's sweet tooth, it was a wonder he still had his original dental work. "I'll keep that in mind should I ever reach your...stature."

Chano winked. "Thank you."

"You're welcome."

Margaurethe cut off the pleasantries. "Can we get this started?"

Puzzled, Castillo nevertheless nodded and returned to his chair. Chano was less inclined to take things at face value, being the eldest and strongest in the room. "We're not waiting for Reynhard and Valmont?"

"No, we're not. Reynhard has been out of town on an errand for Whiskey. Valmont knew the time and place; it's hardly my fault he's a coward." With the acid tone stronger than usual, Castillo wondered again at Valmont's offense. Her next words enlightened him. "Valmont took Whiskey hunting last night."

That impressed Castillo. He wondered what brought that up. "Really? How interesting."

"Interesting?" Margaurethe's sharp word matched the flash of anger in her eyes as she glared. "She bullied her guards into not telling me she'd left, and Valmont took her to Tribulations, of all places!"

"Isn't that the local Sanguire haunt here in Portland?" When Castillo agreed, Chano shrugged. "Not very sensible on his part."

Margaurethe must have assumed the elder's remark had given her tacit permission to rant. "To think how close she came to being hurt or killed... There are dozens of Sanguire using that place as a hunting ground."

"A hundred or more," Castillo corrected softly.

"*Hundreds*!" She seized on Castillo's comment with grim satisfaction. Standing, she paced around the table, forcing the men to crane their necks to keep her in view. Castillo had the sudden vision of being an owl, wondering if his head would twist off like the cap of his favored root beer before she finished. "If she had made a mistake, told anyone who she was, they would have ripped her to shreds. We can't lose sight of the fact that there are some here in Portland who have seen Elisibet during her reign. What if they had recognized her last night?"

"It sounds like both of them were completely irresponsible."

She paused to stare at Chano, gauging his sincerity, then glanced at Castillo. "Yes. Completely." Castillo gave her his full attention, studiously urging her to continue. Margaurethe must have decided their responses were genuine for she returned to circling the room. "How could Valmont be so idiotic?"

"Whose idea was this?" Castillo asked.

Margaurethe's lips thinned further, the muscles in her jaw visibly throbbing in time with the grinding of her teeth. "Whiskey claims it was hers, that she asked Valmont to take her hunting."

Chano narrowed his eyes. "You doubt her?"

Margaurethe waved dismissively. "I believe her, of course. But I know Valmont well enough after centuries. The conniving bastard probably brought the subject up, and made her think it was her decision."

Her statement didn't change Chano's expression. "To what purpose?"

She paused, mouth open, as she considered the question. "To put her in danger, of course! He's never happier than when he's taking risks, and he wants to take risks with Whiskey."

Chano frowned. "I do not understand. Why would he wish to put Whiskey in danger? It would defeat the purpose of what we are doing here, and put him in danger of being hunted by every American Indian Sanguire on this continent, not to mention any other nations currently in negotiations with us."

Margaurethe stood opposite Castillo on the other side of the table. She turned and planted her hands on her hips. "He killed Elisibet." Her words became slow and pointed, as if she spoke to an idiot. "You don't think he plans on doing anything different this time around, do you?"

Castillo mentally rubbed his temples. Margaurethe's distrust of the fifth member of Whiskey's advisory council was bone deep. Valmont could neither do nor say anything to redeem himself in her eyes. It made for an extremely rocky working relationship when she insisted he had ulterior motives every time he did or said something to spark her anger. Castillo spoke carefully, taking time to phrase his statement as politely as possible. "I think Valmont has had ample opportunity to harm Whiskey over the last few months. He would hardly need to take her to a public location and reveal her to others if he wanted her killed."

"He is not an innocent in this!"

"I didn't say he was, *Ki'an Gasan*. I simply mean that he can do more damage alone." Castillo held up a hand to forestall another outburst. "Think about it. Whiskey has Elisibet's memories. If he wished her to be torn asunder, wouldn't it be better to do the job himself, to show her that time changes nothing and he still has ultimate control over her life?" He didn't believe a word of that, but suspected much of her anger was directed at Whiskey for brainstorming this little hunting party. Since getting to know Margaurethe, he had come to realize she held a latent fury toward Elisibet—for putting herself in the position that caused her death, and for abandoning Margaurethe to centuries of loneliness. It wasn't that Valmont agreed to take Whiskey on this expedition; it was that Whiskey had originated the idea and brought it to fruition.

Chano seemed unimpressed with Margaurethe's issues. "What is done is done. Now that Whiskey has had a taste, I doubt she will stop. We are built to track down our prey, induce the desired emotional and chemical response, and take what we need to survive. Once truly blooded, a youngling's very nature will succumb to millions of years of evolution. We should pay more attention to locating safe ways for her to follow her natural instincts instead of smacking Valmont on the butt for his actions in this."

Margaurethe's anger became focused on Chano. "Why are you defending him?"

"I'm not defending him." Chano spoke softly, but no less resolutely. "You are angry, and you have every right to be. But we all know that anger blinds vision. You are only seeing what you wish to see, not the truth."

***

As she made her way to the gymnasium on the third floor Whiskey had much to ponder. Elisibet had been a spoiled brat, pushed through the *Ñíri Kurám* far too early. Many Sanguire philosophers and scientists had used her callous reign as an example of how her early induction into adulthood had permanently warped her. With no other examples on record, the assumption stood. Alphonse and Zebediah too had followed the Strange Path at an earlier than normal age. While it was possible that the argument had merit as both brothers were quite vicious, it was equally possible that their first pack leader, Fiona, had nurtured their bloodthirstiness rather than that they manifested it because of their youth. It was standard practice now to wait for a youngling to reach beyond the age of majority—twenty-five years of age or more—before allowing them to follow the Strange Path.

What if that wasn't the cause? *What if Elisibet was just a bully that no one had the balls to punish when she was being a jackass?* Whiskey rode the elevator in silence, staring at the red digital numbers as they changed, an *Aga'us* beside her. Two hundred years of running the show as a petulant middle-school bully would certainly gain a person a bad reputation. Margaurethe had begun making a dent in Elisibet's brutality before Valmont appeared on the scene. Whiskey recalled scenes of Elisibet wanting to do dire damage only to be persuaded otherwise by Margaurethe's presence. Young Valmont had been fuel added to the cooling fire. Not even Margaurethe's quiet serenity could stop the inferno once it had begun.

The elevator stopped on the third floor, and she stepped out with her escort. The cardiovascular room across from them showed a handful of people on the treadmills and ellipticals. Most were Human project managers getting in a few minutes' exercise between meetings. The window beyond showed that the multiple current pools were well occupied. Whiskey turned right, and entered the gymnasium that took up the majority of the floor's north wing. There her pack gave her a rowdy welcome.

Zebediah, ever the teenager, bounded forward. "Dude! You went to Tribulations last night? How'd it go?"

Surprised, Whiskey looked around at the others waiting to hear about her unauthorized field trip. "How the hell did you know?"

Cora blushed and looked down at her feet. "Anthony got called away last night..."

Laughing, Whiskey approached and took Cora's hands as her pack surrounded her. "Of course. If you see him before I do, tell him I'm sorry Margaurethe stripped his hide."

Cora grinned. "I will, *aga ninna*."

Impatient, Zebediah bounced on the balls of his feet. "Come on. What happened?"

A flash of her victim's fear raced through Whiskey's system. She shoved away the exhilaration, still not wanting to examine it too closely. "Not much. We went hunting, then came home." She doubted that would be enough to sway the cutthroat younglings surrounding her, and prepared for an onslaught of demands for more details.

Alphonse snorted. "Who cares about hunting? What's it like inside?"

His words were a slap to her, derailing her attempt to disassociate herself from the feral joy she had discovered the night before. "What...?"

"Inside!" Zebediah grinned at her. "What's it like inside? We're too young to get in."

Thinking furiously to catch up, Whiskey realized they were more impressed that she had entered the bastion of adult Sanguire than with the act of her first hunt. *Well, duh. They've hunted most their lives. Fiona never bothered with* kizarusi. She found the sudden adolescent turn of the discussion amusing, never having expected to be on this side of it. "It was okay. Nothing like Malice, though. The music was slower, and it seemed more...cultured."

Zebediah grimaced in disgust. "That's it?"

"That's it. They have a series of hidden rooms for Sanguire to have privacy, but other than that—" Whiskey shrugged, and looked around. "What were you expecting?"

"No idea." Alphonse shook his head, grinning at his brother. "Not a milder form of Malice, that's for sure."

"Haven't any of you been inside before?"

"Are you kidding?" Zebediah backed away a step, hands in front of him, palms out. "We'd be mincemeat there. Everybody's more powerful."

Whiskey conceded the point. An adult Sanguire's mental power grew with age, the older the stronger. A youngling of eighteen like Zebediah didn't stand a chance. Sanguire children were a rare gift, but once they hit adulthood they were just another resource for their elders to manipulate. That was why they remained in their familial compounds or banded together in packs. Whiskey hadn't had any trouble because she had been with Valmont. Had she entered alone, she might have been able to overpower anyone attempting to compel her, but that would have certainly blown the lid off her cover. Provided that hadn't happened already.

Chaniya shook her head in the negative. "You Europeans do things in different ways, but even in my country I would not consider entering an adult establishment." She made a strange gesture with one hand, one she had used before as a sign of protection. "Gcwawama is always ready with a malicious prank for the unwary."

"Gcwawama?" Daniel asked, ever the scholar.

"The mischievous trickster in our folklore."

Nupa nodded in commiseration. "Yeah, Iktomi is one of our tricksters. Can't ever trust him."

Whiskey watched the others withdraw from the conversation in disbelief and discomfort. She found the religious underpinnings of the various peoples of the world intriguing, but the European Sanguire in her pack tended to mirror the less spiritual view of their Human counterparts. The American Indians and Africans kept closer to their religious roots. Whiskey wondered if the world would be a better place if everyone believed in their races' original faith. *And here you are with a Catholic priest as your advisor.*

The door of the gym opened, and she turned to see Pacal striding forward with three of her *aga'usi* trailing behind. The guards were the youngest of her security staff, and had taken to hanging out with her pack while off duty. They wore workout clothing since Whiskey had publicized that training was open to all interested parties. It was Pacal's attire that surprised her. At their first meeting he had worn typical modern clothing. Now he was barefoot and bare-chested, wearing a linen breechclout held in place by a thin leather band. Being nearly naked did nothing to diminish his confidence as he stalked across the space between them, well-delineated muscles gleaming in the overhead light. His black hair was loose, and a leather headband kept it from falling forward into his face. When he spoke his voice held an edge of contempt. "Is everyone here?"

Glancing around, Whiskey was happy to see she wasn't the only one startled by his appearance. Even Daniel the Pragmatic stared at their instructor. She also wasn't the only one who didn't care for his attitude as was evinced by Nupa's glower. "Yeah, we're all here."

"Good." Pacal came to a halt, arms crossed over his magnificent chest, feet spread wide. "Who will take me on?"

Whiskey blinked, frowning. Again she looked at her pack, seeing her confusion reflected back at her. The three security guards seemed as baffled, moving to stand with them. "I thought this was our first lesson, not a duel."

"Like any of you could survive a duel with me," Pacal snorted, his lip curling.

Her frown deepened at his arrogance. Still, she knew better than to challenge him to a physical fight. Whiskey had absolutely zero experience with hand-to-hand fighting, having always resorted to flight when she couldn't talk her way out of a confrontation. She hoped this was some weird Mayan way of starting a lesson rather than a reaction to Nupa's presence.

"No takers?" Pacal shook his head, scorn dripping from his words. "You think you're all *malandros*, yet you don't have the balls to take me in a physical fight? I can take all of you on at the same time and win."

No one seemed to know what the strange word meant, but

his tone left no question of its derogatory nature. Zebediah nudged Alphonse. "No mind fucks?"

"Like I'd need to use my mental abilities to win against a scrawny thing as you."

Though Whiskey didn't appreciate Pacal's manner, she had lived years on the streets with arrogant bastards who loved nothing more than provoking others into a fight. Rather than take the bait, she gauged the mood of her pack. Most of them had joined Nupa in glaring at their new instructor, the young brothers visibly trembling with the adrenaline rush. Even Daniel and Cora were close to losing their tempers. Despite the angry tension building around them, the pack didn't attack without Whiskey's permission. Proud of their control, she stepped to one side, hands raised in surrender. "Do what you want. Don't let me stop you." With the leash that held them back cut, the pack split up to surround Pacal. He didn't bother to move, allowing them to orbit him without apparent care. The three *aga'usi* considered one another. Two stepped back as the third joined the others preparing their assault.

There was little testing or feinting, and less forethought. Cora and Daniel were the first on the offense despite Alphonse's and Zebediah's eagerness. Whiskey blinked at their swiftness, hardly able to see them move as they thrust and jabbed at their enemy. Rather than meet force with force, Pacal danced aside, their fists meeting air. Chaniya circled behind with Alphonse and Zebediah. She dropped to the ground and swept in a leg, heel aiming for the back of Pacal's knee. He sidestepped. She whirled back to her feet with a snarl. The boys flanked Pacal, attempting a clothesline tackle from both sides. This time Pacal leapt backward, somersaulting over Chaniya to bounce lightly on the balls of his bare feet. Alphonse and Zebediah crashed together in a heap, swearing as they disentangled themselves.

Nupa had remained clear of the first attack, though he crouched to one side, watching. As soon as Pacal hit the ground behind Chaniya, he closed the distance between them, chest butting the Mayan. They scrabbled for a few seconds as Nupa attempted to gain a wrestling hold on his opponent. Chaniya turned and lent her strength to the endeavor, Daniel not far behind. The others followed suit. The combat had turned into nothing but a mass of younglings overpowering their arrogant master-at-arms. Whiskey smirked. That was quick.

Her mouth dropped open as both Alphonse and Zebediah flew out of the upheaval to land in shameful heaps. The sharp smell of blood filled the air, and Cora staggered away with blood pouring from her nose. The single guard who had joined the fracas cried out in sharp pain, careening out of the fight with an arm twisted into an awkward position. Whiskey's eyebrows crawled to her hairline. Nupa, Daniel and Chaniya continued to struggle, but Pacal seemed to be gaining the upper hand despite the overwhelming odds. Was he cheating? She reached out her mind to taste the essence of the tumult, but found no indication that Pacal was attempting to manipulate the younger Sanguire with his mental strength. In a classic Three Stooges move, Pacal grabbed both Daniel and Chaniya, bouncing their heads off one another loud enough to be audible to Human ears. Both collapsed, dazed, at his feet. Nupa still gamely attempted to bring his opponent down, grappling him around his waist, trying to grab and pin down the strong arms. Pacal dropped back, taking Nupa with him as he somersaulted backward. The change in gravity loosened Nupa's hold. Pacal spun him around and pushed him away. Nupa stumbled several feet from the force, his normally impassive face ugly with anger.

With the most dangerous foes out of the way, Pacal crouched as he tried to keep an eye on all of them as they regrouped for another attempt. His body was slick with sweat, and he breathed heavily, but there was no other indication that he had been attacked. No apparent injuries marred his skin. "Let's play a new game." Fangs bared, he pointed a long arm at Whiskey. "She's mine. Try and stop me."

CHAPTER FOURTEEN

Margaurethe's voice became a growl. "And what is the truth?" She hadn't quite extended her fangs, but she leaned forward in a menacing way.

Castillo forced himself to remain calm as he ran interference. "That Whiskey is as much to blame for what happened last night as Valmont. Yet you show no fury toward her, no complaint with her taking her life in her hands so recklessly. She's as much to blame as he is, probably more so."

Margaurethe scoffed and dropped backward into her chair. "So I'm to be mad at a youngling for acting impulsively as opposed to the more experienced Sanguire man who has the brains of a gnat?"

Relieved his head remained on his shoulders, Castillo fought the impulse to stretch his neck. "She's not really a youngling, is she? She has Elisibet's memories and power. She can decimate the lot of us with a single thought if she wished. Whiskey might react on the basis of her nineteen-year-old self, but the wealth of experience, strength and wisdom come from the Sweet Butcher."

"Wisdom," Margaurethe muttered, looking away.

Castillo decided not to pursue that topic. Until Margaurethe worked past her emotions, it was useless. Her vision remained clouded by idealized love and the denial of facts. He pondered how much Whiskey chafed at the subconscious restrictions put upon her by someone for whom she cared so deeply. It wasn't any wonder she had coerced Valmont into taking her hunting.

A knock at the door interrupted his thoughts. The door opened and one of the security guards politely intoned, "*Sublugal Sañar* Valmont."

***

Whiskey hastily stepped back, shaking her head. *He can't be serious.* The two guards that had stayed out of the initial scrimmage sidestepped to block her from Pacal's view. Pacal took three steps before running into an immovable object—Nupa blocked and seized him, throwing him to the ground. Surprised at his success, Nupa hesitated before he pounced. He hit the treated gymnasium floor, Pacal having used the minuscule pause to flip agilely away. Alphonse had had a chance to collect himself, and delivered two punches to Pacal's kidneys before an elbow rammed back into his chin. He slumped to the floor, unconscious. Zebediah screamed in fury, launching himself at his brother's attacker. With a grim expression, Pacal met him, blocking Zebediah's useless fists, spinning him about and sending him stumbling away with an insulting kick to the backside.

It was Cora who got the first significant hit on Pacal. While he was occupied with the boys, she jumped him from behind, wrapping her arms and legs about him, sinking her teeth into his neck. He flailed at her uselessly for a brief moment. Unable to get a good grasp on her, he toppled, using the weight of his body to crush her to the floor. The tactic drove the air from her lungs, and she released him. Pacal bounded to his feet to keep from being dog-piled by the others. Cora's abrupt removal from his neck had torn the flesh there. Blood poured freely from the wound, though not enough to seriously hamper his energy—he hardly seemed to notice. He closed the distance between himself and Whiskey's guards, his gaze only upon her. She stared back at him over the shoulders of the two men blocking him. *Crap. I don't think he's kidding around!* She trembled, smelling her fear in the perspiration erupting all over her body. *What if he's serious? Is this an assassination attempt because I'm half Indian?*

With no pause in his approach, Pacal kicked out, driving a foot into the nearest guard's groin. The man dropped like a stone, clutching his abdomen and gagging. Pacal stepped purposely over his twisting body, reaching for the remaining professional between him and his target. With a flurry of movement too fast to follow, the *aga'us* defended his *Ninsumgal*. He had more training than his comrades, and it showed as he met Pacal blow for blow. But he was still young and inexperienced enough to fall into the trap of disciplined protocols. He wasn't prepared for the sudden appearance of a weapon. Pacal whipped off the leather strap holding his loincloth in place, lashing it around the *aga'us*' throat. Naked, he took the final step closer, twisting to bring the guard to the ground, incapacitated.

***

Castillo sent a silent plea for strength as Valmont entered the conference room, the door closing behind him. Margaurethe stiffened in her chair, eyes narrowing. For his part, Valmont appeared to realize his shaky position. He didn't exhibit his usual acerbic mannerisms. Instead his eyes were calm, and his hands hung loosely at his sides. He remained where he stood, awaiting an invitation to come or go. Knowing this was Margaurethe's show, Castillo kept silent.

After several moments, she rose with a measure of grace, her expression stony. Stalking toward the new arrival, she paused only long enough to rake her eyes over him. The speed and strength with which she struck Valmont nearly knocked him to the floor. He staggered backward, head reeling from the impact. Castillo smelled the blood before seeing it, and he half straightened out of his chair in response.

Valmont used the door to push himself up, his other hand wiping at his split lip. He shook his head once before taking a deep breath. Squaring his shoulders, he stood without support and faced her. He steeled himself for another blow but didn't raise his chin, didn't yield. Another strike from Margaurethe, and again he stumbled. He had nowhere to go, pressed against the door as he was. He worked his jaw to check for broken bones and stood firm again.

Castillo pushed away from the table and neared them. "*Ki'an Gasan* Margaurethe," he said, his voice gentle. "Please. Stop this."

"Oh, I'll stop this, all right." She prepared another blow. "As I should have stopped it long ago. I knew you were dangerous for Elisibet from the first. But she could never see it, would never hear a negative word of you from anyone's lips, least of all mine. I won't let you destroy her again."

"*Enough*!"

The word was sharp and commanding. Castillo turned to see Chano limping forward with his walking stick, a frightful expression upon his face. Knees weak with relief, Castillo swallowed hard, willing his heart to slow down. His younger age made him the weakest of them, incapable of stopping this brawl no matter his desire.

***

Whiskey attempted to run, but Pacal was too fast. He hooked his arm around her throat, pulling back and turning so she hung from his muscled forearm, shielding him from the reprisals of the remaining fighters. The *aga'us* sat at Pacal's right foot, clutching at the improvised garrote and fighting to breathe. Cora, Nupa and Zebediah hovered just out of reach, bruised and bloodied, looking for any opening. Whiskey's fingers dug into the smooth muscles beneath her fingers, feeling her face heat up from lack of blood flow. *He's trying to kill me!*

An all-encompassing fury exploded in her chest. Without thought, she sank her teeth into Pacal's arm, forcing him to release his grip. In a move she couldn't comprehend, she threw him to the ground, twisting his arm to pop the shoulder out of its socket. His grunt of pain shocked her out of the unnatural frenzy, and she realized the overbearing anger wasn't a result of nearly losing consciousness. She staggered away from the melee, dragging Pacal with her as her mind reached out. It connected with a molten ball of wrath. *That's not coming from me!* "Margaurethe?"

Those still on their feet stared at her, and she released Pacal's arm, backing away. This madness was from Margaurethe. *What's happening to her?* "Stay here!" she ordered the others, running for the door.

***

Margaurethe glanced behind her, fangs still bared. "Stay out of this, Chano."

"No. I will not." The old man didn't blink an eye as he approached, glaring at Margaurethe. "It's a wonder you Europeans ever built an empire and took over this country the way you squabble amongst yourselves."

She opened her mouth to respond, and froze. Castillo reached out with his mind, assuming Chano had compelled her to cease her attack. Instead of the vague sound/sensation of cool rain, the familiar essence of the elderly Indian, he met the essence of roses and blood. His eyes widened as the door to the conference room opened to reveal an angry Whiskey, the door guard and a newly arrived Reynhard Dorst flanking her.

"Step away from her."

Castillo hastily obeyed, risking a glance at Margaurethe. She remained frozen in place, only her eyes moving, hair wild from the physical exertion of her attack. Whiskey had overcome Margaurethe's will barely in time, stopping her from flaying her prey's flesh from his bones. Valmont said nothing but did as ordered.

Whiskey entered the room, looking only at Margaurethe. "All of you, get out."

Castillo bowed perfunctorily, and filed with the others past the two women. Chano grunted in acceptance as he passed. When they were safely outside, Castillo gave a mighty sigh. The guard hesitated a split second before securing the door, and blocking their return. Two newly arrived *Aga'gída* joined him.

Valmont used the back of his hand to wipe blood from the corner of his mouth. The disdainful smirk had returned to his face as he examined the smear. "Well, that was pleasant."

Chano grunted again, an unsupportive response regardless of his apparent position in the conference room. "If you poke a stick at a wounded animal, you should not be surprised when it defends itself."

Dorst interrupted Valmont's attempt to answer by chortling, softly clapping his gloved hands before him. He had been absent since the *Baruñal* Ceremony. Now he wore the usual black leather and metal spikes for which he was known. Gone was the long brown hair, replaced with three black mohawks striping his scalp. "Is there no end to the fount of American Indian wisdom you spout, sir?"

Rather than be put off by the effeminate act, Chano peered at the gaudy caricature beside him. "No. It is as endless and bottomless as the deepest dung pit." His words were rewarded by a rare genuine laugh from Dorst.

Sourly, Valmont stared at Dorst. "I asked about you the other day, but no one knew where you were. Up to your same old tricks?"

Dorst's humor faded into mock seriousness. "I've only been back an hour or so. I've been away on a little errand for our *Ninsumgal*."

Something sparked in Valmont's eyes, in contrast to the lack of emotion he'd exhibited throughout Margaurethe's attack. It disappeared so quickly, Castillo wasn't sure he had actually seen it. He glanced around the lobby. "I'm going to go clean up. Is this meeting over, or are we reconvening?"

"I'm not certain." Castillo glanced back at the closed doors, a sensation of ominous gloom pushing him away. "Perhaps we can get some coffee in the Executive Dining Room until they're... finished."

"Excellent idea!" Dorst slipped his arm through Chano's, guiding them toward the elevators. "Perhaps we can root in that dung pit of yours for more gems, eh?"

Castillo ignored their chatter as he followed, his mind working on the abortive meeting. How were they supposed to guide Whiskey when they couldn't consolidate themselves? And what was that between Valmont and Reynhard? More secrets to learn. Depending on the day and hour, the advisor meetings were a morass of egos, all battling for control. It was sad to say, but the two most qualified people stood firmly at the center of breach. Until Margaurethe and Valmont resolved this schism, what would be the point of adding any new representative nations brought into the coalition? *How can we even think about adding the Mayans considering their enmity with the American Indians?* He stepped into the elevator, pretending polite interest to the ribald discussion between Dorst and Chano. *It'll be a free-for-all.*

CHAPTER FIFTEEN

"I don't have to ask what you were doing." Whiskey released her control over Margaurethe, watching the slender shoulders slump. Some days the strength and intensity of the growing bond between them frightened her, but today she was glad of it. Who knew how far Margaurethe's actions would have taken her with Valmont if she hadn't interceded? She hadn't had time to wonder from where Dorst had appeared. She had only seen blood and Valmont in her mind's eye as she had taken the emergency stairs to the lobby.

Margaurethe remained in place a moment before straightening. She turned to Whiskey, her expression sternly beautiful. "My apologies. I let my anger get away from me."

"I'm not the one you need to apologize to."

Her expression altered, a faint sneer flickering across face. Calmness replaced it. "I'm more than happy to tender my apologies to Father Castillo and Chano for witnessing my lack of control, but don't expect me to do the same with him."

Whiskey lowered her guard as she realized the immediate danger was over. She stepped closer, brow furrowed in concern. "What will it take, *minn'ast*, for you to trust me?" The pet word Elisibet used for Margaurethe seemed to have an effect. She watched confusion cross her lover's face.

Margaurethe narrowed her eyes, looking away. "I do trust you."

I thought we cleared this up last night. "No. You don't." She moved closer, and took Margaurethe's chin in her fingers. "You're pissed off at Valmont for not trying to stop me from doing what I wanted to do. You're convinced he either set me up and I fell for his manipulations, or he should have done more to keep me from my goal." She relaxed her grip, gently tracing Margaurethe's jawline with a thumb. "You don't trust my ability to take care of myself."

"I don't trust Valmont or his intentions." Margaurethe pulled away, lips pressed together. She marched to the chair she usually sat in during board meetings. "He's a traitor and a murderer. You've let him into this company and into your heart. He will be your downfall."

Whiskey frowned. "Even Judas had a logical reason for his actions."

Margaurethe whirled around. "What is that supposed to mean?"

Having put her foot in it, Whiskey refrained from the temptation to retreat. She had done enough of that as a street kid, and had resolved months ago to stop running. The thought tickled her funny bone given the irony of her attempt to run away from Pacal only minutes ago. "You and I both know how monstrous Elisibet was. Her entire reign went from bad to worse. She was a terror as a child, incapable of understanding how her actions destroyed hundreds of people, Human and Sanguire alike." She moved closer. "The circumstances of her death were engineered by her."

"You're saying she planned to be assassinated by her best friend?" Margaurethe was livid, her skin flushed, hands balled into fists at her side.

"Of course not. But her lack of compassionate insight blinded her to reality—her people wouldn't stand still for much more of her abuse. She painted her ass into a corner. There was no way out."

"You are *wrong*!"

Whiskey expected it; Margaurethe's essence was a jumbled quagmire of emotion, but she caught the raw fury seconds before Margaurethe struck. When it came, Whiskey felt the stinging slap on one cheek. Unlike Valmont, she didn't allow Margaurethe to continue. She grabbed the flailing wrists, pressing close to give Margaurethe less advantage. "I was there, Margaurethe. I remember! Elisibet wasn't surprised when Valmont showed up in her quarters with a sword. Don't you think she could have stopped him with her very will if she had wanted to? Just like I stopped you a few moments ago?"

The baldly stated truth broke through Margaurethe's attack. Her actions were no less frantic as she struggled, but her intentions had changed. She no longer fought Whiskey. Instead she struggled against the niggling doubt that had rested in her heart since Elisibet's assassination. Sensing the difference, Whiskey released her. Margaurethe clutched at Whiskey, buried her head in her shoulder, and cried loudly against the pain she had held for centuries. Automatically, Whiskey's mind sought the guards just outside the door, sending a soothing sensation to ease their alarm. She didn't want anyone bursting into the room to witness Margaurethe's breakdown.

"How could she have been so stupid?" Margaurethe gripped Whiskey's shirt, shaking her. "She was the strongest of us! The best. She could have blasted that bastard's mind into ashes if she'd given it half a thought."

"She was tired. She had nowhere else to go, no place to be safe. She wanted it over."

"She had me, damn it!" Her fist thumped Whiskey's chest. "She had me. I would have kept her safe."

Whiskey sighed and closed her eyes. Hugging Margaurethe

close, she felt as weary as Elisibet had so long ago. Her throat was thick with unshed tears. "You couldn't keep her safe, Margaurethe. You knew that then. Just like you can't keep me safe now. Don't blame Valmont for being Elisibet's tool."

The truth was hard, and it sank slowly through the layers of Margaurethe's essence. She no longer fought against her demons. Her tears were hot against Whiskey's neck, her hands firm as they held her close. Whiskey tentatively brushed her mind along Margaurethe's, easing past the acrid self-hatred, and projecting her love and acceptance. They slipped into a bond so deep, Whiskey had no point of reference. She not only felt Margaurethe's emotions but saw her memories as she relived them. A sense of shock whispered through Margaurethe, indicating her awareness of this fundamental change: *What is this?*

An answer came, not a sound but a feeling rising from the well of their joined minds. *I don't know.* The bitter edge of regret and sorrow burned the edge of the thought, indicating it was Margaurethe's answer to Whiskey's question.

Neither knew how long the fugue lasted. Eventually, Margaurethe's recriminations faded as she accepted Elisibet's state of mind. For the first time, Whiskey was able to show the emotions and memories she lived with, the ultimate weariness that permeated Elisibet's soul as events spiraled out of control. Margaurethe shed tears of sorrow and regret for her lover as she had been and as she was now. Whiskey wept as well, releasing some of her self-doubts as she truly saw Elisibet for the first time through Margaurethe's eyes—not the horror and barbarism that forever haunted her, but the thousands of tender moments that had occurred between them, moments to which she hadn't yet become privy.

When they broke from their mutual reverie, the room had considerably darkened with the threat of summer rain. "Are you all right?" Whiskey wiped the tears from Margaurethe's face.

"Aye. I am." Margaurethe took a deep breath. "What was that?"

Whiskey blinked. "You don't know?" As soon as the words were out, she shook her head. "No, you don't. I remember."

"I've never felt that before, not even with Elisibet."

"Maybe it's part of whatever makes me so much stronger than others my age." Whiskey didn't want to hurt Margaurethe's feelings with the idea that perhaps Elisibet's inability to feel compassion and empathy had blocked something like this from happening before. *That has to be it, right? I'm as strong as she was; everybody says so. It's a good thing she couldn't get into her victims' heads like this. Is it even possible for me to do this with someone else?*

"Maybe so." Margaurethe's gaze flickered to the door. "I still won't apologize to him," she said with a trace of her former stubbornness.

Whiskey chuckled. "You don't have to."

"Good." She drew a shaky breath and stepped away, straightening her clothes.

Following Margaurethe's cue, Whiskey rearranged herself and wiped her face. Nothing could hurt her, not with Margaurethe by her side. They had weathered a storm worse than the one building outside, and they were so much stronger because of it. She took Margaurethe in her arms and kissed her soundly. "I love you."

"I love you, *m'cara*." They held the stance for a fraction of time before she pulled away. "I suggest we locate the rest of your advisors."

"I can go find them. Shall we meet back here?"

Margaurethe looked about the room. Other than a cup of coffee going cold on the table and a spot of blood by the door, nothing indicated the violence that had so recently taken place. "No. You shouldn't be fetching your advisors. Perhaps we should repair to the Executive Dining Room."

Whiskey sent a questing tendril out to Castillo, locating the others upstairs. "They're already there. Shall we?" She held out her arm to Margaurethe. As her lover's hand nestled in the crook of her elbow, she remembered the comforting sensation of this same action over the centuries, and smiled.

CHAPTER SIXTEEN

Valmont had heard Margaurethe's mournful cry after using the lobby washroom to remove evidence of her assault. The cry had struck his heart; surprising considering the bottomless depths of his apathy. He had barely mustered a need to defend himself from her attack. What would have happened if Whiskey hadn't intervened? Would Margaurethe now be celebrating his long-awaited demise, pleased to finally have had her revenge upon him? Odd that the thought brought up an image of Bertrada Nijmege, one who held the same vendetta toward Whiskey. At least Margaurethe's lust for Valmont's death was based on fact rather than fancy.

Upon arriving in the Executive Dining Room, he noted the others had settled at a table, and ordered food and drink from the kitchen. He resisted sitting when offered a chair, preferring to loiter near the window. He was still too agitated from Margaurethe's bold attack and news that Dorst had been on an expedition for Whiskey. For the next twenty minutes, he listened to the trio discuss a number of topics that didn't interest him, and one that left his heart cold and a bad taste in his mouth. Dorst refused to reveal specifics about his recent trip except that he had been to Europe. *Did he visit the* Agrun Nam*? What, if anything, has the snake learned?* Dorst's flippant behavior didn't do much to ease Valmont's fears. He constantly glanced in Valmont's direction, his black eyes as teasing as ever, the expression on his gaunt face declaring, *I have a secret.*

Talk was suspended with the arrival of Whiskey and Margaurethe. Chano and Castillo received a request for forgiveness from Margaurethe regarding her lack of self-control. Valmont, dourly noting the lack of apology to him though he had been the victim of the unprovoked assault, found his newly formed empathy for Margaurethe fading. She comported herself as if nothing had occurred, though redness rimmed her eyes. Whiskey's eyes were also lightly swollen, testament to the tears they had shared. Yet both women seemed calm, closer. Whatever friction he had noted between them over the last few weeks had apparently been put to rest. It gave him grudging pleasure. Though Margaurethe hated him, he did wish her happiness. His favorable feelings passed as he recalled his true purpose here, the real threat to Whiskey's safety. Margaurethe's joy would not last long.

Before he could return to his wallow of self-pity, Whiskey spoke. "Well, I'm sure Reynhard has made some smart-ass comment about where he's been."

"Most definitely, my *Gasan*." Dorst's current visage magnified the maniacal aspect of his grin. He made eye contact with everyone. "Though I've refrained from the horridly boring details."

Valmont didn't return the wide smile bestowed upon him. Dorst was a wild card, his abilities to ferret out information legendary. Perhaps Margaurethe wouldn't have to wait too long for Valmont's death after all. "You didn't tell us Reynhard was on a mission."

Whiskey shrugged. "I didn't think to, sorry. I had other things on my mind." Her smile was a secret one, meant to remind him of their recent discussions and outing.

It didn't appease his concern. He raised his chin to her. "Of course."

"It's hardly a matter for you, Valmont." While Margaurethe's immediate desire to eviscerate him had dissipated, she still held on to her enmity. "What Whiskey has her advisors do is for her alone to decide."

He grinned at Margaurethe, knowing how much she also detested the spy in their midst. Her skin reddened, and he knew he scored a point.

Chano harrumphed. "It is still polite to keep everyone aware of each other's tasks."

"Very true, *wicakte*." Whiskey used a Lakota word to indicate honor for the elder. She glanced warningly at Valmont and Margaurethe. "I'm sorry for not telling anyone else. I asked Reynhard to do a little investigating of the *Agrun Nam*. Someone there has attempted to kill me. Now that I'm an official adult in the eyes of the European Sanguire, I thought it was time to investigate the threat more thoroughly."

Her apology accepted, Chano murmured a response.

Eyes alight with eagerness, Castillo turned toward Dorst. "Really? Were you able to discover anything?"

"It's not so much what I discovered as what I didn't." Looking at Whiskey, Dorst lifted his chin. "With your permission?" She waved for him to continue.

He rose with poise, his leather trench coat swirling about his ankles. He bowed low before Whiskey. "My utmost apologies, *Ninsumgal*, for I have failed in the task you sent me to do. I was unable to locate the mastermind behind the plot against your life."

Whiskey faltered at the obeisance, though it was slight. Valmont swelled with pride as she smoothed over her surprise. Even last month, she would have stumbled far more. *She's getting better at this.* Dorst stood erect at a slight gesture from her.

"Do you know why?" Margaurethe asked.

Dorst peered at Margaurethe. "*Ki'an Gasan*, I can only surmise that this traitor is working entirely alone, even against his companions on the *Agrun Nam*. He is a shadow, a wraith; he connects with no one who can be...impressed with the need to confess."

"In other words, you couldn't use your gifts to emulate someone in whom he would confide." Valmont's mouth drew into a frown.

Dorst raised a shaven eyebrow. "Of course. That's what I said."

Castillo gave a strangled cough, and Chano smiled. Valmont glared at both of them.

"You say 'he,' Reynhard," Whiskey said. "Does that mean you've eliminated *Aga Maskim Sañar* Nijmege as a suspect?"

"Oh, yes. That dear woman has far more ambitious plans than to have you murdered so far away."

Valmont paled as Dorst pointedly glanced at him with a smug wink.

"And what plans are those?" Margaurethe leaned forward in her chair.

Heart pounding in his chest, Valmont watched as Dorst turned back to Whiskey. *He knows! He knows of my involvement.* Blood rushed loudly in his ears, all but drowning out Dorst's response.

"Why, she wishes to slay Elisibet the Sweet Butcher all by herself, of course. Since that's hardly possible, due in great part to Valmont's role in our history, she will happily settle for *Ninsumgal* Jenna Davis instead."

Margaurethe swore colorfully.

"All by herself?" Castillo echoed.

Chano grunted. "You mean she wishes to kill Whiskey personally?"

"By her very hand."

Valmont felt weak, and finally sat down. How long would it take before Dorst dropped the next bomb? How long before Whiskey knew just how traitorous Valmont's soul truly was? He swallowed. He knew any moment now Dorst would announce his duplicity in Nijmege's campaign.

"How is she supposed to pull this off?" Whiskey asked.

"Initially, she insisted on bringing you before the *Agrun Nam*. What with the threat against you being so recent, however, they have been unable to gain consensus in the matter."

"I'm surprised they've argued the point." Margaurethe snorted.

"As am I," Dorst agreed. "But *Nam Lugal* Bentoncourt was quite persuasive at the time. He's always insisted Whiskey remain here."

"And now?"

Dorst cocked his head, staring at the ceiling in thought. "Now, my dear *Ninsumgal*, they are indecisive. Months have passed with no sign of threat to you. Bentoncourt continues to expound on your need to stay away. At the same time, Nijmege demands your return to your 'rightful' place."

Castillo cleared his throat. "Have they put it to a vote?"

"Ah, yes! The democratic principle." Dorst's tone was jovial. "It's a wonder anything gets done, honestly. In answer to your question, yes it was. Two for my *Gasan's* return, two against and one abstention."

As the topic steered away from Nijmege, Valmont stared hard at Dorst. *Why does he say nothing? He must know the truth. Why else would he look at me with that covert expression, if not to tell me he has the upper hand?*

Margaurethe's voice interrupted his thoughts. "Given the information you've acquired, who can you eliminate from our list of potential threats?"

"The only one who I can suggest—cautiously, of course—is Samuel McCall. He and *Aga Maskim Sañar* Nijmege are deep in each other's pockets over the issue of her perceived revenge. He has voted with her for your return, *Ninsumgal*."

McCall. Valmont's hazel eyes narrowed. So that was Nijmege's silent partner. He knew nothing of McCall save his family had quite a bit of clout. It was their political connections that had gotten him his position at such a young age. He wasn't much older than Castillo.

"So, that leaves three." Castillo looked around the table. "For the record, I don't believe that *Nam Lugal* Bentoncourt is the one regardless of the evidence against him."

Whiskey cocked her head as she regarded the priest, a vivid intensity in her eyes. Valmont felt a stab of déjà vu as he remembered the same mannerisms from Elisibet. He had seen it any number of times when Elisibet interrogated people for information. "Why?"

Castillo searched carefully for his words. "As you are aware, he was the one to first introduce your existence to the *Agrun Nam* when my...friend acted with indiscretion."

Valmont snorted at the delicate phrase. They were all aware of Castillo's knee-jerk response when first confronted with Elisibet's doppelganger the previous year. Six months after their first meeting, he'd been able to coax Whiskey's true name out of her and had asked a compatriot to do some research. "When your friend blithered far and wide that he was searching for the reborn Elisibet's parents in the records, you mean." At Whiskey's displeasure, he held up a yielding hand.

For a wonder Castillo didn't blush, though he frowned at the reminder of his naiveté. He waited until she gestured for him to continue. "He, of all them, has what would be considered inside information. He hasn't used it to his advantage in any way. In fact, he's still quite adamant about you staying away."

"Quite adamant," Dorst echoed. "Though I believe he's fighting a losing battle."

"What happened to that phrase your people taught mine? 'Keep your friends close, and your enemies closer'?" Chano placed his hands on his thighs, staring at the others. "Why not have Whiskey under his immediate supervision?"

Margaurethe grimaced. "He doesn't want Whiskey to return. He's led the *Agrun Nam* since Elisibet's murder to the present; he'll lose that standing upon Whiskey's official ascension to the European throne."

"Providing there's proof of her right to ascend." Castillo shrugged apologetically at Margaurethe's frown.

Dorst bowed to her, ignoring the deepening scowl. "Of course. But I believe his heart is a bit more pragmatic. He truly believes our people will be better off with a High *Ninsumgal* than an *Agrun Nam*."

"Even if that High *Ninsumgal* is me?"

"Yes." Castillo leaned his elbows on the table. "Your level of power as well as your skills, your ongoing education, and how you rule the few people here has to have been reported to him through various means. It's no secret, and a full half of your Sanguire staff are European with families back home. You haven't locked down communications, so they've written or e-mailed or called home over the months. He has heard nothing of the Sweet Butcher's return, and everything about a young orphan with a good heart learning how to rule wisely."

"That leaves two *sanari* remaining—Cassadie and Rosenberg." Dorst ran his fingertips over the bare skin of his skull above his ears. It was a startlingly odd gesture, as if he were tucking back nonexistent hair. "I've yet to find sufficient evidence against either of them."

"Which puts us right back where we started," Chano stated.

Whiskey's expression became disgruntled. "Though we can now eliminate three of the five with some accuracy."

"There is one other thing."

Valmont glared at Dorst, knowing what he would say. He wondered if he could get away alive. Gauging his proximity to the door, he thought it a distinct possibility. Castillo was the only person between him and the exit, and he doubted the priest would put up much of a fight. The danger would be getting past security stationed outside and throughout the building. *I can drop over the banister, be out the front door before anyone can react.* It wasn't the thought of mortal peril that stopped his heart cold, however. It was the look he imagined in Whiskey's eyes as she realized he had bartered her life away for nothing. Again. Memory of the flash of betrayal in Elisibet's eyes had flayed him to the bone for centuries after his deed; now he would get a fresh glimpse to fuel his damnation. He had almost decided not to run when Dorst spoke again.

"Another assassin has been hired. A professional."

Valmont's blood began pumping anew, and he slumped in his seat.

"A professional? Who?" Margaurethe rose from her chair.

"I do not know. I only know that a certain stranger met with a certain individual who has been known to take on the occasional assassination for entertainment. I'm still trying to locate who this person is, and how they intend to fulfill their contract."

"Understood." Whiskey rubbed her temples. "Keep at it, Reynhard. Any information is better than none."

Dorst bowed deeply. "It's my one priority, *Ninsumgal*."

"Does anyone else have anything to add?" No one answered and Whiskey looked at Valmont. "You've been quiet, Valmont. Have any ideas?"

He scanned the others. Castillo was ever curious, and Chano calculating under his bushy eyebrows. Margaurethe didn't even glare coldly at him, simply examined him as if she saw his flea-bitten soul without a microscope. Dorst's lips curled with a hint of humor, indicating he knew too much and was inclined to keep silent for the moment. Whiskey's eyes were warm, concerned, and friendly. She still worried for him after Margaurethe's unexpected attack. They remained a little haunted, an echo from last night's hunting expedition, yet despite whatever had bothered her it did not reflect upon him. He realized he didn't ever want to disappoint her.

"Valmont?"

"Sorry." He coughed and cleared his throat. "I don't have anything, no."

She seemed to want to say something, but held back with the others present. "Then I guess everyone is dismissed. We'll get back together when Reynhard has more information."

"Um, there is the matter of your education," Castillo said.

Whiskey laughed. "Well, everyone but the padre. Seems I'm wanted in class."

The others chuckled politely, and the meeting broke.

Valmont half wanted to corner Dorst and demand answers. If he was wrong, however, it would tip his hand. The question became moot as Dorst pleaded a need to continue his task, and bowed out of the room. Previous experience held that even when closely followed, Dorst would disappear into thin air at a moment's notice. It was rumored he was a Ghost Walker, a *Gidimam Kissane Lá*, though Valmont knew Dorst was a shape shifter. He didn't attempt to tail Dorst.

Margaurethe didn't deign to look at him as she warmly bid Castillo and Chano farewell. She swept from the room without a glance. Valmont felt a twinge of something missing, and he wondered how their antagonistic relationship had changed. Soon, he stood alone in the dining room. With a sigh, he went downstairs to get his car.

He had some serious thinking to do.

CHAPTER SEVENTEEN

Whiskey felt better for the shower as she entered her home office. Margaurethe had suggested taking lessons here rather than the executive office downstairs, indicating it was easier to lead when a firm line between professional and personal delineated the two aspects. Elisibet's memories supported the idea, and Whiskey had to admit it made sense. Over the months, she had noticed a distinct need to act professional downstairs. "Thanks, Padre. Pacal gave me quite the workout before I had to leave."

Castillo smiled, turning from his view of the river. "Not a problem. Shall we get started?" He gestured toward the seating area where they normally conducted their lessons, collecting his teaching materials from the corner of her desk.

"Actually, no." Despite the denial, she took her seat on the couch. She had never refused a lesson before, and wondered if she would need to push the issue with him. Sithathor had brought refreshments, and Whiskey poured lemonade from a pitcher for both of them. Offering a glass to Castillo, she smiled at his questioning expression. "I've scheduled time for double lessons tomorrow, if you want."

"All right." He sat in the armchair, slightly puzzled, setting the stack of books and paper on the nearby incidental table. Taking the glass, he raised it to her. "What can I do for you?"

Whiskey took a sip of her lemonade, then leaned back as she considered how to broach the subject on her mind. "I want to talk about Reynhard's report."

He nodded, though his eyes widened at the unexpected topic. "I'm hardly the one with whom to discuss it. Your have other advisors with much more experience and political acumen than I."

She laughed. "You're a Catholic priest! You know politics better than I do. Besides, I need a fresh eye that understands the ins and outs, unlike Chano who's even more in the dark than me." He conceded with a grin, and she crossed her legs and cocked her head. "You're sure that Lionel Bentoncourt has nothing to do with this new contract out on me?"

That sobered him. He pursed his lips and studied his glass. "As sure as I can be without speaking to him myself."

"Why?"

He sighed, looking at her. "Had he wanted to block the prophecy, he could have done so from the very beginning. He had all the time he needed to have you killed before you began the *Ñíri Kurám*. He didn't."

As he spoke, Whiskey studied Castillo's being and mannerisms. He believed what he said. Not that she expected him to lie, but since Rufus it had become ingrained to check out everyone she came in contact with on a daily basis for prevarication. Her gifts had steered her wrong only when they sat idle, or she asked the wrong questions. "Are we positive he was the first on the *Agrun Nam* to be told of my existence?"

"Oh, yes." Castillo gave an emphatic nod. "When I spoke with Hollis, the friend who researched your name, I told him the reason so that he'd use discretion." He rolled his eyes. "Not that it worked. In any case, once our situation settled, I took him to task. He told me that Bentoncourt himself had shown up to interrogate him."

Whiskey hadn't known that. The news certainly gave credence to Castillo's opinion. Had Bentoncourt really felt threatened, he would have had Whiskey killed long before she had finished the *Níri Kurám* and become a credible threat. Instead, he had notified his peers on the ruling council, and one of them had made arrangements with Rufus Barrett to assassinate her. According to Reynhard, only one of them was responsible for this. "I guess what I'm asking is, can he be trusted?"

"Trusted with what?"

She chewed her lower lip, gaze drifting out at the heavy gray cloud cover. She'd have to ask maintenance to apply a treatment to the windows soon. Thankfully these windows didn't face south. She'd be roasting in long-term direct sunlight. Shaking away the incongruous thought, she returned her attention to Castillo. "With information."

"While we do have an advantage with *Sañur Gasum* Dorst on our side, you must be aware that the *Agrun Nam* also have an excellent network of informants. How do you know he doesn't already have the information you wish to share?"

"If Reynhard can't find out who hired this new assassin, do you think Lionel would know he existed?" Castillo conceded the point with a faint grin and a wave of his hand. Whiskey set her half-empty glass down and stared at her fingers. "We're almost finished with negotiations with the Mayans. The African and Japanese should fall in line soon, followed by the Indians. Pretty soon, our board of directors is going to be a very eclectic." Whiskey counted the governments on her fingers. "The Europeans are next in line after that, and the most likely to balk."

"Don't count your eggs before they hatch. Anything can happen in politics." He poured himself another glass of lemonade, refilling Whiskey's. "It took months to get the Mayans this far; the others will take just as long or longer. You could be looking at years before needing to worry about the *Agrun Nam's* inclusion in The Davis Group."

"Years of one assassination attempt after another." She uncrossed her legs and sat forward, elbows on her knees. "Sooner or later, one of them will succeed. The only way I can stop it is to have the ear of someone on the Euro council."

"Someone who will work with you rather than against you."

"Yes." Whiskey flopped back in her seat. "It's not only the sharing of information between governments here—"

Castillo interrupted her. "It's also about opening lines of communication that will help make the transition easier when it comes time to bring the *Agrun Nam* into the fold."

"Exactly." Whiskey stared at him with such intensity that he squirmed. Dialing back her apparent vehemence, she forced herself to relax. As much as she wanted everything to be done now she was becoming used to the idea that her plans could take months or years to accomplish. What good was it being a High *Ninsumgal* over all she surveyed if she had to wait for directors and committees? It was easy to see why Elisibet did things the way she did at times like these. She had never sat on her butt, waiting for people to finish talking. "I want you to be the go-between with Lionel. He knows your name, and will listen to you."

Castillo sat back, mouth open in surprise. He closed it. "You want me to be your liaison with the *Agrun Nam*?"

Whiskey grinned. "Yeah. You're a trustworthy man. He's probably had you investigated since you came up on his radar, and he knows that. Can you imagine how he'd feel if I asked Valmont to do the deed?" She didn't bother to mention the other members of her board of directors. Chano was an unknown, Dorst would raise a thousand red flags of warning, and Margaurethe would flat-out refuse if asked. Whiskey needed someone whom Bentoncourt might actually listen to for this task.

He frowned at her words, but gave grudging acknowledgment. "All right, how will I contact him, and what do you want me to say?"

"I've got his home phone number and his private office line." She stood, going back to her desk to retrieve the information. "Reynhard got it for me months ago. I just haven't bothered to call." Castillo took the offered paper with a shaking hand.

Concerned, Whiskey knelt down beside his chair. "Are you okay, Padre?"

"Perhaps a little awestruck." He stared at the contact information. "I've never met any of the *Agrun Nam*, let alone had personal phone numbers or addresses."

A smile curved her mouth. He reminded her of a teenaged girl with her celebrity idol's autograph. "Looks like you're moving up in the world."

"Apparently."

Whiskey patted his forearm, stood, and returned to the couch. "I want you to tell him about the new assassin. Let him know we believe one of his *sanari* are responsible for hiring whoever it is. Nothing else."

Castillo nodded as he carefully folded the paper, and put it into a pocket of his cassock. "He'll ask how we got this information."

"I don't want him to know about Reynhard. There are probably enough rumors as it is. Let's not give him too much."

"You realize he might already be aware of him. *Sañur Gasum* Dorst brought up a major point regarding communication between your people here and their families at home. He played a large part in your *Ñíri Kurám* ceremony."

"Maybe so, but if they haven't figured it out yet, no reason to hasten the news along." She thought a moment. "Tell him what we know about their last vote; that might tip the scales in your favor."

"Okay." Castillo sipped his lemonade. "And you think this will bring the *Agrun Nam* closer to The Davis Group?"

Whiskey gave him a grudging nod. "I do. At the very least, it might force out who's responsible. The sooner we can pin down who's involved, the sooner we can act."

"Act?" Castillo scooted forward in the chair, all traces of awe gone. "As a government, it's *Nam Lugal* Bentoncourt's option to act, not ours. All we can do is attempt to press charges."

A sardonic expression crossed her face. "Which we can't really do, can we? I'm the victim, and I'm not considered European Sanguire. I have no legal basis for bringing suit against any of them."

"Then what will you do?"

Whiskey resisted the desire to look away, instead staring into Castillo's eyes. "I'll legally challenge whoever is responsible."

***

Bentoncourt's private line jolted him from sleep. He grunted, and fumbled for the noisy phone as its piercing tones pealed again. Through sleepy eyes, he noted it was a little after one in the morning. He had only been in bed for three hours. Beside him, his wife of eighty-four years mumbled complaint and rolled away. "Yes?" He rubbed his square face.

"Sir? It's Father James Castillo with The Davis Group. I'm very sorry for the late hour, but there's something you should know."

That woke him. "This is my private number. How did you get it?" Bentoncourt glanced over his shoulder, verifying his wife had returned to sleep. Thanking God for wireless receivers, he forced himself to his feet.

There was a momentary silence. "I have my resources."

No doubt. In seconds, Bentoncourt stood in the dark hallway, the bedroom door closed. "What is it you want, Father?"

"A contract has been put out against *Ninsumgal* Davis, and a professional assassin hired to do the job."

Why did they insist upon calling her *Ninsumgal*? Bentoncourt slumped against the wall, his free hand massaging his forehead. "You're serious."

"Yes, sir. I'm afraid I am. I have it on good authority that whoever attempted to have Whiskey killed several months ago has put out this contract."

Bentoncourt yawned despite himself, scowling at his lack of control. *Why wait until now?* "How did you come by this information?"

There was a long pause. "I can't say."

He raised a dark eyebrow. "Is that so?"

"Yes, sir. We believe it's someone on the *Agrun Nam*. I'm unable to give you specifics until the traitor can be found."

Bentoncourt felt a mixture of pride at Castillo's firm stance, annoyance at his refusal to be more forthcoming, and pleasure at his obvious hesitant tone. "I assume you're telling me this on orders from Davis?"

"Yes, I am."

He had known Castillo had gone over to Davis's camp when he had disappeared from Seattle with her. This simply confirmed his information. "Have you sworn allegiance to her?"

Another slight pause. "Yes, sir. Months ago."

Bentoncourt grimaced. "So everything you report is at Davis's order?"

"Yes, sir."

"Are you playing me?"

"No, sir! What I've said is true. I'm not misleading you in any way."

Disgruntled, Bentoncourt soothed his wounded pride with the fact that Castillo was a supremely honest man; a full background check had been done on him the minute his existence had been made known. He had never been caught in a lie, regardless of the circumstances, and seemed to follow many of the precepts of the Human religion he followed. Which meant any information he gave would be true—or twisted before he received it. "Do you have any idea why this person has waited so long between attempts?"

Castillo's sigh was audible. "I believe it was triggered by the last *Agrun Nam* vote regarding the *Ninsumgal's* return. I've heard it was quite a close call with a divided council and one abstention."

Shock washed over Bentoncourt, freezing his blood. "You know of that vote?"

"Yes, sir."

Unable to remain still, Bentoncourt strode down the hallway and into his study. He switched on the light, mind reeling. Whoever Davis received her information from seemed firmly planted within the *Agrun Nam's* network. Who the hell could it be? Certainly not one of the others. Cassadie immediately popped into his mind. *Would Aiden do this?* He continued to pace the room, phone to his ear. "That vote was secret, Father. Yet your informant seemed to easily get the information. Whoever it is, he or she is damned good."

"Yes, sir. Thank you. I'll relay the compliment."

"Something to consider, however." He frowned. "If your friend can get in and out of the *Agrun Nam* facility without discovery, what's to stop this person from also being the assassin, planting false information?"

The thought had apparently never entered Castillo's mind. He didn't speak for some time, as if thoroughly digesting the suggestion. "Nothing, sir."

"I would suggest you speak to your *Ninsumgal* about the possibility."

"I doubt it's the case, sir, but I'll do that."

Bentoncourt stared at the floor, not seeing the thick carpet beneath his bare feet. "Anything else?"

"No, sir. Whiskey just wanted you to know about the assassin. She asks that you keep your eyes open."

He chuckled mirthlessly. Whiskey? What an infernal nickname. "So I've passed muster, eh? That's good to know."

"I've always insisted you had nothing to do with the attack on her, sir."

"And I've always insisted you're too trusting. Best leave the decisions to those more paranoid than yourself, Father. While it's a horrible way to live, at least you're prepared for any inevitability."

"Of course, sir." He sounded unconvinced. "I prefer to put my trust in God for those preparations."

"Good night, Father." Bentoncourt glanced at the clock on the mantel, calculating the time difference. "Or in your case, good afternoon. Thank you for calling. You've given me much to think on."

"Certainly, sir. Good night."

Bentoncourt dropped the receiver to his desk. He sank into the chair with a groan.

So the mysterious traitor had hired an assassin. He wondered if it was in his name again, or if the original plan to discredit him had been put to rest. He assumed it was a Sanguire, which narrowed the list of likely suspects. A professional, of course. Unlike that hapless Human who was hustled into trying last winter. Not many Sanguire did this sort of thing except for entertainment. Long lives and old money meant for little need of mundane jobs in today's society. Most of those who worked for a living enjoyed their careers far too much to care about the pay.

Davis's ability to ferret out information had increased dramatically. Who had come in contact with her recently? Was it this new assassin, turned traitor against his employer? Or perhaps someone sowing seeds of misinformation to keep his prey off the true trail. Could the existence of such a report be merely rumor given to Davis for some obscure reason? Perhaps one of the other *sanari* had made contact. Nijmege? She seemed the least likeliest candidate after McCall. Bentoncourt couldn't comprehend why she would do such a thing. Her hatred of Elisibet and Davis would make it impossible for her to converse with the youngling. Perhaps she and McCall had hatched some bizarre plot to gain Davis's trust, bring her to Europe, and dispatch her. McCall would have been the one to approach Davis in that case.

Bentoncourt rubbed his temples. So much for getting more sleep tonight. He wistfully thought of the warm bed, the smell of his wife's skin, the texture of the sheets. Damn. He picked up the phone. If he couldn't sleep, neither would his aides. Someone had to know whether or not any of the *sanari* had made contact with Davis.

CHAPTER EIGHTEEN

Whiskey frowned at nothing as darkness stole over the sitting room. The storm that had gathered during the afternoon had reached its full fury a little more than an hour ago, rattling the windows with wind and rain. The power had flickered a little, but everything seemed to have calmed down.

It had been an eventful day—getting her butt whipped by Pacal, Margaurethe's attack on Valmont, Reynhard's report regarding another hired assassin. Everything was colored by Whiskey's interaction with Margaurethe. She hadn't seen her lover since the advisors' meeting she had interrupted. Would the distance that dogged them still be there when they next met? Or would the closeness they had experienced that afternoon remain solid?

She hoped the latter.

Andri crept into the room. "My *Ninsumgal*?" His voice was tremulous, unwilling to interrupt her thoughts.

"Yes, Andri?"

"Dinner will be ready soon. Do you wish to dine in private?"

Whiskey frowned, glancing back at the scared little man. Dinner was normally her chambermaid's province. She delighted in whipping up new and unusual recipes to tantalize Whiskey's rather plebeian palate. "Where's Sithathor?"

He bobbed multiple times as he spoke to his shoes. "She has asked that I serve tonight so that she might finish some tasks."

Since her hiring, Sithathor had found any number of things to keep herself occupied. Whiskey had to wonder if Sithathor's gift was the same as Valmont's, the ability to move things with the mind. Telekinesis would do wonders as a housekeeper. Whiskey felt that the whole concept of "keeping house" was as arcane as alchemy, and twice as confusing. The one time she had argued with Sithathor over the placement of furniture, she had lost. Better not to repeat that little episode. "Thank you. That will be fine, Andri. Maybe *Ki'an Gasan* Margaurethe will join me."

"As you wish, *Ninsumgal*." He seemed pleased to accommodate her as he backed away, nearly prostrating himself in the process before closing the door.

Regardless of her distaste with his constant fawning, Whiskey was glad Andri had turned up. At least she knew a servant had survived the Purge after Elisibet, not just the ruling classes. It would be nice to learn about his experiences, but he was far too skittish yet. Whiskey had spent most of the week trying to ease his nervousness to no avail. Odd how quickly she had grown accustomed to his submissiveness, much as she disliked it. She couldn't figure out whether she treated him as a servant because he acted as one, or because she had fallen into Elisibet's thoughtless habits.

Elisibet's power and sense of entitlement were seductive, and Whiskey sometimes wondered if she was strong enough to withstand the inherent temptations. Imagining a life as a world ruler was fine for daydreams, but Whiskey's life expectancy had multiplied tremendously. Providing she remained reasonably wise about her health and security, she could live for several centuries instead of a few decades, leaving her much more opportunity to make mistakes. And a long time to live with them.

Andri was one of Elisibet's mistakes. The poor man had been under the Sweet Butcher's thumb for several hundred years, having been assigned as Elisibet's servant at her birth. He had learned his lessons well. It made sense that he expected the same from the woman who looked almost identical to his previous monarch. *Why come back if Elisibet treated him so poorly?* She assumed it was his age, having known many broken homeless people in her time on the streets—they returned to what was familiar and comfortable, even if it was abusive. Apparently, even Sanguire fell into that mindset if the maltreatment lasted long enough. Whiskey consoled herself with the fact that he had only been here a few days; she had plenty of time to undo the damage Elisibet had wrought.

A knock at the door interrupted her gloom. "Come in." Margaurethe entered, and Whiskey smiled welcome. Receiving an easy one in return blunted her concern. Whatever had happened in the conference room continued to affect them both.

Margaurethe wore her dressing gown, her feet bare as she padded across the carpet. "Andri has informed me that dinner will be served in a few moments." She sat without invitation in an armchair.

Whiskey's gaze wandered lazily over Margaurethe. "You look comfortable."

"I am," she said with a smile. "I spent the afternoon grilling your employees. It doesn't look like any of them are this unknown assassin."

Considering how Whiskey's chambermaid and Margaurethe got along, it was no wonder Sithathor had found a project for this evening. Margaurethe had probably personally taken care of that interrogation. "That's good to hear, though that's a lot of people. Did you get to everybody?"

"Those I didn't know personally before they came here. Reynhard and Chano assisted, as well, so we were able to eliminate all of the *Aga'gída*, and quite a number of the general staff."

Andri interrupted them as he knocked and entered, carrying a tray laden with food.

"Over there, Andri." Margaurethe waved at a small table.

"Yes, *Ki'an Gasan*."

While he set out dinner, Whiskey said, "I told the Padre to report news of this assassin to Lionel. Whether or not he tells any of the others on the *Agrun Nam* is up to him."

Margaurethe took the news well, though she wrinkled her nose. "I don't like it, but it's sound judgment. I'm beginning to believe that Lionel truly is an innocent in this." She fingered the cuff of her robe in thought. "Does he know of Reynhard?"

A loud clatter drew their attention away. Andri hastily gathered the dropped silverware, and polished it with a napkin. "My apologies, *Ninsumgal*," he whispered.

"It's all right, Andri. Accidents happen." Whiskey hated his naked fear of her. She resolved once again to try and change his opinion. Returning to the conversation, she said, "No. I don't want the *Agrun Nam* knowing of him until they figure it out for themselves. That's one more ace up my sleeve that Bertrada hopefully doesn't know about."

"Good. I had planned to suggest it to you."

"My apologies, *Ninsumgal*. Dinner is served."

"Thank you, Andri." Whiskey stood, reaching for Margaurethe's hand. "You can go. Take the rest of the night off."

He bowed and scraped his way toward the door. "Thank you, my *Gasan*."

Whiskey sighed after he left. "I've got to break him of that habit. It's annoying as hell."

"It's expected." Margaurethe led her toward their meal. "Shall we?"

***

Whiskey and her pack spent the next few days furthering their education—savage forms of combat with Pacal within the limitations of their injuries, politics with Margaurethe, and other subjects with Castillo. Dorst had resumed his lessons in intrigue, as well. Other than one breakfast with her American Indian relatives and her brutally violent lessons with Pacal, Whiskey seemed surrounded by European Sanguire. The focus of her education was Eurocentric in the extreme, something she hoped to change in the future. She couldn't hope to serve all the races in this growing coalition if she didn't know anything about them. The board of directors did most of the work of the corporation's business, and she was rarely needed for major judgments unless it came time to put a decision into place, or break a tie vote. It had been days since anyone had brought anything to her attention, not even about the ongoing political negotiations currently underway. She had no problem with that, though she sometimes felt the part of her that was Elisibet chomping at the bit in the desire to get more involved.

Needing to escape her apartment, she decided on a public breakfast in the Residents' Lounge on the fifteenth floor. It was sheer happenstance that Chano arrived at the same time. Smiling, Whiskey joined him at the buffet. "Good morning, *wicakte*." She pulled out a tray and placed two plates on it. "How are you?"

He vocalized acceptance of her aid, and smiled. "I am well. And you?"

She stretched her back a little, rubbing her shoulder. "Very sore after yesterday's fighting lesson, but okay."

Chano laughed, a graveled rumble emanating from his chest. "It is good for you to feel pain. It reminds you of what not to do."

"I'll say." She flipped some pancakes from the heating tray onto her plate, doing the same for him when he nodded acquiescence to her questioning look. "Pacal's been vicious, but I think I might actually be learning something these days."

"Nupa has told me he is quite harsh. You are strong and intelligent. You will learn."

Whiskey smiled at his matter-of-fact belief. She wished it were that easy. Pacal seemed to have other ideas. The injury he'd sustained in their initial lesson had slowed him down somewhat, but his arrogance and thinly veiled dislike of Nupa wore thin. It didn't help that some of that disfavor seemed to be directed at her. Whiskey could only assume it was because of her American Indian heritage and Pacal's inability to see past his racism. She'd be damned if she'd complain to Margaurethe, though. One of the earliest lessons she'd learned on the streets was that the whiners were first to be taken out. No, she'd keep her mouth shut and learn. What better way to thumb her nose at Pacal than to defeat him at his own game?

She and Chano worked their way through the buffet, and she carried their mutual tray to a table. Others greeted them, both Human and Sanguire, and she acknowledged their words and nods. She knew everyone on sight now, though still struggled with some of the names and positions. She relaxed once she sat down, knowing no one would approach while she ate unless it was an emergency or one of her pack. "I think I'm going to ask about expanding my lessons."

Chano peered at her over his plate, pouring his syrup. "I have heard they are quite extensive already. What do you believe is missing?"

She briskly buttered her pancakes. "Indian Shamanism? African culture? Mayan history?" Spreading jam over the pancakes, she looked up at him. "For starters."

"For starters." He barked a laugh, shaking his head as he set aside the syrup dispenser, and cut into his breakfast with a fork. "Do you think you will learn it all?"

Whiskey finished a mouthful of food. "Probably not. Once I get through those, I'll have to start on Japanese economics and the subcontinental Indian caste system." She chuckled as he raised his chin in concession.

"You make an excellent professional student."

She nodded, keeping her attention on her plate. "I'd much rather be an excellent ruler."

"You have the makings of one."

Warmed by his confidence in her, she risked looking at him. "Can you tell me something?"

"If it is within my knowledge and power."

Whiskey thought back. "When Margaurethe attacked Valmont in the conference room, something happened to me... to us. I haven't been able to find anything in the European books about it, so maybe it's something else."

Chano placed his silverware down, giving her his full attention. "What was it?"

She frowned, thinking of the right way to phrase the occurrence. "We connected on a very deep level. Much deeper than I've ever seen before. I could feel her emotions. I was able to see what she saw." In a moment of brilliant revelation, she remembered seeing Valmont through Castillo's eyes in Seattle. *Oh, my God! It's happened before.*

"That is known to happen when two people are profoundly in love."

She struggled to return to the conversation, setting aside her furious thoughts. It hadn't been love for Castillo that had caused the last occurrence. It had been fear and anger. Her face warmed as she registered Chano's words, and she knew she was blushing. "So you know about this...whatever it was? I haven't found anything anywhere, and I've been really digging in the Sanguire literature."

He fixed an aged eye on her, tilting his head. "What you describe is a...a melding of the two egos, a blending of emotion and thought. Your people, the Lakota, call it *mahasanni*, second skin. The European Sanguire do not strike me as being of a romantic nature." He returned his attention to his breakfast. "It makes sense that you are unable to find anything in their records."

Whiskey frowned, wondering if she or Margaurethe were being subtly insulted by his prejudice. Elisibet had loved Margaurethe with all her being, and hadn't been able to do such a thing. *Yeah, but Elisibet wasn't much in the empathy department. That's got to count for something. And it doesn't explain what happened with the Padre.* "I can't believe that no one has mentioned it in all the centuries of documented history. Are you sure that's all it is?"

Chano chewed on a piece of bacon as he considered. "I have heard that it can be something learned, though few have attempted it. The stronger a person, the more ability they have to penetrate the deeper levels of another's mind."

That made sense. Considering he was one of the oldest Sanguire she knew besides Sithathor, she had to ask. "Can you?"

He laughed aloud, drawing the attention from other tables. "Oh, no! Not I. If such were the case, my wives would have me under their complete thrall. I would be making their breakfast rather than eating my own."

She smiled. *I bet Reynhard can. I wonder if Sithathor...* Remembering the vision she'd had through Castillo, she began to eat again. *Or maybe not.* "I heard her thoughts in my head."

"Yet another reason I have never attempted this with my wives."

Whiskey chuckled. "I guess I can see why no one mentions it in the scrolls and books. Wouldn't want any spouses to get funny ideas." Or spill a secret weapon that could give other people ideas, either.

"Agreed."

They passed the rest of the meal in silence, giving Whiskey ample time to consider their conversation. When the merging first happened between her and Margaurethe, she was under the impression that her lover was as surprised as she was over the matter. Since then, they'd been able to repeat the procedure, each time becoming easier than the last. Oddly, they hadn't discussed it aloud, preferring to marvel at the superb sensations as they occurred rather than analyze them. She wasn't even certain that Castillo knew she had seen his initial meeting with Valmont. Still an untried youngling, not even finished with her stroll along the Strange Path, how could she have done something like that to begin with?

Yet Chano acted as if the ability were a normal thing among his people, though one reserved for true lovers. Whiskey wondered how many other nations had their own understanding of the talent. Had any of the Sanguire races done research on this ability? How many older, stronger Sanguire had trained themselves to access others' memories and thoughts? She decided that Dorst did not have this talent. If he had, he would have turned up the *Agrun Nam* counselor responsible for the current assassination contract. Nothing could be kept secret from someone with this kind of ability.

Thank God Elisibet never knew about it!

CHAPTER NINETEEN

"I'm going to drop this rock over the side. Bet I could hit that Human in the red baseball cap!"

Slightly alarmed, Whiskey sat up in her lawn chair, bare feet scraping the rough stone tile of The Davis Group's roof. "No, you're not!"

Zebediah gave her an aggrieved look, pausing in his attempt to properly aim his projectile. "Why not? I probably won't get him anyway."

Whiskey wondered when she had become a parent and how to change the fact. Before she could respond, Daniel spoke for her. "Dropping a rock from this height is just as damaging as shooting a bullet."

"Nothing heavier than ping-pong balls." Whiskey gave Zebediah a stern look. She relaxed when he grumbled at the restriction and returned to hanging half over the side of the sixteen-story building to watch pedestrians and traffic below.

In an attempt to discover new scenery today, the pack had taken over the roof. Electrical cords snaked from the elevator shaft tower behind them, powering a high quality stereo and a small bar refrigerator, both appropriated from Whiskey's apartment. *Ugula Aga'us* Anthony had made an emergency trip to Costco, his purchases resulting in a wading pool, several deck chairs, a barbecue grill and assorted lawn toys. He had nixed the outdoor fireplace, the weather being too warm. Besides, tenants and workers in the surrounding taller buildings might overexcite themselves at the sight of fire on their neighbor's roof. The pack had set up their impromptu camp on the opposite side of the building from Whiskey's apartment, revealing the unfamiliar view of the city and the northwest hills. Though the day was warm, the overcast sky gave them a break from painful shards of sunlight. By the looks of things on the horizon, it wouldn't be long before the cloud cover would burn off. Soon, sunshine would drive them back inside. Until then it was a perfect morning.

Whiskey smiled, taking a drink from her beer. *All we need is some sand, and we can have a beach party.*

To one side Daniel taught Chaniya the fine tradition of lawn darts with the aid of Alphonse. They'd had to improvise, removing the tips from the darts so as not to damage the decorative stone layering the rooftop. Nupa had come up with the idea of using pool chalk from the recreation level to more easily mark where a dart landed. He sat beside Whiskey, nursing a bottle of beer. The only pack mate missing was Cora. Whiskey assumed she was with her current paramour, Anthony. He had disappeared soon after delivering his purchases, content with the presence of six *Aga'gída* scattered about the roof alert for any threat. In any case, it had been a couple of hours since his disappearance. Whiskey had sent Andri off in search of both of them when he had delivered sandwiches a little while ago.

"What happened there?" Nupa pointed the neck of his bottle at a large bruise on Whiskey's thigh.

Whiskey rubbed the injury. "Just something I picked up this morning at practice. You were there." Though freshly wounded, the bruise had already succumbed to her Sanguire metabolism, appearing yellow-green rather than the livid black and purple it had been early that morning.

"Pacal doesn't pull his punches much."

"No. I think he believes pain gets the point across much better."

Daniel, taking a break from the games, appeared unimpressed. "There are other ways." He opened the small cooling unit, and pulled out a bottle of water. Cracking it open, he took a deep draught before gazing at his pack leader.

Nupa grunted agreement. "That's what I say. I don't think he's teaching you anything but how to take a beating."

Whiskey blinked. Nupa rarely gave an opinion unless asked, and even then it was difficult to get him to speak. Despite the fact he was of the Tillamook tribe and that his immediate people had had nothing to do with the Mayans, he still felt the hatred that had been ingrained from centuries of border feuds hundreds of miles south. Naturally he held strong prejudices against Pacal, and had always been the most savage of the pack in their combat sessions. She picked at the label on her bottle. "Are you sure that's the case, and it's not a cultural thing? Different training techniques?" She smiled at him to ease the bite of her words. "I'm the one with the least experience or knowledge. Once I learn to defend against his attacks, I'll get hurt less."

Nupa dipped one hand in the wading pool, watching the water play across his skin. "I don't think so."

Daniel remained close. "Why?"

After a moment's regard, Nupa shrugged. "I've had training, not just my peoples', but formal martial arts. I've never seen an instructor consistently pair others of like abilities, and then focus all his expertise on the one with the least."

Chaniya sidled over, a lawn dart still in her hand. "He's right. In my country, you teach moves to the student and allow her to learn to use them with others of her proficiency level." She flopped bonelessly into a deck chair. "Just because you are a ruler does not mean you are to be coddled, certainly. But no other culture does this with their martial arts."

Whiskey took a moment to digest this information. As stated, she had no formal experience. Neither did Alphonse or Zebediah who were most often paired in training. Daniel was the eldest among them, even older than Nupa. Despite his underprivileged childhood he was one of the better fighters in the pack, having had a more formal education. "What do you think?"

"Could be they have a point. Pacal does appear to target you more often than anyone else."

His words held more weight than any of the others'. "But why? To what purpose?"

Nupa gave a contemptuous snort. "Who knows how a Mayan thinks?"

Whiskey gave a little shake of her head. "That's racism, and it's got no place here." Nupa became stone-faced in response to her sharp annoyance. She gently caressed his essence to ease her words, tasting sea salt on her tongue. Chaniya's touch on her arm pulled Whiskey's attention away.

"Maybe so, maybe no, but you can't dismiss the possibility from his viewpoint. They've been battling off and on for as long as either of their people can remember. Their racial hatred can't be dismissed because you're trying to forge a conglomeration of nations."

Finding her argument valid, Whiskey raised her chin. "So you think it's because I'm half American Indian?"

Alphonse shrugged. "Why not?"

"What if it's something else?"

Whiskey looked at Daniel. "Like what?"

He ran his hand through his loose mohawk. "You said the Euros had hired an assassin. What if Pacal's that assassin?"

Mouth open, Whiskey gaped at him. Zebediah swore and the others exclaimed. Before they could build up a head of righteous fury, she raised her hand to stop them. With ease she gathered up their essences, holding them lightly to remind them of her strength. One thing she had learned over the last few months was that she had to keep her people firmly controlled. They had the capability for serious damage without a steady hand. "That's stupid. He's had plenty of opportunity to do the job. Training accidents happen all the time. Why wait and drag on the farce?"

Because he's Sanguire, and Sanguire have plenty of time to play their little games. The thought blindsided her, and she considered it as the pack mulled over her question.

Alphonse slouched over to his brother and leaned against the edge of the building. "Okay, so maybe it's not him. Maybe he's got a different agenda. What if he's working with that *Agrun Nam* chick who's out to bring you to Europe?"

"That still wouldn't explain why he's beating the shit out of me every lesson." Whiskey disliked the petulant grumble in her tone. Forging on, she pushed aside her irritation. "How would they have met? Do the Mayans have treaties with the Europeans?" She looked to Daniel, the only Euro Sanguire in the bunch.

"We've had some dealings with them, but nothing extensive." Daniel shrugged with one shoulder. "Just trade for the most part. Some travel regulations between the two nations."

"Hey." Zebediah cut into the conversation. "Doesn't your buddy Valmont have a ranch or something in South America? And he's the asshole who killed you the first time, right? Maybe Pacal is working with him and that *Agrun Nam* chick."

Chaniya gave a grudging nod. "It's possible. The Tibetans rule farther south, but Brazil is part of the Mayan territories. Maybe this whole assassin story is just a smokescreen to confuse you to Valmont's true intent."

Whiskey had to admit it was a decent scenario, but it felt wrong. Valmont had sworn fealty to her months ago, and had done nothing to endanger her since. *He swore fealty to Elisibet, too. Look where that got her.* "So the consensus is that Pacal's not an assassin, but working with Bertrada to kidnap me?" She chuckled. "You know, this paranoia thing is a bitch. I'm getting confused at all the ins and outs and possibles and maybes."

Nupa gave her a slight smile, opening his mouth to speak. He was interrupted by the slam of a distant door, and a whimpering. The two immediately visible *Aga'gída* closed in on Whiskey and her pack, alert as the mewling grew closer. Andri shambled around the corner of the elevator shaft with three guards behind him. He threw himself to the stone tile at Whiskey's feet, prostrating himself. "I'm so sorry, *Ninsumgal*! I only just found her. Please, have mercy!"

"What the hell?" Whiskey and the others rose to their feet. "Andri! Calm down! What's happened?"

"My *Gasan*?" An *aga'us* moved closer, one that hadn't been with the others on the roof. He looked decidedly uncomfortable as he chewed his lower lip. "Your friend, Cora. She's been found in her quarters. With *Ugula Aga'us* Anthony."

Whiskey's heart thumped. "And?" she asked, not wanting to hear the answer.

"They're dead, *Ninsumgal*."

***

Whiskey sat alone in her apartment. The curtains drawn against clearing sky, they masked the sunlight, hid the sharp pain that awaited Whiskey and her kind. She felt numb, a miasma of antipathy that insulated her from thought. Visions of Cora's and Anthony's blood-spattered bodies cropped up at the oddest times, as if some higher power lay in wait to shock her. At least they hadn't suffered much pain. Valmont's experience and keen eye had been a boon; he informed Whiskey that both had died quickly.

Had the tragedy never happened, she would be teasing Cora about her frivolous romances over lunch, their friends surrounding them. That would never happen again. *How many others will die because of me?* This attack upon her pack, her people highlighted the death threat hanging over her head. At any moment it could indiscriminately slop over onto those closest to her. The thought of Margaurethe or Castillo lying in a puddle of blood flashed unwanted through her mind. She shook her head to dispel it, barely succeeding.

Whiskey had allowed herself to become complacent, settled herself too deeply into the pampered lifestyle Margaurethe had constructed for her. She had trusted Margaurethe's in-depth scanning of Whiskey's staff, ignoring the fact that despite her lover's actions Margaurethe hadn't the level of mental strength as Whiskey. Had Whiskey done the job, there would be no doubt who could be trusted. *I've been too busy playing the spoiled rich bitch. I haven't paid attention.* Her imagination relentlessly substituted her aunt or grandmother for Cora. There was a killer on Whiskey's ass, and she had assumed everybody would protect her, that nothing would befall her or them. *Why the hell didn't I think of this?*

She heard a knock, and ignored it. As expected, the door opened. *Interesting that being* Ninsumgal *means people come and go as they please.* Whiskey barely acknowledged Andri as he eased into the room.

The poor man's terror had persisted. He must have felt responsible for her pain, having been the one to discover the grisly remains. The dishes on his tray rattled as he trembled. Still, he eased closer, sliding the tray onto the table beside her. "My *Ninsumgal*," he whispered. "My apologies for the interruption, but *Ki'an Gasan* Margaurethe insists that you eat."

Whiskey glanced at him. His flinch cut her to the quick, and she looked away. "Thanks, Andri. Go away."

His swallow was audible. Bowing, he backed away. He paused at the door. "I'm so very sorry, my *Gasan*." He didn't await a response, slipping out of the room. What could she say to him? He was probably happy to still be alive. Had this happened with Elisibet, he would have suffered either a torturous death or simple maiming as she released her anger and grief.

And there was anger. Despite the apparent indifference she projected, she felt it. It beat against her with fists of fire, demanding to be free, to avenge Cora's completely needless murder. It desired to be quenched by the life's blood of the assassin responsible, to rise again from the killer's ashes and destroy the person who hired him. To succumb to it would be so easy. Whiskey only needed to open the door, to stand aside as the rage boiled up to become the monster that controlled Elisibet for so many centuries. So easy.

It would never be worth the price. As much as she longed to give in, she fought it, not succumbing to the desire to slash and rip and tear flesh. Elisibet's mistakes all boiled down to her indiscriminate lashing out. Whiskey couldn't afford to do the same. It was a bitter pill to swallow.

Someone else knocked on the door. Again she ignored it, and again it opened regardless. A stab of fury sliced through her emotional lethargy, clean and pure, before succumbing once more to the heaviness. Margaurethe and Castillo entered and approached. For a change, he didn't react as a petitioner toward his monarch. With no invitation, he pulled an armchair close to hers and sat, watching. Margaurethe knelt at her feet, for the moment not touching.

Whiskey vaguely recalled telling Castillo to inform the leader of the *Agrun Nam* of recent events. Now she couldn't dredge up interest at Bentoncourt's response. She wondered if she disregarded them, would they go away?

"Are you all right?"

Well, that answers that question. "Fine and dandy, *minn'ast.*" Her voice cracked. She cringed from it. Not wanting her words to sound weak, she continued, forcing them out of her throat. "One of my friends, someone under my protection and living under my roof, has been murdered by someone targeting me. Why wouldn't I be all right?"

"It's not your fault, Whiskey."

She barked out a laugh, surprising herself as tears finally burned her eyes. "Keep telling yourself that. I kept her here, I let others do for me, protect me, fight my battles. She'd still be alive if I'd sent her and the others away like you wanted me to months ago." The muscles between her eyebrows twitched as she tried to control her tears, tried to force them back behind the apathy. Her throat stung from the effort.

"If it wasn't Cora, it would have been someone else."

"Then it should have been someone else!" Whiskey gave up the struggle, and leapt to her feet to pace the room, nearly trampling Margaurethe in her haste to get past. She hugged herself tight, as if fearing she would explode. Her tears were acrid, burning her cheeks. They both stood with her, watching her storm about the room.

"You can't take the blame for everything that happens around you. Cora's and Anthony's deaths were sudden, unplanned. The killer was surprised by their presence; if they'd been on the streets with friends, it could have happened just as easily. Where we receive the Angel of Death is written on God's heart. It was their time."

Swearing, Whiskey let Castillo know exactly what she thought of that. She rounded on him, teeth bared, tears streaming across her cheeks. Margaurethe intercepted, wrapping arms around her. Whiskey felt the bestial anger surge forward. Her lip pulled into a sneer, her will lashing out against both of them. Despite the fact Margaurethe had been prepared, Whiskey shredded her defenses, focusing all of her rage upon that which kept her imprisoned. Margaurethe's grip tightened, and her eyes rolled up into her head as she convulsed from the invasion. Her physical reaction sent icy tendrils through Whiskey. Horrified, she mentally reeled back. As Margaurethe's body sagged, Whiskey supported her, guiding the limp form into the nearest armchair.

Castillo was there beside her, a pained expression on his face. Margaurethe appeared dead. Before Whiskey could fully articulate what happened Castillo called out to the guards in the hall.

"I just...I was so angry...She tried to stop me!" She watched Castillo check for a pulse. "I didn't mean to!"

"Shhh." Castillo stood and took Whiskey into his arms. "She's still alive. Calm down."

Three *Aga'gída* rushed inside. As Castillo held the sobbing Whiskey, he directed them to move Margaurethe to her apartment, and call Daniel at once. When they were gone, Whiskey found herself sitting on the edge of the couch, Castillo still holding her as she cried. "Will she be all right?"

"We'll see. She's alive. That's what counts. And Daniel has experience with this sort of thing." Castillo brushed Whiskey's hair away from her face.

Whiskey wiped her face with a sleeve. A handkerchief appeared in Castillo's hand, and she took it. A fresh wave of guilt washed over her, the tears beginning anew. "I've fucked it all up. I got Cora and Anthony killed, and now I've tried to kill Margaurethe."

Castillo pulled her close, rocking. "No. You didn't get anyone killed. They were simply in the wrong place at the wrong time."

"I did it! I should have sent everyone away as soon as I knew about the assassin."

"Whiskey, you can't blame yourself for not being omniscient. We had no idea that the assassin would attack so soon or go after someone not targeted. Valmont is of the opinion he didn't strike by choice. Cora saw something she shouldn't have, and that's why it happened. Anthony came upon the aftermath, and had to be eliminated."

"Is Margaurethe going to be okay?" Whiskey felt juvenile for needing the assurance.

"I don't know." Castillo clucked at the fresh spurt of tears. "She'll probably have one hell of a headache. Chances are good you didn't cause permanent damage; you let her go as soon as you realized what had happened."

The guilt was too much to bear. Whiskey curled up, her very soul in agonizing pain. "I don't want to do this anymore."

Castillo eased back, pulling her unresisting form with him. He continued holding her close. "She won't leave you, Whiskey. She trusts you to do what's right. We all do."

Her weariness at all the emotions cascading through her made a response hard. "I don't trust me."

"You will. I promise."

Bittersweet chocolate stole over her. It was a measure of her emotional bankruptcy that she didn't have the energy to deny him. Instead, she allowed Castillo to ease into her mind and caress her soul.

CHAPTER TWENTY

Cassadie was the last to arrive at the emergency meeting. He wore a black tuxedo. "I do have tickets to the ballet with my paramour." He tossed a hat and a pair of white gloves onto the table. "Let's make this quick so I don't end up paying for my absence over the next decade, shall we?"

Rosenberg looked him over with a humorous eye. "Top hat and gloves, Aiden? Didn't they go out of style about seventy years ago?"

Snorting, Cassadie sat in his chair. "Tell Genevieve that. 'When one goes out in public, one must be exemplary in appearance at all times.' She's hooked on etiquette and fashion these days."

"Let's get this over with." Nijmege, impatient with the flippancy, turned her attention to the head of the conference table. "Why did you interrupt our dinner plans?"

Face grave, Bentoncourt said, "Father Castillo has informed me that the assassin has struck."

Nijmege half stood up from her chair, her complexion paling. McCall and Cassadie both exclaimed in shock, but Rosenberg remained silent. Bentoncourt watched their responses carefully, hoping to surprise the traitor into a misstep. He wondered if the assassin had been able to report. If so, Rosenberg's response could be construed as foreknowledge. He held up his hand to halt their rapid-fire questions. "Davis was not harmed. A Sanguire friend of hers was murdered under her roof, as was the captain of her personal guard. Whether it was by accident or intent is currently unknown."

Sinking back into her seat, Nijmege closed her eyes. Bentoncourt imagined she was overcome with relief that her perceived vengeance remained on track.

Beside her, McCall's face flushed. "This is ridiculous! How are we to protect Davis if we refuse to bring her here?" His black eyes snapped, and he thumped the table with a fist. "Order *Ki'an Gasan* Margaurethe and *Sublugal Sañar* Valmont to return with her. Now."

"It certainly seems as if their ability to protect Davis is slipping," Rosenberg said.

Bentoncourt scanned the others. Even Cassadie's expression was apologetic as he nodded an agreement with the others. It occurred to him that by being the lone dissenter, by not wanting Davis to return in order to facilitate her assassination, he would appear to be a traitor. He exhaled, and frowned. "I'm not certain you understand—"

"What's to understand, Lionel?" Nijmege glared. "O'Toole is deluding herself if she thinks she can keep her precious little *Ninsumgal* safe. Two needless deaths have occurred. The assassin is playing with them, letting them know he can come and go at will, that he has the ability to slay Davis with ease."

"What you don't understand," Bentoncourt said, pinning her with hard eyes, "is that no matter what we vote on here, Davis will refuse to relocate."

McCall sneered. "What matters that? We can send a force in to arrest her."

Unable to help himself, Bentoncourt chuckled. "You're working on the assumption she's not who she says she is. Her strength of will has multiplied tremendously since her *Ñíri Kurám*. She is Elisibet reborn, and will be able to sway anyone attempting to take her by common sense or force." He laughed again, waving dismissal at their youngest member's suggestion. "And I won't even go into the legality of arresting an American Indian Sanguire for transport to Europe. We still have no clue as to her paternal parentage."

"It doesn't have to be an arrest. At the very least, we can appeal to her sense of self-preservation," Cassadie argued. "Certainly, when she hears the nature of our precautions, she'll understand she's safer here."

"She's the spitting image!" Nijmege thumped her fist on the table. "I don't give a fig about her parentage. She's Euro whether we have genetic proof or not."

Bentoncourt shook his head, remembering his discussion with Castillo. "If anyone moves, it will be the *Agrun Nam*. I believe Davis will remake her court in today's image, and center it where she feels most comfortable."

Cassadie tilted his head. "I move that we vote to bring Davis to the heart of her people by ordering *Ki'an Gasan* Margaurethe and *Sublugal Sañar* Valmont to bring her here."

"I second the motion!" Nijmege slapped her hand on the table, her muddy brown eyes alight.

Unable to deny the motion, Bentoncourt ground his teeth. "All right. All those in favor of demanding Davis's return?"

As expected, Nijmege and her conspirator, McCall, raised their hands. When Cassadie did, as well, Bentoncourt felt his heart lurch. Everyone stared at Rosenberg.

"Davis must know she cannot thwart tradition. She appears to be attempting to unite all Sanguire under her banner." He raised his hand. "This is where the center of her people originates; this is where she needs to be."

"I don't think we need to continue." Nijmege's aquiline face seemed almost feral with the toothy smile she displayed.

Bentoncourt looked away from his companions. "No. We don't. I'll notify Castillo of our decision tonight. Tomorrow, I'll have one of my aides send letters to *Ki'an Gasan* Margaurethe, *Sublugal Sañar* Valmont and Davis with orders to return posthaste."

With the meeting concluded, the others rose to leave. Soon only Bentoncourt and Cassadie remained. "You know, I haven't seen Bertrada that ecstatic since the birth of her grandchild." Cassadie picked up his gloves and hat. "It's for the best, Lionel. We can keep her safe here."

Bentoncourt stared off into space. "I think you're wrong. Bringing her here only furthers Bertrada's warped goals."

"Please. We all know what she wants." He gently hit the edge of the table with the gloves. "It'll never happen despite her most ardent wishes."

"You're deluded, Aiden." Bentoncourt finally looked at his friend. "You're working under the assumption that Davis will be as malleable as every European Sanguire who comes under our rule."

Cassadie cocked his head.

"What you fail to understand is Davis knows her place in the scheme of things. And we've just confirmed it."

"And her place is...?"

Bentoncourt felt a well of laughter spring up inside him. He couldn't help but chuckle. "She's our ruler, of course, destined to destroy and unite us. She and we both know it."

"So." Cassadie blew out a breath. "You're saying regardless of our order, she'll disobey?"

"Listen to yourself! 'Disobey.' It is presumption that what we say has anything to do with her. She's our ruler in all but fact. We're not hers."

Cassadie blinked. "How do you figure?"

Bentoncourt quoted Nijmege. "'She's the spitting image! She's Euro whether we have genetic proof or not.' This vote has put us in the position of granting her a European lineage. And while we're here making all sorts of important decisions about Davis, she's across the water doing what needs doing to forge her crown." Bentoncourt laughed again. "Bertrada had better enjoy her sense of victory. It won't last long once she realizes that this vote seals Davis's rule over the European Sanguire."

They stared at one another in consternation before Cassadie pulled out a silver pocket watch. "Damn, I might actually make the second act." As he put the timepiece away, he stepped toward the door. "I'll think on what you said, Lionel. You may be right. If you are, we're all going to get a rather rude awakening, aren't we?"

***

Margaurethe lay abed, eyes closed. Every muscle in her body ached from the sudden seizure that had occurred when Whiskey had attacked. Her head pounded and her eyes screamed at the smallest hint of light. Daniel had informed her how fortunate she was to still have all her mental facilities. She thought Whiskey lucky, as well. Reports from Castillo told her how badly Whiskey had taken the reflexive attack. Margaurethe would need all the political and psychological weapons in her arsenal to ease Whiskey's guilt over the accident. Regardless of how personal the attack felt, she knew it had only been a reaction to her foolhardy attempt to give physical support.

Centuries before she had learned to avoid Elisibet when she became enraged. Elisibet had enjoyed her many negative moods, and had no difficulty in exposing them to the people around her regardless of their station. While she had never outright attacked Margaurethe, there were moments early in their relationship that had scared Margaurethe enough to know when to make herself scarce. Up until now, Whiskey had never shown such a tumultuous emotional storm. She had her moments, as everyone did at her age, but rarely were they violent. The deepening of the bond between them, this newfound ability to feel one another's emotions and hear each other's thoughts, had caused Margaurethe to forget Whiskey's potential—the same potential that Elisibet had exploited on a regular basis. Intercepting Whiskey on a grief- and anger-stricken tear had been the epitome of suicide. The only reason Whiskey had stopped was because Margaurethe was the one whom she had attacked.

Margaurethe heard a gentle tap on the door, and closed her eyes tight against the impending pain. "Come in." Even the stab of weak light against her eyelids increased the ache in her head. She forced her expression to pleasantness, not wanting to give Whiskey the least indication of her discomfort and more fodder for self-flagellation.

"*Minn'ast?*"

She smiled at the whispered endearment, and waved Whiskey forward. "Close the door behind you. Come sit by me." Once the dangerous illumination was hidden, she opened her eyes and watched the silhouette approach.

Whiskey sat gingerly on a chair beside the bed. "How do you feel?"

"Like I've been run over by a carriage." She chuckled to offset her words. "But Daniel says I'll make a full recovery in a day or two."

Leaning forward, Whiskey placed one hand on the edge of the bed as she stared. "I am so sorry, Margaurethe! I never meant to do anything to harm you. I swear." Her voice was edged with earnest panic.

Margaurethe took her hand, and held it firmly, conveying a subtle message that she remained strong despite what had happened. "I understand. Apology accepted. And I apologize to you, too." Whiskey's hand jumped as she tried to pull away. Margaurethe held it securely, and Whiskey capitulated, probably worried about causing more pain.

"You have nothing to be sorry for. I was angry and weak. You didn't do anything wrong."

"Oh, I think I did." Margaurethe forced herself to laugh though it hurt her head, holding their hands between them. "Barging into a wounded lioness's den to give her a hug, and not expecting to be mauled for the effort is the ultimate in stupidity. I should not have physically interfered."

"You didn't know."

"Actually, yes, I did. Elisibet spent many nights on the verge of violence. I simply didn't recognize the signs coming from you; it's been so long since I've seen them." She watched Whiskey digest the words, apparently not taking them well. *Of course. Now she's dealing with her fear of becoming Elisibet.* Margaurethe swore at the slip, but there was nothing to be done for it now. Her mind was too fuzzy. She couldn't argue herself out of a paper bag at this point. "In any case, we're both more educated on matters of your emotions and abilities. A reccurrence can easily be avoided."

"Is it that simple?"

Margaurethe smiled, and squeezed her hand again. "Of course." Whiskey appeared unconvinced. Margaurethe gingerly pulled the covers back from the bed, and tugged on their joined hands. "Come here." After an initial attempt to withdraw, Whiskey crawled into the bed, pillowing her head on Margaurethe's stomach. A tentative sense of relief stole over Margaurethe, and she closed her eyes. At least this hadn't been completely destroyed. They lay together for long minutes, Margaurethe gently caressing her lover's hair. The unending throb in her head was the only thing keeping her awake. Even with the painkillers Daniel had given her, Margaurethe still felt the sledgehammer and maul attempting to split her skull. Fortunately, Sanguire healed quickly, even from wounds of this nature. Tomorrow she would be much better, but this conversation couldn't wait. "How are you feeling? Still furious?"

Whiskey's shoulders stiffened beneath Margaurethe's fingers. "Not as bad, but yes."

"Anger will do you good if you can control it. If you can't..."

"I'll be just like *her*," Whiskey completed the sentence.

Margaurethe tugged a lock of Whiskey's hair. "No, you'll never become her. I have faith in you. You are leaps and bounds ahead of her." Her next words caused as much pain in her heart as was rocking her head. "The more I see of you, the more I know you'll do the job so much better than Elisibet ever could have imagined." *Odd, this sense of betraying my heart. Yet the sentiment is true; Whiskey will do more than Elisibet ever could have. And she is my heart and soul, just as much as Elisibet ever was.*

Whiskey scoffed, the sound muffled against Margaurethe's abdomen. "You say that even after I attacked you?"

"Yes, for one simple reason." Margaurethe forced her aching muscles to support her as she sat up, displacing Whiskey. "When you realized what you were doing, you stopped."

They stared at each other. "I won't attack you ever again, Margaurethe. I promise that."

"No." Margaurethe's palm cupped Whiskey's cheek. "Never promise something of which you can't be certain. Who knows what the centuries will bring? We could find ourselves at odds over some decision or other. I could go off the deep end and become a depraved serial killer or something."

Whiskey snorted unwelcome laughter at the thought. "That will never happen. I'll become one before you will." The truth of her fear drove the tentative humor out of the conversation. She leaned into Margaurethe's hand.

"Impossible," Margaurethe whispered. "You're too compassionate, too kind. You're a youngling with volatile emotions, and someone dear to you has been taken away. You have every right to feel this pain, this anger." She leaned closer, brushing her lips against Whiskey's, tasting the salt of tears on her skin.

For a moment Whiskey became pliant, then stiffened. She pulled back, Sanguire eyes reflecting the minimal light in the darkened room. "I can't feel you!"

Margaurethe frowned fuzzily until the rising panic in Whiskey's expression prodded her. "It's all right! I'm fine. You did no lasting damage." She grabbed Whiskey's upper arms, stilling the trembling shoulders. "Daniel gave me medication to numb that area of my brain since it received the brunt of the attack, nothing more. I'll be fine."

"Medication? Why?"

She felt so tired. She needed sleep, but Whiskey required an explanation for peace of mind. Leaning back on her pillows, Margaurethe sighed. "If you receive a bruise, you allow it a chance to heal. Prodding it will make it worse, not give it a chance to rest and repair itself. Such is the same for mental injuries such as this."

Whiskey digested the information, still sitting up on the bed. "I...bruised your brain?"

Margaurethe smiled. "In a manner of speaking. Tomorrow I'll be much better, but we'll need to go slowly for the next few days." Her eyes drifted closed of their own accord. The brush of Whiskey's lips on her temple roused her. "I'm sorry. I'm exhausted. The medication..."

"It's okay." Whiskey laid beside her, gathering Margaurethe into her arms. "Sleep. I'll be here when you wake."

Comforted, Margaurethe allowed Morpheus to take her, knowing she was safe in Whiskey's arms.

CHAPTER TWENTY-ONE

Hours later, Whiskey eased out of Margaurethe's bedroom. She almost stumbled across Margaurethe's chambermaid seated just outside. Maya leapt to her feet to give proper obeisance. "My *Gasan*." The Human girl, a *kizarus*, glanced at the closed door. "Will she be all right?"

"She'll be fine." *No thanks to me.* Whiskey stifled her recriminations. There was an assassin in her home, and two friends were dead. She had no time to become a hot mess. "Stay close. She'll probably need blood when she wakes."

"Yes, *Ninsumgal*." She paused. "Father Castillo wishes to speak with you when you are available."

"Thank you."

Whiskey left Margaurethe's apartment for her own, feeling surprise as she gazed out the windows of her sitting room. It seemed like days since Andri's gruesome discovery and her temper tantrum. The sun that had threatened to end the late morning rooftop party had indeed burned off the clouds. The Willamette River drifted lazily in shadows as lights began to come up on the east side, and the last bit of rush hour traffic whisked across the bridges and highways. Hardly any time had passed at all.

"*Ninsumgal*?"

She turned to see her chambermaid at the door leading in to the rest of Whiskey's apartment. "Sithathor."

"I imagine you're not hungry, so I've prepared a cold dinner for you to eat at your leisure. It's in the kitchen refrigerator."

A ghost of a smile quirked Whiskey's lips. "Thanks. Take the rest of the night off."

Sithathor curtsied, her powder-blue sari gracefully shifting with her. "Please do not forget to eat, my *Gasan*. *Ki'an Gasan* Margaurethe will be most displeased."

Whiskey couldn't dredge up the least amount of interest in food, nor the potential haranguing she would receive from her uppity chambermaid should she ignore the repast. "I'll eat. I promise."

"Yes, *Ninsumgal*." Accepting the assurance, Sithathor curtsied again and disappeared inside. She, like Andri, lived in the apartment with Whiskey, always within calling distance. No doubt Andri cowered in his tiny room right now, afraid to poke his bulbous nose out the door for fear of reprisals.

Whiskey discarded the thought of trying to ease his fears. She didn't trust herself not to cause another scene. Instead, she turned back to the windows, staring as the blue sky deepened in color. After an indeterminate time, she recalled Maya's message. Picking up the nearest phone, she told whoever answered that she wanted to see Castillo. His knock came so quickly, she thought he must have been waiting in the hall at the security station.

"*Ninsumgal*."

Disgusted at his bow, Whiskey waved at him. "Stop that! Get up. I don't deserve it."

For a change, he lowered his chin rather than concede. "That's for me to decide."

Not used to outright defiance from him, Whiskey simply gaped. She didn't have the mental wherewithal to argue the point, feeling old beyond her years. "Whatever." Turning away, she didn't complain when he stepped inside and closed the door. "So, what did Lionel have to say?"

Castillo sat uninvited on the couch. "The *Agrun Nam* has used the news of Cora's and Anthony's murders to call for a new vote. *Ki'an Gasan* Margaurethe and *Sublugal Sañar* Valmont will be in receipt of orders to return you to them immediately."

It made sense. With the discovery of a snake nesting in her home, what else could they do? Even had they not been involved in engaging the assassin they would want to move her to safety. Her people had made no secret of The Davis Group's political aspirations, and it would improve the *Agrun Nam's* standing to appear as if they held the power in any worldwide Sanguire conglomeration. She looked over her shoulder at Castillo. "Do we know if any voted against?"

"*Nam Lugal* Bentoncourt says he was the lone dissenter." He shrugged. "They believe you'll be safer there than here."

"Better under their thumb, you mean." *My, what big teeth you have, grandmother.*

"You say tomato."

Whiskey's agitation forced her to start pacing. "Do they expect me to be the good little European Sanguire and come running?"

"I believe so."

"What world do these people live in?" She paused to glare at him.

"A very closed one in which they've been in political power for centuries."

She ran both hands through her hair. "I hate politics."

Castillo smiled, having heard her say the same countless times during their lessons. "Unfortunately, it's what makes our world go 'round."

Whiskey dropped into an armchair. "So, tell me, Padre, do they have a legal precedent for ordering me to attend them?"

"None of which I'm aware." He frowned. "Even if they have confirmed you're European through your father's side, you technically outrank them. They cannot order or compel you to do anything."

"But...?"

"But, they haven't actually accepted you as their monarch. I'm not certain if it's necessary for the *Agrun Nam* to officially accept your ascension or not. They brought Elisibet's father into power to begin with, so that is somewhat relevant." He gave her an apologetic shrug. "About the only 'official' thing you have going for you is your likeness to Elisibet Vasilla, and the fact that you've already begun amassing a following and an army."

She stared blankly at him. "An army?"

"Your security force, the *Aga'gída*." He overrode her derisive snort. "A standard corporation doesn't have near the amount of firepower. The *Agrun Nam* has to be concerned at how much you've amassed in such a short time."

It was too much to deal with on top of everything else. Whiskey set his words aside for the time being. "Where would I go to find out the legalities of my claim?"

He frowned in thought. "There might be something in the library. I'll have a look."

"Do that. I'll draw up a personal letter to the *Agrun Nam*, refusing their...offer." Whiskey massaged her temples with her fingertips. Too much to think of, too many loopholes and contingencies, not enough knowledge. Frowning, she looked up. "Where are Reynhard and the others?"

"*Ki'an Gasan* Margaurethe notified all your advisors, and Valmont arrived this afternoon. Chano has offered spiritual counseling if you would prefer him to myself." His gaze became distant. "I'm not certain about *Sañur Gasum* Dorst. I haven't seen him at all today. I thought you'd sent him on another errand, or that he was lurking about in some capacity."

"I didn't send him anywhere." Even given Dorst's secretive proclivities, she doubted he would investigate the murders without checking in with her. Digging her cell phone from her pocket, Whiskey gave his number a call, but it dropped immediately into voice mail. "No answer." She picked up the house phone.

"This is Sasha, *Ninsumgal*."

"Has Reynhard Dorst been in today?"

"Let me check the visitor's log." There was a pause as the new *Ugula Aga'us* of Whiskey's *Aga'gída* looked up the information. "No, *Ninsumgal*. He left the building last night, and has not returned."

Whiskey thanked Sasha and set the phone down. "Where the hell is he?" She had half a mind to return to Margaurethe and ask when she had called him, but held off. Even with the drugs Daniel had given her, it had taken a long time for her to move far enough past pain to sleep. Margaurethe needed rest, not more prodding.

"Perhaps he already has a lead on something?"

"Or perhaps he's the one responsible."

Whiskey whirled to see Valmont in her door. He had entered without knocking, and stood politely in place with a very pale *aga'us* standing behind him. With a wave of his hand, he released his mental hold on the much younger Sanguire guard. "I'm sorry for the rudeness, but when I heard that you'd called the priest, I assumed you were taking visitors. Unfortunately, this gentleman took exception to my attempt to speak with you."

The guard slumped a little, hand to his head as he came to his senses. A moment later, he flushed and snapped to attention. "*Ninsumgal*! I'm sorry! I—"

She waved off his apology. "No matter. Go...report to Sasha. Leave us." Once the door was closed, she scowled at Valmont, the unremitting fury barely contained. "If you ever compel someone in my home again, I will eviscerate you. Is that understood?"

Valmont blanched at the violence lurking beneath the veneer of normalcy. "Of course. This was just a way to expedite my visit."

Whiskey stared at him until he blinked and raised a chin high in concession. "What do you mean Reynhard's responsible? Why would he kill Cora and Anthony?"

Realizing he had escaped a potentially messy death, Valmont relaxed. A little. "I meant to say, how do we know he isn't the hired assassin?"

"*Nam Lugal* Bentoncourt said much the same." Castillo gave Whiskey an apologetic look.

"You're joking." Whiskey grimaced and turned away, leaving Valmont at the door to follow or not.

"Who knows what he thinks?" Valmont ventured farther into the room. "What has he been doing since Elisibet's demise? Where has he been? How do we know he hasn't branched out into other avenues of entertainment?"

Castillo frowned. "Like assassination for sport?"

It took an iron will for Whiskey to control her temper anew. Forcing herself to step back from her immediate response, she looked at the situation from Valmont's point of view. While her historical education was of a more general nature, she had searched the growing Sanguire library for more information on all the players from Elisibet's reign. That data coupled with her insight into the Sweet Butcher's thoughts and feelings gave her a much larger picture than anyone else. "Reynhard has never enjoyed killing for killing's sake. In fact, the only time he refused an order from Elisibet was when she asked him to kill someone he didn't believe deserved death."

Valmont frowned, moving to stand at the window. "Blaylock, wasn't it?"

A vision filled Whiskey's mind of a younger Dorst looking much aggrieved and apologetic. "Yeah."

"He refused and still lives?" Castillo raised his eyebrows. "I find that intriguing. I'm surprised she didn't rip his throat out."

Whiskey smiled wanly. "It was a close thing. But Reynhard was more useful alive than dead."

"In any case," Valmont said, "it's been hundreds of years. People change. Perhaps he's found a taste for blood. We can't be certain."

Whiskey thought back to her experiences with Dorst since he arrived in her life with a bag of hamburgers. She had been a homeless teenager, ignorant of who and what she was. He had treated her with honesty and kindness—feeding her, offering a safe haven, and guiding her along the Strange Path. He'd been the first to swear fealty, long before she'd finished the *Ñíri Kurám*, long before she understood the scope of her destiny. Even then she had known him to be...if not a friend, then the next best thing. Since he had sworn fealty he had followed her blindly, just as he had followed Elisibet. Seeing him through Elisibet's eyes, she saw the truth. Dorst had been in love with Elisibet, a doting father figure twisted about the Sweet Butcher's little finger. She sighed, and looked at Valmont. "You're wrong. It's not him."

"Don't let sentiment blind you—"

"It's not him." Whiskey sniffed. "Didn't you just say last month that he was a dog in need of a master? That his life wasn't complete without someone to 'rule over him, and pat him on the belly' when he did a good job?" She jabbed a thumb into her chest. "I'm his master, you can't deny that."

"Not a very charitable view," Castillo murmured.

Whiskey shot him a glance. "I don't have time to be charitable, Padre."

Valmont brought his hands up, palms out, to indicate surrender. "It was but a thought."

"Not a good one." Whiskey turned her back on them, hands on her hips, as she attempted to regain some control over her anger. "Do either of you have anything useful to add?"

Castillo's cassock rustled as he stood. "No. I've made my report. Do we know where Cora and Anthony are?"

It surprised Whiskey that she had no idea what had been done with the bodies. Sasha had allowed Whiskey and her advisors into Cora's quarters long enough to witness the devastation. After that, she'd chased everyone out to do a full investigation.

Valmont's voice cut the silence. "They're down in the clinic right now. Once your new *Ugula Aga'us* finished with her photographs and such, she transferred them there for autopsy. Daniel was assigned."

Whiskey sighed and turned back. Daniel had inherited the job of house doctor due to his training and experience. As much as she hated the idea, she couldn't let him suffer alone as he cut into his friends. "I should be down there, too."

"It's too late." Valmont's tone was gentle, an unfamiliar sympathy in his eyes. "He's finished. You'll have to talk to Sasha about his findings."

Swallowing past the lump in her throat, Whiskey nodded. "All right. You two go get some sleep." She glanced outside to see it was still light out. "Or whatever. I'll call you if I need you."

Castillo bowed, a quick bend to forestall her argument against it, and left the room. Valmont lingered a few moments longer. "I'm staying nearby. In case you need me."

Whiskey nodded, her feeling of apathy already putting her actions back on automatic. "Of course. Thank you. I'll call if I do."

He paused, a pained reflection in his eyes. "Good night, *Ninsumgal.*" He bowed, and left, closing the door behind him.

Whiskey let out a shuddering sigh, feeling very much alone.

CHAPTER TWENTY-TWO

"I say, these emergency meetings are becoming quite tedious." Cassadie strolled to his chair and flopped down. Most the others were already there. "What's this one about?"

Bentoncourt opened his mouth, but was interrupted by a new arrival. "What is it now?" Nijmege demanded, marching in to the main council chambers. She didn't bother sitting down. "Has there been another attempt?"

"Do be seated, Bertrada." Cassadie gestured at the chair before the perpetually annoyed woman.

"I'll stand, thank you." She pointed her hawk nose at Bentoncourt. "Well?"

Rather than speak, Bentoncourt slid several sheets of paper toward his peers. "We've received a response regarding our last vote. I thought you'd want to see it for yourselves, so I made copies."

Nijmege snapped up the offering, staring at the text. Her chin dropped to her chest, and the sound of her teeth grinding became clearly audible. A vein throbbed at her temple.

"A direct response from Davis herself?" Rosenberg frowned. "Have we heard from Valmont or Margaurethe?"

"No."

McCall looked up from his copy. "What about that priest you've been talking to? Castile?"

"Father Castillo. No, I haven't heard from him since he updated me on the investigation into the current murders." Bentoncourt waved at his peers. "This has been the only response to our demand for her to attend us."

Nijmege crumpled her copy, tossing it to the floor. "Then we send a team to extract her."

"We are not going to dispatch a covert operation on foreign soil without permission from the *Wi Wacipi Wakan*." Bentoncourt sat up, eyes flashing beneath his dark brows. "And since she's at least half-blooded and currently on their rolls, I doubt they'll give it."

"If we don't retrieve her, we will appear weak!" Nijmege aggressively leaned her weight on the conference table, hands spread wide.

Unimpressed, Bentoncourt shook his head. "You should have thought that before you all decided upon this course of action."

"Sour grapes, Lionel?" Cassadie shook his head. "It's not the first time you've lost a vote. Certainly you have something a bit more constructive to bring to the conversation."

"For this discussion?" Bentoncourt scoffed, unable to hold back his annoyance any longer. "Are you all daft? This entire line of reasoning is nothing but folly." He forced himself to his feet, emulating Nijmege's aggressive stance as he leaned over the table. "We are weak, and have been since the Purge! We barely kept our people together during those dark times, and continue to struggle to this day. We're under constant probing from China, India and Russia. All our military forces are tied up in keeping our nation from falling apart piecemeal, and you now want to throw them at a woman who's destined to reunite our people? You'd drain our resources for an act that couldn't possibly succeed, and leave our borders unprotected against an invasion!" He slapped his hands on the wooden surface. "What is wrong with the lot of you?"

Before anyone answered, he pushed away from the table, putting distance between himself and his political comrades. "What's wrong is that we are falling apart at the seams—not just the *Agrun Nam*, but the European Sanguire as a people. We've attempted to lead as a council without a monarch, and we are failing. Our people are either blissfully complacent, or they are in collusion with our enemies for profit. Mahar prophesied that Elisibet's return would cause much strife, but that she would unite a divided people. We can't divide much more before there's nothing left to unite!" Bentoncourt glared at them, gauging their responses.

Cassadie, ever the optimist, had raised his chin slightly in concession, expressing contrite alarm. Master of the Office of International Affairs, he had apparently never thought of the situation in this manner before, preferring to enjoy the illusion that the all-knowing *Agrun Nam* remained firmly in control as he wandered from one social event to another. Elisibet's father had assigned Cassadie this particular seat on the council. He had been a force of nature on the battlefield when Elisibet's father fought for his throne, a man of action not diplomacy, a vital commodity in a violent time. The centuries and the growth of Human civilization had softened him.

Rosenberg's thick-lidded eyes were narrowed to slits as he considered Bentoncourt's statement. Bentoncourt would have preferred him in Cassadie's position, but the *Nam Lugal* held no power to shuffle job functions. That was a power held only by the *usumgal* or *ninsumgal* ruling over them, an adjustment that hadn't been brought up for amendment since Elisibet's demise. So Rosenberg remained in the position that had been open upon his installation, the Office of Finance. His was the quiet, brooding demeanor that promised somber consideration and resolute action. There was no telling which way he would jump. Once his decision was made, however, the Devil himself wouldn't be able to convince him otherwise, not without some serious evidence.

The youthful McCall frowned, studious as he watched his peers. It was rare for him to speak out, and he remained true to form. Bentoncourt had hoped that after a century of experience the boy would have opened up a bit. At age four hundred, Bentoncourt was carving out a nation with his best friends at his side—Aiden Cassadie and Elisibet's father, Maximal Vasilla. It seemed those times and those sorts of people didn't exist any more. McCall's attention to detail served him well in the Registry Office, but he lacked fire in the belly.

"You sound like you want the Sweet Butcher to return," Nijmege accused.

Bentoncourt regarded Nijmege. "No, I don't want a tyrant to return. But then, I don't assume that a physical resemblance has anything to do with personality. You've seen the same reports I have. Can any of you recall a time that Elisibet acted as Ms. Davis does?" He realized that McCall and Rosenberg had never known Elisibet. Waving at Cassadie, he said, "Well, Aiden? Think about it."

Cassadie shrugged and nodded, leaning back in his chair. "She was a petulant little bratling as a child. Maximal spoiled her horribly after her mother died." He sighed. "She got worse as time passed, only beginning to mellow when *Ki'an Gasan* Margaurethe came into the picture."

A sense of validation loosened the tightness in Bentoncourt's chest, even if he'd had to damned near impel the admission. "And let's be honest Bertrada. No one here believes you want Davis brought here for her safety. As soon as she arrives, you'll attempt to challenge her or have her murdered. The only reason the vote went through was because the others think they can keep Davis safe from you."

Nijmege gasped and sputtered as she paled. Her gaze darted around the room at the others, not finding support to deny the statement.

A rueful grin softened Cassadie's face. "You're not quite as devious as you think you are, Bertrada. You've been quite the fire-breathing dragon since news of Davis came to us."

She flushed, glaring at the rest of them. It took a moment for her to regain some control. "Perhaps so."

Bentoncourt resisted the urge to scoff at her. "There's one other thing of which you should be aware." He stepped back to his chair, and pulled sheets from his stack of reports. Handing them out, he ignored Nijmege's stubborn glower. "One of the building security officers has family here, and has been sending regular correspondence. I think we know how Ms. Davis is gaining her information about our meetings and actions."

"Dorst? Reynhard Dorst?" McCall straightened in his chair, mouth dropping open as he stared at the report. "He's alive?"

Nijmege swore.

"He was her *Baruñal*." Bentoncourt seated himself. "He's been working for her from the beginning, and was the first to swear fealty."

"That certainly makes things stickier, doesn't it?" Cassadie dropped the report onto the table. "Do we have any intelligence regarding his actions since he surfaced?"

Bentoncourt shook his head. "Not really. He conducted her *Baruñal* Ceremony—the one we refused to attend—and is working with a handful of younglings that Davis has taken under her wing. I've no doubt he's reprising his network of espionage and training a new cadre."

"Like we don't have enough problems." Nijmege turned and marched out of the room.

McCall half rose to follow, then sank back into his chair. He looked at those remaining. "How sure are you of Davis's intentions, Lionel?"

Bentoncourt's eyebrows raised. *Is this the type of crisis it will take for young Samuel to come out of his shell?* "I firmly believe that the only threat she'll be is to whoever threatens her and her friends. Yes, her very existence causes strife and chaos, but I don't think Mahar meant Davis would personally cause it."

Rosenberg spoke. "Is Davis still under the impression that this recent assassin has been hired by one of us?"

"Yes, she is." Bentoncourt shook his head. "I've heard the evidence, and I can see where she could come to such a conclusion." He raised his hand to stop Cassadie's reaction. "That doesn't mean it can't also come from any of a half dozen other factions, I know. I've passed on what intelligence information I could without going in to too much detail."

McCall studied him a moment. With a curt nod, he stood and left the room.

"I believe I need to conduct some research on *Sañur Gasum* Reynhard Dorst. If this meeting is over...?" Rosenberg waited for an affirmative nod before exiting.

"Looks like the party's starting. Too bad we threw away our invitation, eh?" Cassadie shook his head.

Bentoncourt sighed. "We still have the chance to make things right, Aiden. We don't have to crash the gates. Davis appears to be somewhat amenable to change, unlike certain members of this august gathering."

Cassadie chuckled. "Yes, well, I can't see Bertrada running with open arms to welcome Davis home. You may have publicly unveiled her here, but her plans haven't changed."

"I know."

"I have a prophecy of my own."

Bentoncourt snorted. "You've become an oracle?"

"Oh, no. I'm far too visceral for that." Cassadie grinned, though his eyes were serious. "I predict that our dear Bertrada will die at the hands of our dear Jenna Davis."

The wry humor faded from Bentoncourt's heart. "You think so?"

"I do. Bertrada is driven." Cassadie drew to his feet, pushing his chair in and standing behind it a moment. "She won't wait until the reunification is complete before attempting what her heart desires."

Bentoncourt could only agree.

***

It was almost over. Cora's vigil service and funeral liturgy were finished, and Whiskey stood at the graveside awaiting the rite of committal. Having a priest as an advisor made moot the decision of what sort of funeral to have. Clouds blanketed the sky, and the rain had stopped, leaving behind the scent of damp earth. Whiskey had selected a cemetery plot near a line of pine trees, and the only sound beyond the gentle murmur of mourners was the steady dripping of water onto the wet ground. A large awning had been erected over the grave to protect them from further showers. A hundred people huddled against the damp, roughly half from Whiskey's *Aga'gída*. The rest were her pack, her advisors, and a number of others—Human and Sanguire alike—here to pay respects to the dead.

As Father Castillo read from his book, Whiskey scanned the attendees. Had Margaurethe had her way, the security staff would have outnumbered the mourners, two to one. As it was, their presence still made the Humans nervous. A number of them were senior management, there more to pay respect to Whiskey than the wild-child Cora. They stood with faces pulled into expressions of sympathy, huddling beneath wet umbrellas, their eyes watching and watching and watching. *Is one of them the assassin?* Whiskey forced herself away from her ever spiraling thoughts. She recognized the paranoia, having witnessed many such thoughts from Elisibet's memories. No Human had been involved in the murders, no Human had the stamina or the physical strength capable of the act that had occurred. No, the paranoia came from recognizing their insincerity. Whiskey had heard the platitudes after the service as they all drifted by in ones and twos to take her hand. She saw the falseness they portrayed. Few of these people had known either Cora or Anthony. How could they act so heartbroken and concerned?

The same question filled her mind as she studied the Sanguire mourners. Each diplomatic retinue currently in negotiations with The Davis Group was represented, most with the chief envoy and two or three aides. In deference to the solemn proceedings each entourage kept themselves separate from the others. Pacal stood with his people, a vaguely condescending expression on his face. *Is it him? Is he the assassin?* The disdain sparked a flash of fury within Whiskey's chest, and she thrust the emotion away, her gaze falling upon the coffin before her. She wouldn't turn Cora's funeral into a bloodbath.

Castillo finished his prayer. Margaurethe gently nudged Whiskey's elbow, urging her forward. Someone tripped the mechanism holding the gleaming cherry wood casket, and it slowly sank into the ground.

Whiskey's eyes and throat burned with tears as she dropped a white rose onto Cora's casket. Those that personally knew the deceased followed suit—Nupa and Chaniya each added a fetish derived from their peoples' spiritual beliefs, and Daniel a rose so red it was nearly black. Alphonse and Zebediah caused a ghost of a smile on Whiskey's face as they each pulled out a flask, took a deep draught, and poured the remainder on their fallen comrade. A few of the more conservative Humans muttered imprecations, not realizing how easy it was to be overheard by the people they were there to impress. Whiskey glared at them, startling them into silence.

"Come away." Margaurethe gently led her from the gravesite.

Unable to see through the angry blur, Whiskey allowed herself to be guided to the limousine. Phineas held the door for her, his cheerful smile missing. Margaurethe, Valmont and Castillo climbed in after her. As the limo pulled away, Whiskey stared out the window.

"How are you, *m'cara*?"

"Fine." Everyone knew she lied. No one called her on it, and she continued to watch traffic as they made their way to the wake.

She had personally spoken with Anthony's parents in Europe to tell them of his honorable service and unfortunate death. They had requested his remains be returned to his family, and Margaurethe had seen it done. Whiskey had promised to punish whoever was responsible for taking their only son away from them. As for Cora, there had been no news from the private detective Whiskey had hired to locate her parents. All anyone knew was that she had been raised in the United States. Daniel had known her for thirty years, and hadn't gotten much more from her beyond that. The least Whiskey could do was let them know where their estranged daughter was buried. The company hired to erect a headstone had been paid and only awaited a phone call from the family to determine what it should say. She had done everything she could. It wasn't enough to appease the guilt.

Whiskey almost wished for Elisibet's ability to not care, not feel. The entire issue would be easier to deal with without her Human sympathy getting in the way. It seemed odd to find something in Elisibet for which to yearn. For over a year Whiskey had denied everything to do with her previous incarnation, finding the Sweet Butcher too repulsive to emulate.

Somewhere an assassin lay in wait for her. She wondered who would be the next to die. Would it be her? Or another innocent victim?

The limousine stopped and the door opened. Her driver, Phineas, offered his hand. "My *Ninsumgal*." Whiskey accepted his assistance, Margaurethe following her out. Valmont exited from the other side, and Castillo already stood on the sidewalk, having ridden in front.

Against her advisors' wishes, Whiskey had insisted that Cora's wake take place at Club Express rather than in the function area of The Davis Group building. The argument was that she could be better protected on her home turf. Though a valid consideration, Whiskey pointed out that the last place she wanted to celebrate Cora's and Anthony's lives would be on the premises where they had been brutally murdered. After much grumbling, cajoling and outright shouting, she reminded them that she was *Ninsumgal*, and they the advisors. Chano was the first to capitulate, followed by Castillo. Realizing she had been left siding with her nemesis, Valmont, Margaurethe decided to agree with the others on the condition that Whiskey went nowhere in the club without at least two *aga'usi*. Whiskey didn't care for the restriction, but had agreed. Valmont had thrown his hands up in the air, and remained staunchly against the entire affair.

The owner of the sex club met them at the door, a tub of a Human with an oily air about him. Whiskey always thought of him as unwashed though he always smelled clean enough. Upon her arrival from Seattle, she couldn't take her pack into regular youth clubs—her people were too young and rough, wolves slavering at the hundreds of Human lambs patronizing the various establishments. With Margaurethe's money and Castillo's organizational skills, they had rented Club Express a number of times over the months to blow off steam before Margaurethe's arrival.

"It's good to see you again, Father." The owner grasped Castillo's hand. "It's been several months."

"Yes, well, we've been busy elsewhere." Castillo extracted himself with grace. "Did the caterers arrive?"

Jovial, the owner chuckled. "Yes, indeed. Quite a spread you ordered. A lot of people have already arrived. What's the occasion?" His greedy eyes wandered over the gathering people waiting to enter.

"A wake for a couple of dear friends."

A parody of sorrow crossed the man's face. "You have my condolences for your loss."

Disgusted, Whiskey left Castillo to his job of making nice. If she had to put up with the ugly man for long, she might do something everyone would regret. She didn't need her ability to see a lie to know the Human didn't give a damn about why they were there; his thoughts remained completely focused on the final tally of the tab that would be paid when the wake was over. Four of her *Aga'gída* exited the building, indicating it had passed their scrutiny. They surrounded their ruler with casual, evident menace. As they reached the entrance, she glanced across the street. A couple of homeless men hovered in a darkened doorway, eyes gleaming with hungry desire. She felt a sharp pang of remembrance. When was the last time they had eaten? It might be high summer now, but the weather had been capricious and autumn would arrive too soon. "Padre, how good's my credit here?"

Castillo interrupted his conversation, following her gaze to the vagrants. "Everything's covered, Whiskey. A woman of your standing shouldn't be required to handle something as lowly as money."

She grinned at his tone, allowing herself to play along with the royalty act for the club owner's benefit. "Can you see that each of them gets twenty bucks?"

"Yes, it would be my pleasure." He melted away from them to follow her command.

"They're only Humans." Valmont's voice wasn't as disgruntled as his feigned expression.

A frisson of irritation whispered through Whiskey. "Maybe. But I was once one of them."

He shrugged.

She and her entourage entered the club. A DJ took up residence on a small stage normally reserved for more prurient entertainment. A poster-sized enlarged photograph of Cora and Anthony hung on the wall behind him, the only known photo of them together. Whiskey smiled, recognizing the man onstage as one that Cora had found particularly intriguing a few months ago. They had bonded over music. It was fitting that someone had invited him to be here, and she suspected Castillo had been the one.

"Something to drink, my *Gasan*?"

She considered her options. Her last time here was the evening of Margaurethe's arrival, surrounded by her pack and a layer of anonymity. Now she was surrounded by a Sanguire security force, and several of her guard were peppering the crowd in various states of civilian attire. Despite the added threat of an assassin, there was also added protection. Even with a couple of drinks, she had confidence she could mentally take on the eldest and most powerful Sanguire in residence. "Yeah. How about a Jack and Coke?"

"Yes, *Ninsumgal*." The guard peeled away from the others to visit the bar.

"We have a table reserved near the dance floor." Margaurethe guided her forward.

Valmont held chairs for both women, and Whiskey looked around to see the immediate tables occupied by her top staff—her advisors, her pack, the handful of *kizarusi* that had been in her presence, and her Human senior managers. Extending her mind, she found more Sanguire security ranging throughout the club, a couple even standing on the edges of the stage to afford a clear field of fire. Weapons weren't prominently displayed, but Whiskey knew that her people were armed to the teeth, pun not intended.

"*Ninsumgal*."

A drink was placed before her, and she thankfully took a sip. She smiled as she remembered Cora pouring shots of whiskey in a Seattle club last year. That had been the first time Whiskey had gotten drunk on her namesake drink, nearly falling on her face when she had attempted to stand. That was the night she had met Dorst. Her mind scanned the club. *Where is he?* Her first advisor hadn't been seen or heard from since the murders. His continued absence was beginning to worry her.

A waiter approached the table, and retrieved orders from the others. Castillo arrived in time to ask for a root beer, and sat down beside her.

"Mission accomplished?" Valmont asked.

"Yes." Castillo leaned close to be heard over the music.

Valmont snorted. "They'll just find a liquor store and swill it away."

"Or buy food. Or pay for a night in a flophouse, or get their first decent meal in three days." Whiskey eyed him. "Adult homeless have a tougher time than kids. Not as many services or as much money." Margaurethe's hand on her arm cooled her burgeoning anger, reminding her of the number of times she'd done the same with Elisibet. The comparison didn't ease Whiskey's emotions. Their drinks arrived, halting conversation.

Never ones for introspection, Alphonse and Zebediah promptly dragged Chaniya and Aleya onto the dance floor. Zebediah drank deep from a bottle of vodka he had appropriated from the bar. "To Cora!"

A roar from the rest of the pack echoed his toast, and Whiskey shot to her feet, joining them. "To Cora! To Anthony!"

"To Cora and Anthony!"

Several hours later, the party still surged on with the younger set. Of Whiskey's advisors, only Margaurethe stayed. All the older Sanguire had left, stopping by her table to bestow their sympathies upon Whiskey before departing. Even Pacal had given his somber condolences, his dark eyes seeming to sparkle in the light. The remaining Humans were the young *kizarusi* attached to Whiskey's pack and those working the club. Considering the number of delegates courting The Davis Group, it was no surprise that half of the strangers were from a number of different nations—children of the Japanese, Mayan, Indian and African diplomats. The DJ had set up a microphone at the corner of the stage, and every so often someone would tell a story about the fallen. Some were funny, some heartbreaking, but the whole idea was for them to celebrate their friends' lives, to honor their highs and lows, to put some closure to the devastation left in the wake of their deaths.

Drink in hand, Whiskey didn't quite stagger up to the microphone. The buzz of alcohol dulled her senses, and Margaurethe stabilized her as they walked. Whiskey tapped the mic, a heavy *thock thock* interrupting the flow of music. The volume decreased, and everyone turned to see who wanted to speak next. Whiskey released Margaurethe and straightened, taking a deep breath.

"The first time I saw Cora Kalnenieks, I was getting my ass handed to me by a bunch of punks. She proceeded to take one of them down with a single punch, becoming my hero." Alphonse and Zebediah grinned in remembrance. "A week or so later, she and Daniel stood up to their pack leader, a woman twice their age, to protect me during my *Ñíri Kurám*." Whiskey raised her glass to acknowledge Daniel, who nodded back. Nupa jostled him with a smile. "She suffered—they both did—and she became my hero once again. All she ever wanted from me was for me to remember her, to remember who helped me in the beginning." Whiskey stared down at her drink with a frown. "We had our differences of opinion. My upbringing was different than most of yours, and sometimes that was glaringly evident. But I could never forget her sacrifices or her friendship.

"Anthony came to me with Margaurethe a few months ago. He took over as *Ugula* of my *Aga'gída*." She grinned up at the audience. "What a thankless job that was, huh? I'm surprised the lot of us didn't give him an aneurysm. He took it in stride, though, never shirking in what he thought was right to protect me—when he could find me." Another chuckle reverberated around the room. "When I heard that he and Cora had become lovers, I was happy for them. It looked like Cora was thinking about settling down, and I couldn't think of anyone more trustworthy or courageous for her to be involved with."

Whiskey raised her glass, feeling the tightness in her throat. "To Cora and Anthony. They will be sorely missed." She tossed back the shot while the others echoed her toast. Setting her empty glass down on the edge of the stage, she stumbled away, eyes blurring. She didn't want to break down in public. "I need to get to the restroom."

"Of course." Margaurethe went with her toward the back of the establishment. The two nearest guards flanked them as they walked, one speaking into the radio mic at his wrist.

Whiskey bit back a drunken snicker at the absurdity of a personal escort to the toilet. The silliness didn't ease as several other *aga'usi* emerged from the crowd, clearing the way to their intended destination. A few of the revelers tried to gain her attention as she passed. It was a futile effort. The loud music and level of alcohol in her bloodstream made even her Sanguire hearing suspect, and she heard nothing but noise. At the restroom, she was forced to remain outside with her *aga'usi* while Margaurethe swept the interior for potential danger. Whiskey's bladder became more insistent in its demands. She leaned against the wall by the door, six burly men and women keeping the others at bay. A sudden popping noise interrupted her melancholy.

Everyone moved in slow motion. She heard two more pops, and watched her security turn their heads toward the sound. One of them crumpled to the ground before her, his companion reaching out to stop his fall. The others surged around her, blocking her view as they put their bodies before hers. The people clamoring for attention turned away, attempting to leave the suddenly claustrophobic area, a neat trick considering how tightly packed the crowd had gotten in Whiskey's vicinity. She saw the ripple of movement, like someone had dropped a rock in a still lake. But where was the rock?

A man materialized from the cringing mob, an automatic pistol in each hand. He shot another of the *aga'us*, leaving the way open to his intended target, her.

They stared at one another for what seemed like forever. He was unfamiliar, someone she had never seen, someone Elisibet had never known. He was Indian and Sanguire, looking a little older than Whiskey, which—considering the much longer lifespans of the Sanguire—placed his age anywhere between twenty- and sixty-years-old. His face was contorted into a savage snarl, at odds with the dull look in his eyes. Despite the expression on his face, his eyes told the true story. *Compelled.* Taking careful aim, he said something, but Whiskey couldn't hear him over the screams of the crowd trying to escape, the yells of her remaining

Aga'gída as they aimed weapons to protect her. She felt the wall solid against her back, knowing there was nowhere to go, praying to God that Margaurethe wouldn't come bursting from the restroom and get herself killed as well. Whiskey closed her eyes, pushing backward as if she could simply step through the solid concrete construction that had gone into the making of this building. With an almost fatal calm, she awaited the next pop, knowing that bullet would be for her.

It didn't make a pop this time. The sound was muffled, almost impossible to hear. In fact, all sound became smothered. She wondered if this was what happened when one was shot to death. That didn't seem right; she had detailed memories of Elisibet's death. If anything, sound sharpened toward the end. She felt no pain, just a sensation of being cocooned, followed by a smell of sanitizer, and a cool draft of air.

"Whiskey?" a baffled voice asked.

She opened her eyes to see Margaurethe in the process of opening the bathroom door to go out. Startled, Whiskey scanned her surroundings. "What the hell?" She stood inside the restroom, having pushed *through* the wall. Somehow, she had entered this safe haven, and had left no evidence of her passage.

The door burst open, revealing Sasha. The sound of radio chatter and general chaos entered with her, and she had to shout to be heard. "*Ninsumgal*? Are you hurt?" Too confused to speak, Whiskey stared. Sasha closed the distance between she and Whiskey, quickly running her hands over Whiskey's body. "She appears uninjured." Sasha shouted, "We have to get her out of here!"

While Margaurethe and Sasha arranged the abrupt exit of their ruler, Whiskey reached out a shaky hand. Cool unmarred concrete met her fingers. *What the hell just happened?*

CHAPTER TWENTY-THREE

Margaurethe, Sasha and every security person under her command surrounded Whiskey, and hustled her through the chaos to the waiting limousine. She barely had time to hear the owner's strident tones as he disavowed any knowledge of danger to her before the door slammed, and Phineas drove away from the bedlam. Whiskey tried to piece together what had happened. How had she gotten inside the restroom? She had been completely helpless, watching her killer aim the pistol at her head. Then she'd stood on the other side of the wall, safe from harm, as confused as Margaurethe.

Two *Aga'gída* rode in the back of the limo with her and Margaurethe, and Sasha had hopped into the front seat. One of those seated across from Whiskey listened intently to the earplug connected to his radio. "*Ninsumgal*, Captain Kopecki wishes you to know that all your friends have been accounted for, Human and Sanguire alike. The shooter only hit the *aga'usi*."

Still fuzzy from the alcohol and excitement, Whiskey nodded. "Thank you." Her mouth was dry, and she wished she had a drink of cool water. She cast her eyes around the interior of the limousine, fumbling with the small refrigerator that held refreshments.

Margaurethe was less confused, jaw tucked to her chest as she glared at the two men across from her. "Were we able to apprehend the assassin?" Her words were lightly slurred, not from drink but because her fangs were unsheathed.

To his credit, the ranking man of the two didn't tremble at her fury. "No, *Ki'an Gasan*. We're not certain whether he died as a result of our actions or if he killed himself. In either case, he's no longer a threat."

Margaurethe cursed.

Who was he? Whiskey stared out the tinted window, chewing her lip. She remembered his lips moving, watching the slow motion replay of memory. Was he defending someone, maybe even avenging a dead family member? "*This is for...*" But his eyes had held no life, no consciousness, no spark of emotion.

"We're here." The limousine pulled off the street, and bypassed the front apron of The Davis Group. Normally, they would stop at the main entrance to disembark. Due to the emergency they proceeded down the ramp to the bottommost of the two parking garages. There was a single express elevator there to carry her to her apartment. Looking out the window, Whiskey saw what looked like every member of the security personnel in the building guarding the entrance. It was something similar to what she had seen on documentaries of attempted presidential assassinations. It stunned her to realize that it was all being done to protect her. The magnitude of the situation took her breath away. *Am I truly that important?*

Within seconds, Phineas had the limo pulled over near the elevator. Whiskey reached for the handle, only to be stopped by the *aga'us* across from her. He shook his head, waiting for radio confirmation. The elevator opened, several guards pouring out of it to circle the vehicle. Only when all were in place did he open the door. Whiskey and Margaurethe were surrounded and hustled into the elevator. Four security officers blocked the entry as the door slid shut. It seemed ludicrous. What did they think could happen here?

Sasha plugged an unfamiliar code into the keypad on the elevator.

"What's that?"

"It tells the system to bypass all other floors. It's an express code." True to her word, the elevator didn't stop until it reached its destination. The doors opened, disgorging the occupants onto the dark marble. The sixteenth-floor foyer bristled with more guards, many armed with automatic rifles. Sithathor stood at the open penthouse door, and Whiskey was ushered inside.

Sithathor closed the door. Margaurethe pulled Whiskey into her arms. "Are you all right? Shall I have Daniel brought to examine you?" Her voice trembled along with her body. She thoroughly examined Whiskey, turning her this way and that in search of injury.

"I'm fine." When Margaurethe ignored her, continuing her examination, Whiskey grabbed her lover's wrists. "I'm not hurt, *minn'ast*. Really! I'm okay."

Tension flowed out of Margaurethe, causing her shoulders to slump. She closed her eyes, and a single tear spilled over. Her wrists remained captured by Whiskey. Rather than free herself, she pulled them close, resting her head in the crook of Whiskey's shoulder. Whiskey wrapped her arms about Margaurethe. They held tight to one another, both understanding how close they had come to history repeating itself. Though Margaurethe's body shook with restrained emotion, she didn't weep beyond the one tear.

After several moments, Sithathor broke the silence. "Can I get you anything, *Ninsumgal*?"

Whiskey sighed, pleased to feel Margaurethe relax. She looked past her lover to see the worried expression on her chambermaid's face. She offered a smile to Sithathor. "Yes, please. Juice for me." After a fraction of a pause, she added, "And a stiff drink for Margaurethe." The woman in her arms gave a chuckle, one tinged with hysteria but not overly out of control. Sithathor bowed, though her body remained tense as she proceeded to the bar.

"I'm all right." Whiskey pulled back to peer at Margaurethe.

She sniffled, but appeared in command of her emotions. "What happened?"

"I don't know exactly. Everything was fine until you went inside. While we were waiting, someone came out of the crowd with a pistol, and started shooting."

Margaurethe's normally olive complexion turned pasty yellow. Her frantic gaze traveled across Whiskey's body once more, searching anew for possible wounds. "How the hell did someone get in there with a gun?"

"Again, I don't know. Security was doing searches at the door, but maybe they missed somebody." Whiskey turned away, removing her jacket, tossing it onto a chair.

Margaurethe's anger slowly began to boil. "This is Reynhard's fault! Off on one of his little jaunts—he should have been here. Here! You're damned lucky that assassin didn't smuggle in a bazooka!"

Whiskey raised her hands in surrender. "I have no idea where Reynhard is, and I'm not concerned about it." The alcohol and adrenaline faded away, and she sank with some force into an armchair. "But that wasn't the weird thing."

Sithathor returned to place a tray on the coffee table. "*Ninsumgal*," she murmured, making certain her employer knew of its presence.

"Thank you." Whiskey didn't give the woman a second thought as she continued the conversation. "I mean, the guy had me, dead to rights. He shot two of my guards. I had nowhere to go—I was trapped by the *Aga'gída* around me, and a wall behind me."

Margaurethe halted her furious pacing. She paled again, puzzled. "Yes, what happened? How did you get into the restroom? I had just checked the last stall when I heard the commotion outside."

Whiskey remembered the sensation of everything being

muffled as she cringed away from her killer. "I closed my eyes, waiting to die. And then I was inside with you."

"Someone shoved you through the door."

"No!" Whiskey jerked her head up to stare at Margaurethe. "I had my back to the wall, and then I was standing inside facing the same wall."

Margaurethe's eyes narrowed. "That's not possible."

"But it is."

Both of them looked at Sithathor who had remained in the room. Her smile was unexpected, at odds with her previous pinched expression. It was benevolent, with a hint of smugness. She stood in a bubble of calm, her hands clasped before her.

"You are *Gidimam Kissane Lá*, *Ninsumgal*. You have finally discovered your gift."

Whiskey recognized the words, but they didn't register. She stared uncomprehending at her chambermaid, barely hearing Margaurethe's gasp.

"Ghost Walker?" Margaurethe's voice sounded somewhat strangled. "You think she's a Ghost Walker?"

"Yes, *Ki'an Gasan*." Sithathor's smile widened. "It seems obvious considering the situation." She turned to Whiskey who still gaped at her. "Did sound become dampened when you passed through the wall?"

"Yeah, it did." Somewhat belatedly, Whiskey made the connection to the familiar words. "You're saying I'm a Ghost Walker?" She pressed her lips together in irritation. Even to her, she sounded like an idiot, repeating what had already been said. "That's impossible. The *Gidimam Kissane Lá* haven't been seen or heard from in centuries. I've asked around, and they disappeared almost worldwide at the same time."

Sithathor knelt before her. "This is true, my *Gasan*. But we deemed it necessary to remove ourselves from society long ago."

Still confused, Whiskey asked, "We?"

Her chambermaid's skin flushed slightly. "My apologies, *Ninsumgal*, but the Sweet Butcher's desire to exploit our abilities was only one of many wishing to do the same. In the beginning our gifts were slight, but they have strengthened over the centuries. As our abilities grew, so did the desires of many rulers. Only the oldest and most powerful could defend against compelling. We thought it best to remove the temptation."

Whiskey's mind flashed to a memory of Elisibet, a rage in her heart as she ransacked a building with her men in the hopes of locating just one of the elusive Ghost Walkers. To have one at her beck and call would make her privy to many state secrets. She could use them as assassins and spies, ultimately becoming the ruler of all Sanguire, not just the Europeans she currently led. She reeled back from the recollection, the fury washing away to numbness. "Smart move."

"You're one?" Margaurethe demanded.

"I am." Sithathor placed her hand upon the table, and Whiskey watched with fascination as it slid through as if the wood didn't exist. Sithathor waved her hand back and forth just beneath the surface of the table, appearing to be caressing a puddle of water rather than a solid chunk of wood. "Were I to solidify myself, I would do irreparable damage to both my hand, and the table. The two sets of molecules are not mutually exclusive; they cannot exist at the same time in the same place." She removed her hand, looking at her audience.

Whiskey linked with Margaurethe, finding a swirl of conflicting emotions; residual anger at the nearly successful assassination attempt, disbelief of Sithathor's words, a tentative joy at the discovery of Whiskey's gift, and fear of unknown capability. "Nobody knew my father. If you've been working on this stuff for centuries, he'd have to be part of it." Whiskey shook her head. "My family would have told me if this talent came from my mother's side. I might not be the best student, but at least I know enough biology for that."

Sithathor, her hands clasped neatly in her lap, smiled. "We do know your father, *Ninsumgal*. Gareth Davidson—son of David Sceadson and Enid."

***

"What the hell do you think you're doing?"

He held the phone away from his ear, a smile on his face. The ranting continued for a solid minute before his employer paused to inhale. "I had no choice. The youngling saw me. Wrong place, wrong time. Very unlucky for her."

"Very unlucky for you! Because of your idiocy, the *Agrun Nam* has voted for her to return at once."

"Oh?" He raised his eyebrows. A waitress arrived with his drink, and he sent her away with a flick of his wrist. "I'm intrigued. Do they actually believe she'll bow to their whim?"

There was no response. He refused to fill the emptiness, twirling the liquid in his glass with a thin straw. From the sounds of it, his employer had yet to hear of the attempt at the club last night. He considered not answering his phone after this, just to avoid another verbal tantrum.

"How should I know?" came the reluctant answer.

He grinned, knowing he had scored a point. Here was rudimentary proof that his mysterious employer indeed worked for the esteemed ruling council. He wondered what the chances were of him actually being one of the *sanari*. It made sense considering the identity of his assigned target. "I thought you might have more information than I." He sipped his drink. *Ah, a Bloody Mary. Or was it Susan? Perhaps Gretchen.* The alcohol swept over his tongue, leaving behind the tasty hint of blood. "The news I get here is weeks old."

"You don't need news. You need to get the job done!"

"Of course. But if you don't mind, I'd much rather do it and survive than sacrifice myself. It seems when I took this assignment, you failed to mention the target's well-trained security escort and the presence of a certain eccentric spy in her employ."

"She's nothing. An upstart."

He chuckled at the lack of reaction to hearing Reynhard Dorst was involved. "Aye. An upstart who just happens to have a massive security detail around her and at her estate at all times."

"Not all the time. It seems she went out hunting one night with only *Sublugal Sañar* Valmont. You would have had the perfect opportunity if you had paid the slightest bit of attention."

Leaning back in his chair, he scanned the interior of Tribulations. Though only afternoon, the place boasted being open twenty-four hours a day. Several Sanguire were scattered about the room. Very few Humans braved the club before evening hours; those that did were fully cognizant of his people's existence. "Actually, I followed them. They have a rather marvelous club here."

"You what?"

He smiled at the muffled curse on the other end. As he took another drink, his employer sputtered until regaining a modicum of control.

"I hired you to do a job. Now do it!"

"Aye, you hired me to do a job. And I will. In my own time."

"If you don't kill her before she can be returned to the *Agrun Nam*, you'll have failed. Not only will you not get the remainder of your fee, but I'll see to it that you'll follow her into the grave."

He felt his expression stiffen, and he leaned forward. "You threaten me?"

"You're a dog I've sent to attack a rabid animal. If you fail, you're useless to me, and a danger to everyone else. I'll put you down. Count on it."

He remained silent, eyes closed, teeth gritted. Finally, he spoke. "Your job will be done, and you'll pay me what you owe." He paused, opening his eyes. "But you'd better consider 'putting me down' anyway, guv. Because I'll be looking for you next."

Disconnecting the line, he tossed the phone onto the table. "Cheeky bastard." He nursed his drink, ordering another when it got low.

The longer he investigated Davis, the more inclined he was to believe what was said of her. She was Mahar's Prophecy embodied; the Sweet Butcher's soul lived and breathed within hers. What else could account for her mistaken but successful mental attack of her Margaurethe O'Toole last week? That woman was older than Davis by seven hundred years! No normal youngling had the strength of will to do such a thing.

It was too bad, really. He had actually come to like the girl. Unlike the Sweet Butcher, she had compassion. If left to her own devices, she would have made a tremendous positive impact on their people. He remembered living during Elisibet's time—the backbiting, the squabbling over her attentions, and the fear of attracting her jaundiced interest. Given what he had observed so far, he doubted those evil years would be repeated. Unless his employer preferred to step into the Sweet Butcher's slippers, of course, which seemed a likely prospect.

Very unfortunate it was that he hadn't gotten all the information available before accepting the job. He had a certain level of honor, probably more so than many of his ilk. He had hired on for the job, he would do it, and he would regret it. Such was his long life. But he would also discover who hired him. The thought of publicly taking his employer down warmed his heart. First find him, then unveil his intentions and actions. They both might die as a result, but it would be well worth the cost of his life, knowing that the man who had stopped the reputed Golden Age of the Sanguire from happening would join him in hell.

Satisfied with a plan of action, he stood, drained his drink, and dropped money on the table. It was time to return to the estate and arrange things. After the ill-timed attempt at the club last evening, Davis wouldn't leave the estate alone. The incident had been more a test of her security than anything else, one where his toy had failed to achieve the desired result. To enact his plan, he needed to procure a new bit of bait. The last one had died with her burly boyfriend when her kidnapping had been interrupted. *Pity that. Cora had been a darling.*

CHAPTER TWENTY-FOUR

Castillo sat in his office, peering at a book. He set aside the tome and turned his office chair to scan the shelves behind his desk. He had a smaller yet more extensive collection than Whiskey's private library, books he had gathered over the centuries as he followed the precepts of his church. It hadn't done him much good for his current task. So far, neither he nor Whiskey had found any legal precedent for the *Agrun Nam* to insist she go to Europe except upon arrest for crimes against the realm. That was a fairly new law put into place not long after Elisibet's demise.

To his mind, the search went well. Except for the one aforementioned ruling, nothing among the laws of the Sanguire allowed for the *Agrun Nam* to order anything of their *Ninsumgal*.

Castillo felt surprise at this lack. After Elisibet's atrocities, he assumed they would have given themselves more power to keep a future ruler in check. Perhaps they were so relieved at the Sweet Butcher's death, they simply hadn't taken her reincarnation into account, despite the prophecy. Certainly they had attempted to negate it entirely by taking control of the realm sans monarchal leader.

With a sigh, Castillo stood and picked up the book he had been scouring, intent on returning it to its place. He heard an unfamiliar scratching and paused, looking over his shoulder at the door. Since moving into The Davis Group, he had requested and received permission to conduct prayer meetings for the faithful. He wondered if someone needed religious guidance. He answered the door and his dark eyebrows rose.

"Father Castillo." Andri hovered in the hall, wringing his cap in his hands.

"Andri! What a pleasant surprise." Castillo stepped back to allow Whiskey's valet entry. "Please, sit down."

The homely man took a hesitant step into the room. He couldn't seem to make up his mind whether to stare at the floor or the window or the books, his eyes occasionally darting to the priest.

Castillo softened his voice. "You're not here as a servant, Andri. Please. Sit down." To illustrate his point, he returned to his desk and resumed his seat.

Andri's Adam's apple bobbed once before he gave a curt nod, and perched on the edge of a chair.

Offering Andri something to drink would probably unnerve him more, so Castillo refrained from the hospitality. Instead, he studied the man, surprised he would knock at all. To Castillo's knowledge not a single Sanguire here followed the Human religion as he did. "Can I help you?"

Andri cleared his throat, eyes always on the move, never letting his gaze rest anywhere long. "My *Ninsumgal* has given me the day off, sir. She mourns her friends."

"Yes. Cora was one of her best friends among her pack, and Anthony her *Ugula Aga'us*. It's been difficult for her."

"Yes, it has."

"But that doesn't explain why you're here, Andri, unless you wish to partake in a prayer meeting? I was unaware that you were a believer."

Andri's nervousness ratcheted up another level as sweat beaded on his upper lip. "No, sir. I'm not."

Castillo watched him, and decided not to press the issue. A gentler hand was needed to urge Andri to trust. His time with Elisibet had all but destroyed him. Castillo wondered why Andri would put himself into the position of repeating the past by working for Whiskey. "Tell me what's on your mind."

Andri's fidgeting grew more pronounced, and he stared at the edge of Castillo's desk. "The day of the murders...I saw something."

Castillo's pleasant demeanor faltered. He leaned forward, studying his visitor with intensity. "What did you see, Andri?"

There was explosive movement as Andri yanked a handkerchief from his coat pocket and wiped his face. "I would have told my *Ninsumgal* but...she was so angry." His eyes, naturally reflective, shone brighter with a dab of wetness as he glanced at Castillo.

Having been the emotional punching bag for someone more powerful in the past, Castillo well understood Andri's reluctance to pursue the matter. "I understand." His voice soothed over the edge of panic emanating from his visitor. "Tell me what you saw. I'll be glad to speak to Whiskey on your behalf."

Andri paled. "I don't...I don't want her knowin' it was me," he whispered. His fingers gripped his cap with such strength, his hands shook from the exertion. He'd had centuries of experience with Elisibet. Only centuries more with Whiskey would break through his conditioning.

"I can't promise not to tell her where the information comes from, but I swear to do everything in my power to convey to her your role as innocent witness to whatever it is you'll tell me. It's the best I can do."

Several moments passed as Andri considered the offer, his shoulders hunched so high, he looked like a small, brown turtle. His swallow audible, he peered at Castillo and nodded.

"What did you see?"

Andri's mouth worked before his voice actually caught up with it. "It was the morning of the murders. I had been released from my duties after I set clothes out for my *Ninsumgal*." He dropped his gaze. "I was going to the Resident's Lounge when I saw someone going into that girl's apartment. It was that man—"

Castillo blinked, his heart thudding. "What man, Andri. Whom did you see?"

Refusing to look up, Andri cringed. His voice was so faint, Castillo barely heard him. "The *Sublugal Sañar*."

Valmont? Castillo slumped into his chair, mind whirling. *Why would Valmont go into Cora's quarters? Was he even on the premises that day?* He distinctly remembered Chano insisting that Valmont be called after the security lockdown had been put into place, and Valmont's arrival thirty minutes later. What would be the point in targeting Cora? He returned his attention to his visitor. "What did he seem like? Was he upset? Calm? Can you tell me?"

Andri wilted further under Castillo's concentrated scrutiny. He shrugged, a weak gesture of his already strained shoulders. "He seemed normal, I guess. I don't know."

"You're certain it was Valmont?"

"Yes, sir. Very certain." Despite his adamant answer, Andri shivered. "I've seen him in the residential section a few times now. There's no mistaking him."

Residential section? "Was security with him?"

"No, sir. He was alone."

Castillo frowned. To his recollection, Valmont had refused an apartment in the building, preferring to live elsewhere. He hadn't been friendly with anyone who did, either. Despite Whiskey's attempt to alleviate security where Valmont was concerned, he had never been allowed to roam the residential floors without an escort. How could he have gotten there, and why? "Define 'a few times,' please."

***

"I don't believe it."

Castillo took a deep breath, letting it out slowly as he faced Whiskey. "I didn't think you would, actually. But who else could it be?"

It was the day after the wake, and Castillo had requested an audience with Whiskey. Even being one of her advisors hadn't exempted him from a thorough body search before being allowed into Whiskey's apartment. They now sat at the dining table in her sitting room, joined by Margaurethe and Chano. Dorst was still missing.

Whiskey rose from her chair and circled behind it, grasping the wood frame. "I know Valmont. He wouldn't have killed Cora."

Chano resorted to a grunt of assent, using the standard non-verbal response of his people before choosing to speak. "Perhaps the man you remembered wouldn't. But none of you has been close to him in centuries. Who knows how he lived? Time and regret change a man."

"I still don't believe it." Whiskey hated the unfocused anger at the murders, and the sick uncertainty that she may have been wrong about Valmont's intentions. Valmont had changed from the man Elisibet had known, but would he have done this?

"I have to agree with Chano." To Margaurethe's credit, she didn't show her pleasure at the justification of her concerns regarding Valmont. "You know I've never trusted him. We've done a thorough sweep of all Sanguire allowed access to The Davis Group, and he is the only major security issue we have. Who else could it be?"

"Maybe Andri is wrong. Perhaps he saw someone else."

"Andri's Sanguire, just like the rest of us," Castillo interrupted. "He might be emotionally damaged, but he's not blind."

"He is old, as old as me." Chano frowned, his face becoming more craggy in the process. "Elder Sanguire do suffer the same dimming of the senses that Humans do."

Margaurethe shook her head. "Speculation is getting us nowhere. Perhaps we should call Andri in to report his sighting."

Castillo raised one hand in a placating maneuver. "That would probably be best, but he's terrified of incurring his *Ninsumgal's* wrath." He met Whiskey's gaze. "We know you're not Elisibet, but he firmly believes you'll punish him severely for what he saw."

"In other words, tone it down." At Castillo's nod, she took a deep breath and forced herself to relax. "All right. Bring him in, Padre. I'll be gentle." A burble of sadistic humor soothed the rage seething beneath the surface. Margaurethe's hand and mind on hers further mellowed her. It took a few moments for Whiskey to restore her equilibrium.

Castillo escorted Andri into the room with a firm hand on one elbow, not releasing him until they stood before Whiskey. Andri's iron-colored hair presented itself to her as he stared at his feet, shoulders hunched, awaiting a sharp blow. He visibly shivered, the wave of fear radiating off of him thick enough for even a nerve-deadened Human to smell. Whiskey couldn't demand answers from him in this state. She had tried for weeks to settle him in her presence, to no avail. Something drastic needed doing to get through to him. She stood and walked around the table. Andri cringed away, but his training held firm; he didn't evade her approach, probably assuming she would physically attack him as Elisibet had habitually done in the deep past. Instead, Whiskey knelt at his feet and took his cold hands into hers. Castillo backed away.

Andri gaped at her, a horrified expression on his face. His fear of her fought his solidly entrenched idea of royal etiquette. He tried to pull his hands from hers, tried to step back, shaking his head, but Whiskey refused to release him. Andri could stay where he was or drag his liege across the floor on her knees. An almost silent sob escaped his lips as he steeled himself to remain still, staring at their joined hands.

"I need you to tell me what you saw that morning, Andri."

His jaw jumped as he worked his mouth. He had difficulty finding his voice, but it came in a bare whisper. "After you released me for the morning, I went to the Residents' Lounge for my breakfast. When I finished, I returned to the elevators. That's when I saw him."

When he stopped, Whiskey gave his hands a light squeeze, ignoring his nervous jump. "Saw who?"

Andri swallowed. "Your friend, the brown man, though he wasn't the brown man in the past."

Whiskey felt her expression harden. Only one man could be considered the "brown man." "You mean Valmont?" She received a jerky nod in response, chilling her heart. "What was he doing when you saw him?"

His quivering increased as he recognized the danger signs. "He was going into *Gasan* Cora's apartment, my *Ninsumgal*."

"Did he see you?"

"No, *Ninsumgal*. I don't believe so."

"What happened next?"

"I returned to my quarters, *Ninsumgal*."

Chano spoke. "Are you certain it was Valmont?"

As Andri nodded assent to the question, Whiskey considered her options. It seemed wrong that Valmont was involved. He had never had anything to do with the pack, their activities and interests so far removed from his youthful experience that they bored him. *And why kill Cora? He's had ample opportunity to kill or kidnap me over the months. It doesn't make sense to murder an innocent victim. Why now?*

She had to see what Andri had seen to confirm his report. There was only one way to do that. The inadvertent discovery of her ability to see and feel a memory of Castillo's, and the discussion she'd had with Chano over the noticeable lack of information regarding such a skill in the European Sanguire records, made the decision for her. She felt trepidation at the thought of invading Andri's mind. He had been through so much as Elisibet's valet—she doubted she'd be able to find the recollection without hurting him. She shook his hands, bringing his attention back to her. "I have to see, Andri. I won't hurt you, but I have to see for myself."

His craggy features crunched into an expression of confusion.

"What do you mean?" Margaurethe asked.

Whiskey glanced back at her. "You know what I mean." Her gaze swept over the others. "You all do. Padre, I saw your memory of meeting Valmont back in Seattle when you found me with Alphonse and Zebediah. That's how I knew you'd seen him."

Castillo blinked, his mouth dropping slightly open at the revelation.

"And Chano tells me that some Sanguire—the very strong ones—have this ability."

"I thought—" Margaurethe looked aghast, hand to her heart. Whiskey wondered if perhaps the sharing of visual memories between them was more one-sided than she had thought. "That's preposterous!"

Andri's complexion turned pasty, his eyes widening as he understood Whiskey's intentions. With Sanguire strength, he wrenched his hands from hers, wrapping his arms around himself in a parody of protection. He didn't step away. Pleased he didn't attempt escape, Whiskey remained on her knees before him. "I know this is a tough thing I'm asking, Andri. I know how much Elisibet hurt you. I remember what she was like when she was angry." She stared at him until his glance flickered to hers. "I won't hurt you, I swear. I won't go where you don't want me to go. I just have to see what you saw that morning. I have to know."

Terrified tears spilled down Andri's face as he closed his eyes, nodding.

Permission given, Whiskey reached out with her mind, allowing the barest edges of it to wash over Andri. As much as she wanted to know now, she refused to push. This connection might go a long way in helping Andri realize she was not her predecessor, an added benefit. She soothed his fears, and let him feel her awareness. He emanated the sensation of rough stone, cool but abrasive if rubbed against. It didn't feel the least bit familiar, and Whiskey took a moment to relish the unexpected newness. A quick scan of Elisibet's memories indicated no knowledge of Andri's essence. He had been such a nonentity to her, at her side since birth, that she had never bothered to register what he felt like when she had become an adult. Her gentleness lulled Andri into a sense of normalcy, and Whiskey reinforced the link. His mind fluttered under hers, a delicate butterfly banging against the glass jar imprisoning it. She paused, hating the excruciating slowness, knowing she had no choice. She let Andri get used to her presence in his mind, not sifting through memories, not taking control of his will, not attacking. "Show me, Andri. Show me what you saw in the hallway the day Cora and Anthony died." Several moments passed before he strengthened the connection, tentatively reaching out with a mental finger to touch the surface of her essence.

She felt power radiating below the surface of Andri's mind, and was reminded that despite his appearance of lowly servant, he was an aged Sanguire, strong in his own right. Whiskey had no idea how old he was; in Elisibet's earliest childhood memory he was a full adult. Quick calculation surprised her. Andri had to be at least nine hundred years old. Technically, he should have the strength to mentally snap her in half. She put herself on guard. She didn't believe he would attack, but his excessive fright might cause him to attempt to repel this invasion. It wasn't inconceivable that he could lash out in defense after a misplaced nudge on her part. Better prepared than dead.

In her mind's eye, she saw a black cloud hover where their essences met. She focused upon it, watching it solidify into a picture. It was the fifteenth-floor corridor, blanketed in grayness. As her attention narrowed to the scene, it rapidly grew until she was in the shadows, standing near the elevators. The transition felt odd, and she blinked and shook her head. Cora's murder occurred in the morning, but the dimness made it feel like twilight. Beside Whiskey, Andri stood near the elevators. He seemed at ease, something she rarely saw when dealing with him. Despite the semidarkness, he had no candle or flashlight; but then, perhaps his eyesight was going bad because of his advanced age. *Chano was right; Sanguire do age like Humans. We lose our eyesight and hearing as a matter of course before we die of old age.* A gentle scuffling noise drew his attention. Whiskey watched as he rushed from normal man to scared mouse. Andri's eyes widened. He scanned the foyer as he slipped closer to the elevator doors.

She turned to see what caused the sound. Valmont stood at a door down the hallway.

The connection wavered as she stared intently at him, knowing what was going to happen once he entered that apartment. Her flare of anger derailed Andri enough that the contact faltered between them. Whiskey quickly suppressed her emotions, sending him an unspoken apology. When things settled once more, she looked back at Valmont's form.

Everything had frozen as if someone had hit the pause button on a video player. Valmont had the apartment door open a mere inch. His attention elsewhere, he glanced over his shoulder to where Andri huddled just out of sight. Whiskey realized it had been sheer luck that Andri hadn't been discovered. Slowly, as her valet returned to the memory, Valmont turned as he opened the door, scanning the hall as he stepped backward into the apartment. Once the door firmly closed behind him, Andri slipped quietly into the Residents' Lounge and relative safety.

Whiskey resisted the urge to plunder Andri's mind for more. She could tell he thought the same, his mind trembling before her as he prepared for an assault. Reluctant, she pulled back, severing their link as gently as possible. "Thank you, Andri."

He shivered, tears freely flowing down his face.

A wave of disgust for Elisibet washed over Whiskey. "You can go, Andri. Take the rest of the day off, okay?" Andri barely managed a nod. He backed away, giving a half bow before fleeing the room. Whiskey sat back on her heels, shoulders slumped.

"Well?"

Looking up at Margaurethe, she said, "It was Valmont. He almost saw Andri, too."

Castillo frowned. "It's a good thing he didn't, else there'd be three murders on our hands."

"And a bigger mystery," Chano added.

"I can't believe I was so stupid."

Margaurethe came to Whiskey, taking her hand and helping her rise. "You're not stupid. You're young and inexperienced. You'll make mistakes and learn from them as time goes by."

"How many innocents will pay the price for my mistakes?" Whiskey ignored the glances between her advisors. They worried about her looming depression with good cause.

"Some," Castillo said bluntly. "But you'll never make those mistakes again, and fewer will die as a result."

Whiskey resisted the urge to respond in anger. She knew Castillo wouldn't defend himself if she attacked, regardless of what it would do to his mind. He was one of the innocents paying for her mistakes, as was Margaurethe. Perhaps Castillo was right; she certainly remembered that particular lesson.

"Now what?"

Inhaling deeply, Whiskey set aside her black melancholy. Her head ached, and she rubbed the bridge of her nose. "I'm tired. This can all wait until tomorrow. Valmont must realize we'll be on our guard for the next few days, even if he doesn't have a clue we're onto him. I'll deal with it later."

"But, Whiskey—"

"Tomorrow!" she snapped, standing. "Leave me." Unable to ignore the implicit order, Castillo took his leave, Chano following closely behind. Regret filled her heart after they left. "I shouldn't have yelled."

Margaurethe took her hand. "It's to be expected. You've had a very trying few days. Let's see to lunch."

Whiskey allowed herself to be led into her apartment.

CHAPTER TWENTY-FIVE

Margaurethe had insisted Whiskey turn on the lights in her apartment. Instead of brooding in the dark, she moped before a cheery gas fireplace as night fell outside. She sat alone. Margaurethe had gone to the office in her apartment to attend a couple of things with the promise of her return by dinner. Whiskey wasn't hungry, but doubted Margaurethe and Sithathor would let her get away with not eating anything.

How could her world fall apart so quickly?

Cora and Anthony murdered, Valmont witnessed at the scene, funeral rites, assassins, uncontrolled attacks—was it only a handful of days ago that everything felt right? It seemed so much longer. She couldn't believe her level of exhaustion, like she hadn't slept in a week. Of course it had only been that long since things had begun to unravel. Her to-do list mounted faster than she had time to think. Needing the distraction, Whiskey went to her office to locate a pad and pen.

Once more slumped in her living room armchair, she began writing. Valmont needed to be taken into custody first thing in the morning. His actions didn't make any sense, but Andri had seen him at the scene of Cora's and Anthony's murders. If necessary, she would forcibly wrest the memory from Valmont. She shivered, greasy revulsion slipping through her gut at the prospect. It was an abuse of power to take such a gift and pervert it so. But what other choice did she have? She had to confirm that he had been in the building without escort. Was this how Elisibet's atrocities began? Whiskey negated the useless thought, knowing the Sweet Butcher had been a bloodthirsty tyrant long before she had passed out of childhood.

Staring at the paper, she wracked her brain for a distraction. The assassin. Sasha had reported that the Sanguire that had taken a shot at her in Club Express had died from his wounds, never having regained consciousness. He had been one of the India delegates, a low-level aide brought in as an assistant to the assistant of the ambassador. The delegation had extended its utmost apologies for the incident, offering any number of gifts in recompense, up to and including the dead man's family for torture. Whiskey had authorized Chano to respond with thanks, and to sway them from punishing anyone in their party connected with the man. He had been young, barely two hundred forty years old. She was certain he had been compelled by someone older. She remembered his face, the snarl of hatred as he yelled, his eyes dulled of intelligence. "*This is for—*"

Whiskey shook her head, banishing the sight, tapping her pen against the pad. Then there was Sithathor. Whiskey put her free hand flat on the surface of the paper, willing herself to reach through it to the arm of the chair. She tried to recall how she had felt when pressed against the cement wall of the club the night before, losing herself in an unfamiliar tingling that didn't quite make her itch. Focusing on the feeling, she felt it spread across her palm, noting with odd disconnection when her fingers sank through the first layer of paper. Mouth open, she stared, wiggling her fingers to dabble in the almost liquid quality the paper had become. With a jerk, she pulled her hand free. The tingling disappeared, and she rested her palm on the now solid pad.

Whiskey had a lot of questions for her chambermaid, Sithathor. She spoke of the *Gidimam Kissane Lá* as "we," indicating an ongoing society of Sanguire who remained in contact with each other. The fact that she'd known Whiskey's father and grandfather hadn't been a coincidence. Distracted by that thought, Whiskey spoke them aloud for the first time, treasuring the sound. "Gareth Davidson, son of David Sceadson and Enid." She wondered if that made her Jenna Davidson or Garethsdottir, like they named children in Iceland.

Forcing herself back to the present, she jotted down questions for Sithathor, questions she hadn't asked out of initial shock over the assassination attempt and the revelation of her talent. If the Ghost Walkers had knowledge of her father, then why hadn't any come forward to find her when he had died? They were a tight-knit group that had wrapped themselves in secrecy to avoid the world. Had they decided she wasn't one of them, not worth the effort if she couldn't walk through walls like the rest? Had they even been able to come close to finding her in the Oregon foster care system? A jumble of emotions rumbled in her chest—she felt dismay that they had failed to locate her, and a sense of abandonment that they hadn't tried hard enough.

The one question that had always puzzled her—as well as the caseworkers she had been assigned—about the accident that had killed her parents had finally been answered. The same thing had occurred at Club Express last night. She had fallen through the booster seat and chassis of the car, hitting the road as her parents smashed headlong into a semitruck. Why didn't Gareth Davidson try to escape? Wasn't his skill strong enough? Did he decide to stay with his wife in death rather than raise his daughter alone? Whiskey grumbled to herself. She didn't even know if Nahimana Walker was a Ghost Walker. Neither her aunt nor grandmother had actually mentioned her mother's skill. Maybe Nahimana had had no choice but remain in the vehicle that had killed her.

Whiskey stared at the paper. Lots of questions, few answers, and no end in sight. Forcing herself into a practical state of mind, she jotted down people to whom she needed to speak: the India ambassador to accept apologies and suggest his low-level aide wasn't as duplicitous as he assumed; *Ugula* Sasha Kopecki regarding security issues and that convenient express elevator code she had used the night before; her pack needed gathering and reassurance before they went off half-cocked in a misguided attempt to "protect" their leader. She shook her head. "And where the hell is Reynhard?"

With a sigh, she glanced at the clock on the mantel. Margaurethe had been gone for three hours. Whiskey's frown, fast becoming a permanent expression, deepened. A look outside showed full dark, and she smelled something cooking in the kitchen. A tentative probe revealed Sithathor fixing dinner. Margaurethe had said she would only be away for a few minutes. *What's taking so long?* A spark of alarm flared across Whiskey's nerve endings. The loss of Cora had taken place literally under the noses of building security, and they had somehow missed a weapon being brought to the wake. Not liking this train of thought, Whiskey cast out with her mind, searching for the familiar sensation of her lover in the neighboring apartment.

There was nothing there.

Whiskey shot up from her chair, expanding her search to include the entire building. She easily picked up the Sanguire in residence, as well as those still working in the labs down to the fifth floor. From there her coverage was spotty, even for someone of her strength. A sick feeling developed in her belly as she grabbed the nearest phone. Dialing Margaurethe's downstairs office directly, she received no answer. Panicked, she bolted from her apartment, throwing open Margaurethe's door and rushing inside. She searched every room, scaring Margaurethe's Human chambermaid partaking of a light supper alone in the kitchen.

"Where is she?"

Maya leapt to her feet and gave a quick curtsy. "I thought *Ki'an Gasan* was with you, *Ninsumgal*. She said for me not to make dinner for her."

"When?" Whiskey demanded, fear and impatience flaring as the Human stuttered. She moved with preternatural speed to grab Maya by the upper arms, not quite shaking the trembling woman. "*When?*"

"Two hours ago, *Ninsumgal*."

Two hours. Releasing Maya, Whiskey backed away. *Two hours?* She pointed a shaking finger at the chambermaid. "You are not to leave this apartment until Sasha or myself tells you so. Got it?"

Terrified, Maya stared at the floor. "Yes, *Ninsumgal*."

Whirling, Whiskey ran from the apartment and to the security desk in the corridor. "Margaurethe O'Toole is missing! She's either unconscious or she's been kidnapped." She glared at the *aga'us* blinking at her. "Lock down the building. I want an immediate and full physical search of the building."

"Yes, my *Ninsumgal*!" He spoke two words into his radio. "Code Four, *Ki'an Gasan* Margaurethe O'Toole. I repeat, Code Four, *Ki'an Gasan* Margaurethe O'Toole."

Whiskey felt both pleasure and dismay that her *Aga'gída* had trained well enough to have a predetermined radio code for a missing person. Within moments her *Ugula* and a half dozen senior officers came out of the break area tucked behind the security station. Sasha and one other remained with Whiskey, the others dispatched to begin a floor-by-floor search. Sasha ushered Whiskey into the guardroom.

"When was the last time you saw her, *Ninsumgal*?"

Swallowing, Whiskey scanned her surroundings, having never seen its interior before. "About three hours ago. She left for her apartment to check on a few things." The station out front had video feeds from security cameras in the corridor, fire exits and elevators. This area had even more extensive information-gathering equipment, making it the nerve center of her personal guard. She felt a moment's surprise at her house sigil painted on one wall. Written in Latin beneath it was the phrase *In Omnia Paratus*.

Sasha spoke into her radio to convey the information to her team.

Whiskey grabbed Sasha's tunic sleeve. "She's not up here. I scanned all the way down to the R&D system labs and didn't find her."

"We still need to check every floor, *Ninsumgal*. She may be here, but unconscious."

Feeling like an idiot, Whiskey released Sasha, rubbing her face. "Yeah. Right." *I knew that.*

Sasha guided her to a folding chair at a large table. Coffee cups, snack wrappers and paperwork littered its surface. Apparently, they had been having a meeting. "We're doing everything we can to find her, *Ninsumgal*."

Whiskey planted her elbows on the table, and put her face in her hands, fighting the fear beating in her chest. "I know. Find Castillo and Chano, make sure they're safe." She jerked her head up. "And my family! The pack!" As Sasha gave orders over the radio, Whiskey added, "And find Valmont and Reynhard, for Christ's sake. I want to know where they are, and where Valmont has been tonight."

As much as Whiskey wanted to be fully involved in the search, she shut up and stared blankly around the guardroom. Contingencies were in place. One thing Margaurethe had taught her was the need to step back to let her people do their jobs. So she waited, ignoring the coming and going of a number of people, not paying attention when Sasha slipped out to take over the search, praying to God that this was just an embarrassing mistake on her part.

CHAPTER TWENTY-SIX

The hour was late. Whiskey and her advisors had taken over the sixteenth-floor guardroom since no one wanted to allow her to roam the building. Her aunt, grandmother and the members of her pack had been moved to her apartment for their safety. Those governmental delegations that had accepted her hospitality were secure in their quarters until further notice. The search had turned up a number of inconsistencies—the body of a security guard in the garage, a missing vehicle and another absent Sanguire. No one had been able to locate Whiskey's valet, Andri. It was assumed he had been kidnapped along with Margaurethe. Building security had a video from the parking garage, showing Valmont driving the absconded car out of the garage.

Whiskey stared out the window. "I know they hate each other, but how could I have been so wrong about him?" It felt like Rufus Barrett all over again; she'd had faith in him to some degree, and had almost died as a result. *How can I lead if I can't even trust my own judgment?* She saw movement in the window's reflection as Castillo shifted.

A scowl had fast become a permanent addition to the priest's handsome face. "I feel the same. I can't imagine what possessed him to do this. It just—" He ran both hands through his curly hair and leaned back in his folding chair. "It just doesn't seem like him at all."

"Perhaps we should wait to judge him or our supposed failings until we hear his side."

Grimacing, Whiskey turned. She leaned her hands behind her on the windowsill as she looked at Chano. "Which side is that?" She waved at the screen that held the frozen image of Valmont's face behind the windshield of the stolen vehicle. "That he sneaked on the property without checking in with security, went to the garage, and took a car? What would be the point unless Margaurethe and Andri are unconscious in the backseat?" *And why now?*

Chano grunted, a sound with which Whiskey had become familiar over the months. Valmont's caustic wit and flippant reactions had often elicited this response—disapproval. "What would he have to gain?"

"Well, that's it, isn't it?" Whiskey returned to the window. "Nothing. He's had plenty of opportunity to harm me. Maybe he ran into Margaurethe and they got into another argument. Maybe they fought." She refused to voice her darkest concern, but the thought couldn't be denied. *Maybe he killed her, and is running to conceal it.* Apparently no one else wanted to bring up that particular idea, since neither of the men suggested it.

"*Ninsumgal.*" Sasha stepped inside the door, finger against the bud in her ear. "*Sublugal Sañar* Valmont is in custody, and is being transported here. He'll arrive in five minutes."

The news didn't improve Whiskey's mood. If anything, she felt worse than before, adrenaline increasing the tremors in her hands. "Bring him in when he gets here."

Sasha bowed. "As you wish, *Ninsumgal*." She paused a moment, and lifted her chin. "We've found something else."

Whiskey ignored the sick feeling in the pit of her stomach. *Who else is dead?* "Tell me."

"*Sañur Gasum* Reynhard Dorst checked in with security about two hours before *Ki'an Gasan* was noticed missing. He hasn't checked out, and we've been unable to locate him in the building."

"Reynhard?" Whiskey struggled to make the connection. "He hasn't responded to messages in over a week. Why would he turn up tonight and not speak to me?"

Sasha swallowed, chin still raised. "I don't know, *Ninsumgal*."

Rather than torture her *Ugula* with the threat of a royal temper tantrum, Whiskey waved her away. "Keep looking. Enlist anyone who knows his essence, scan every person in the building, Human and Sanguire. If he's hiding here, we'll find him that way."

"Yes, *Ninsumgal*."

As soon as the door closed, Whiskey stared at the others. "If Reynhard's here, why hasn't he checked in with me?"

Castillo chewed his lower lip. "Perhaps he wasn't here."

Chano rumbled in his chair, hands clasped over his belly. "Shape shifter?"

The priest nodded. "Yes."

Whiskey felt disconnected, light-headed. When was the last time she ate? She leaned heavily against the window frame. "You think someone breached security, a *Gúnnumu Bargún*?"

"It would make more sense than *Sublugal Sañar* Valmont sneaking on the property to kidnap your valet and your woman." Chano hooked his thumbs in the belt of his jeans.

Castillo rubbed his forehead with one hand. "That might not even be Valmont." He pointed at the damning evidence of Valmont's treachery, the frozen video of his face in the stolen car.

The only other person Whiskey had reason to suspect was her man-at-arms. "What about Pacal? What talent does he have?"

Chano stared at her. "The Mayan? You think he has something to do with this?"

She swallowed, not wanting to play into the American Indian's prejudices but unable to think of anyone else who had regular access to the building and possible motive. "I don't know. He's very…rough in training. He seems to target me and Nupa more than any of the others."

"He's not a shape changer." Castillo shook his head. "His talent lies with weather."

"But how do you know?" Whiskey considered the evening's multiple disturbances. "I can't believe Reynhard would put a crack security department together without paying attention to some sort of precaution."

"He didn't." Castillo dropped his hands to his lap. "That's why I so rarely leave the building. All *Gúnnumu Bargúni* living here are registered, and all Sanguire are put through a rigorous examination before being allowed re-entry. That's how I know Pacal isn't one—I've seen him come and go without the need for the extra testing."

The news startled her. Curious despite the current circumstances, she studied Castillo. "What sort of examination?"

A knock at the door precluded his response. Sasha entered, holding the door open for Valmont and four of Whiskey's *aga'gída* to enter.

"Whiskey? What is the meaning of this?" Valmont raised his handcuffed wrists, affronted. "I was having dinner at Tribulations when these goons descended upon my table and arrested me! None of them will answer my questions."

Great. I didn't think to give them different orders if he was in public. Rampant rumors had probably spread throughout the city that the budding *ninsumgal* was arresting her advisory council. *Shades of the Sweet Butcher. As if I don't have enough to worry about.* "Where were you for the last three hours?"

"What?" Valmont yanked his arms from the grip of the guard on his left. "I just told you. I was having dinner."

Castillo cocked his head. "For three hours? How many courses did you have?"

Valmont sneered. "No one's speaking to you, eunuch." He returned his attention to Whiskey. "So I had a couple of drinks beforehand, and was looking for a little snack after. What of it?"

Whiskey walked to the computer screen on the security panel and pointed. "According to that video, you were here just over an hour ago, and stole a car from the garage." As he stared in shock, she added, "There's no record of you checking in with security, we have visual evidence you stole a car, three people are missing, and one is dead."

The indignation drained out of him as he took in her words. "Who's dead?"

"One of the security staff stationed in the garage. His neck's been broken. Not a drop of blood spilled."

"And who is missing?"

It took every ounce of control Whiskey had to keep from attacking him, or anyone else. "Reynhard, Andri and Margaurethe."

Valmont stared blankly at her, lips silently moving as he repeated the names. He attempted to step forward, but was held back by a guard on his right. Tugging, he glared over his shoulder at the man.

"Let him go."

As soon as he was free, Valmont took two steps, staying well out of reach of Whiskey as he knelt to the floor. "You have my word, my *Ninsumgal.* I had nothing to do with this. I wasn't here."

Whiskey studied him. This was the first time he knelt in her presence of his own accord; even his oath of fealty several months ago could have been considered coercion. She let the sight of him blur in her gaze. The telltale indication of a lie wasn't there. He told the truth as he knew it. What if someone stronger compelled him, like Reynhard? Was it possible to plant false memories? She hated the thought, but Dorst's sudden reappearance was suspect. Though the idea of the betrayal hurt almost as bad as losing Margaurethe, she had to consider that her master spy might have changed his allegiance. "I can find out. I can look inside your mind, Valmont."

Trepidation cleared his features, and he leaned back on his heels. When he spoke, his voice was droll, as though he didn't believe her. "Really?"

"Yes." She moved closer to him, waving back the sudden surge of guards preparing to surround her. "We can do this the hard way, or not. I'd prefer to not hurt you."

Valmont studied her, a worried frown on his face and what looked oddly like relief in his eyes. After long thought, he raised his chin. "All right. Do what you need to do."

Whiskey paused, then ordered security from the room. Castillo and Chano joined forces, preparing to give her the added strength she would need should Valmont decide to revoke permission to enter his mind. "Just relax. It's kind of like joining to some degree. Then I'll go a little deeper to look at your most recent memories." Sweat had popped up on Valmont's forehead. Whiskey frowned. Considering their mutual past, it was no wonder he was almost as nervous as Andri had been with the prospect. "I won't go digging around, okay? Just the last few hours. Maybe the day of Cora's and Anthony's murders."

Valmont gave her a stiff nod, then raised his chin.

The difference between this excursion and Andri's was stark. With her valet, it had been a dim and tenuous thing, always seeming on the verge of collapse. Here, Valmont actively strengthened their bond though he didn't control it. She looked out of his eyes as he ate a serving of beef stroganoff, tasting the mushrooms that flavored the dish. The night was young, and she had no meeting scheduled until the morrow. As she finished, a waitress arrived to top off her glass of burgundy. Feeling sated, she leaned back and swirled the glass, watching the sweet young *kizarusi* on the dance floor. *Perhaps a little snack.*

Another odd tidbit to file away; with Andri, Whiskey had been a third party witnessing what occurred. Here she became Valmont, seeing things from his point of view as he went through his day. She wondered if this changed from person to person.

Valmont told the truth. He'd had nothing to do with kidnappings and killings, didn't even have a care in the world regarding knowledge of an attack. Whiskey scrutinized the memory closer, sifting through his thoughts. Something about Bertrada Nijmege caused anger and sorrow, not unexpected considering their past. The sight of an African contingent at a nearby table brought up cold calculation over recent disagreements during treaty negotiations. Disdain for a number of what he considered low-lifes hanging about the bar. Nothing more.

Prodding a bit, she introduced a vision of Dorst into his mind, and received an instant ripple of fear. That surprised her. Had Dorst threatened Valmont? As much as she wanted to delve into the topic, she had promised to leave him his privacy. She had confirmed his alibi as well as proved to herself that he'd had nothing to do with tonight's abduction. She eased back out of his mind, until she was conscious of sitting on the floor in front of him. Whiskey took a deep breath, and stretched. "Get someone in here to release him. He has nothing to do with it."

Several minutes passed as Valmont's handcuffs were removed. Whiskey returned to her station at the window, staring out over the city, feeling hollow. When they were once again alone, she turned to study them.

"Do we have any leads?" Valmont asked, his voice stern with fury.

Whiskey found his response familiar. "The only solid one we had was you showing up on video." An odd sense of peace drifted over her at his outrage. Many were the memories of just such an incident, Elisibet furious at some slight or other, Valmont standing beside her, righteously echoing her sentiments. This was as it should be. It felt right. *And there lies the danger. Regardless of Elisibet's friendship with him, he's still an unknown.*

Chano grunted. "No, we have more. Reynhard checks into the building after being missing for so long. He doesn't respond to messages or phone calls, yet cannot be located within."

Castillo pursed his lips as he stared at the video image of Valmont. "And he is *Gúnnumu Bargún*. He could have assumed Valmont's shape to throw off pursuit."

Andri remembered seeing Valmont going in to Cora's apartment. Was that Reynhard, too? Whiskey fought the sudden urge to rage and cry.

"So what do you think happened?"

"That's rather obvious, isn't it, Padre?" Valmont said. "Margaurethe ran into Reynhard, and the valet showed up at the wrong place and time. The guard was killed when he interfered in Reynhard's escape."

Castillo, perhaps becoming inured to Valmont's caustic wit and older strength, scoffed in derision. "Where did Margaurethe meet her abductor? It's possible he got the jump on Andri, but Margaurethe would have known something was wrong."

Whiskey's thumb tapped restlessly on the windowsill. "Unless he looked like the guard. If he's a shape shifter, he could have taken any form and Margaurethe wouldn't have had a clue unless she tried to scan him."

"True. Even among others of my talent, Dorst's abilities are legendary," Castillo murmured.

Valmont growled. "We have to find him before he does her any harm."

"And how do we do that?"

Whiskey forced herself to remain composed when all she wanted to do was attack something. "Reynhard might be able to come and go anywhere he pleases and in whatever disguise he prefers, but certainly he doesn't hide his travels elsewhere around the city. Someone is bound to have seen him; who could forget it with his clothes and hair?"

Eagerness lit Valmont's expression. "Let me hunt for him."

"No." She shook her head at his flash of anger. "I think his ability to shift is extensive and automatic. He changes from one person to another in the time it takes one of us to walk one step in front of the other. If he sees you before you see him, by the time you turn around, he'll be someone else."

Valmont ground his teeth, but accepted her refusal, exposing his throat.

"Then who?" Castillo asked. "He knows all of us. Besides, it's one thing for a priest to wander the streets at night to reach the unfortunates. It's quite another for one to saunter into Sanguire nightclubs and the like."

Whiskey stared at him.

"What?"

"It couldn't be that simple." She turned to Valmont.

He picked up her thought. "It could be. I know of two other establishments in town, but it's for the less...extravagant of our people."

Chano tilted his head. "You think Dorst has been hanging out at another club in his current guise?" Their expressions gave him the answer.

"But, that's ridiculous! Why would he do something as idiotic as that?" Castillo held his hands in front of him, palms up. "He can look like anyone, why would he remain in his current form in a public place?"

"Reynhard has always liked games, Padre." Whiskey stopped drumming the sill. "It would be just like him to set me a trail of breadcrumbs to locate him."

"And Margaurethe is the bait?"

At Valmont's words, a surge of rage pounded against Whiskey's containment. *If he's responsible for this, if he's hurt her...* She gritted her teeth to keep from baring her fangs. "Very effective. Reynhard never misses an opportunity."

"Then what happened to Andri?" Castillo wondered aloud.

"Who knows?" Valmont shrugged. "The mouse no doubt stumbled onto the abduction. It wouldn't take much for Reynhard to overtake him."

Whiskey remembered the depth of power she felt in Andri earlier. She would bet that he and Reynhard were very close to one another in strength. Would it have been so easy for him to be thwarted? She felt a stab of guilt, knowing it was entirely possible; Elisibet had broken Andri so well he might not defend against attack by his "betters."

"Padre, I want you to gather your resources. Send contacts into Tribulations and anywhere else Valmont knows. We need to locate Reynhard, or at least get an idea of where he's holed up. I doubt Margaurethe is there, but it could give us a place to start."

Castillo stood and bowed. "Anything else?"

She didn't want to say it, but knew she had no choice. "If you could search the morgues and hospitals, as well? I don't think I can."

"Of course." Castillo raised his chin. "I'll put out the word for Andri, too. Perhaps he did see something, and ran in fear. I'll need to use a phone."

Whiskey didn't want to be in the room to overhear those calls. She strode across the room and opened the door. Four *Aga'gída* jumped to attention in the hall. Leading her entourage down the now crowded corridor, she stepped into the foyer joining her residence with Margaurethe's. "There's a phone in

Margaurethe's apartment, Padre. Take your time. I'll be in mine when you're finished."

Castillo nodded and slipped inside.

Valmont pulled a cell phone from his pocket. "If you don't mind, I'd like to make a couple of calls, as well?"

"Sure." Whiskey gestured to Margaurethe's door. "You can do it in there. There's plenty of room. I'll see you when you're finished?"

"Oh, yes."

Whiskey stood in the tiny foyer, not alone. Her guards hovered close, a constant reminder of how bad things had gotten in such a short time.

CHAPTER TWENTY-SEVEN

Once he had given Castillo the locations of the appropriate businesses, Valmont slipped into another room to make his call. He ignored the Victorian dining room, scanning it only long enough to confirm he was alone. The cell phone was new, bought a day or two after destroying the previous one. He had been out of contact with Nijmege long enough for her to have become irritated, no doubt. This call wouldn't be a pleasant one. Considering what he wanted to tell her, he didn't think she would take his news well anyway. As her phone rang, he calculated the time, knowing it would be late morning there.

"Ah, Bertrada! You're home!"

"Valmont?"

He grinned at her sharp tone. After centuries of association, he easily saw her in his mind, bristling with agitation, pacing whatever room she occupied as she twisted her thick braid with one hand. "How have you been, Bertrada? Well, I trust?"

"How dare you!"

She seemed a bit more put out than usual, too much so for his lack of communication. Puzzled, he decided to play the game. "Well, you know me. I'm a daring kind of man."

"You're no man at all! I wish to God Nahib had never met you, never brought you into our home. You were a traitor then and you're a traitor now."

Thoroughly confused, Valmont sat on the edge of a spindly chair. He hadn't heard that sort of vitriol from her in some time, not since Elisibet had executed Nahib, a deed which Valmont had been unable to stop. "You're not making sense, Bertrada. Maybe you should start at the beginning."

"You bastard! How could you have taken her hunting when you've told me time and again you couldn't get her away from the estate?"

Valmont's eyes closed. *Shit.* "Who told you?"

"I have my sources."

"I'm sure you do," he said, annoyed. "Was it your new little friend on the *Agrun Nam*? McCall?" She didn't respond immediately, and Valmont knew he had scored a point.

"I don't know what you're talking about." Her outrage cooled.

Valmont's smile was crooked. "I'm sure you don't."

"If you're calling to gloat, Valmont, I suggest you hang up. You have bigger worries ahead."

Her words set off alarm bells. "Bigger worries? What do you mean?"

"I mean that soon our young *ninsumgal* will know exactly what kind of man you are."

The threat caused his mouth to go dry, and he stood. He refused to give her the satisfaction of reacting, though his thoughts were spinning. "Is that so? Well, I suppose she'll be happy to know the true merit of two of the *sanari* she'll be dealing with, as well."

Nijmege laughed, a nasty sound that skittered across his spine. "Like she'll believe you! Chances are good you'll be long dead by the time she realizes the truth. I know what she did to Margaurethe; you think she'll stop when she attacks you?"

Valmont swallowed, the recent experience of Whiskey rooting through his mind a grim reminder. For decades after killing Elisibet, he had puzzled over why she had refused to mentally defend herself. It wasn't as if he had any more defenses than anyone else. He had eventually come to the conclusion that she had iron control from years of experience and truly didn't want to destroy his mind, despite the fact that he destroyed her body. Whiskey didn't have that level of control to refrain from blasting his mind into a bubbling gray mass. Nor did she have centuries of loyalty and friendship to dissuade her.

That may be a blessing.

"Maybe she won't stop, but I'll be damned sure she knows about the plot you have against her, Bertrada. I'll give her all the gory little details. She'll know everything I know and everything I suspect about you and your little playmate. Hell, I'll even tell her you have something to do with Margaurethe's kidnapping as a bonus."

"What? What kidnapping? I don't know anything about a kidnapping!"

It was his turn to laugh. "Certainly by now you have some idea who's working behind your back to kill her. The priest is making calls now; I expect one of them will be to Bentoncourt. We believe the assassin may be Reynhard Dorst and that he kidnapped Margaurethe tonight."

"Dorst?" Her shout was loud enough that he jerked the phone away from his ear. "That's preposterous!"

A mirror on the wall showed his grin was more a death's head grimace as he sank back onto the chair. "He knows about you and me, Bertrada. How else did I find out about McCall?"

Silence. He didn't know how to feel; terror for his impending exposure, relief that the game would soon be truly over, or gritty happiness at possibly thwarting the plans set in motion so long ago. He would receive his punishment for killing Elisibet, a richly deserved reward to end his monotonous existence. And maybe Whiskey would live to be a better ruler. "I called to tell you I quit," Valmont said. "I plan on spilling my guts—both figuratively as well as literally, if necessary—to Whiskey as soon as we locate Margaurethe and get her back. If Whiskey can use the information against you, all the better. You've become a crazy and bitter old woman, Bertrada. Elisibet is dead. Killing Whiskey will not make things better. Nahib is gone. Accept that."

She sputtered her fury over the phone, unable to speak.

A wave of sadness swept over him, coupled with a bone-deep exhaustion. "Nahib would never have wanted to see you this way."

That ended the discussion. She shrieked at him and the line went dead.

Nahib wouldn't have wanted to see his protégé this way, either. Valmont turned off his phone and slipped it into his pocket. He felt hollow, as if he didn't know who he was anymore. But then, he hadn't been himself since Elisibet had executed Nahib for speaking common sense. Slowly rising, feeling his true age of six hundred plus years, he went to the door and opened it.

Castillo stood quietly on the other side. The expression on his face was alien and it took Valmont a few moments to place it. Anger.

"Are you going to tell Whiskey or am I?"

***

Castillo braced himself for an attack. He didn't know if he'd survive it, but consoled himself with the fact that at least Whiskey would know of Valmont's actions by the evidence of Castillo's death. Hopefully, she would realize the second traitor in their midst.

He had finished his phone calls quickly, only having a few to make. One was to an associate on the police force to begin the process of locating Dorst, the other to a woman on the city council who would search various outlets for Margaurethe's wounded or dead body. Upon hanging up the phone, he had overheard Valmont's argument with someone he called Bertrada. There was only one Bertrada with whom he could be fighting.

"I'll tell her." Valmont's voice sounded weary.

Castillo blinked. At the very least he had expected denial, at the most a desperate attack. This quiet acceptance was foreign to his experience with the volatile man before him. Was he playing with him, perhaps hoping Castillo would change his mind or take pity?

"If you overheard enough, you also know that I planned on telling her anyway." Valmont closed the apartment door and proceeded through Margaurethe's sitting room.

"Wait." He circled Valmont to stand before him. "You'd do that? You'd confess to her all that you know, all that you're involved in?"

Familiar impatience curled Valmont's lip. "That's what I said, Padre."

Castillo's thirst for knowledge far outweighed anything in his life, running an embarrassingly close second to God Himself. Here was a puzzle to which he had to know the answer. "Why?"

"Because she deserves better than to be stabbed in the back twice," Valmont said, his tone long-suffering. "She deserves to have people like you and Chano around her, good and honorable people. Not worn-out old traitors like me." His minimal levels of tolerance at an end, Valmont shouldered past and continued on his way.

Castillo ruminated over Valmont's words. By the time he hastened to catch up, Valmont was already in the foyer leading to Whiskey's quarters. Two *aga'gída* stood in the corridor, and Whiskey's seething anger and worry blanketed the area. Castillo sped after him, reaching the door at the same time as Valmont. "Wait!"

Valmont stopped in place, shoulders slumped, eyes looking askance at the ceiling. "What?"

Mindful of the attentive security, Castillo took Valmont by the arm and pulled him back the way they had come. He was surprised when Valmont acquiesced, following his lead. Once back inside Margaurethe's sitting room, he closed the door. "Why did you come here at all?"

Valmont's exasperated expression cleared, a smile growing. "You always have questions, Padre. And all those books. You're a research junkie, aren't you?"

Castillo called up his previous anger at Valmont's duplicity. "You're evading the question."

Valmont raised his hands in a supplicating gesture. "All right. Bertrada Nijmege called me when word of Whiskey reached the *Agrun Nam*. She insisted I ascertain whether or not Mahar's Prophecy was coming true."

"And?"

"And—" Valmont pursed his lips in thought, no longer seeing the priest standing before him. "I didn't believe it. Didn't want to. But then I saw her." He clicked his tongue and shook his head, eyes sparking with humor. "She's the mirror image of Elisibet. It's like seeing a ghost, Padre; a living, breathing ghost."

Castillo said nothing, letting Valmont remain caught up in his recollections.

"But the ghost has memory loss. Half the time she scares the hell out of me with the things she says. I remember my friend, I can see her, alive and well despite my actions. The rest of the time, she's so innocent, so naive. She's nothing like Elisibet and I very much doubt she ever will be." Valmont's eyes focused on Castillo. "That's why I planned on telling her about Bertrada. Whiskey doesn't deserve to die before she's had a chance to prove what she can do. And I'm certain she can do so much more for our people than Elisibet or the *Agrun Nam* ever did."

Too many months of dealing with Valmont's snide attitude and sardonic humor had done its work. Castillo wasn't sure whether to trust this information or not. Was it truly what Valmont felt, or was this a ruse to keep him off guard? "If that's the case, then why did you stay?"

Valmont shrugged one shoulder, his countenance darkening. "I still don't truly believe it. Besides, what difference would it make? She's dead the minute the *Agrun Nam* get their hands on her. I didn't expect her to refuse to go or to keep me around. When that happened, Bertrada insisted I find a way to secretly return Whiskey for her version of revenge. It was easier to agree than to argue with the shrew."

Castillo glared intently at the man before him. "What's *changed*?"

They stared at one another.

"I murdered my *Ninsumgal*, my best friend. Whiskey is my *Ninsumgal*, almost literally the child of my best friend. I will never, ever do such a thing again. In my grief and anger, I made a horrible mistake and I refuse to do so once more."

"Even if it causes your death?"

"Even then."

Castillo inhaled deeply, his stern expression softening. "Maybe you should tell her that."

A familiar grin broke out on Valmont's face. "You're funny, Padre. Why did she want an oath from an oath breaker? Unless you think the process amused her? It was good for a giggle the day I swore fealty, and probably will be several decades down the road."

"Perhaps. But I know Whiskey to be a kind person, one to give her people opportunity to rectify their errors. As you said, she's not Elisibet."

A knock on the door interrupted them.

"Sirs? *Ninsumgal* Whiskey awaits you in her sitting room."

"We'll be right there," Valmont called out. Returning attention to Castillo, he studied the man. "What are you suggesting? That I bow my stiff and prideful neck, give her another vow of loyalty?"

"Yes."

"My vow is no good. She remembers the first one I broke."

"She also remembers why it was broken. I've had plenty of opportunity to discuss history with her. Whiskey feels that Elisibet was a horrible person, and she struggles daily to be better."

"Elisibet wasn't horrible," Valmont said in automatic defense. "She had her reasons for being what she was, some of them revolving around me."

"Perhaps." They stood in silence. "We'd better go before she comes looking."

Valmont nodded and opened the door. "Let's see if I survive the next ten minutes."

"I think you'll be surprised."

His laugh held a slight edge. "Or you'll be, Padre."

CHAPTER TWENTY-EIGHT

It took a quarter hour before Nijmege calmed herself enough to speak coherently. Valmont's betrayal laid waste to her current scheme. Without someone inside Davis's organization to seize and deliver her to Nijmege's doorstep, little else could be done. She should have pushed to accept the *Baruñal* Ceremony invitation.

She caught sight of herself in her dressing room mirror and stared. She had never been considered a beauty—the strong lines of her nose and jaw gave her face a masculine cast she had long rued. After one too many lonesome dances seated along the wall with the other unattractive girls, she had made the decision to prove her worth in other ways. Logical discourse, political rallying and a potent wit had become her weapons of choice. Her disdain for courtly prattle garnered the attention of Nahib, the *Nam Lugal* of the ruling council. With him Nijmege had never felt ugly.

Her muddy brown eyes shone with unshed tears, and the lump in her throat burned. "Enough of that!" Nijmege turned away from the mirror, pushing away the crippling depression. She gathered her anger about her, carefully wrapping it about sorrow, protecting it from exposure.

With her emotions under control, she searched the room for the cell phone she had thrown across it. Fortunately, it hadn't broken in her rage, having squarely hit the clothes hanging in an open wardrobe. She found the thing amongst her shoes and dialed a number from memory.

"Mmm, yes? What is it?" The voice was furry from sleep. The hour was still early enough that those who preferred a lazy sleep-in could partake of one.

"I've just had a call from Valmont." Nijmege closed her eyes, cloaking her vision in order to focus.

There came the sound of rustling as McCall came awake. "Does he have her?"

Nijmege gritted her teeth. "He quit."

After a pause, McCall said, "Excuse me?"

"He quit! He said he wouldn't do it. I confronted him about the hunting trip he had taken the bitch on, and the bastard told me he wouldn't bring her to me! He said he was going to tell her about our plot against her. And that's not all."

"What else?"

"Apparently Margaurethe O'Toole has been kidnapped. The snake said he was going to tell Davis that I was somehow responsible for that, too."

"What?" McCall's voice came sharp and clear, no hint of sleep in its tone.

"They think Dorst did it." She shook her head, gripping her braid tightly in one hand. "Though I don't see how that's possible. Dorst had been in love with Elisibet since she was a child." She tugged her hair hard enough to cause little stabs of pain in her scalp. "He's been at Davis's side for this long; I thought he believed her claim."

"As did I."

A tone came over her phone, and she pulled it away to check the caller ID. "Lionel's calling. That blasted priest probably reported to him. I guarantee he'll be setting up another emergency meeting."

"Talk to him. I'm getting dressed now. I'll see you in chambers."

They had worked together long enough that there was no need for standard farewells between them. Nijmege disconnected the call, her cell phone immediately ringing through. She took a deep breath, calming herself, and answered. "Yes?"

"Bertrada? If you were sleeping, I'm sorry to wake you."

She almost snorted her derision as she looked around the dressing room. "I was already up."

"Oh." Bentoncourt paused a moment. "I've just heard from Father Castillo in Oregon. It seems someone has made another attempt on Davis's life, and has abducted Margaurethe O'Toole."

"You're joking." She rolled her eyes and began searching for something to wear.

Bentoncourt was oblivious to her scorn. "We've nothing scheduled for today. I'm calling an emergency meeting to discuss this. When can you get here?"

"I must dress first. An hour?"

"Good. I'm already here; hadn't left the office yet. I'll call the others."

She frowned, pausing in her hunt. It was nearly ten in the morning. He had spent all night in the office? Whatever for? "All right. I'll be there."

They said their goodbyes, and she tossed the phone onto the nearby table. Perhaps she would be able to salvage something of this mess. *If I can't reach her from outside the country, perhaps I should arrange a personal visit.* The thought cheered her as she pulled out her clothing.

***

He gritted his teeth as he dialed the number from memory. The heated interior of the limousine was soundproofed; he had no worry that his driver would overhear the conversation.

"Hello?"

"What the hell do you think you're doing?"

"Why, I'm doing the job you sent me to do, guv."

The response held a flippant note and the muscles of his jaw jumped. "You've kidnapped *Ki'an Gasan* O'Toole, you idiot! You'd better not harm her, or you'll wish you had never met me."

Laughter. "Oh, no worries there, certainly! I already wish I'd never met you. Unfortunately, I gave my word and I'll do the job."

His nostrils flared. "Why did you kidnap her?"

"Well, you did say I'd have an easier time of it if I got the target away from her estate. What better way than to steal the love of her life? She'll come running, make no mistake, and the job will be done." The assassin's tone of voice implied the rest of the sentence; that he would then be free to follow through on his threat to his employer.

"I was told you were a professional, but ever since I hired you, you've mucked things up! You let at least one golden opportunity to complete your contract get away. Now you've created a situation to put Davis's entire security on guard against you. How do you expect to do the job now? Can you turn invisible? Walk through walls? I thought you were *Gúnnumu Bargún*, not *Gidimam Kissane Lá*."

"Calm down, guv! You didn't have all these stipulations when you hired me, you know. You wanted the job done, and I said I'd do it. Now butt out and let me do my work."

"Then do it. Time's running out." He hung up the cellular phone, knuckles whitening as he held it tight. Staring out the window, he tried unsuccessfully to regain his equilibrium. Until he could control his anger, he couldn't return to the *Agrun Nam*.

Pending Davis's death, his plans remained on hold. He'd never expected the youngling to drop everything in Portland and come running upon command, unlike most of the council who seemed to believe their word remained law. Despite this, his plan couldn't continue forward until she was dead. Once the deed was done, he could produce evidence that Bentoncourt was responsible for murdering the last best hope for the Sanguire people. That would destabilize the Europeans enough for him to take control. His Russian allies only awaited his word. If it didn't happen soon enough, however, the *Agrun Nam* might uproot themselves and move across the ocean to begin political negotiations with the upstart, ruining all for which he had worked.

This assassin turned rabid worried him. He knew the man was a shape shifter, able to make himself into anyone he wished. It would be easy for him to slip inside the security net and make good the threat he had made at their last contact. But would he? After an exhaustive background check, he had learned that the assassin was the quintessential professional. That was the only reason he had been hired for the job.

Ah, this was getting to be such a mess! If Davis didn't die soon, it would all be moot. If this assassin attempted to bite the hand that paid him, he would have to hire someone else to take care of it. Would that person be as unpredictable and willing to ruin future reputation by attacking an employer? If, if, if! And what of Bentoncourt? What if he convinced the others to displace themselves and attend Davis in the New Country? If this final bid to remove Davis failed, perhaps it would be best to leave Nijmege to her revenge. At least the deed would be done, though he'd be no closer to his goal of becoming the ultimate authority over the European Sanguire.

Calming somewhat at this turn of thought, he glanced at the phone in his hand, surprised to see blood. He had squeezed so hard, the plastic had cracked, sending a shard into his palm. With a mild curse, he dropped the useless electronics onto the floorboard, and pulled a handkerchief from his pocket to wrap the wound. His concern had always been that Davis would stand before the *Agrun Nam* and sway them with her presence; that with word and deed she would make them understand the truth of who she was, and compel them to follow her. If the assassin failed, perhaps he himself should assist Bertrada in her goals. Not only would his goal be met, as well as hers, but the *Agrun Nam* would begin its fall with the murder of their young *Ninsumgal* directly staining their hands.

Alternate plans and thoughts filled his mind, the ache in his hand hardly noticeable. Tapping on the window between he and the driver, he indicated his desire to head to the *Agrun Nam* offices. Perhaps this would all work out for the best.

A grim smile crossed his face as he stared unseeing at passing scenery.

***

Whiskey didn't have the patience to deal with anyone, and her people prudently understood that. The younger members of her pack had taken over the sitting area, playing a violent video game and making bets on who would kick whose ass next. The absence of Cora still echoed across the pack to the point that the armchair Cora would have normally occupied remained empty, though the couch was too crowded by far. The older Sanguire—her aunt, grandmother and Chano—sat around the dining table, drinking strong coffee. They were entrenched in a conversation with Sithathor who was learning the fine art of making Indian fry bread. Equidistant between gatherings, Whiskey fought her fear and fury, forcing herself to stillness lest she shake apart from the urge to destroy everything and everyone.

She surged to her feet at the appearance of Castillo and Valmont. The adults quieted, but the younglings continued their game, perhaps becoming a little rowdier at the potential for bad news. Whiskey gestured for the two to follow her into her apartment, nodding at Chano's quizzical expression to include him. Once in her office, the door closed behind them, she spun around. "Well?"

"I've made the necessary phone calls, my *Ninsumgal*." Castillo bowed. "We should hear soon from my contacts."

Some underlying current in the room felt odd. Whiskey wondered if her fury had anything to do with the priest's deference. Here in the privacy of her office, she thought he would abandon his formal behavior as he had in the past. Chano gave Castillo a searching look, before hobbling to a chair to sit down. Whiskey looked at Valmont, and frowned. Did he seem stiffer?

"I've made my call as well, my *Ninsumgal*."

She blinked at the title coming from his lips. A trickle of dread ran icy through her heart. Automatically, she mentally scanned them both, relieved neither was Reynhard in disguise. "What's wrong? Why do you call me that?"

Valmont didn't answer. Instead, he approached and knelt at her feet.

Fear mixed with her trepidation. He had willingly bent his knee to her once tonight, and now again. She glanced at Castillo, finding intense compassion in his eyes. "Get up, Valmont. There's no time for this."

"If I don't do this now, *Ninsumgal*, I never will. Please. Allow me the opportunity."

Castillo gave a slow nod, guiding Whiskey through the puzzling circumstances.

She returned her attention to Valmont. "Say what you have to say."

He sighed, whether from relief she would listen or resignation, she couldn't say. "I once gave this oath to my best friend and *Ninsumgal*, Elisibet. At the time, I was young and impetuous. I didn't understand the true meaning of the words, or that I'd break that vow so thoroughly."

Whiskey recalled the first time Valmont had been presented to Elisibet and shrugged. "That's in the past, Valmont. And you've already sworn allegiance to me. What does it have to do with the situation now?" What indeed? Her mind worried the connection.

He peered up at her. "Please, let me finish." When she didn't interrupt, he dropped his gaze to the floor and continued. "I've had centuries to contemplate my actions and mistakes. I've changed considerably from those rash decisions, from my inability to control my emotions. I want you to know, I refuse to break my oath again."

Whiskey realized he somehow felt responsible for Margaurethe's kidnapping. Why? They'd already confirmed he had nothing to do with it. She held her mental breath as he spoke, teetering on the razor's edge of emotion where she could tumble either direction—destructive fury or an implosion of grief.

"I told Elisibet I had a willingness to follow her to the ends of this earth and beyond. But I didn't follow. I ushered my friend into the darkness of death with betrayal and the sword with which I had sworn to protect her. I've lived with that knowledge too long." Again he breathed deeply, his shoulders slumping. "I offer this solemn oath from an oath breaker, *Ninsumgal* Jenna Davis. I know I've done this already, but I think it needs doing again. I, *Sublugal Sañar* Valmont, swear that I will never raise my hand against you and yours, that I will die at your hand or at your behest or in the defense of you and yours, that I will follow you beyond should you pass the veil before me."

The grief seemed to be winning as her vision blurred. She cleared her throat, working past the knot there. "And I swear to treat you with all the integrity and honor with which you treat me, *Sublugal Sañar* Valmont." She faltered a moment, glancing at Castillo and Chano. Much as she would love to add that she would never attack Valmont, she couldn't say such a thing. Circumstances could change, just as they had in Elisibet's time. Sniffling, she added, "I swear to treat you honestly and fairly in all things, no matter the cost."

Valmont's chuckle was dry and weak. "You might want to renege on that last."

Regaining her emotions, Whiskey wiped at her eyes. "Get up, and tell me what the hell is going on here."

He didn't rise though he boldly met her gaze. "I throw myself on the mercy of your court, *Ninsumgal*. My mission here has been traitorous toward you."

The immediate thought that he had something to do with Margaurethe's disappearance after all lit a fire in her heart. Only supreme effort kept her rational enough to remember his echoing fury at the kidnapping. "Clarify your statement, Valmont."

"I knew of *Aga Maskim Sañar* Nijmege's plans for you. She originally contacted me to come here and verify your existence. When it proved you were Elisibet reborn, she insisted I help return you to her so that she might gain the revenge she so dearly seeks."

Whiskey stepped away, confused. This had nothing to do with Margaurethe. "Why are you telling me this now?"

"Because the phone call I made was to tell her I quit. I'll not be party to the killing of an innocent, which is what you are." Valmont watched her as she leaned against her desk. "And because I believe Reynhard knew of my connection with Bertrada and didn't tell you."

"What?" Castillo sounded shocked.

"Yes. When he reported about the assassin, he made mention of Bertrada's goals and all but told me he was aware of my duplicity." Valmont raised his chin to Whiskey. "Why wouldn't he tell you such a thing? At the very least, he would have told you privately about his suspicions, wouldn't he?"

Was this further proof of Dorst's true nature, or simply an indication of his enjoyment of the game? It would be just like him to toy with Valmont this way. There was no love lost between her advisors of old; aside from Valmont and Margaurethe who had been the best of friends before Elisibet's murder, all her other advisors had been at each other's throats. Elisibet had fostered the dissension among them to retain control. If anything, the news of Valmont's involvement with Nijmege pulled Whiskey from her angry funk. Valmont still knelt on the floor, and she felt a stab of irritation. "Oh, stand up, Valmont. My knees ache just looking at you."

Slowly, he stood, frowning. "I'm willing to accept any punishment."

"I'm sure you are, but I don't see any reason to punish you. You did what you thought was necessary." Whiskey lifted an eyebrow. "We start from here." She almost laughed at the expression on his face, one of dismay mixed with a healthy dose of wonder. "Besides, I need you strong and healthy when we find Reynhard. Once we locate him, we find Margaurethe and Andri, and get our pound of flesh."

"Each?" Chano asked.

Whiskey's twisted smile expressed her opinion. "He'll be lucky to have any flesh left when I'm through with him."

***

Whiskey paced her office. The phone sat ominously silent on her desk. Castillo had pulled a few books from her private library, and sat surrounded by open volumes on the couch around him. Chano perused one of them, occasionally murmuring ideas and suggestions to the priest. Valmont paced at the other end of the room, still edgy from his confession and oath.

She still felt the shock of surprise when she looked at him. It had never occurred to her that he would work for Nijmege again after the last fiasco. Of course, it put everything into clearer perspective. Her sudden concern and distrust at Tribulations during their hunting lesson had been valid. He had still been seated on the fence's edge regarding whether or not to carry through with Nijmege's plan. Whiskey was glad to know her instincts had been right; it eased the growing doubts she had experienced over recent events. Regardless of the justification, it didn't help now. Those much-touted Sanguire instincts still insisted that Dorst had absolutely nothing to do with Margaurethe's kidnapping, regardless of all the evidence against him. But why else would he not tell her of Valmont's deceit? While it was true that Dorst enjoyed his little games, would he have withheld information that could have been dangerous to her? If he was the assassin, then indeed he would. But if he wasn't? Could it be because he already knew Valmont well enough to know that Valmont wouldn't follow through?

Her heart flipped when the phone rang, both she and Valmont freezing in their tracks to stare at it. Castillo stood and strode across the room to snap up the receiver. "Yes?" Whiskey extended her hearing to catch the report despite the rudeness of eavesdropping.

"Sir, we've had reports of a man matching the description you gave us living at the Hollywood downtown."

She almost bit through her lip in surprise and pleasure. The Hollywood was a ramshackle, low-income hotel. The business rented rooms by the week. Junkies, punks and the occasionally flush street person resided there. Even Whiskey had spent a night or two at the Hollywood in her early days to take the rare shower when panhandling had paid off exceedingly well.

"Do you have a room number?"

The voice gave one and, before Castillo could even hang up the phone, both Whiskey and Valmont were heading toward the door.

CHAPTER TWENTY-NINE

"I'll not be left standin' at the car." Phineas stood with his arms tight across his chest. "Beggin' my *Ninsumgal's* pardon, but that's my cousin the bastard's nabbed."

Valmont rolled his eyes, his lips twisted into a grimace, and Whiskey found another reason to appreciate his presence—he exhibited all the negative emotions she couldn't. They stood on Northwest Couch Street, five blocks from the sluggish Willamette River, the same river that Whiskey saw every day from her apartment. The limousine hadn't quite caused raised eyebrows in this neighborhood, though it was a near miss. A few old establishments remained, the Hollywood Hotel being one. Previously dilapidated buildings had recently been renovated into upscale apartments and expensive shops, making the vehicle not too blatantly obvious.

Sasha spoke into her microphone, and reported, "We have the building surrounded, *Ninsumgal.* There's no evidence of *Sañur Gasum* Dorst, but we haven't closed in on the hotel room."

"Don't get too close. We don't want to tip him off if he's here." Whiskey turned to Phineas, fighting to keep the exasperation from her voice. "Phineas, I understand your concern." Her urgent desire to locate Margaurethe safe and sound made his demand an unnecessary delay.

"I'm sure you do, my *Ninsumgal.* I just want you to know where I stand." He paused, thinking about what he had just said. "And it ain't out here!"

Castillo stepped between them, ever the voice of calm and reason. "Perhaps Phineas can accompany us inside? He could keep an eye on the exits, to ensure Dorst doesn't escape?"

Phineas frowned, knowing he was being thrown a bone of appeasement, but didn't argue the suggestion. "It's better than sittin' in the damned car."

"Whatever you decide, Whiskey, it needs to be fast." Valmont studied the windows of the hotel. "I doubt Reynhard is defenseless. He may already know we're here despite our not advertising ourselves."

Whiskey sighed, glancing behind her at the two sedans that had carried her personal guard to this location. "All right. Phineas, you stay in the lobby and keep an eye on the stairs and elevators." She smiled grimly at his satisfied air. "I've been here before. You'll be able to see the street, as well. I'd suggest you mentally scan the first floor; the back door is behind the front desk."

"Aye, then. Let's get to it." He cracked his knuckles, apparently ready to move.

Warm air gusted out the glass door as Valmont opened it, redolent with mildew, cigarette smoke and the meaty smell of sweat and alcohol. The five of them stepped into the foyer, joined by three more guards. The only apparent difference between the interior and exterior was the level of light—regardless of bright lamps, the lobby appeared darker and damper than the street. The windows faced west, and morning illumination hadn't yet crawled high enough to illuminate the lobby. Brown carpet beneath their feet sucked in the light, holding a multitude of indecipherable stains. To one side sat several moth-eaten couches and armchairs, mismatched in style and color. An old man lounged in a rickety wheelchair, staring out the picture window, tongue lolling as he drifted in and out of sleep.

At the front desk, a relatively young man studied them. His head was bald and tattoos peeked from the collar of his button-up shirt. A nose ring glinted in the light of a small television. "Whaddya want?"

Castillo stepped closer. "We've come to see a friend."

The clerk jerked a thumb at a sign behind him. "No visitors allowed. Can't you read?"

Valmont grinned. After receiving silent permission from Whiskey, he sidled forward and leaned against the counter. "Who's going to stop us?"

Looking the newcomer up and down, the clerk sneered. "Please, old man. You ain't packing. Give me any shit and the cops will be all over you." He pointed at the camera parked prominently above and to one side behind him, and then patted the top of the small television. "You think I'm watching Oprah on this thing?"

"I don't think you're watching anything." Valmont gave the camera a glare, concentrating.

Whiskey smiled. Valmont was telekinetic, able to move physical objects with his mind. It was child's play for him to turn the camera off.

The clerk stared as his television went to snow and static. "What the fuck...?" He paused long enough to slap the machine, not seeing any change in reception. He glared at Valmont. "I'm calling the cops."

"Here, let me help." Castillo reached across the counter and took the receiver before the clerk could. With little exertion, the molded plastic shattered in his hand, and he gave the young man a contrite look. "I'm so sorry! Sometimes I don't know my own strength."

Whiskey smelled the beginnings of fear, her mouth watering. It didn't help the bloodlust for revenge already pounding in her heart. She gruffly pushed aside the hunger reaction, "Come on. We're wasting time. Phineas, keep an eye on him."

"Aye, *Ninsumgal*." Phineas grinned, all teeth and just a hint of fang as he stepped forward. "Don't be pulling one o' those newfangled phones out of your pocket, son. I don't know my own strength neither."

Castillo dropped the pieces of phone onto the desk, shrugging apologetically. Valmont winked at the clerk, his smirk a promise of more to come before moving to rejoin Whiskey. Sasha was already at the elevator, holding it open for them.

Whiskey stepped inside the car. "Valmont, you and Sasha come with me. Padre, if you don't mind?" She indicated a door marked Stairs.

"Certainly. Shall we race?"

Regardless of the seriousness of the situation, Whiskey chuckled. "No, Padre. You'll win. This elevator is slower than hell. When you get to the fourth floor, wait for us. Don't approach the room."

"As you wish." He disappeared up the stairs, another guard in tow, leaving two in the foyer with Phineas to keep control.

The elevator door closed with a groan. Valmont raised an eloquent eyebrow. "You sure this thing can hold us?"

"I'm sure. It's stronger than it looks." Whiskey expanded her awareness to include the exterior of the car. She didn't want to miss Dorst should he be in the elevator shaft itself, already aware of their approach. When she pushed the proper button, she wasn't surprised when it didn't light up. With a grunt and a rattle, the elevator began its ascent.

"You realize, of course, he's probably not here. He's not stupid."

"I know." Whiskey's tone was distracted as she concentrated on their immediate surroundings. "I'm hoping he left a clue about where he took Margaurethe. Since he hasn't called me, he has to leave a message somehow. Otherwise, he'll never have an opportunity to trade her life for mine."

Valmont sucked his teeth a moment. "Have you considered that he may have already killed her?"

Fury flashed icy fire through her veins. "Reynhard is an intelligent man. The only thing to keep him alive will be Margaurethe safe and well."

"I agree."

Their gazes met, a rush of emotion and communication transferring between them. This richness in their connection was new to her, probably a result of her in-depth scrutiny of his thoughts, coupled with the clearing of his conscience. It resounded through her soul with familiarity. Elisibet had shared this type of bond with him. It held a different texture than the link Whiskey shared with Margaurethe, though the intensity was as strong. It smacked of consuming flame and terrified screams.

It was oddly comforting.

The elevator creaked to a stop and the doors opened, breaking their subliminal connection. Sasha promptly stepped out first, and scanned the dingy corridor. Whiskey shook her head in amusement as Valmont followed suit. So now he had appointed himself her protector. How long would it be before she disabused him of this notion? Following him out, she sent a tentative scan through the immediate area, not pushing herself as far as Dorst's room. She picked up Castillo and the guard just inside the fire exit door, waiting for them. At her mind's touch, he opened the door and they stepped out. Castillo idly glanced at his watch to indicate how slow they had been to catch up. Whiskey saw Valmont give him a grimace, and tried not to laugh.

The smell of cigarette smoke and urine was stronger here. Whiskey didn't think the window at the end of the hall had ever been opened. A quick glance at the room numbers around them told her which direction to go, and she glided past Sasha and down the hall in silence, her advisors and security flanking her. She refrained from scanning Dorst's room until they arrived at the entry. If he was still inside and unaware of their presence, she didn't want to tip him off. The room stood at the rear of the hotel. Unless he had assistance from spotters or cameras, he wouldn't know how close they were.

Taking a deep breath, she guarded herself against a potential attack. Then she stabbed her consciousness into the room, searching with sharp and vicious thrusts for any Sanguire presence. She almost fumbled when she realized Dorst was inside. Surprised, she pounced on his mind and held firm. "He's here!" Something didn't feel right, the link seemed hazy and indistinct compared to the rich amber and steel to which she was accustomed.

Valmont needed no further urging. He pushed Whiskey aside, and crashed through the door into the squalid room. Sasha and the guard flowed through to clear it, weapons drawn. Castillo remained beside Whiskey, his attention on the hall and surrounding doors in case of ambush.

As Whiskey entered, she realized that Dorst hadn't fought her control, didn't struggle. His essence slithered and flopped in her mental grasp in a revolting manner. She frowned at the odd sensation, not comprehending. She watched Valmont grab the form on the bed and haul him to his feet before she understood. Dorst was unconscious, his arms and legs tightly bound with chains. A partially full intravenous bag hung from a nail in the wall above the bed, the tube snaking down and entering the IV shunt expertly taped to the back of his hand.

"What the hell is this?" Valmont shook the spy's limp form.

Castillo backed into the room, quietly closing the door before turning to regard them.

"What is that?" Whiskey asked.

Valmont eased his bundle back onto the bed. "I'm not liking this." He touched the IV at Dorst's wrist, lightly drawing his fingers up the tubing.

"He's been drugged." Castillo walked over to a cracked plastic table where he picked up an empty bag. There was no writing upon it, no indication of what sort of narcotic it had held.

"But why? And who could do it?" Whiskey's mind rushed through her preconceptions, washing away the fallacy. She came up with an answer to her question at the same time as Valmont.

"Reynhard isn't the assassin."

Whiskey felt wobbly, and she sank onto the foot of the bed. While it was good to know her instincts had been correct about Dorst, this new knowledge shattered any plan she had to regain Margaurethe safe and sound. Where was her lover? And who had her? The only name that came to mind was Pacal's, but she couldn't see how he'd be involved if he couldn't shape shift. All the evidence indicated the culprit was a *Gúnnumu Bargún*.

Valmont roundly cursed in several languages, pacing the tiny room.

Forcing herself to attend to the present, Whiskey looked at Sasha. "Stand down." As her captain relayed the order, she went to Dorst's side. Crimping the tubing, she pulled it from the IV shunt. "Think we can get him awake?"

Castillo set the drug detritus down. "It's possible. He's a spy. No doubt he has all sorts of concoctions and antidotes on his person. Search him, and I'll start looking through his things."

While Sasha and Castillo searched the room, Valmont explored Dorst's body. Whiskey found the small valve on the tubing, and stopped the flow of liquid. A drop sat on the pad of her finger, and she raised it to her nose to get a whiff. Even the scent of it made her feel slightly foggy around the edges of her mind. She quickly wiped it from her skin.

Castillo's extensive thirst for knowledge was beneficial. It didn't take long for him to identify the drug—a psychedelic anesthetic brewed specifically to stunt a Sanguire's mental facilities combined with a morphine drip—and a likely antidote among Dorst's belongings. It was the same drug Margaurethe had been given to facilitate her healing after Whiskey's inadvertent attack a few days ago.

Eventually, Dorst sat groggily on his bed, the chains removed by Valmont's ability to open the locks. "Dear gods, I'm hungry," he muttered. With shaky hands he found his mohawks in disarray, making a small noise of disgust in his throat as he attempted to straighten them.

"I'll find a *kizarus* for you." Castillo cocked his head. "The poison you were given has used a lot of your physical resources. You'll feel better after a meal and some real sleep."

"Make the call downstairs. And let Phineas know what's going on."

Castillo bowed to Whiskey and left.

"What happened, Reynhard?" Valmont's voice and eyes mocked the victim. "Someone duped you, the master spy? Not something you'd want people to know about, eh?"

"I'm honestly not certain."

Whiskey glared Valmont down. "What's the last thing you remember?"

Dorst was slow to respond, his thin lips pursed and his hairless eyebrows furrowed together. "I remember speaking with you about the *Agrun Nam*. I spent the evening here."

"You were here, eh?" Valmont snorted. "You didn't decide to hang out at the estate, did you? Perhaps sneak around in another's guise and murder people?"

The frown deepened. "No. I'm positive." Dorst's normally musical voice was as pale as his visage. "I had begun plans to return to the *Agrun Nam* to see what else I could find about the assassin."

"What happened?"

Dorst released a breath, his black eyes staring at Whiskey. "I don't know."

"How convenient."

Whiskey shot Valmont another fierce glance. Margaurethe's life was on the line. She had no time for his jealousy and sarcasm. He seemed to understand her expression, and tilted his head in a request for forgiveness. Returning her attention to Dorst, she said, "Let me in."

He understood her meaning. "Of course, my *Ninsumgal*."

His easy surrender gave Whiskey harsh satisfaction. She was correct, he meant her no harm and was willing to subject himself to her will, no questions asked. The knowledge both pleased and scared her. Such a level of submission easily led to abuse. As with Andri and Valmont before, she put up her guard before entering Dorst's mind rather than invite an attack. Despite her pleasure at his apparent obedience, he still had several hundred years of experience and strength behind him. Of the same opinion, she felt Valmont's essence bolstering hers, staying close and ready should she need his assistance.

It was easier this time. The skill improved with each successful endeavor. In less than a minute she was in Dorst's head, watching through his eyes as she sifted quickly through the memories, skimming past the personal thoughts and experiences of what transpired after their meeting. She invaded his mind for a purpose and saw no reason to delve into his privacy. Dorst was a spy and full of illicit information. She had no doubt he would allow an in-depth examination by her, but she knew how destructive that could be. He would be worthless to her ever after.

As she neared the time in question, she slowed her search.

She sat in her room with a single lamp on the table illuminating her work. She looked through Dorst's eyes as she doodled on a notepad, the action aiding her thoughts as she made plans for another incursion into European territory. She looked over her shoulder at the sound of someone knocking, felt immediate suspicion at the interruption. No one knew she was here. Who could be at the door?

Whiskey eased a tentacle of thought toward the door, finding nothing on the other side. Obviously a Human, as Sanguire were unable to touch them in such a manner. Assuming some drunk was lost, she rose and went to the door. Opening it, she stared at the clerk from the lobby. "What do you want?" She heard Dorst's voice instead of her own.

He shrugged, his nose ring flashing. "Not a thing."

Alarms rang in her head as he turned and walked away. Before she could close the door, she felt another presence, a Sanguire mind rolling over her own.

Whiskey recoiled from the blackness that followed. She tumbled, Valmont grabbing her elbow to keep her upright. Her hand massaged her forehead as she separated Dorst's memory from her own, collected herself from their joining. When she stood on her own, she looked at Dorst still sitting on the bed.

"Well, that was unpleasant." A hint of his jovial demeanor leaked through the exhaustion. "It seems our assassin knows who and where I am."

Valmont released Whiskey. "What happened? What did you see?"

"Someone paid off the front desk clerk to knock on the door. Reynhard was put off guard, and the Sanguire was able to overcome and compel him." Whiskey inhaled deeply. She felt rough around the edges, and sat upon the only chair in the room, the same one Dorst had been in before he had been attacked. Glancing at the scribbling on the notepad there, she felt the déjà vu of the pen in her hand, knowing it was Dorst's memory.

"Do you know who it was?"

She shook her head. "Not really. But I'm betting it's who has Margaurethe. He has to be damned strong to take on Reynhard and win."

"*Ki'an Gasan* Margaurethe?" Dorst asked. "What are you talking about?"

She stared out the window, lost in thought, so Valmont answered. "Someone kidnapped Margaurethe and Andri from The Davis Group last night. We thought it was you."

"Me?" Dorst sounded affronted. "I would never do such a thing! I gave my oath to my *Ninsumgal*."

Something about her walk through Dorst's mind puzzled her. She compared it to the other times she had done similar, while Valmont and Dorst talked around her.

"Regardless of your oath, Reynhard, we had evidence to suspect your involvement."

"And what evidence was that?" Dorst's voice became stronger as his anger burned bright.

Whiskey remembered the connection with Margaurethe, only a few short days ago. Every time they had bonded, she had seen something about Elisibet that her lover had encountered. And every time, that event was from Margaurethe's point of view, Whiskey riding silently behind her eyes as she watched, listened and felt what the woman experienced.

Valmont scoffed. "For one, your reputation precedes you. Only you have the ability to come and go at will despite the guards."

"Oh, please. I'm not the only *Gúnnumu Bargún* in the world. Some others are even as good as I."

She heard Margaurethe's voice, a conversation she had had with her lover the night of the murders.

"I spent the afternoon grilling your employees. It doesn't look like any of them are this unknown assassin."

"That's good to hear, though that's a lot of people. Did you get to everybody?"

"Well, those I didn't know personally before they came here."

Pacal was Whiskey's man-at-arms. He might have chosen to reside with the Mayan delegation, but he was still an employee of The Davis Group. Margaurethe had to have investigated him.

"Perhaps," Valmont said. "But you're the only one that knows the security setup. Someone has been parading around in my guise. I've been accused of three murders this week. That interloper stole a car from the garage after killing a guard, and was caught on camera."

"Murders? What murders? And my *Gasan* already saw what happened to me that night. I wasn't there. Who is this witness?"

Whiskey saw memories with Margaurethe's eyes. She saw with Dorst's eyes. Even when she purposely attacked another, as with Castillo and Valmont, she saw glimpses of their thoughts through their eyes.

But she had not seen through Andri's eyes.

Swallowing a sudden rage, she turned icy eyes on her advisors. "It's Andri. He's not who he seems."

CHAPTER THIRTY

Margaurethe struggled toward consciousness. Her vision blurred as she forced her eyes open. Several minutes passed until they focused, revealing her location.

She lay sideways on a cot in a dusky little room. Light glowed from beneath the door, the only illumination. She stirred, trying to sit up, realizing in the abortive attempt that her arms and legs were firmly chained. Strangely groggy, Margaurethe tried to puzzle out what happened to her. She tasted blood in the back of her throat, smelled it in the air about her. The aroma was familiar, and she realized it was her own.

Whiskey. She had been talking to Whiskey, and then she had left to check something in her office. Margaurethe searched her memory, piecing together the fuzzy scenes into a comprehensive recollection. A vague sensation of irritation flickered through her in distant sympathy with a memory. Margaurethe had finished her business and found herself in the empty foyer. She firmly recalled setting a guard on Whiskey no matter where she traveled within the building as a precaution against another attack.

Valmont. He was the one suspected of killing the others. Yes, it was coming back to her now. But Whiskey, fresh from Cora's funeral and wake, recently discovering her talent, didn't want to further investigate the matter. Instead, she fled to her quarters to distance herself from the pain and anger. That was why Margaurethe had set the guard—her young lover might be loath to deal with the realities of the situation; she was not.

There had been no expected *Aga'gída* in the foyer, though he had been there when she had passed through earlier.

Margaurethe stretched as much as her bindings would allow, noting the pain coalescing at the back of her head and neck. Still on the hunt for her elusive memory, she put the ache out of her mind. She had stepped inside Whiskey's sitting room, searching for the guard, figuring he had taken position there. He hadn't been. She most definitely had a thing or two to say to him when she found him. Not wanting to upset Whiskey, she had extended her mind in an effort to locate him, but found nothing. As suspicion had clouded Margaurethe's mind, Andri had quietly entered the sitting room from Whiskey's apartment. He seemed agitated, scared. Quickly darting to her side, he had said something. What was it again?

"Ki'an Gasan! *We must hide. The brown man I saw, the one in that poor girl's apartment, he's here!*"

Margaurethe's head pounded as it did then, though for an entirely different reason. She licked dry lips, realizing her nose had bled at some point, causing the taste in her mouth. She remembered telling Andri to go into the hall, to find Whiskey's personal guard and send them in. She had only taken a few steps away before pain had exploded in her head. Everything had gone dark.

Clearing her throat, Margaurethe shifted once more. She saw movement in front of the door, a shadow crossing the light.

Extending her senses, she picked up the sound of footsteps. Her nose only found dust, and she fought against a sneeze. She pressed her face into the dirty mattress in an attempt to stifle the explosion. It worked for the moment, but the tickle in her sinuses indicated her failsafe wouldn't last long. It was Andri who had hit her from behind. Had Valmont enlisted the terrified little man to his cause, somehow knowing that his cover had been torn away, and he was revealed for the traitor he was? Margaurethe opened her mouth to breathe and alleviate the impending sneeze.

Despite the memories coming together, Margaurethe still felt stuporous. Most of her senses seemed to work fine. She tried to focus her mind on the shadow beyond the door. She couldn't. Swallowing a stab of fear, she tried again. She concentrated on scanning around her, but found herself unable to get out of her head. The sensation nauseated her, an essential part of her spirit completely hobbled. As if in answer to her prodding attempts, the door opened, a shaft of light spilling across the room and making her squint.

"Ah, it's good to see you're awake, luv," a familiar voice said.

Margaurethe stared at Andri, finding the confident expression alien to his countenance. She swallowed and attempted to speak. "Who are you?" Her tongue felt overlarge and dry.

He grinned, his features flickering, his body lengthening, as he changed into a stranger. "No one you know, sweetling. Though it has been quite fun, hasn't it?"

"You're the assassin."

"My, aren't you the smart one?" He winked at her. "I'm surprised it's taken you this long to realize I wasn't who you thought I was. You knew the original Andri Sigmarsson, you and *Sublugal Sañar* Valmont both. Yet neither of you deigned to give me a going-over. Very sloppy, that."

She cursed to herself, remembering in-depth scans of everyone new to her after Dorst had reported an assassin being hired. Cora's and Anthony's murders had interrupted her plan to scan the remainder of the staff the following day. "Since I'm here and alive, I'm assuming you haven't been able to murder Whiskey."

He leaned against the doorjamb, crossing his arms over his chest, his smile casual. By all appearances, he loitered and chatted with a dear friend rather than a hostage. “Not yet, though I expect it will be soon. I’ve been waiting for you to awaken before I called her.”

Margaurethe snorted once and finally sneezed. She ignored his mild “bless you,” sniffling. “Don’t think I’ll speak to her on your behalf.” She wished her tone were more firm instead of tremulous from another potential sneeze. “If you give me the phone, I’ll tell her to leave me with you and to live.”

“It won’t make much difference, will it? She loves you dearly, *Ki’an Gasan*. She’ll not rest until you’re safe and I’m dead. Or she is.”

She knew it to be true, and hated that he knew it as well. “How much are you being paid? I’ll double it.”

His chuckle was a pleasant one. “Now how far do you think I’d get in my profession if I turned on my employers that easily, eh? I’d be out of work in no time. No.” He shook his head. “I gave my word I’d do the job, and I will.”

Anger flared, giving her enough strength to push herself up to a sitting position. She twisted until her bound feet touched the floor, pleased to see him stand erect in preparation for a potential attack. “Do you realize who she is? You’d be murdering our final hope!” Her head pounded.

“Oh, I’m perfectly aware of who she is, luv.” His lips turned down with regret. “As I said, however, I’ve already given my word. If it’s any consolation, I plan on finding my employer and giving him a dose of the same.”

“It’s not a consolation.” Again she tried to break through the haze in her mind, attempted to strike out at him. Her head throbbed once in response, a stab of agony shooting behind her eyes and another wave of nausea forcing bile into her throat.

She must have given some indication of what she was doing. “My apologies, *Ki’an Gasan*, but you’ll find yourself quite unable to use your gifts against me.”

“What have you done to me?” Margaurethe remembered hearing horror stories of Sanguire who, after sustaining head injuries, were forever unable to use their gifts or mental abilities. Had he done the same to her? Had he crippled her beyond measure when he had knocked her out? What would she do?

"Only a psychedelic anesthetic." His earnest expression conveyed truthfulness. "Something to protect me from your talents. When the *Ninsumgal* arrives, I don't wish to be fighting on more than one front."

"She's stronger than you think."

"Aye, I'm aware of that. And she's aware that I'm older and more powerful than her. Granted, she's got strength, but I'm certain I'll have no problem. I did well enough when she rooted around in my head for my 'memory' of Valmont's treachery. She thinks I'm a hostage just like you."

Margaurethe closed her eyes, ignoring the shape shifter's change before her. Whiskey's soft spot for Elisibet's valet was no secret among the other staff. If Whiskey thought Andri was as much a victim as herself, she would be in even more danger. With Margaurethe's mind numb, there was no way she could convey the truth to her.

"You're probably tired," he said in Andri's voice. "Lie down and get some sleep. It will all be over soon."

Margaurethe glared at him. "You'd best kill me, too. I'll not be a witless mourner this time."

He cocked his head. "Then you'd better queue, luv. My employer has first dibs, I hear." Before she could demand more information, he gave a familiar bow and stepped out of the room, gently closing the door behind him.

In the dark once more, she slumped. What could she do?

***

Whiskey stared out the Town Car window. Valmont sat at her side, fingers tapping against his leg. Phineas had taken the wheel, and Sasha sat beside him, keeping tabs on security via a cell phone. Castillo had remained behind to see to Dorst's injuries. Dorst had been given his fill of a *kizarusi*, and had promptly fallen into a fitful slumber. Considering how old Andri was, Whiskey had insisted that Dorst be moved to The Davis Group immediately, and they had taken the limousine. She didn't know if the assassin had been checking on his victim, and didn't want Dorst in his weakened state to be there. If the man could overpower Dorst, Castillo would be child's play.

The car idled on the top floor of a parking structure. It had been an hour since discovering Dorst and still no word from either Castillo's sources or the assassin.

Chewing her lower lip, she watched a trio of crows bickering on the edge of the building nearby. There was nowhere else to go until or unless she was contacted. Why is it taking so long? Margaurethe has been gone for over twelve hours. Surely the assassin had a deadline. Her cell phone rang. Everyone turned to stare at her a moment. Whiskey swallowed, heart racing, and pulled it from her pocket. The caller ID said, Margaurethe. "Yes?"

"Listen carefully."

The voice belonged to a stranger. Whiskey gritted her teeth to keep silent. She heard the phone exchange hands.

"My *Gasan*?" a tentative voice said.

"Andri?" Her immediate emotional response was concern for her fainthearted valet. She forcibly reminded herself of the different bond they had shared, that he was the assassin and hadn't truly connected his mind to hers. He had fed her a vision, a lie.

"Aye, *Ninsumgal*," Andri's tone held a combination of relief and worry. "I'm sorry! I'm so sorry! I don't know what happened."

Whiskey closed her eyes against the desire to comfort him. A touch on her leg brought her back to the present, and she stared at Valmont. "It's okay, Andri. There was nothing you could do. Are you okay?"

He sniffled. "Aye, my *Gasan*. But *Ki'an Gasan* Margaurethe... she's been hurt!"

Whiskey's mouth twisted into a snarl, and Valmont recoiled from the expression on her face. The assassin obviously thought she didn't know of his ruse. "Give the phone back to him. Take care of Margaurethe as best you can. You'll be free soon."

"Aye, *Ninsumgal*."

She tasted ashes in her mouth, feeling all the world as if she was condemning her timid valet to his death. Whoever the assassin was, he was good at his job.

"I think you know what I want."

"Yeah, I do," she said, her voice icy. "Where and when?"

"Tonight. Say, about midnight." He rattled off an address in north Portland. "And come alone."

"I'll be there."

He paused. "I'll have your word as *Ninsumgal* that you'll come alone." When she did not immediately answer, he added, "Or either the *gasan* or the valet will take your place. Do you really want another innocent to die for you?"

Her tone gruff, she said, "I swear I'll come alone. But if anything happens to them, you'll regret every remaining minute of your miserable little life."

"I understand. I'll see you there."

Whiskey hung up the phone with great care. It was either that or slam it on the door and break the thing. "We have an appointment set up. She may or may not be there." She ignored Valmont's indignant look. "Phineas, take us back to The Davis Group. We have plans to make."

"I won't let you go alone. Don't dare ask it of me."

A grin cracked Whiskey's stony visage, and she raised her chin slightly at Valmont. "I wouldn't ask it of you, my friend. I said I'd come alone, I didn't say I wouldn't be followed."

Phineas gave a gusty sigh of satisfaction, and turned back to the steering wheel.

CHAPTER THIRTY-ONE

Whiskey had no need for subterfuge. The time and place of the meeting was known to both of them. She didn't restrain her essence as she approached the dilapidated house on foot. Instead, she kept a constant scan of the immediate area, stretching wide to be certain she would survive long enough to see Margaurethe safe. Sanguire might live longer than Humans, but a well-aimed sniper rifle could still do the job with satisfaction; she had no illusions about her mortality.

It had begun raining not long after she had left The Davis Group. Her hair dripped into her eyes, and she slicked it back from her forehead. She wore a leather trench coat, not unlike Dorst's, that repelled most of the rain. Hidden beneath it, tucked safely into her belt at the small of her back, was a Glock 9mm pistol. Valmont had given her a rudimentary lesson in its use, hopefully giving her a better edge against the unknown assassin.

The house was a mossy green, trimmed in white, its paint peeling to reveal gray wood. It looked like the perfect flophouse. She wondered why the street kids hadn't found it yet; the location was close to a grocery chain and bus line, a prime spot. Of course, a Sanguire in residence would deter even the hardiest of Humans.

Her mind touched his, and she tested his defenses, though not with any true effort. She felt him do the same. If she'd had any doubt of Andri's role here, it was gone. This was the same mind she had connected with to see Valmont's supposed entry into Cora's apartment. A bubble of humor broke against her as he realized she was aware of his acting, yet still he didn't attack.

Whiskey stepped into the carport, out of the rain. The assassin had picked a good place. The yard was fenced and a stand of trees along the back and sides kept prying eyes away. Sniffing the air, she smelled faint oil and wet concrete. The building hadn't been used for some time. The back door gaped open, deeper blackness in the dark. Bracing herself, she gave a final glance to her surroundings before mounting the steps.

Cool dustiness assailed her nose as she visually scanned the long hallway. To her immediate left was an open door, steps leading down into a moist basement. She tried to pinpoint his location with her mind, finally resolving he was on this level and not downstairs. Easing down the hall, she tried to locate Margaurethe, hoping he held her here. It was odd, but she could almost feel her lover. Gentle hints and emotions flickered just out of reach—anger, fear, love. Deciding Margaurethe was here and probably incapacitated in the same manner as Dorst, Whiskey solemnly continued forward.

At the end of the hall, she found an open area with a dryer hose still dangling from the vent. A darkened room was beyond it to her right and another, shorter hallway led to the front of the house on her left. The linoleum was cracked and dirty with trash and animal feces scattered about. It seemed that Humans had not found the place, but the local feline and rodent population had. Stabbing her mind toward the darkened room, she found nothing. She turned left.

The hall opened into the main living area. To her right was a large living room, its white walls long since succumbing to graffiti artists. Before her was a dining room, flanked by windows to let in light on sunny days. A pane of glass had been broken out, and someone had set up a planter with crawling ivy in the opening. From the looks of the thing, it had been growing quite well in the humid weather, spilling onto the floor and outside in a riot of life. Whiskey slid along the wall until she could look around the corner into the dining room, seeing the kitchen beyond. No one awaited her. She saw the street from where she stood, watched a car slowly drive past, windshield wipers squeaking as the rain gave way to mist. She turned her attention to the empty living room.

Halfway down the length of it, a hallway opened and she padded that direction. While there was no reason for silence, she winced at the creaking of the ill-cared-for wood flooring. Three doors opened off the short hall. One she identified by the powerful aroma of rusty water; the bathroom. The closest door stood open and she peeked inside, seeing a spacious bedroom and nothing else. That left only one door, and she stopped before it.

Taking a deep breath, Whiskey reached for the doorknob. It rattled in her hand as it turned, and she opened the door. Golden light spilled out of the room.

"How good of you to come, *Ninsumgal*." Andri bowed deeply, his eyes never leaving hers. He held a pistol in one hand, though he didn't aim it at her. "Please come in. We've much to discuss before we can put an end to this."

Whiskey lowered her chin. "Thank you, Andri. Or should I call you something else?" She left the door open behind her, and went to the empty chair across from him.

"Andri will do."

"Then let's get down to business, shall we?"

Andri smiled. "Aye. Let's do."

***

Valmont paced beside the Town Car, glancing at his watch every few moments.

"D'ye think she'd be upset if we went a little early?"

He snorted at Phineas's question. "If she's anything like Elisibet—and she does have her moments, let me tell you—you wouldn't be asking."

Phineas frowned, shoulders dropping as he sat in the driver's seat, car door open. "How long should we wait then?"

"Until she's had time enough to get there and make contact."

Obviously disgruntled with the answer, Phineas's lips twisted into a grimace.

True to her word, Whiskey had gone to the meeting alone. And her words to Valmont were also true. He knew in which direction she headed, watching her disappear into a driveway about two blocks down the street. They would follow soon. Phineas had been ordered to locate and release Margaurethe if she was there while Valmont was to back up Whiskey.

He had better plans than that. If that filthy snake hurt either of the women, Valmont schemed to tear him limb from limb. Slowly. And with great relish.

***

Margaurethe's weariness vanished as she heard someone moving about upstairs. It had been hours since the man masquerading as Andri had left her. He had long since quieted. As best she could tell, this was someone else walking stealthily across the floor.

It had to be Whiskey.

Margaurethe struggled into a sitting position, trying in vain to break her bonds. Of course, the chains held firm; the drug holding her mind also robbed her of her Sanguire strength. She groaned in protest.

Another attempt to expand her awareness past herself resulted in a fierce headache. She bent over as her stomach spasmed. When the sensation passed, tears of frustration stung her eyes. *I have to find a way out of here!*

***

Whiskey turned the chair around and straddled it, one arm propped on the back, the other fist planted on her hip. "There's really not much to say, is there? You have something I want, and I have something you want."

Andri also sat, the pistol held loosely in his lap. "Actually, it's not what I want, but what my employer desires. If it were left to me, this wouldn't be happening."

"It still doesn't need to."

"Ah, unfortunately, I do have ethics, young Jenna. My career might be of a less savory nature, but I have scruples."

"That's too bad. Though I can understand your point of view." She wondered how long it would take for Valmont and Phineas to get there. Would they find Margaurethe easily enough? Would they arrive in time to stop her death?

"So what are we waiting for?"

He raised an eyebrow. "Are you so eager to die?"

"Hell no. You can smell my fear as well as I can. But you've given me no choice. If I'm to see Margaurethe safe, I have to give myself to you."

"You would succumb willingly to your execution?" He leaned forward, watching her.

Whiskey squinted at him. "What? Is this a test or something?" She sat straight, bringing her arm down from the chair, planting that hand on her hip as well. "You have your ethics; I have mine."

"You realize, of course, that my employer is most likely attempting to take over the *Agrun Nam*?"

"So?"

He appeared perplexed. "So? Your people teeter on the edge of chaos. If the prophecies are true, you are the main hope to see true order restored."

Whiskey stared at him. "And?" she urged impatiently.

He shook his head, disgruntled. "I thought you'd be more concerned for your people. Apparently, I was wrong." He rose and walked to the window, dividing his attention between her and his thoughts. "You played a good game, I'll admit. I guess you can take the girl away from the streets but not the streets out of the girl."

She grinned. "You're disappointed." Her voice held a measure of delighted awe. "You expect me to be noble and sacrifice my love for my people—a people I know next to nothing about."

"Well, we can't all be perfect, can we?"

Her smile widened at the acid in his tone, her fangs slipping from their sheathes. "If you're looking for a fight, you have one. But not until Margaurethe is safely away from here."

He cocked his head and looked at her. "How do you know she's here?"

"Because I felt her when I came in."

"You felt her? Impossible."

His pronouncement caused her heart to stumble. "Why is it impossible?" Her humor disappeared into an ominous growl.

***

Valmont slipped in through the open door, Phineas close on his heels. Keeping his mind in check, he attempted to discern in which direction Whiskey had gone. He didn't have to use his mind to locate her; he smelled her passing. Wavering slightly, eyelids half closed, he decided she had continued on this level. With a glance and a nod, he directed Phineas down the basement steps, a whisper touch of his mind admonishing silence.

The chauffeur nodded and disappeared into the darkness.

Gliding through the murky hallway, Valmont took great care to keep quiet. At the junction of the hall, he paused again, ignoring the squeak of a mouse scuttling nearby. To the left then.

Another junction, another choice. Leaning close to the wall, he almost saw Whiskey's scent rise from the cracked paint. She stopped here, pushed against the wall. He did the same, looking around the corner to see a kitchen in disarray, appliances long since stolen, and cupboard doors removed. The house wasn't that large. Valmont knew the places she could be were dwindling. With nowhere else to go, he directed his attention to the living room.

His ears picked up voices, and he smiled in satisfaction. Very close. They were just up ahead. He picked up his pace.

***

A scratching at the door interrupted Margaurethe's panicked struggle. Metal on metal. She fine-tuned her hearing, but couldn't increase it much. It sounded as if someone was picking the lock. Valmont had no need for such subterfuge, having the ability to move objects with his mind. Margaurethe wasn't certain Whiskey would know how to open a lock. Margaurethe almost laughed. Whiskey was a Ghost Walker; she would simply pass through the door.

If this was some fool Human looking for something to steal, she would be ready.

Margaurethe heard the solid snick of the lock, and a faint sigh of relief from whomever worked the mechanism. She sat on the edge of the cot, bringing her chained legs close, muscles tensing as the doorknob gently rattled. The door opened and she pounced, tackling the person on the other side. Both of them fell to the concrete floor, her savior letting out a grunt as she knocked the air out of him. Rolling away, Margaurethe struggled to get to her feet, a tough proposition without her arms to assist her.

"Gods, cuz," a voice whispered. "I missed you, too."

Margaurethe stopped, raising her head, and staring. "Phineas?"

The young Sanguire grinned, his face red as he regained use of his lungs. "Shhh. We're supposed to be quiet." He picked up his lock pick set, waggling the metal tools at her. "Let me get you out of those."

"Where's Whiskey?" She forced herself to barely breathe the words.

"Probably talking to that ass who created this mess."

"Hurry! I've got to get to her!"

"Be still!" he hissed. "And keep it down. *Sublugal Sañar* Valmont should be there."

CHAPTER THIRTY-TWO

Andri held up his free hand in a placating gesture. "No worries, luv. Your consort is quite alive, and no doubt very angry. I simply meant that the drug I gave her is supposed to suppress her abilities." He sniffed his opinion of the medication. "Obviously that batch is a bit stale."

Whiskey swallowed a sense of relief, confirming Margaurethe was here and not hurt. She had to keep him talking if she were to give Valmont and Phineas time to find her. Having risen from her chair, she shoved it out of her way, fangs still extended. "So tell me, did Andri ever really come here?"

He scrutinized her carefully. "No. I was given a dossier with his information. He hasn't been seen in two hundred years or more."

She found the information disconcerting. Was Elisibet's valet dead or in hiding? Would he someday turn up to avenge all the hurts his liege had done to him? Or would he understand that despite her appearance, she wasn't the evil woman who had dominated him through the centuries? Whiskey ran her tongue over her fangs. There were more important things to consider right now. Like whether or not she would live through the next few minutes. "How do we do this? You release Margaurethe, and I allow you to execute me?"

A smile crossed his face. "Ah, now, don't be thinking I'll fall for that sort of act. You might be perfectly willing to give your life for hers, but a body has a will of its own. Regardless of your word, I know you'll fight your death. They all do, no matter how helpless they feel."

"Whatever." Whiskey held her hands out with a slight shrug. She took a step closer. "But don't doubt I will take you with me if you don't let her go first."

The floor in the living room creaked.

Andri took a step back, and raised the gun. Aiming at Whiskey's heart, he glanced beyond her, smile gone. "You said you'd come alone! You gave your word."

Whiskey shrugged again, forcing a bravado she didn't feel as she stared down the barrel of the pistol. "I did come alone."

"Then who the blazes is out there?" He raised his voice to be heard.

Another creak, and Valmont stepped in, an unrepentant grin on his face. "I followed her." He held a pistol, as well, pointed at the nervous assassin.

Whiskey's spirits rose at Valmont's presence. Even if she didn't survive this, it wouldn't matter. His being here meant Margaurethe would be safe. "You never listen to me," she said to Valmont.

"I never call, I never write," he added in feigned boredom.

She chuckled.

"Enough of this." The assassin cocked his gun. "Get out of here or I'll shoot her."

"Like you aren't planning on doing that anyway?" Valmont asked, scorn in his voice.

The assassin's was equally acid. "And then I'll shoot you."

Valmont scoffed. "You'll die before you pull the trigger."

"Do you want his blood on your hands, *Ninsumgal*?"

Whiskey's mind searched for options. "What, are you stupid? Of course not." She turned to Valmont. "Leave us."

His gaze barely flickered from the assassin. "You're joking."

Yes, I am. Smirking, she reached out to caress his mind. Even as strong as she was, she didn't think she could take on a Sanguire of Andri's apparent age alone. *But maybe with Valmont's help, I can.* "You heard me. Get out."

Valmont's face twisted with a mix of emotion, his jaw setting stubbornly as he lowered his chin. "Fat chance, my *Ninsumgal*." He adjusted his grip on the pistol, cocking the hammer.

The sensation of their essences melding together wasn't lost on the assassin. He took another step back, raised the pistol to Whiskey's head. "Don't even think about it!"

Whiskey stabbed out with her mind, hoping the shock and pain of it spoiled his aim.

***

The time it took for Phineas to open the locks stretched far too long. Her legs finally free, Margaurethe glared ineffectually at her cousin as he worked on the one at her waist.

"It's hardly my fault." He worked with diligence as he whispered. "Bastard made a right mess of things, buying these locks. Special, they are. Takes a bit more to get through 'em."

Upstairs she heard more movement, and discerned faint voices through the ceiling. It sounded like Andri and Whiskey, but then she heard Valmont's distinctive tones. "Just hurry!"

***

Sharp pain pierced Whiskey's head as he defended himself with surgical precision. There was no wasted energy, no fumbling as he thrust his mind against her attack, the barrel of the gun still aimed at her head. Despite having Valmont's strength to draw from, she scrambled to keep herself shielded, amazed at her opponent's mental discipline. Her only other experience with a duel had been Fiona Bodwrda—a Sanguire no more than a hundred years old. The differences in ability between her and the assassin staggered Whiskey. *God, it's no wonder Margaurethe went into convulsions when I lashed out at her!*

He seemed content to continue in this vein, though his finger remained solidly on the trigger. Just as she found a way to block his advance in one area, he switched tactics and engaged another part of her mind. Her body shook from the mental exertion, her vision clouding as she and Valmont struggled. It was so hot, sweat beaded on her forehead and upper lip. She barely noticed that she had thrown off her trench coat, and taken a physical step closer to Andri as she concentrated on staying alive. She tried to flank him, to surround his mind with hers as she had done to others. A tendril of his thought slid out to cut off her advance with no lessening of power in his frontal attack. Again and again he met her, strength with strength, defeating her at every twist and turn.

Whiskey felt Valmont weakening, heard him groan at a particularly vicious counterattack. She pulled her mind inward, not able to shield herself alone, not able to put the assassin on the defense. Frantic, she searched Elisibet's memories for anything, anything to help her. All she saw was a young Margaurethe hovering over her dying Elisibet, and cold, darkness filling Elisibet's vision. "*No!*" Gathering up every shred of her might, she surged forward. She grabbed at the gun in Andri's hand, but it was almost as if he saw her actions before she took them. He brought his arm down, closed the distance between them, and planted the pistol in her gut. *I can't die! I can't do this to Margaurethe again!*

An alien thought entered her mind, a whispered response from her enemy. *My apologies,* Ninsumgal. *But this is something I have to do.*

His mental invasion angered her. She grabbed his throat, glaring into his eyes as she fought for her life. He stared back, face reddening as she cut off his oxygen, no fear in his eyes, no remorse. "No!" So close were their minds, she saw his intention as he thought it. Glancing down, she saw his hand wrapped around the grip, felt his finger tightening on the trigger. She growled as she tightened her hold on his throat, feeling a familiar tingle settle in her torso. A gunshot echoed loudly in the small room. Valmont swore as the bullet punched into the wall beside him.

Whiskey felt nothing but the tingle in her gut. She dug her thumbs into the assassin's throat, crushing his windpipe, nails burrowing into the flesh. His mental attack faltered when she didn't weaken. Taking the initiative, her mind pounded against his, sensing the narrow margin of his endurance beginning to ebb. His mental shielding began to shred, tatters of uselessness through which she slipped. She felt confusion in his mind, watched his mouth gape in search of breath, felt the flesh part beneath her fingers. A godawful ripping noise filled her ears and blood spilled hot across her hands, spraying her face. She held him until his eyes rolled up into his skull, and his mind turned sluggish, swirling down into the dark. Disgusted, she tossed him aside.

Valmont staggered into view as he circled her, looking down upon the dying man. Sweat slicked his dark skin, and he had bitten his lower lip hard enough to draw blood. His eyes trailed up, carefully examining her torso. "He shot you. I saw it."

Whiskey took a deep breath to calm herself, though her gore-ridden hands still shook from adrenaline. "I'm *Gidimam Kissane Lá*."

He stared. "Ghost Walker?" Before she could answer, he burst out laughing. "Why not? Of course you are!"

A smile crawled across her face at his laughter, the sound chasing away her fear and revulsion. Footsteps rapidly approached the room, and she turned to see Margaurethe and Phineas rushing in.

"Margaurethe?"

CHAPTER THIRTY-THREE

By the time Bentoncourt arrived at the meeting, everyone else was there. The glares he received were odd, and he frowned as he took his place at the head of the table. "So, what is this all about?" he asked Cassadie.

The others shared puzzled glances. "Why are you asking me?"

Bentoncourt stared at his longtime friend. "Because you called us here."

"No," Nijmege said. "You called us here. At least that's what my note said."

"And mine," McCall agreed.

"Whereas my note came from you." Rosenberg's heavy-lidded eyes stared at the woman.

Nijmege scoffed. "I most certainly did not call this meeting."

"What the hell is going on?"

The door popped open, interrupting them. A man entered, his garb and hair that of a black-and-white clown. His skin was pale and three mohawks graced his otherwise bare scalp. "Ah! You're already here! My apologies for being late." He moved to the other end of the table from Bentoncourt.

They stared for a second in shock. No one but the *Agrun Nam* entered this room. It just wasn't done.

"Who are you?" Nijmege demanded.

The stranger's face twisted into a petulant frown, his long fingers fluttering over his heart. "I'm crushed, *Aga Maskim Sañar* Bertrada! You don't recognize me?" He scanned the others in the room. "Well, I suppose it's to be expected, though I daresay one of you should have an idea."

Bentoncourt tilted his head, listening intently to the man's voice. Leaning forward, he peered at the man. "Reynhard?"

A grin of delight quickly replaced the frown. "Oh, very good, Lionel!"

"Who?" Unlike the others, McCall didn't immediately make the connection.

"Before your time, I'm afraid." Dorst's manner was conspiratorial. "Though I'm most pleased to make your acquaintance, Samuel."

While the others tried to catch up, Bentoncourt said, "Davis brought us here."

"Oh, two for two. Very good." Dorst produced a laptop and blithely set it up as he chattered. "She most certainly did, though I suggested the subterfuge. I seriously doubted some of you would appear if you knew." He gave a small shrug, beaming at them. "I could have been wrong."

Nijmege, jaw moving as she gritted her teeth, rose to her feet. "I'll not be at some pipsqueak's beck and call. I'm leaving."

"Oh, I think not." Dorst's tone remained pleasant. A pistol had appeared in his hand, pointed at her. "You see, I've been given permission to use any and all means at my disposal to ensure your cooperation for this little meeting. You'll find the door locked." He tsked in apparent concern. "And I've put a guard on the door for the duration. Let's all have a seat until my job is complete. It will be much less messy, don't you think?"

"Sit down, Bertrada," Bentoncourt said. "Let's get this over with."

She looked as if she would fight the order until McCall reached out to touch her hand. Their gazes met, something communicated between them, and she returned to her chair.

"Very good. Thank you so much. I do so hate bloodshed." The pistol disappeared and he finished whatever he was doing. "I present to you, my *Ninsumgal*, Jenna Davis." With a flourish, he turned the laptop around.

Davis stared back at them. Having only seen still photographs of her, Bentoncourt couldn't help but be fascinated by her image, hardly noting the choppiness of the transmission. When she spoke, her voice was a bit tinny, more from the speakers than anything else, but the sight and sound of her brought back all the memories of Elisibet. There was no way any of the others could doubt her veracity now.

"My apologies for going about things this way, but I'm pretty sure it was the only way to get you all together at one time."

"It's a pleasure to finally meet you, *Ninsumgal*." Of course Cassadie would be the one to remember protocol and politeness.

She grinned, obviously thinking the same. "Thank you, Aiden. I remember you from before this, however." Her eyes didn't move, but Bentoncourt assumed she looked at all of them on her computer. "I remember all but Mr. McCall."

Nijmege was pale as death. "Then you remember me, as well," she snapped.

"Yes, I do, Bertrada." Davis's expression softened. "What happened to you was one of the worst things that could happen to anyone short of death. While I had nothing to do with Elisibet's decisions, you have my heartfelt sorrow at your loss."

Her mouth opening and closing, Nijmege looked like a fish out of water.

Bentoncourt took back his role as *Nam Lugal*. "Since you've brought us together, *Ninsumgal*, perhaps you could tell us what you wanted us to know."

Davis nodded. "Of course, Lionel. I know you're busy with the day-to-day operations of your people. I'll be brief." She paused a moment, collecting her thoughts. "This is your official notice. You will stop harassing me. I will not be coming to place myself before the *Agrun Nam* and beg your protection and assistance. Whether or not you believe who I am means nothing."

"I believe it means a lot," McCall muttered.

"Perhaps so, Mr. McCall," Davis said. "But you are no more a *Sañar* than I am. If you recall the laws of the European Sanguire, only royalty can assign a member of the *Agrun Nam*."

He gaped at her.

"I hereby demand that the *Agrun Nam* prepare a delegation for travel. I'll give you three months to assign a representative to attend me in Portland, Oregon. I've already found a fairly nice complex of buildings for your offices and residences should you wish; you don't need to reside at my headquarters if you don't want to." Davis paused to stare at them. "This is not up for debate. At least one of you will attend me. Is that understood?"

Bentoncourt scanned his companions, all apparently speechless. "We understand."

"Good. Then I'll see you in a few weeks. Reynhard?"

Dorst, who had been smiling pleasantly at the gathering, turned the laptop around. "Yes, my *Gasan*?"

"I'm finished here."

"Of course, *Ninsumgal*. I'll see you soon."

He busied himself with disconnecting the computer from the data line and putting it away as everyone stared at him. When all was ready, he strutted to the door. "Have a nice day!"

Bentoncourt almost smiled at his shell-shocked peers. His eyes met Cassadie's, and he remembered the last time they had spoken. He had said then that Davis wouldn't attend them, that she would demand their relocation instead. It was with great diplomacy that Bentoncourt refrained from saying, "I told you so."

***

It was with great care that he closed the door. He stalked across his office, standing for a few minutes before his desk.

Nijmege's "pipsqueak" had displayed a steel backbone and shrewd political insight. Her use of Dorst as her messenger boy was a calculated move to impress the *Agrun Nam* with her resources at hand, and it had succeeded. None of those fools realized how close to the edge of the precipice the *Agrun Nam* sat. Having now seen Davis almost firsthand, he still wondered how much of Elisibet's memories she truly had and how much was coaching from O'Toole and Valmont. If the latter, the situation might not be as dire as it seemed.

But the insult!

With a growl, he released the fury he had held in check throughout the unscheduled meeting. In one smooth motion he bent, sweeping his arms across his desk, savoring the crash as everything fell to the floor in a jumbled heap. The sound echoed the chaos of his anger, but didn't appease it. He raised his fists over his head, locking them together and bringing them down with all his Sanguire strength. It wasn't enough to completely shatter the solid oak, but it gave a satisfying *crack* as a split opened across its surface.

There'd been no word from his assassin since the day before. He'd assumed the man had completed the job and was en route to fulfill his promise of destroying his employer. This message from Davis put lie to that supposition. She lived. Whatever that buffoon had done, Davis was now on the offensive. Maybe she thought Nijmege was involved, and this forced delegation would flush the saboteur out of hiding. There was nothing and no one linking he or Nijmege to any of the assassination plots—he'd made certain of that. The only option Davis had was to get each *sanari* under her thumb long enough to interrogate them. To go to her now would most certainly ruin his plans.

Or would they?

He stood before the wreck of his desk, ignoring the aches in his wrists as he considered his options.

The phone rang, interrupting his mulling. He frowned, staring blankly at the empty space on the desk where it resided. It rang again, and he moved around to find that the receiver had miraculously landed in the cradle. He picked it up. "Yes?"

His secretary's voice was timid; she'd obviously heard his temper tantrum and was loath to interrupt it. "*Aga Maskim Sañar* Nijmege is on line one for you, sir."

He didn't bother thanking her. Reaching down he placed the phone base on the desk to pick up the call. "Bertrada?"

"If I can't get these *ñalga súpi* to bring that bitch here, then I'm going there."

Samuel McCall nodded to himself. "Of course. I concur. What do you need me to do?"

CHAPTER THIRTY-FOUR

Whiskey quietly shut down the computer. She was alone in her apartment office, the only place currently deemed safe by her *Aga'usi* and advisors. Despite the fact that the assassin had been discovered and personally dispatched by her, The Davis Group was still in security lockdown. From her apartment office she could see the *Aga'gída* stationed on the roof, patrolling directly above her.

From this vantage point she also saw movement in her sitting room. Her pack, family and advisors idled there, the younglings chafing at the imposed restrictions this threat had caused. Whiskey hoped that her demands of the *Agrun Nam* would allow their reins to be loosened. Whichever one of the *sanari* was responsible for the multiple assassination attempts should be backpedaling now, trying to regain control of the situation before the impending departure of the European delegation. That would allow her pack the opportunity to break out within the bounds of her responsibilities, have some fun and mourn the loss of their comrade. She had no doubt that the person ultimately responsible for Cora's demise would be one of the European delegates. After both a Human and a Sanguire assassin had failed to kill her, she anticipated that the mystery mastermind would come to see the job done properly. She looked forward to that. It would be nice to put a face to the bastard before she destroyed him.

Whiskey set aside the visceral anger, forcing her teeth to sheathe. Was it only last year she had first discovered her heritage? She remembered the terror of those fangs sprouting in her mouth and her inability to make them go away. A smile quirked her lips. A lot of things had changed since then.

Picking up her desk phone, she said, "Send in my advisors." Through the glass she watched as the message was conveyed. Margaurethe, Valmont, Castillo and Chano rose from the large table. Moments later Whiskey's lover, protector, priest and elder filed into her office.

Margaurethe came behind the desk, her hand settling on Whiskey's shoulder. Whiskey covered it with her own, looking up to receive a kiss. Since arriving in the aftermath to discover Whiskey had dispatched her attacker and survived a bullet, something indefinable had changed within Margaurethe. She seemed less forceful in words and action, as if she had come to terms with Whiskey's abilities to protect herself and no longer needed to waste energy in worry over the matter. Whiskey found Margaurethe less combative and more inclined to listen, even to Valmont. While the change was a bit of a relief, Whiskey didn't want Margaurethe to regress to the woman she'd been with Elisibet. She liked the strong professional Margaurethe had become.

Valmont took up position at the window, his casual stance somehow revealing a deeper level of peace within him. His expression was more open than Whiskey was accustomed to, the last couple of days taking its toll. She liked the switch, finding him incrementally closer to the Valmont of Elisibet's memories, less acrimonious, less inclined to sarcastic flippancy. His confession had been good for his soul, his second swearing of fealty a balm against the punishment he'd meted out against himself for murdering his best friend. It would be stupid for Whiskey to ignore his history, but this easing of his acerbic nature did wonders for her ability to forgive him for past actions.

Castillo, too, had changed, his bearing more confident than it had been over the months. He bowed to Whiskey and sat in a chair across from her. He carried himself taller, assured of his place on her board of advisors. Although the others were strong enough to destroy his mind on a whim, he had come to trust in his capabilities and those of his companions'.

Chano sat beside the padre, easing his old bones into the second chair and leaning his cane against the arm. Whiskey hadn't known him long enough to see any alterations in his behavior, but that didn't matter. He was there, a wise voice to offset her first youthful inclinations and a level head bringing balance to the group as a whole.

Together they made a formidable team, one that would take The Davis Group far and wide. Whiskey remembered the old *Agrun Nam*, the one of Elisibet's time. They had been strong together, as well, but the death of their *Usumgal* and centuries of manipulation by the Sweet Butcher had weakened them. They had fought each other when they should have banded together against her. *Nam Lugal* Nahib had realized this truth, and had taken steps to correct it. His actions had come too late, the disastrous repercussions still ringing to this day. From what Dorst had reported to Whiskey, things hadn't changed much in their council chambers. They still fought and clawed against each other to keep their shreds of power. Only the appearance of Whiskey, their *Ninsumgal* reborn, had begun the change in their power structure. She was certain that this was exactly what Mahar's prophecy meant. *I will bring order to chaos, compassion to corruption, and peace to warring people.*

She smiled.

Glossary

Aga Gasan - lady crown, ["the crown" and "lady"]; term used for a princess of the blood.

Aga Maskim Sañar - Bertrada Nijmege's title; Judiciary of the High Court of the *Agrun Nam.*

aga ninna - fearsome crown ["the crown" and "fearsome lady"].

aga'us/aga'usi - security, policeman, soldier ["the crown" and "to follow"].

Aga'gída - the Ninsumgal's personal guard ["the crown" and "just" and "to protect". Literally - to protect the just crown].

Agrun Nam - council ["inner sanctuary" and "fate, lot, responsibility"].

Baruñal - midwife to the Ñíri Kurám process.

gasan - lady, mistress, queen.

Gidimam Kissane Lá - ghost walker, a talent, able to move through solid objects.

Gúnnumu Bargún - shape shifter, a talent, able to change appearance.

Ki'an Gasan - Margaurethe O'Toole's title ["beloved" and "lady, mistress, queen"].

kizarus, kizarusi - vessel ["large vessel" and "to tap" and "blood"], vessels.

lúkal - dear one.

m'cara - beloved (not Sanguire, but an affectation of Margaurethe O'Toole for Elisibet Vasilla).

minn'ast - beloved (not Sanguire, but an affectation of Elisibet Vasilla for Margaurethe O'Toole).

Nam Lugal - Lionel Bentoncourt's title; leader of the *Agrun Nam*.

Ninsumgal - lady of all, sovereign, dragon, monster of composite power; official title of Elisibet.

Ñíri Kurám - the change, the turning ["path" and "strange" and "to take/to traverse"].

Saggina - local magistrate for European Sanguire.

sañar/sanari - councilor of the *Agrun Nam*.

Sañur Gasum - eunuch assassin ["eunuch" and "I will" and "to slaughter"]; Reynhard Dorst's title.

Ugula Aga'us - Captain of the Ninsumgal's personal guard, the Aga'us.

Usumgal - lord of all, sovereign, dragon, monster of composite power; official title of Elisibet's father.